GW01458662

The Eye of a Dragon

The Dragons of Dorwine Book 2

Jack Adkins

Honor Bound Books

Contents

KENTARI

Acknowledgments

Writing *The Blood of a Dragon* was an incredible experience. It was one of those achievements few people get to cross off their bucket list. I poured the sum of my knowledge and experience as a writer and human into that book. Then I sat down to do it again.

It's a humbling thing to try to catch lightning in a bottle a second time. I truly hope you enjoy *The Eye of a Dragon* because it was born of sweat equity. This story is far from the place I imagined it while writing the first book. The point of view characters changed. The story's structure changed. As late as a month before release, I made noticeable changes to this book. And I loved it.

I want to thank Jim, Chris, and Chilton for inspiring some of the new characters in this book. We should have another uke jam session. To Brock and Brandon, who have molded me and my work through the decades of our friendship.

Without the help of my amazing wife, Alicia, I would be just a silly little man haplessly smashing keys on my keyboard. Thank you for bringing form and discipline to my scattered musings.

I am eternally grateful to my Lord and Savior, Jesus the Christ. Apart from whom I could do nothing. (John 15:5)

.

Prologue

"Sum Buck!," Anuka complained, tossing a small tin cup against the bulkhead. It ricocheted and bounced harmlessly to the deck of the goblin's tiny room. *That would have breached the hull on the Sea Pocket*, he thought. A little of his rage drained away, and he chuckled. His fond memories of being enslaved seemed to have happened a decade ago. Now he was rotting in the belly of what used to be the Brinery. Bull Man now called it the *Calcium* or some other stupid Minothos word. *Whatever.*

Anuka couldn't help his dour mood. He hadn't been up on deck in three days. Not since High Ball, the greasy little crewman manning the crow's nest, had reported a sky full of Silver Dragons to the west. Circling Kentari like buzzards, he guessed. *So all the Silver Dragons want me dead. Big deal!* Anuka didn't mind being accused of things, except on the rare occasions he was innocent.

It was funny that despite his distinct lack of love for water--he wasn't afraid of it--Anuka missed the cool sea mist spray on his face while he explained to Kikkabar's crew how everything worked in the world.

At the first sight of a Dragon, they had stuffed him in this box. Although there weren't any Dragons in his room, Anuka had trouble feeling gratitude. Offund and Kelios were holed up as well, but Anuka was sure he was way more miserable than his companions. Kelios had his own bathtub!

Anuka had planned on entering Kentari in disguise. But with the sky full of Dragons everyone had insisted he hide in his quarters. *Stupid Dragons.* Once he found Rigby, it would all work out. Anuka's hand went to his vest and he stroked the letter in his pocket.

"I'm comin', Papa."

The seas had smoothed just after his interment and Anuka thought he had felt the sleek vessel break inland up the brackish river toward their destination. It would be their first port in a week. The previous stop had been solely for repairs.

The little red goblin slipped the ruby eye from his pouch and turned it over in his hand. He had used it to control a baby Dragon and cripple Brine, a sea wyrm twice as long as this ship. Anuka didn't understand what made it work but when he positioned it like a monocle he saw the world differently through it. He could see the insides of any Dragon. It had some sort of invisible power that the allowed the user of the ruby to control a Dragon like a puppet. It gave him full power over any Dragon.

It was an incredible feeling. He had felt ashamed to use it on the baby Bronze, especially since he was Crenthys's little brother or something, but it had to be done. It had saved them all. Using it on Brine had also felt wrong, even though that old sea wyrm was an evil slive. Wrong in a different way. Like learning the girl you've been kissing is a close cousin. *Nasty!*

When Anuka thought about his plans for the ruby, he pushed down his guilt and set his jaw.

His swinging foot clanked against something metallic and he remembered the ugly device under the bed. Anuka hauled it up to his lap. It was a wicked contraption with a cruel, barbed needle the size of Anuka's wrist on the end. An evil Sea Elf and his goons had used it on Crenthys's brother--*sands but he wished she would have named that poor Dragon*--to harvest DragonsBlood. Anuka had kept it on a whim and had been careful to hide it from his friends. He hoped he would never need it for anything, but at least it wasn't in Wave's hands. His palm itched when he thought of the Sea Elf. Anuka's best dagger had followed that Sum Buck through a magic portal just as the elf fled. He'd resolved to get Wave after he found Papa.

Anuka reached into his vest and pulled out the crisp letter his Papa had left him. With a shuddering breath, he calmed his racing heart. He could feel his skin heating. If he lost control, he could burn down the boat. He exhaled slowly and carefully slid the letter under his thin mattress.

The boat had slowed and, based on the muffled commands being issued, he guessed they were mooring. Anuka was eager to get off the boat but knew he would have to wait his turn and be careful. He sighed.

"Anuka!" someone called above deck. Placing a hand on his dagger, he moved toward the door.

"Anuka, got somit for ya, right."

High Ball. His overbite was so bad the kid's bottom jaw didn't really matter. Anuka jerked the door open and started toward the lanky human. At least it looked like he had been cleaning his teeth regularly. "What is it? Can't you see I'm...recreating?"

High Ball looked past Anuka into the goblin's room to see if he could discern what 'recreating' meant. A smack on his leg got his attention.

"Oh. Right." The lanky teen jerked his head to one side and flung his long hair from his eyes. Then he pulled out a leather pouch and offered it to Anuka. "This came straight away. Crane post. We's barely docked."

Anuka took the thin leather pouch, gave it a squeeze, then opened it. With a shaking hand he pulled out a crisp letter. A familiar design was impressed in the wax seal. "Papa," Anuka breathed.

Chapter 1

Guess Who's Back

The Year 983 Dragon Anum

As crossbows raised and swords hissed from their scabbards, Crenthys regretted reverting to her DragonKin form. It was Anuka's idea. Zanderon, the Bronze Dragon she had ridden from Usban, had suggested she remain in her Sea Elf disguise until she had made explanations. After all, the last time she was in Clover Crisp, some of these same guards had tried to kill her. *Oh well. Nothing for it now.* It was better to deal with this straight away than hide behind a disguise and deal with lying about it later.

Her companions stood with their backs to her, hands raised. Tabir's slender jaw was set determinedly, though his posture was calm and non-threatening. Coltimar was relaxed. Almost bored. Ember seemed ready to spew forth a torrent of unintelligible words, as he was prone to do in such situations. Crenthys needed to say something or the Malkin might get them all killed.

Before she could start her defense, Zanderon, the gigantic Bronze Dragon they had ridden on from Zhazie boomed, "Put those away, Brinka is our guest."

The guards jerked in surprise. They turned their heads up to see the enormous seething beast glaring down at them. Some fumbled with putting their weapons away like scolded children at the end of playtime, while a few still stood their ground.

"Brinka," the Bronze boomed, causing her companions to jump, "this is foolishness. What were you hoping to accomplish, deviating from the plan?"

Despite the rock-hard knot in her stomach, Crenthys swallowed and straightened her back as she faced the Dragon. "I didn't want to begin my time here under false pretenses. And please address me as Crenthys."

The Dragon straightened to his full height and harrumphed. "Crenthys. This is not your given name. If you don't wish to operate under pretense, then I suggest you shed this false moniker as well."

"I am not the frightened, heartbroken creature they tried to kill a decade ago," Crenthys said in a firm but quiet voice. She heard her blood pulsing in her ears as she ground her teeth behind her leathery snout.

"So be it." Zanderon turned and strode back toward the landing field.

Crenthys sighed. She had no shortage of enemies here. She could not afford to lose the one friend she had. Zanderon was trying to help. "Master Zanderon!"

The Dragon stopped walking but it did not turn back.

"Thank you. For everything." Crenthys said.

With the slightest dip of his head, the massive Bronze Dragon continued walking until he came to stand by her frightened brother.

Coltimar, the broad-chested human who had accompanied them from Zhazie, came jogging toward them. Crenthys wasn't convinced he was human—not fully. He addressed the cadre of guards still barring their path. "It would be unwise to continue to brandish those weapons against someone Master Zanderon has declared to be a guest."

"Coltimar does not rule here," barked one guard—a captain, based on the markings on his uniform.

"But he is an ally, Faluvio, and deserves our respect." The voice came from behind the soldiers. A large Dragomyr, like Crenthys, dressed in a deep crimson uniform glided through the crowd.

A wave of vertigo washed over Crenthys as the guards parted. The voice of the newcomer, paired with his appearance, burned with familiarity.

Judging by how he stared, he knew her as well.

"Brinka. I can't say I am happy to see you. My last orders concerning you were to apprehend, dead or alive."

Some of the confidence returned to the guards, and they gripped their weapons more firmly.

"Kilkus?" Crenthys blurted before she could think.

The barrel-chested Dragomyr snorted. "You remember. I don't know if I should be flattered or insulted."

"What do we do with them, my Lord?" Faluvio asked.

Kilkus absently dug at an old scar amidst the bronze scales on his arm with one clawed finger.

Something told Crenthys that scar was her doing.

"This is Council business. Vodinar's mess. Detain them and send him a message to come deal with it." He turned to walk away but paused to look back at Crenthys. A vulpine smile spread across his face and he said, "Unless you intend to resist."

It wasn't an invitation she was eager to accept. Coltimar stepped to her side and exchanged hard looks with the Dragomyr. *What human stares down a Dragomyr?*

"No," Crenthys barked. "We didn't come here for trouble. We will cooperate."

"Why did you come back?" Kilkus asked, naked disgust on his face. "Not your mess, remember?"

The big Dragomyr nodded.

"What about him?" Faluvio pointed eagerly at Coltimar.

"Let him go. Locking him up won't do any good." Kilkus sauntered back toward the gate to the upper city.

Some guards stepped forward to lead Crenthys and her friends away.

"What did he mean 'won't do any good', Master Coltimar?" Ember asked.

The big human smiled coyly. "I am resourceful. Don't worry. I am going to speak to Vodinar myself."

Crenthys sighed as the guards lead her, Tabir and Ember to spend their evening in a jail cell.

———◦———

"Why do Dragons have guards?" Ember asked.

Tabir and Crenthys regarded him dubiously. He had held his peace for nearly an hour, but the question niggling in his mind finally broke free.

Ember suddenly felt small, as he often did when his mouth ran amok. It was a legitimate inquiry. When no one answered, he continued. "I mean, the Dragons have nothing to fear. They sit atop the predatory hierarchy. And if they did have natural enemies, mortal guards would be of little use. Is civil unrest an issue?"

"Not typically," Crenthys said in a flat tone that hinted she wasn't fond of this line of questioning.

"Is it for psychological reasons?" Ember asked. His tongue licked his upper lip excitedly.

"Explain." Crenthys said.

Tabir's expression smoothly shifted from annoyance to curiosity.

"Well, thick walls make for good neighbors, as the expression goes. That is of Mobetarian origin, I believe. Anyway, if the Dragons present an armed policing force, that visible presence would deter crime. She-bathian states that 'no good resides within mortals, save for the good they demonstrate for fear of reprisal'. I rather agree with him. Having spent the past weeks studying humanity closely, I—"

"Ember," Crenthys said impatiently.

"Right. My point. Well, the guards represent a relatable reminder to the citizens of Clover Crisp to behave. Being eaten by a Dragon for stealing bread is hard to visualize for most people. But having armed guards that might chop off your hand for stealing bread... Well, that's more realistic. Kind of like the walls around the city proper. All for show."

Crenthys resumed staring at her feet.

Ember sighed. *Crenthys is distraught and I'm rambling again.* It was a big risk for her, coming back here, but the baby Dragon needed to be with his people. Crenthys had been nearly been killed by these people a decade ago over the death of her creator: a Dragon called Belendurath. She had hoped tensions would have eased. So far, it appeared they had not.

Ember made several observations about the cell they were in. The room was large. *Likely it was built to house DragonKin. Or would they be called Draconis Mortalis here? Or, perhaps Vessels? Or maybe that was what Gold Dragons called them?* The room was also exceptionally clean. As a frequent prisoner of late, he had several examples to compare. His time in the custody of Jhaldus, the Dark Elf slaver, was particularly foul. That memory made him shudder. But through that experience, he met his new friends. His only friends. Ember doubted many prisoners cycled through this room. The walls were unmarred and free of graffiti. The wrist-thick iron bars that formed the door still held their silver-gray coloring. Their thickness seemed like overkill, but would be necessary if containing something strong—like the Draconis.

The area outside their cell was quiet. While he wasn't certain, Ember didn't think any other prisoners were down here.

"This is truly an excellent facility," Ember said cheerfully. When his friends looked blankly at him again, he realized that his previous observations had taken place inside his head. His friends weren't privy to the conclusions he'd already made. He did that a lot. Based on the looks from his companions, he let that chain of thought die.

Crenthys got up from the thick stone slab seat and paced around the room.

The lock on this door must be amazing. Anuka likely could pick it, given the correct tools. Ember had learned a lot about lock picking from the little red-skinned goblin. Technically, Anuka was Filgenium. His mother was a Djinn from the adjacent plane of fire. But he didn't like to talk about that. "I miss Anuka."

Crenthys spun on a massive clawed foot and stopped in her tracks. "What?" The incredulity in her voice matched the look on her face.

Tabir put a reassuring hand on Ember's back. "Ember. I know you have a brilliant mind, but sometimes it's difficult for us to follow your chain of thoughts."

The Gold Elf was always comforting. Well, High Elf was a better term. He wasn't from Dorwine and wasn't technically part of the

Golden Elves. Maybe that was why he was so kind. Most elves Ember had met were cold and pretentious.

"I apologize. I've never been in a prison this nice. And when I was appreciating the craftsmanship of the lock, I thought of Anuka. I imagine he could pick that lock in short order. That thought made me wonder if I could open it. I have been studying his methods, and while my education is purely theoretical, I feel that I have a decent grasp of the base concepts of lock mechanics and—". They were staring again. "I'm sorry. Now you know why I said I missed Anuka." Ember wished for a hole to crawl into. *Why was knowing so many things so easy, but saying the correct thing so hard?*

"Wait," Crenthys said, taking a step toward Ember.

She was much larger when she wasn't transmuted into a pretty Sea Elf. And now that she had reverted to her true form, her teeth, claws, and reptile eyes made her visage quite terrifying. Ember backed into the corner.

Crenthys softened her approach. "Did you say that you thought you could pick this lock?"

"Theoretically," Ember said.

Tabir looked sharply at Crenthys. "Cren. What are you thinking?"

"I'm not sure I want to wait and see whether we will be executed or not."

"Executed?" Ember squeaked.

"When I left here ten years ago, there were a dozen Dragomyr chasing me with spears and axes." Crenthys said it matter-of-factly, but a muscle in her leathery neck twitched.

Dragomyr! That's what the Bronze call them. "Time heals wounds no salve can mend. Also Shebathian," Ember said. He felt it important to always cite his sources.

"No. Dragons have long memories. What is ten years to a six hundred-year-old DragonLord?" Crenthys knelt down beside Ember. "What do you need to open this lock?"

"Umm," Ember calculated his chances of success and weighed them against the moral implications of a prison escape. He also factored in variables such as getting caught, being killed for treason he didn't commit, and what he might learn from the experience. He leaped up and exclaimed, "Let's inventory our assets and I'll make do with what we have."

Voices in the hallway sent Ember hiding guiltily behind Crenthys.

An older human lady peered into the cell. She had graying hair pulled into a bun and a severe look on her hard brown face. The dark yellow of her uniform marked her as a member of the DragonLord's guard, and the knots on her shoulder identified her as a captain.

"Brinka Belendurath?" The woman asked in a raspy voice. Two younger human guards, in similar attire, stood at attention on her flanks.

Crenthys raised her chin and took a deliberate step toward the bars. She met the captain's gaze. "I am."

The older woman held Crenthys's stare for many moments. "Master Vodinar has summoned you."

Chapter 2

New Old Friends

Twenty years as a professional thief should have made a blade to his throat less frightening. It hadn't. Rigby clenched his teeth together and exhaled slowly through his nose.

"You're late old man," the young Biazo noble accused while his guard held the blade against Rigby's neck. The noble's expression was smug and bored. The scent of Tent Weed lingered in the air. Ru Biazo sat on a heavy table with neatly wound bolts of silk cloth stacked around him. He looked like a king on a throne of silk. In fact, that wasn't far from the truth. Ru Biazo was heir to the Biazo Patriarchy. His father, Herin, was the wealthiest of Bog's mercantile Patriarchs. The Black DragonLord had made the Biazo family responsible for nearly all clothing trade in rural Zhazie.

Patriarch was a position Ru would inherit from his father one day, but the ambitious son didn't intend to wait. That's why they were all here tonight.

"I've done what you hired me to do, Ru," Rigby said. His throat had gone dry, but he controlled his voice.

"Have you?" Ru asked. He waved and the guard holding the dagger on Rigby released him. Then Ru nodded to another slightly smaller human guard on Rigby's flank.

The guard moved toward Rigby with an outstretched hand. Rigby produced a small dagger from his belt. It had a worn bronze handle protruding from a dull wooden sheath. The guard passed the dagger to Ru. He barely glanced at it before handing it back to the guard. With a nod, the guard returned the dagger to Rigby.

"Master Biazo...?" Rigby began. He proffered the dagger back toward the young nobleman.

The boy's eyes were like glass and the skin of his neck was red from constant scratching. Tent Weed made the user feel like their skin was constantly shedding. "Save it!" Ru barked, hopping off the table and stepping close to Rigby.

Rigby thought of three ways to escape the situation—two of which involved the noble being cut with his own guard's dagger. *No. That was not the way out of this.*

"A Barclov, is it?" Ru asked. The shock that flashed across Rigby's face made the noble smile sadistically. "That's right. I know your tricks. It's a move you've made famous if I understand it right." Ru paced the narrow aisle in front of Rigby.

Rigby's eyes darted from guard to guard and then to the side exit. The guard with the sword tightened his grip on Rigby's arm to let him know he saw the movement.

"So, with a Barclov, you steal something for me, at my direction, but give me a fake, instead. Then you take the genuine item to the church and get paid twice."

Before Ru finished speaking, a figure stepped slowly from the shadows, and Rigby gasped.

"Fabian," Rigby said in a near whisper. "What are you doing here?"

The human wore a smug grin framed by tight blond curls. He wasn't as handsome as Rigby, but was ten years his junior. "As Master Biazo says, you're late. While you were dragging your feet, Master Ru contacted me and I stole the dagger for him. That night."

"That was my job!" Rigby spat, stepping forward. The guard with the sword brought the blade to Rigby's throat. He stopped short but barked, "I have a contract."

"Wrong!" Ru said, barging back into the conversation. "We had an agreement. You took too long. If I had waited any longer for you to steal the dagger, I could have just waited for father to die of old age."

It was a terrible job to start with. The son, itching for power, wanted to disgrace his father by having the family's prized heirloom stolen. The dagger, reported to have the power to sever magical enchantments, was a major source of the family's political power. Without it, Ru's father would be shamed into stepping down and his governorship would pass to Ru. Once in power, Ru would produce the dagger and begin his own rise to power. *It's always bad to get involved in family politics.*

"So, Rigby, the dagger you are holding, and the dagger we would find if we were to search you more thoroughly, are both fake." The hawk-nosed noble briskly patted his breast, and Rigby heard the soft clank of metal under the velvet vest. "I have the real dagger."

Rigby didn't think Ru could hurt him. Not without serious consequences. Bards were some of the best tools the great DragonLord Bog had for keeping his servants in check. They placated the commoners with their magically enhanced music, and most of them also worked as thieves or con artists who harassed the nobles. Bog loved political intrigue. It would displease him if something happened to one of his most effective tools. Ru wouldn't risk Bog's disfavor while vying for the Patriarchy.

"Cheer up, my friend," Fabian said with a flourish. "You are retiring, I heard. Not too soon. A man of your age can't keep up in this game forever."

Rigby fixed Fabian with a level stare, but offered no argument. Rigby was well into his fourth decade. He was feeling it: he moved a little slower; bumps and bruises gained on the job took a little longer to heal; and he didn't have the hunger he once had. Those weren't the reasons he was retiring. The actual reasons were not for Fabian or anyone else to know.

Rigby sighed. "Then I can go?"

Ru barked a laugh, "Yes, you can go. Never come to me again. I don't think I could stomach the disappointment."

The guard holding Rigby at sword point shoved him roughly. Even he had a sneer for Rigby now. There had been a time when he would not have tolerated disrespect from a lowly house guard. Those days were gone. Rigby shuffled past the guard without looking up.

"You know," Ru started, prompting Rigby to turn back. "My father said that you were once the best there was."

Rigby swallowed a retort his old goblin friend would have been proud of and said, "Once." Then he walked out the door, and disappeared into the night.

———◄○►———

Rigby smiled as he turned the real Biazo dagger over in his hands and admired its quality. "You did well, Felin." The Wood Elf looked at Rigby curiously, like he had never heard a compliment before. Most people lived a long time without receiving a simple compliment, Rigby supposed. Especially in the swamp. *That's sad.*

"Thank ya," Felin replied, looking away. The young elf suddenly seemed not to know what to do with his hands.

"When did you get it?" Rigby asked as he held the magical weapon near the dingy room's lone candle to inspect it further.

"'Bout a week ago." Felin looked at Rigby. The dark skin of the elf's face turned a shade darker. "I got it on Eleventh Day. Everyone was... distracted."

Eleventh Day. The people of Zhazie worked hard for ten days and got wasted on their first day off. The aging thief fished a coin knot with a nice heft to it from his vest and tossed it to the elf.

Felin bounced the string full of square coins and nodded his satisfaction.

"What you are going to do with that thing?" Felin pointed his pinky at the dagger as Rigby slid it into his belt.

Elves never used their first finger to point. Wood elves used their pinky and Rigby didn't see how that was any different from any other finger. He had better things to do than figure out the way of elves. "I'm going to turn it in to the church, as I am mandated to do with all magical items I recover." He felt bad lying to the elf, but the truth was too dangerous.

Felin smiled. "Okay, then. Just be careful not to mix the fake one up with the one what's real."

That is the trick, I guess. Knowing the difference. Rigby just smiled in reply.

"Let's do it again sometime, eh?" Felin slipped the coins into a slender pouch and smiled widely. "Great to work with you. You're everything I've heard 'bout you. A real legend."

Rigby smiled at that. *Legend.* Even after twenty years, it was still satisfying to dupe stupid, rich nobles out of their valuables. He didn't have the heart to tell the elf he was retiring.

Felin stepped quickly out the front door of the small meeting room and into the street.

The bard rubbed his jaw. His face ached from smiling. It had been a while since he had anything to smile about. Everything about Felin was entertaining. From his odd accent to his prodigious skill at thievery and acrobatics. The elf seemed to take well to the criminal life. It had been that way for Rigby. But that seemed like ages ago for Rigby. Now everything was a little tougher than it had once been. The normal bumps and bruises of a good burglary took a few extra days to heal. Even a long night of playing music left his throat sore and hands aching the next day.

Rigby rubbed the dagger as he considered what his friend Anuka was planning. After giving Felin enough time to slip away, Rigby stepped out into the night and moved into a nearby alleyway. Only a few people were out on the streets at this hour. Those who were moved quietly about their business. Since the skies had filled with Silver Dragons, the Church installed a soft curfew. Soft meant you better have a good reason to be out and about after dark. Otherwise, Bog's thugs would find the soft spot in your skull with their clubs.

Rigby feared neither the PeaceMen—the church's legitimate law-keepers—nor an alleyway cutthroat. The church ignored, even sponsored his career as a thief. Bog saw the pilfering of his nobles as a good way to keep them sharp and agitated. Even so far from the Capital, Rigby's reputation preceded him. His notoriety, coupled with a career's worth of victims, would make retirement difficult. He had no shortage of enemies.

Rigby's mind drifted to a fifteen-year-old girl with his dimples and her mother's eyes locked away inside the vaunted church building. If the bard truly meant to keep the girl safe, he would have to execute his plan carefully. He squeezed his eyes shut and tried to put those things out of his mind. There would be time to worry about that later. First, he needed some sleep.

Before Rigby got three steps toward his soft bed, a dirty human boy skittered to a stop at the mouth of the alley. He looked both relieved and terrified when he saw the bard's face under the sick green light of the street lamp. When the child saw the dagger in the dangerous bard's hand, he ran.

Seas. Rigby put the dagger away and yelled, "Stop".

The urchin stopped and hung his head.

"Come here, boy," Rigby said, struggling to hide his irritation. It was bad luck to raise a weapon against a child. He traced an "X" inside his boot with his toe and spat to the side.

The urchin shuffled to Rigby, dipped his head in his best imitation of a courtly bow and said, "Master Rigby, sir, I'm sorry for startlin' ya'."

The boy was searching for someone, and Rigby suspected he was the boy's quarry. "Say, where are you off to so late?"

After a moment, the boy said, "I delivered a letter, sir. Jus' tryin' ta get off the street before them PeaceMen get me."

"Who was the message for?" Rigby asked.

The boy shrugged. "Dunno, sir," he replied breathlessly.

"You don't know who you gave the message to?"

"Oh, um. Tara, sir. Hammerhead club. But I don't know who the letter was for." The boy made another clumsy bow.

Rigby knew the place. Seedy tavern by the docks. He knew of Tara, as well. The child was still lying. "You didn't read it?" the bard asked with a note of accusation in his voice.

The boy paused for a beat before replying. "Oh, no, sir. I've not got my letters."

"Have you not?" Rigby asked curiously as he inspected the boy. He couldn't gage the lad's age, but knew the boy was old enough to read.

The boy shook his head briskly and tugged on his ragged knee-high trousers.

That's a bad tell, the bard thought. Rigby produced a coin and held it up for the urchin to see. "Two things; first, don't tug your pants. It's how I know you're lying. Second, tell me who asked you to find me and this is yours."

Rigby saw the battle taking place in the child's mind. He didn't want to betray his first customer, but Rigby's coin was likely much bigger than the other fellow's.

"Just point me in the right direction," Rigby said.

Sighing, the boy looked Rigby in the eyes. "The part about Hammerhead was true. Big old bast—er—fellow in a cloak. Something wrong with his skin. It's green, I think."

The boy's street accent had dried up suddenly. "Very well," Rigby said, fishing out a second coin. "Take this to Madam Poral and tell her I said you need your letters."

The boy stared at Rigby, the possibilities in his head swimming on his face.

"Do you want the Educators to send you back to the streets to live?" When he shook his head, the bard offered him the coin. "Then take this and get your letters. Go on."

The boy snatched the coin and murmured his thanks before dashing off the way he had come.

"And stop working for criminals," Rigby yelled, watching the boy go. It was unlikely that he would use the extra coin for tutoring, but that was his business. Rigby felt he had done his part. Bog sent all the children from the entire province of Zhazie to the Capital for education. If a child could learn a skill or was useful to the Dragons in some way, they would be put to work and provided for. An illiterate human boy from Kentari would likely never return. Or worse, he would return as a thief.

Rigby rubbed his lucky pendant and went searching for a big green-skinned man in a dark alley.

—◦—

From his perch on a short barrel in a dark alley, Kelios strained to hear the subdued conversations inside the tavern. The place had nearly emptied after dark and the din of noise inside had almost died away. That made little sense to the Triton. In Usban, places like this came alive after dark. During his brief time on the Fareth Tore Enclave—the F.T.E. for short—he had noticed those cities also coming to life at night. Kentari was different. It had a strange vibe that was unsettling. Only a handful of people scurried about and they moved with purpose.

Closing his eyes, Kelios inhaled deeply. That had gotten easier as his lungs grew more accustomed to breathing air instead of water. The bitter scents of smoke from potbellied stoves lay like a blanket over the myriad of other smells of the city. The stench of the bog that surrounded them tainted everything. He smelled the unwashed bodies of the sweaty laborers in their nearby homes. Though the shutters were perpetually open, they found no relief from the heat as the moist air clung to the town.

Kelios no longer smelled the children he had hired to find Anuka's friend. He had expected at least one to have returned by now. Thinking of Anuka made him think of Crenthys. Truth be told, everything did. A few days back, he would have chalked his feelings up to the effects of his shape-shifting into the bear. Irana, as he had named her, changed him emotionally each time he summoned her. It was not necessarily bad, but the spirit of the bear inside him wreaked havoc with his own emotions.

But no. Kelios couldn't blame Irana for how he felt about Crenthys. It was well beyond primal attraction. He snickered at the irony. Crenthys was DragonKin. He hadn't been brave enough to ask, but according to legend, DragonKin could not reproduce. They were humanoid creations of the Dragon they served. Tall and powerfully built, Crenthys was as tall as Kelios. She was also covered in bronze scales that shone like honey in the sun. He had thought her beautiful when she was disguised as a half Sea Elf. But he found her stunning as a DragonKin. And yet, he did not pine after her in a lustful manner. He was captured by her spirit. Crenthys had a warrior's heart: she spoke her mind, held firm to her convictions, and was a loyal friend. And he had told her they could never be more than friends.

Whether Kelios had spurned her to protect her, or because he still dreamed of returning home and raising a Triton family, it didn't matter. He was a fool for letting her go. Kelios smiled. Her mind was made up, and he had no way to stop her. He should have joined her. Instead, here he sat, commiserating with Irana. The bear's lingering spirit enhanced his sense of smell. He checked again for the children and smelled tobacco.

"Rigby, I presume," he said, his eyes still closed. He sensed someone nearby. Another gift of his bear companion.

"And you are?" asked a steady voice from the shadows.

Kelios opened his eyes and slowly turned to peer down the alley. A human clad in fine, dark clothing stood clutching a dagger. *The bard.*

"I am Kelios Verromath."

"Well, Kelios Verromath, what do you want with me?"

"We have a mutual friend. Traveling has become difficult for him of late, so he sent me." Anuka hadn't told Kelios to be circumspect, but it seemed prudent.

"Anuka?" Rigby asked. There was alarm in his voice and he tightened his grip on the dagger he held.

"Yes. He told me to ask how things went at the Biazo's."

Rigby mulled the information over before replying. "Is Slobbers with him?"

"Who?" Kelios hadn't expected that question.

"Slobbers. Savage little honey badger. Tries to eat your face off."

"No. I don't know what a honey badger is."

Rigby loosened his grip on the dagger and exhaled. "Fine. Things went fine with Ru. He's an idiot, and I'm a professional."

Kelios found it odd that the bard didn't seem worried about saying Anuka's name in the streets of a town owned by a DragonLord who wanted to kill the goblin. But he seemed terrified that the little pirate may have someone named Slobbers with him. The Triton made a mental note to ask Anuka about that later.

"Anuka is early. I wasn't expecting him for weeks." Rigby stowed his weapon and rubbed a pendant around his neck.

"We have been in port for a week already."

"A week? Sands." Rigby was calculating something in his mind. "Wait, did he send the letter from here? From Kentari?"

Kelios nodded and Rigby grew agitated as he mulled over the information.

"Are the rumors true? The absolutely crazy, unbelievable rumors that I am hearing out of Usban?"

Kelios pursed his lips before saying, "Anuka asked me not to spoil his fun. I think he wants to share the details of our... adventures himself."

"Fine. Good grief. Where is the little fire monkey?"

"I don't know. He was on our ship when I left this morning. When I checked back in this afternoon, he and Offund were gone."

"Wonderful. Well, let's get out of the street. We'll find him tomorrow." Rigby walked past Kelios and headed down a side street.

With a sigh, Kelios followed.

———— ◆◆◆ ————

"You sure this is working, bubby?" Anuka said out of the corner of his mouth. "I feel kinda naked out here."

"When has feeling naked in front of people ever bothered you?" Offund asked dryly.

Good point. Anuka glanced around, pleased that the people buzzing around paid them no mind. "Maybe not, but I'd rather not get arrested and boiled in Dragon acid if it's all the same to you."

"No one can see what we look like. We appear as children."

"Excellent." The goblin relaxed with the knowledge that the Hob's magic was concealing his bright red skin and dashing good looks. If they were recognized by some priest or DragonMan it would end poorly. Killing one of Bog's oldest allies and burning down a lucrative sea port put him at the top of the Black DragonLord's hit list. Anuka had a mission, and he needed to connect with an old friend, but that could wait. Right now he needed to collect some information.

The streets of Kentari were as sodden and stinky as Anuka recalled. The dank, earthy smells of the swamp hung thickly in the air. This far inland there was no sweet brine smell to cover the odors of the frogs, snakes, and crustaceans that filled his nostrils. Even the streets of the city teemed with life as vegetation waged its constant war on civilization. Despondent workers rushed from task to task, eager to please their foremen or escape punishment. Everyone in Zhazie worked or they didn't eat. Remembering that, he quickened his pace and bade Offund to follow. They didn't want to be seen lollygagging.

Anuka and Offund arrived at the city square and took in the sights. Not much had changed in the year or so since he'd last been here. Dead vining plants clung like skeletal hands to the light posts and support beams of the state-run buildings. Caretakers had killed them with some alchemical spray, leaving only their bones behind. These buildings, places where Bog's highest ranking administrators lived and worked, were taller and better built than the other structures. Rows of little huts lined one side of the courtyard. They contained merchants providing food and supplies, primarily for the use of the government workers.

Anuka moved along the row of merchants until he came to a solid but well used little shack with fruit for sale. Some fruits, like oranges and mangos, only grew in the West and were expensive. Other hardier fruits like apples grew in the mountainous regions of Zhazie and were a treat in Kentari. The only thing that grew in this swamp was Sprick-berries and they gave you the runs.

Fishing out a few coins, Anuka bought a few apples and stuffed the least shriveled one in his pocket. Then he lead Offund to the steps of the biggest, most ornate structure in town; the church.

Churches in Zhazie were like banks in most other places, and the priests were accountants. They didn't run on goodwill, either. So when a burly young acolyte, some might call him a guard, held out a hand to stop Anuka and Offund, the little goblin held up the apples for him to see.

"My offering to Master Caustimis and his holy priests, sir." Anuka's voice was pitched a little high, so it wasn't hard to approximate a child speaking.

The thug in a clean robe scowled at the pitiful offering but stepped aside so the two children could enter. "Leave your boots. Wash your feet."

They did so and the cool tiled floor felt good on Anuka's feet. He would do without boots if it wasn't for their practicality and how good they looked with all of his outfits. The main hallway led straight into the high-ceilinged antechamber where followers came to worship Bog. Two-thirds of the room was reserved for various altars and large bronze urns for collecting coins. The remaining third was for seating. *Bog must prefer active worship to having his followers sitting around.*

Only a handful of people were scattered throughout the large room. Four or five were at the altar praying or lobbing coins into the big jars. There was a severe-looking priest watching over them. The look on his face could turn milk to cottage cheese. He was probably there to discourage miserly giving. Two young acolytes moved among the seating area, polishing the wooden benches with a cloth.

"What are we doing here?" Offund whispered at his side.

"There is something I need to see for myself," Anuka said. "Here, go make our offering. I'm gonna meditate or something." The goblin dumped his apples into Offund's tiny arms. The Hob fumbled the fruit but got control, dropping none. When Anuka took a seat nearby, the little sorcerer waddled down the sloped floor to the altar.

Anuka tried to be nonchalant as he inspected the acolyte nearest him. She was a human girl. Pretty with dark hair and dark eyes. It was hard to tell with humans, but she might have been twenty years old. The girl smiled at him when she noticed him staring. *Oh, right. I'm a little kid.* Anuka gave her a silly wave, then turned to search for the other acolyte and found her standing right next to him.

It required all of Anuka's willpower to swallow the curse that almost slipped past his surprised lips. A squeak came out instead, and the girl jumped.

"Oh, dear," the girl squealed, covering her mouth with her hands. "I'm sorry. I didn't mean to frighten you." She knelt down and gently put her slender hand on Anuka's. The girl frowned at him and put the back of her hand on his forehead. "Are you sick, sweetie? You are burning up."

"I'm fine. Just been working." He tried to smile, but it likely looked pretty weird. His eyes searched her features, and he felt his mouth fall open. She was mixed blood; elf and human. Common, or low blood elf. Her eyes were auburn with flecks of green, like her father. Locks of silky hair spilled around her face as she looked down at him with concern. Red hair with streaks of dirty blonde mixed in—it was distinct. In fact, Anuka only knew one Sum Buck with hair like that. *I'll be the son of a sea captain. If this girl ain't Rigby's daughter, I'll eat my hat.*

Chapter 3

Welcome Home

Crenthys felt like she was being led to the gallows. The streets of Clover Crisp were lined with rows of human onlookers. Mostly farmers or craftsmen by trade, they had left their fields and forges to witness the disturbance the newcomers had caused. It was unlikely they had this kind of excitement often. The relative peace of the Bronze Dragon cities stood in stark contrast to the shadowy menace that plagued the streets of Usban. Bog pitted his servants against one another in an unending war for power, or at least survival.

The veneer of peace and harmony in the Bronze cities was well polished. Although Crenthys remembered little prior to her master's death, she had experienced firsthand what was beneath that shiny surface.

She resisted the urge to sneer at the nosy crowd, but none of this was their fault. They were just curious, and maybe a little frightened. No, her quarrel was not with these people, but rather, it has been with the Dragons.

Crenthys knew Vodinar, or likely had. Those memories were lost to her. Vodinar was to the Bronze DragonLord, Dovondes, as Celebris had been to the Silver DragonLord, Shimmer.

Sadness touched her then. A sense of loss that was deep. Like many of her emotions, it made little sense to her. Perhaps she had known Celebris, a DragonKin like herself, in her previous life. He had died in Usban Port just weeks ago. Wave, a deranged Sea Elf possessed by an evil spirit, had killed the Ambassador. He had tried to blame Bog, the Black DragonLord, for the murder by framing Anuka. Wave's aim was to start a war between the Dragons. Based on her reception in Clover Crisp, she imagined he was on his way to hitting his mark.

Celebris had been an imposing figure. He had the build of a great warrior and an honorable heart. By reputation, Vodinar was different. Tall—taller even than the towering Celebris had been—but with a slight frame. He was closer to Ember in build than a Dragomyr, and he was shrewd. If Vodinar had summoned them, it wasn't a good sign. He had likely directed the assault group that had chased her from the city a decade ago.

The crowds thinned as they moved closer to Wrythmar, the walled seat of the Bronze government.

Ember's question about Dragon guards had been annoying, but he had a point. The guard was an ornamental body serving as police for a docile human population. It was an homage to a bygone era, where mortals built massive armies and fought great wars. The guard was a reminder to the people of the violence from which they had been liberated by their Dragon masters. The rhetoric had once seemed a matter of pride to Crenthys. Having lived among those being ruled for a decade, she now had a different perspective.

The human woman, the one the guards called Captain Kiterin as they saluted, led them into a building shaped like a large gazebo with a hexagonal roof of red clay tiles. The building connected to another rectangular building twenty feet from the great wall dividing the human settlement of Clover Crisp and the Dragon city Wrythmar.

Two humans in silky, dark yellow robes greeted Captain Kiterin as they entered. One was a human man of similar age to the captain. He had a salt and pepper beard on a dark, worn face. He wore a black cap that covered his hair, save for a few rogue locks of silver that spilled out the back. The second human was a young man, who had likely seen fewer than twenty seasons. He wore an identical robe and tight black cap. His thin mustache and patchy beard would not survive two licks of a cat. The acolyte bowed to the captain, then stood behind the older priest.

Captain Kiterin exchanged some business with the priests and turned to face her captives. She had to crane her neck to look Crenthys in the eyes. The captain gave a nod and left the building without a word. Crenthys could sense the woman's frustration, but didn't understand it. Perhaps the context was lost in the sea of her forgotten memories. The two guards followed the captain from the building, leaving Crenthys and her companions alone with the priests.

"Greetings, mistress Belendurath," the older man said with a bow. "I am Dula Nerie. This is my apprentice, Nove Arte." The young man bowed as well. "Welcome. We are sending you to Master Vodinar. Are you prepared for the journey?"

Sending? Oh. A fresh memory burgeoned in her mind. One didn't simply walk into Wrythmar. Crenthys turned to her companions. "We will be traveling. The way Wave did."

Ember's eyes went wide, and a smile blossomed on his face. Tabir nodded a reluctant understanding.

"We are prepared," Crenthys said.

With another bow from each man, they moved through a beaded curtain dividing the two rooms. Nearly every surface of the wall in the rectangular building was covered with hand-written markings. *Venerations.* Another memory. Citizens of Clover Crisp were permitted an audience with members of the Bronze Council, or their representatives. Each would pass through this place and many would leave prayers scribbled on the walls with charcoal—usually prayers of thanks or adulation for the Dragon they served.

At the other end of the hexagonal building was a large portal rimmed with hammered bronze. The metal was twisted ornately and resembled a wave or perhaps the blowing wind. It was unnecessary, but Crenthys supposed it provided an air of mysticism for the mortals who used the portal.

Arte, the younger of the priests, carried a jade dish resembling a canoe with a lid. Based on the way the acolyte handled the container, Crenthys could guess at its contents. With reverence, the young man removed the green lid and slid it into a long pocket on his robe. Meanwhile, Nerie fitted a metal claw to his index finger. Once done, he and Arte bent low to the ground and chanted softly. The words were a prayer, and spoken in very poor High Draconic. The language was too complex for mortals, but some words were used in ritual ceremonies, like this one.

The older man stood and went to the other side of the portal rim. Arte moved to stand at his right side, proffering the jade dish. Dula Nerie dipped the metal claw into the dish and drew it out. The tip of the claw was covered in blood: DragonsBlood.

With an incantation and a sweeping motion, the blood tipped claw cut a thin line in the space between the companions and the priests. Like cloth severed from a tapestry, the fold of space cascaded down. Crenthys could no longer see the priests. A well lit room resembling an amphitheater loomed ahead.

Drawing a breath to steel herself, Crenthys stepped through the portal. She could sense her friends following her.

Passing through the portal wasn't pleasant, but the experience was not new to Crenthys. It was like walking through a thick spider web or an unseen curtain. The claws of her feet scraped against smooth stone. It was marble or polished granite. The room was warm and bright: portraits and decorations lined the walls; exotic plants filled pots hanging from the ceiling or resting on short pillars.

The ostentatious display of wealth stirred old feelings within Crenthys. It was a strange mix of dread and homecoming. She noticed Vodinar, flanked by two other Dragomyr, watching her closely. The ambassador's face wore a regal mask of passivity, but his eyes betrayed darker emotions.

Tabir entered the room behind her. He stumbled with a moment's disorientation, but composed himself quickly. Ember staggered through the portal, collapsed to his hands and knees, and wretched noisily.

Crenthys felt the heat of embarrassment creep up her neck as she bent to help her companion. "Brinka Belendurath," Vodinar said in a voice that rang with a hint of satisfaction. "Welcome home."

———◦———

Crenthys didn't know how to respond. Was that a genuine statement from Vodinar? Hard to imagine, given how things had ended a decade ago. If it was sarcasm, why was he smiling? In her mind, she had played over the likely outcomes of her return a thousand times during their flight from Usban. In none of those scenarios did she imagine being told 'welcome home'.

Servants came and cleaned up the mess Ember had made. When she realized she hadn't replied to Vodinar, she bowed at the waist and said, "Thank you, Master Vodinar." She wasn't sure what else to do.

"Lord Dovondes wishes me to inquire about your health, and to make sure you are comfortable." The tall Dragomyr inspected Crenthys from head to toe and added, "And properly clothed."

A detail she had forgotten about Vodinar was his presentation. He always dressed immaculately in the finest attire. Today he wore light brown trousers cut just above the top of his sandaled feet. They had a neat crease from his ankle up that disappeared beneath his dark yellow silk jacket that buttoned smartly up the front. The jacket was lightweight and held a lustrous shine. The cuffs and lapel were of the same material, but had a matte finish. *What type of silk is that? Ember would know.* She glanced to the side where Ember was apologizing to the servants. When the Malkin stopped mid-sentence to admire Vodinar's clothing, Crenthys smiled.

Whatever the emissary thought of her tattered travel clothes, Crenthys was thankful he didn't seem apt to harm her or her friends. At least not right away.

"Quarters are being arranged for you. In the meantime, Sorpa and Leena will escort you to a place where you can clean up." Vodinar gestured and one of the Dragomyrs on his flank moved to the room's exit, beckoning Crenthys and her friends to follow.

Crenthys moved to go, but paused. "Master Vodinar."

The tall Dragomyr was still standing primly, watching them go. "Yes," he asked, sufferingly.

"I am well. I did not lose my mind or fly into a rage." She wanted to say more, or at least say what she meant. When a DragonKin lost their master—from whose blood they were created—they either died or went insane in short order. There was no good explanation as to why, but she had not.

Vodinar nodded and said, "We shall see."

As Crenthys turned to catch up to her friends, he called, "I am glad you are well."

The words were almost tender. She didn't stop, didn't want him to see the newest layer of confusion to cloud her mind. Instead, she sped up, walking as fast as she could without running. But the distance she put between her and the administrator didn't stop her from wondering what her relationship to Vodinar had been.

⸺⸺◦⸺⸺

The scalding hot water was the best thing Crenthys had felt in ages. It flowed between her scales and washed away weeks of dirt and grime. Aromatic spices and medicinal oils rode the clouds of steam into her nostrils.

Tabir sat on a bench nearby, waiting for his water to cool. The heated pools for Dragomyr weren't suitable for others. Ember had declined a bath and instead requested a bucket, a cloth, and a soft bristled brush. *He is crazy,* she thought. *This is amazing.*

For the past decade, she had been able to keep the frustrations of her missing memories in the background of her busy life. Now, literally sitting in the heart of the Bronze government, some memories were bubbling forcibly to the surface. It was an odd sensation to find something familiar, yet have no memory of it. As her body relaxed, she carefully explored those memories. Ember suggested that, with time, her memory might return. Crenthys wanted to remember some things, but she was sure there were other things she dared not recall.

As if the Malkin was privy to her thoughts, he asked, "Do you recall much of Vodinar, Crenthys?"

Had the perceptive Malkin heard Vodinar's parting tone? Ember was very good at hearing something, yet understanding much more. "I only recall him in generalities. I think he was responsible for sending the hunting parties after me. Apart from that, I only know of him by reputation."

"Vodinar is ancient. Over three hundred years old." Ember was a fount of endless knowledge that he frequently shared with others.

Crenthys hadn't known that.

"Despite being one of the most powerful Dragons of Dorwine, Dovondes has only created one Dragomyr."

Crenthys could hear the smile on the Malkin's face as he tried out the word. He had been listening. DragonMan, or DragonKin were the most pedestrian terms for what she was. The terms bordered on insulting, but were tolerated. Bog didn't care what DragonSpawn were called in his territories. Things were different in Dirzal. Dragomyr were respected and treated as extensions of their master's will. For that reason, rogue Dragomyr were dealt with swiftly and severely. As they had done with her.

"What else have you learned, my scholastic friend?" She kept her tone light, because she really did value Ember's observations.

"That he knows you. Or he did. I doubt anyone here is aware of your... condition. If my guess is correct, it won't be long until we are called to give an accounting of the deeds in Usban Port. We likely should make sure we tell the same story." Ember had grown somber.

She thought about what Ember had said. "No. Neither of you will be called to give an accounting—*only* me. Your opinions don't matter here. No offense meant, but the word of a Dragon, or DragonKin, is worth ten times the word of a non-Dragon mortal. I would not be surprised, however, if they sent someone to observe you both."

"Spies?" Tabir asked as he eased himself into a nearby pool. He made a face like he was stepping into lava.

"One thing Dragons do well is collect information. They have magic, incredible strength, and breathe fire. But they rule the world with knowledge. You will need to be careful." Crenthys let her friends digest her warning but she worried her words had not been strong enough to convey the truth. They were all in grave danger.

⸺⬦⸺

As Tabir finished his morning prayers, he could hear Ember grilling Crenthys about many things concerning Dragon life. He smiled. The Malkin had been very respectful of their friend while they traveled. Considering her memory issues, and the fact she had kept her true nature a secret from them, that was considerate of him. But now, he grilled her like an over-zealous jailer.

Tabir rubbed at the indentations the fine carpet had left on his knees and looked around the room. Their accommodations were incredible. Each of them had their own bedroom in the housing complex. In a different context, perhaps on his home continent, these would have been soldiers' quarters. The countries on the continent of Dorwine didn't have armies, as far as Tabir knew. So he wasn't sure for whom this place was designed.

The bed was enormous and very soft. No doubt designed for one of Crenthys's kind. Dragomyr, she had said. He would have to remember that. The sheets were silky, with interesting patterns on them.

A clean basin of water awaited him on a small podium. The walls were covered in smooth wooden paneling. This was the nicest place he had slept in for... decades. Has it really been that long? He thought back to his home, a mansion compared to most dwellings he had seen in his life. The extravagance had been lost on him then. To be honest, he cared little for it now. More than a century of life had shown him the horrors of poverty and disease. Living in luxury while others lived in squalor seemed distasteful to him.

Tabir was grateful for the current provision, though he longed to learn why Rathune had brought him here. His god had never failed him since delivering him from a city full of demon-possessed elves. Their passions had been their undoing. Thousands of elves, his kin, had died at the hand of Rathune's judgement. There was nothing to learn inside this room. He gathered his meager belongings and stepped into the common room.

Ember looked at him appraisingly and Tabir felt very self-conscious. The clothing provided for him had likely cost more than he had spent on his wardrobe in a decade. His friend smiled at him and came to greet him.

"Good morning, Tabir. Um, you aren't aware of the latest fashion trends I gather."

The Malkin meant no offense. His mind was constantly in motion and he loved solving problems. Tabir's outfit qualified.

"I am not. Could you help me?" Tabir asked, extending his arms to Ember.

His friend beamed and Crenthys, who was helping herself to a breakfast tray, smiled to herself.

Ember began by unrolling the sleeves of the voluminous, silky shirt to hang below Tabir's hands. Before the elf could protest, the Malkin rolled them again to form square cuffs and connected a button on a length of silk to a button hole inside the shirt. The sleeves now hung between his wrists and elbows at a comfortable length.

Tabir nodded his approval. Then Ember untucked the shirt from his trousers. "Ember," the elf protested.

"You can't tuck it in. That is for nobility or on-duty guardsmen. In fact, if you see a guard with his shirt untucked, don't bother them. They are off duty."

Tabir allowed his friend to continue to fuss over him, even letting Ember bind his long blond hair in a ponytail with a strip of silk.

"There ya' go. You will fit right in." Ember smiled.

Tabir did not fit in, but that was okay. He had long grown accustomed to that. He sighed.

A knock at the door startled everyone. All eyes went to the main entrance. They were all wound pretty tightly, Tabir supposed. Crenthys opened the door a crack and spoke to someone on the other side.

"Tabir," Crenthys called, "Your escort to the Golden Consulate is here."

He tried hard not to notice how beautiful his escort was. It was difficult. Her name was Tanila. Her angular Elven features were hidden beneath a sun veil she raised to make introductions. The skin of her thin face was like porcelain. Her eyes were the color of the lightest part of the sky and seemed as big as saucers. *This is a Golden Elf*, he thought. Though High Elves—such as himself—shared ancestry with Golden Elves, Tanila's radiance set her apart from any elf he had known.

Tanila spoke Low Draconic with a strange accent. It reminded Tabir of a fawn frolicking. Her diction would slow to a crawl, then race forward in a torrent of words. It was interesting to follow. He said his goodbyes to his companions and followed Tanila into the street. When he learned there were elves in the city he had gotten excited, and a little fearful. When an invitation to visit the embassy arrived, he was ecstatic.

Tanila didn't look back as they meandered through the neat streets of Wrythmar, but he sensed that she noticed his eyes on her.

Tabir sought something else for his eyes to do. His heart was racing and he felt moisture on his palms. The dryness in his throat had nothing to do with being thirsty. A smile spread across his face as he understood the significance of the moment. He basked in the normalcy of it. Tabir had followed Rathune faithfully for over seventy years. For most of that time, he had avoided moments like these. His work was too important. All of mortal kind teetered on the brink of disaster and didn't know it. The time for recompense was at hand. Rathune was coming to collect what was due him. Still, people moved about their lives without a clue. Decades of standing between the creator god and his wayward creation had nearly driven the life from Tabir. Yet he still walked, talked, and breathed.

He had known for a long time that his life would be sacrificed for the mortal races. That didn't mean he was already dead. Things like joy and happiness, even embarrassment, were far too valuable to be dulled by the weight of his duty. How much have I yet to learn?

"Please forgive me for staring," he began.

She didn't stop, or even slow, but inclined her head in his direction slightly.

"It isn't often I encounter one of my kind."

Tanila placed a hand to her mouth as if he had said something amusing.

"What is so funny about that?" Tabir asked.

"I am sorry. Your manner of speech is so... strange. I mean no offense."

"I'm not offended. I confess I thought the same of you when you spoke."

She glanced back at him, a small smile on her thin lips. "You are from where?"

That's a tough question. "Far from here. Far from Dorwine. From another continent. Above the line."

She stopped and grabbed his arm. Shock replaced amusement. "Above the line? Over the mountains?"

"Yes. I... it's a very long story."

"I would like to hear it, sometime. I did not know we have people in that part of the world. Rumors say nothing civil lives there." When she realized her hand was still on his arm, she pulled away quickly and resumed leading them along the well-paved road.

Tabir wasn't looking forward to explaining how nearly all of his people had bonded with demons, gone insane, and been destroyed by Rathune. Perhaps he could avoid that conversation. He frowned as he considered that these elves could also fall into those sins. Perhaps he was here to prevent that from happening.

He saw their destination plainly ahead. The building was small compared to the hulking structures surrounding it. But it was no less grand. His chest tightened when the sweeping architecture came into view. Using Borch and Haylock wood, they had constructed an immense facade of incredible artistry. The front of the building appeared to be carved from a giant tree with random twists and turns in the gnarled branches. In truth, every surface appeared crafted with intricate design. His home had been much the same.

A pair or ornate doors in the center of the building stood open and a slender elf clad in elegant clothing stood regally watching them. A half dozen elves, three on each side, knelt along the clean-swept stone courtyard. Petals from pale violet flowers lined the path from the street to the front door.

When they drew near, the regal elf bowed deeply. "Tabir Nalvir, of House Nalvir. I am Payris eth Druindar. Welcome to our home." A wry smile played on his face as he stood.

Chapter 4

This is Anuka Sandbar

Rigby and Kelios spent most of the morning looking for Anuka and Offund. Several hours ago, they had stopped by a rundown tavern and picked up a dark-skinned elf Rigby introduced as Felin. He was an associate of the human and carried himself like a thief. *Anuka would not like the competition*, Kelios thought. Despite the elf's help, they found no sign of the little red-skinned goblin. The group stopped for a moment, and Kelios leaned against a crooked tree. Sweat beaded on his head and ran down his face. His heavy hooded cloak made the stagnant heat unbearable. It was necessary, however, to hide his green-skinned features. He doubted there were many Tritons in Kentari. They hadn't yet encountered another.

Kelios followed Rigby and Felin through the back door of the massive warehouse Rigby had made his lair. A skittish human let them in and glanced around to see if anyone had followed them before closing the door behind them. They had just removed the watertight swamp coverings from their boots when the nervous human reappeared.

"Everything okay, Timmun?" Rigby asked as he tossed his shoe covering onto a pile of them.

"Huh? Oh, yeah. Great." Timmun fiddled with a small sewing hoop he wore on one arm.

By the looks of the place, the bard had supplied his hideout amply long ago. Kelios found that curious. How long had Rigby known Anuka and his band of troublemakers would come to Kentari? If he hadn't known until recently, why would he already have a well-stocked hideout?

Rigby's base of operations was in a small, hidden room inside one of Bog's many manufacturing warehouses. They made the uniforms for the entire country here. The room he rented from the factory manager was concealed. Timmun seemed eager to get back to the fifty men and women who were sewing on the other side of the building. Rigby thanked the man and walked down a long, slender hallway that lead to his office.

"His skin is red?" Felin asked.

"Yes," Kelios confirmed.

"Then how can he hide so good?"

Felin doesn't know Anuka. The Triton reminded himself. He was glad they had stopped and collected the elf. "Well, he's small and pretty smart. Sometimes. If he doesn't want to be found, he won't be."

"One time in the Capital he—" Rigby froze when he noticed the door standing at the end of the hallway was ajar.

A thin line of flickering light spilled into the hallway. Rigby and Felin exchanged looks. The bard crouched and silently led them down the hallway.

Rigby had assured Kelios the church's PeaceMen were seldom a problem and basic security was part of what Rigby paid for. But there was little to keep a rival crew leader from raiding his office. A dozen possibilities ran through Kelios's mind—each was more terrifying than the last.

They stopped right outside the door and Rigby moved like a slug to peer into the room. *It has to be about Anuka. Bog must know he is here. That would mean that he knows about me as well.* What they saw in the room confirmed his fears.

Rigby opened the sturdy door with his boot and listened for signs of an intruder. He saw none. The bard squeezed his long-bladed dagger in his fist as he flung the door open and rushed into the room. Felin, wielding a dagger of his own, followed close behind.

The room was a mess. The chairs were overturned and papers had been strewn about haphazardly. Rigby stood in the center of the room and spun around to complete his inspection.

Something caused Rigby to whip his head back toward the door. Kelios mirrored the motion, but only Felin was there completing his own inspection. Kelios heard a noise at his back and spun again, but saw nothing. Only shadows from the flickering candle danced along the wall.

The bard took a step toward the origin of the noise. Felin stood on his flank.

"Hands in the air, criminals!" a voice behind them bellowed.

Felin drew his dagger arm back, ready to launch a deadly throw. Beside the door, stood a small red figure.

Rigby grabbed Felin's wrist before he could launch his lethal attack. "Don't, Felin!"

The wood elf spun and fixed Rigby with a fierce questioning glare. An unmistakable peel of laughter erupted from the doorway.

Releasing Felin's arm, the bard stepped around the elf to see a howling, red-skinned goblin rolling on the floor.

Kelios bent over to rest his hands on his knees. His panic shifted to embarrassment. Offund stood behind Anuka, his eyes wide open and his back pressed against the wall. *One day Anuka's antics will get one of us killed*, Kelios thought.

"You," Anuka began before another wave of laughter took him. "You Sum Bucks. If you could have seen your faces. You boys need the privy? Or is it too late?" Another wave of laughter overwhelmed the little goblin.

Rigby sighed. "Felin," the bard said with a gesture toward the cackling goblin. "This is Anuka Sandbar."

Anuka hadn't laughed so hard in ages. The look on Rigby's face could scale a Dragon. The elf with skin like Zeminy chocolate turned as white as Tabir. His tiny goblin heart was racing and his skin was turning bright red. Tufts of smoke were rising from his workers' outfit, but Anuka didn't care. It felt good to laugh. And to fear. Through tear-filled eyes, he saw Rigby comforting the elf. Sum Buck had been within an ace of chucking a dagger at his head. From the looks of the boy, he might have hit Anuka. It was so good to feel the rush of nearly dying again. His sides aching, he barked out the last dying guffaw and pushed himself to his feet. With an effort, Anuka calmed himself and his skin's glow receded. "I needed that."

"Oh, we are glad to entertain you," Rigby quipped.

Anuka wiped snot on his borrowed sleeve and blew out a deep breath. "Boys, this here is Rigby. No last name. Just Rigby. Rigby, this is Kelios the Fish Man and Offund the secret sorcerer. I don't know the elf."

Kelios and Offund looked at Anuka incredulously. The Triton gave a nod. "We have met."

"This is my associate, Felin," Rigby said.

Felin made a weird elf gesture.

Offund rubbed at his pants and made an awkward bow.

"Associate means he's a criminal. Like us." Anuka beamed.

"How come I didn't see you? I looked when I came in. Right where you were." Felin asked softly.

"Well bubby, it's a secret," Anuka said seriously. Then he whispered, "My little friend here is DragonBlooded. Don't tell nobody."

Offund's eyes went wide.

"Anuka," Rigby began, stepping closer. "Why are you here?"

Rigby always was slow. "I sent you a letter, dummy."

"No, I mean—why are you here? In my hideout. How did you even find this place?"

"Oh. That." Anuka whipped the bola hat from his head and rubbed his scalp. "Well, I wanted you to see the Brin—er' um, the Karmax—"

"*Kargarak*," Kelios and Offund said in unison.

"*Kargarak*, whatever," Anuka barked at his companions. "I wanted you to see our ship."

"The Minothos ship?" Rigby asked.

"Yeah. She was mine for a day or so."

"An hour," Offund corrected.

"Would you shut up? The grownups are talking." That Hob had been full of himself ever since he killed the Red DragonMan. "Anyway. PeaceMen started snooping around and we had to bail."

"I'm sure it's a lovely boat. And I assume you stole it," the bard said with a smirk.

Stolen? Anuka felt like he just had a fart go wrong. Rigby was supposed to be his friend. *Why would he think I stole her? Sum Buck.*

"I'll have you know, I killed Onan Swet all by myself. I won that ship. Fair and square!"

Rigby looked a little impressed. "You killed Swet?"

Instead of answering, Anuka folded his tiny red arms across his chest and fixed the bard with a stern glare of defiance.

"Anuka, what really happened in Usban?" Rigby asked.

I thought you'd never ask... "Nothing, really. Certainly not what you've heard. Ok, me and my buddies were captured by pirates, sold as slaves, took a job for Shimmer's DragonMan. We freed some slaves, stole a boat, the karmannghia—"

"*Kargarak!*" Kelios and Offund shouted again.

"Do you want to tell this story?" When his friends didn't reply, Anuka continued. "We killed some of Bog's people, and rescued a Bronze Dragon... oh, and killed Brine." Anuka smiled widely.

The room was silent for a few moments. Anuka reveled as the tension swelled.

"That's... exactly what I heard, Anuka." Rigby's eyes were wide, and he was shaking his head in disbelief.

"Oh. Word travels fast, I reckon. And I know what you're thinkin': 'No half measures for old Anuka.'. Well, you'd be right on that score".

"Anuka..." Rigby seemed to claw around in his brain for the right words to say. He looked like a constipated seal. "Are you going to tell me what this is all about? You are up to something. I know you."

"Well, did you get the thing I asked you to get?"

Rigby chewed on this lip. Then he rubbed at the stupid little pendant around his neck. "What do you need it for? What are you planning?"

Anuka didn't answer. He elected to fold his arms and tap his foot instead.

Rigby sighed and pulled something from a secret compartment in the wall. He unwrapped a white cloth to reveal the Biazo dagger to Anuka.

"You are a beautiful man," Anuka said. "Does it work?"

Rigby wrapped the dagger back up and gave the goblin a look of incredulity. "How am I supposed to know if it works?"

"Didn't you test it? With your wizard buddy, Xylathar."

"Xanavor, and no. I told you. He isn't a wizard. His powers are... different."

"Oh. So he's special?" Anuka asked.

"He isn't a sorcerer or DragonBlooded or anything like that. Look, this is the authentic Biazo dagger. Whether or not it does what the rumors claim, I don't know."

"It dispels enchantments, yes?" Offund stepped into the conversation.

"That's what the rumors say." Rigby said.

Offund nodded and snapped his hands quickly together, then drew a big circle in front of himself. He snapped his hands apart and a luminescent rope appeared. One end of the rope twirled around Anuka's feet and the other hurled into the air. Before the goblin could protest, he was hanging from his feet by the glowing rope.

"Muk-qwef!" Felin cried and drew a dagger.

Rigby stepped warily around the dangling goblin, inspecting the enchantment.

"You Sum Bucks! Let me down!" Anuka barked, struggling uselessly against the magical rope.

"Felin," Offund said. "Bring your dagger. Cut him down."

The dark-skinned elf stepped up and sawed at the rope, to no avail.

Sensing what was next, Rigby took out the dagger, slid it from its sheath and stepped forward. Seeing the blade, Felin stepped back.

With a flourish, Rigby raked the blade cleanly through the rope, sending Anuka tumbling to the floor with a thud.

Kelios nodded his approval at the display, and then, bending down, helped Anuka to his feet.

"I would say, yes. This is your dagger." Rigby laughed and Felin joined in.

"Ok. Ha ha. Gimme that." Anuka held his hand out and Rigby passed him the dagger. After inspecting the weapon for a moment, he passed it to Offund. "Here. Put this someplace safe."

The Hob took the blade with a nod, then cut a half circle in the air about the size of his head. It was like taking a knife to a portrait. The part of the air Offund cut flapped down, revealing a cabin aboard the *Kargarak*.

"Keit and Tor!" Rigby swore when Offund plunged the dagger into the hole. The bard looked to the Hob and then to Anuka. After a moment, the hole in the air stitched itself up as if nothing had happened.

"Neat trick, eh?" Anuka beamed.

"Where did it go?" Felin asked.

"Look, it ain't that I don't trust you, but the less you know, the better." Anuka gave the elf a wink. "For now, we need to discuss some things."

Rigby still looked shaken. "Anuka, what are you planning?"

The goblin gave his grandest smile. His near-perfect teeth gleamed. "Relax, boys. I've got it all figured out. Um, Rigby, I'm gonna need you to see the Victorin about that big secret job he needs done."

"You mean the one I turned down because I am retiring? And because it's a suicide mission?"

"Yup. That's the one. You have suddenly had a change of heart."

"Some friend you have," Felin said as he walked through Kentari with Rigby.

"Yeah. He's a handful, but I owe him my life. And he helped me pull off the biggest job of my career."

Felin nodded. He could understand owing a debt. He owed much of his own success to Rigby. *Now he has a daughter. That changes everything.* Felin thought of his own mother. They hadn't spoken in seven years. She had abandoned the family path and taken up the lover path again. It was the way of his people to move from one path to another every dozen years or so, but it still hurt. He had come to the city then to begin his own new path: city dweller. He learned the language and started his career. Thinking of her still made him sad. Rigby's daughter would likely feel the same way. Now they were heading out to do something very stupid. *Does he even know what it is like for her? How she must feel? He must know.*

"You can't change things, you know? With the girl. You can't change what's already happened." Felin looked at Rigby. The bard's face grew solemn. Humans changed more easily than elves—even Wood Elves—but they could be stubborn.

"I know," Rigby said.

It seems he does not know, Felin thought. "It's good to do the thing what's right, for the girl. But don't expect to fix what's done been."

"I know," Rigby said more firmly.

Felin grabbed Rigby's arm and the bard reflexively tried to pry the elf free. Felin held fast until Rigby looked at him. "We gonna do what we do. Maybe you come back and maybe you take that little girl away from here. Then the rest of your days are about loving and protecting her. What's done is done. You can't be Rigby, the bard legend or Rigby, the thief master. Do you see that?" Felin thought his heart would burst. The weight of his words seemed to reach Rigby, so he released the bard. There was so much more to say, but Felin couldn't say it without explaining his own childhood. He would not go there. Instead, he left Rigby staring at his back as he took his position at a merchant stand near the church.

He couldn't look at the bard. Maybe that was a stupid thing to say to Rigby. Maybe it would ruin their friendship. It wasn't his place to say such things, but he wasn't thinking of how it would make the human feel. He thought of a lonely, half-elf girl locked away in a stone building. Alone and afraid.

<hr/>

Rigby reminded himself for the fifteenth time why he was sitting in the waiting area outside Victorin Lebarin's office. *Aridelle*. When he agreed to come back and accept the impossible job, he had done so to shut Anuka up. Three hours later and Rigby didn't care if the little red goblin sprouted wings and flew into the sun. But his daughter...

He had been afraid of seeing her, or of her seeing him when he came today. It was funny to think about how many days he came by this district hoping to see his daughter. No, he prayed she would not see him. What would he say to her? Did she know about him? She had to. Rigby was a famous bard. He doubted Amaria could have kept such a secret for so long.

What would he say when they met? He would have to talk to her eventually. His entire reason for being here, for taking this impossible job, was to secure her freedom. Rigby had asked himself a thousand times why she was here. He didn't like the only logical answer he could think of: she is Blooded. Not like Offund, who Anuka said had Dragon's blood in his veins. Or even like Xanavor who had... who knows what. Some people have a wisp of magical power in their blood.

No one is supposed to use magic apart from DragonsBlood, but some were taught to do incredible things with training and access to the powerful substance. The church worked hard to control the users of this power. They tested everyone for it. Almost every priest was able to use DragonsBlood. If his daughter was here, that meant she was Blooded.

If that was the case, freeing her from Lebarin's grasp would be difficult indeed. *Focus, Rigby: one more job.* He busied himself by taking inventory of the ornate waiting area. The honey-colored bench he sat on was plain, but well made. Likely from Alder wood or something similar. Probably was made locally. Rigby knew he would find nothing but Borch, Haylock, and Rosewood beyond the Victorin's door.

At a long, narrow desk outside Lebarin's door sat a stooped, reed-thin human who had tufts of red-gray hair sprouting from his scalp and ears. Rigby didn't know the man's name, but he whistled every time he made an 's' sound.

The walls were bare save for a small mural above Rigby's head. The painting was of a Black Dragon, presumably Bog, curled around a map of the country of Zhazie. Standing to get a closer look, he noticed something odd about the Dragon. It had one blue eye. Maybe it isn't Bog, then.

A bell rang above the clerk's head, and he scrambled through the door by his desk. A moment later, he emerged with a familiar figure in tow. Fabian. Rigby didn't know what the rival bard was doing here and didn't much care. Unless he was here to discuss the Biazo dagger.

Fabian's smile was nearly a smirk as he exited the waiting room. Rigby nodded. *Prig.*

"Come, Master Rigby. We musn't keep his holiness waiting." The stooped clerk spoke with forced cheer punctuated by a pair of whistled 's' sounds.

Could I be walking into a trap? Rigby always wondered this whenever dealing with the old high priest. It was rare for anyone to deal directly with the Victorin. *If it's not a trap, perhaps I should be flattered.*

This office was nothing like Rigby expected. The walls were bare, the decorations sparse, and plain. Even the simple wooden desk in the middle of the room was austere and smaller than the secretary's. It was like a front office Rigby and his crew would hurriedly put together for a job. The aged man sitting placidly behind the desk was neither sparse nor plain.

Victorin Lebarin was a tall human with a thin frame. The pale skin that hung from his bones was speckled with liver spots and a ring of thin, gray hair left a bare spot atop his head. Rigby had never before seen the man without his towering ornamental hat. Even combined, the ravages of age did little to diminish the man. Lebarin stared at Rigby as the secretary led him in. His eyes were like the swamp. Dark and menacing. Calm on the surface, danger lurking beneath. The priest sat with his elbows on the desk, one hand atop the other. The glow of the magically powered Blood lantern caught the array of extravagant rings adorning each of his fingers. His nails glistened black. Whether the nails were black from paint, or use of magic, Rigby could not guess.

"Thank you, Qavini," the Victorin said, his voice a rich baritone.

Rigby found the high priest's smooth vocal timbre to be off-putting. When Lebarin spoke, his honey-smooth voice covered the venom of his words.

"Master Rigby, I heard you were retired." The Victorin stood and proffered his left hand to Rigby.

Rigby's insides churned as he took the old priest's clammy hand and stared at the giant onyx ring. It was a holy symbol. An ornament that denoted Lebarin's considerable rank. It was also disgusting. Rigby hated touching dirty things. The thought of putting his lips on that nasty gem where untold hundreds of other lips had been nearly made him retch. The moment drug on and Rigby swallowed his revulsion. Dipping his head, he quickly placed a poorly aimed kiss on the gaudy ring. He tried to look nonchalant as he stood. The urge to wipe his mouth with the back of his hand was overwhelming. It was like ignoring a fire ant in your boot.

Finally, the Victorin lowered himself into his chair and said, "Have a seat. This will be a short meeting. I have many other appointments today."

As the elderly priest settled into his padded desk chair, Rigby made a show of moving to the ladder-backed chair to his right. He made one good swipe at his mouth with his forearm and instantly felt relieved.

"Yes, your holiness. I will be brief. I would like another chance at the opportunity you offered me," Rigby said.

"The opportunity you turned down?"

"Yes, Victorin. I've reconsidered." Rigby's palms started sweating, but he kept his face neutral and his voice steady. He was a professional who frequently worked with people who could easily kill him.

"What if this opportunity is no longer being offered?" The Victorin sat up straight in his chair and stared at Rigby.

"I... I hadn't heard that—"

"Your nosy ears are keen, Mister Rigby, but they only hear what I want them to hear." Lebarin sucked on his bottom lip as he continued to stare a hole in the bard. "Why do you want this job?"

"This is the opportunity of a lifetime. It's a job to hang a successful career on. It's the perfect—"

"Mister Rigby," Lebarin cut in, "if you came here to lie to me, go now."

Rigby was afraid it would go this way. Lying was pretty easy for the bard. He had made a career of it. Telling the truth was harder. You always wanted to mix some truth in with your lie to make it believable. But telling the unvarnished truth made things way too personal. No one knew the extent of the powers of a DragonPriest. Some said they could read your mind. That sounded stupid to Rigby, but he didn't want to take a chance. This was too important. *One more job.*

Steeling himself, Rigby met Lebarin's stare and said, "I want to free my daughter."

The old priest smiled. It wasn't a knowing grin or a small celebration. It was an Anuka smile. Full toothed and a mile wide. His entire face smiled. Everything but his eyes. The goblin would admire the priest's teeth, Rigby thought. His friend had a thing for teeth and Lebarin's were perfect. They were obscenely white, perfectly straight, and he had every one of them. There was no way it was natural, which made it hideous.

"Your daughter."

The way the priest said the word made it sound filthy. Like the word held some lurid meaning Rigby wasn't privy to. The urge to reach across the desk for the Victorin's throat swelled within him. He tamped it down. His fingers were strong from decades of playing a host of different stringed instruments. He could crush the old man's windpipe before help could arrive. Rigby pushed those thoughts aside.

"I assume you were planning to merely steal her from me. Is that so?"

That smooth, condescending voice brought Rigby back to the moment, and he relaxed his grip on the arms of his chair. *What had he asked?*

"I consider your silence as assent," Lebarin said. "When that seemed impossible, you decided what? That you would buy her from me? Do you have any idea how much a beautiful girl of her... talents is worth to me?"

Rigby had thought about those things and knew they were futile. If he simply stole his daughter from the priest, they would live the rest of their lives hunted by Bog's people. No place would be safe. All of Rigby's earnings wouldn't approach the value of a Blooded Priestess.

"Instead, you want to make an exchange?" The Victorin leaned back in his chair and let his smile fade away. "Tell me, Master Bard, how will you pay your crew if I pay you in flesh instead of coin?"

"Let me worry about that." Curse the old bird. Rigby felt like a fool. As if the old man knew he would come.

"This is not a job for old men, Mister Rigby." The smile returned, but without its previous intensity.

"I employ young men. They do the heavy lifting for me."

"Sharing trade secrets? I've heard of these young men you employ. They also seem quite inexperienced."

"They're quick studies. I am old enough to make up for their inexperience." Rigby gave a forced smile of his own.

"It is too bad Mister Sandbar isn't here to accompany you. He has quite the reputation."

Rigby's heart sank. *Did Lebarin know about Anuka? Is he toying with me?* He imagined PeaceMen dragging the goblin and his friends out of Rigby's hideout. "He was something else."

"Was?" Lebarin countered.

Again, Rigby detected the slightest hint of innuendo in the priest's voice. *Is he messing with me? What does he know?* Pushing the questions down, he continued, "I had heard that Anuka got into some trouble in Usban. I assumed he was on his way to the gallows now."

"Very nearly," Lebarin said confidently. He fixed Rigby with another predatory stare and the room was uncomfortably quiet for a long time until the priest said, "very well. Someone stole an item of unspeakable value from the church. I need you and your team to retrieve it for me.

I can provide some details, requisition rights to the church's supply stores, and several detailed maps."

"And four smears of DragonsBlood?" Rigby asked.

"No. I cannot."

That was surprising. Four smears would only amount to a few hundred gold coins. Providing access to the magical substance was standard when working with the church. They controlled all the DragonsBlood. "May I ask why?"

"The Silvers have created a shortage. We must carefully ration our stocks. Besides, using DragonsBlood inside the keep would be very dangerous.

"The keep?" Rigby asked.

"Yes, Master Bard. You and your team will travel to Barith Shir."

The priest's tone was unnervingly solemn. It set Rigby's nerves on edge. What's more, he had never heard of Barith Shir.

Chapter 5

Wrythmar

Ember sulked for a quarter hour after Tabir left, wondering what he would do with himself cooped up in their apartments all day. Then Vodinar came to collect Crenthys and gave him the best news he could imagine: he had permission to use the city's massive library. The Bronze emissary pinned a short chain with a small metal chit to Ember's lapel and instructed him to present it to the library staff.

Now the Malkin moved as quickly as possible without sprinting, nearly bursting with excitement. He had spent most of the past five years in a secret library containing a wealth of information believed to be lost to the world. As grand as that place was, it was desperately short on mundane information. Local histories, minor philosophers, and regional religious peculiarities were of little value to his former teacher. The urge to run washed over Ember anew as he rounded a corner, and the towering spire of the Intellecis came fully into view. *Where would he start? What were the options?* Vodinar had mentioned something about a guide. Would that person be adequately knowledgeable, or would they saddle him with some acolyte or archivist? He tried to stem the flow of questions, but it was no use. His feet ached from the pounding he gave them as he marched along.

A wide set of stone stairs led to a platform outside a tall set of double doors. The stairs were twice as wide as Ember was used to. A Malkin's legs were much like a human's, but their stride was different. He likely looked ridiculous with the long strides he took up the wide stairs, but he didn't care. When he reached the landing, he panted and his legs were wobbly. He paused just a moment to catch his breath. As a patron exited the library, Ember could see a severe looking older human glaring out at him. Sometimes he forgot he was a Malkin, an exotic creature that the uneducated thought to be a fable, and the educated thought to be extinct.

"Excuse me," called a breathless feminine voice. "You must be Ember."

Ember checked and, sure enough, he was. So he turned to regard the petite human girl bounding up the awkward stairs. She was winded when she reached the top, though not as bad as Ember had been. She was the only light-skinned human he had seen since they landed the day before. Her hair was an oddity. It was long and blonde. Not yellow like many humans who call themselves blonde, but pearl white. It hung in waves over her shoulder, nearly reaching her waist.

"I'm sorry I'm late," she said.

"As am I." It was probably a strange thing to say, but Ember always hated when someone was in an unfortunate situation.

She pursed her lips and smiled with a chastised look. "I was supposed to beat you here, but you must have run."

The pieces fell into place. "Oh, you are my escort."

"Yondi," she said with a small curtsey, "Yondi Fick."

Do they curtsy in Dirzal? He wouldn't have thought so. "It's a pleasure to meet you, Yondi. I am Ember. Just Ember." He gave a stiff bow.

"So, the library. What interests you here?" she asked.

"Everything," he gushed. "I'm sorry. But books are my life. Well, the study of what is in the books has comprised the majority of my time for many years. That is a more appropriate statement. Do you know the library well?"

"Yes, I do. C'mon then. Let's get started. Book worm, eh? You will love it here. There are books on every subject you can imagine." She noted something on his shirt. Before he could see for himself, she had snatched the pin with the chit on a chain. She held it up and smiled. "We won't get far without this." She strode toward the double doors and he followed close behind.

The strange way she moved her hips was also unlike anything he had seen here. He would have to ask Crenthys about these oddities this evening.

The attendant took a great deal of convincing before he would let them into the library. He objected to Ember's hair, saying that he would leave hairballs everywhere.

Just as Ember poised to stiffen his spine for an encounter with the brute, Yondi put a slender finger in his face and changed his mind. She used a few words Ember had never heard a lady utter and made a mental note to ask Crenthys about those as well.

Beyond the atrium, the room opened to the most glorious site Ember had ever beheld. Columns of tall bookshelves lined every wall, and shorter rows of the same were placed neatly throughout the expansive room. While the library he was raised in had important tomes, their total number wouldn't fill this floor. This tower had six levels, by Ember's estimation. The scale of it made his head swim. He grabbed the nearby bust of a Dragomyr—nearly toppling it—to steady himself.

"Are you ok?" Yondi asked, coming to his aid.

"Yes, apologies. It's just... a lot." He closed his eyes and breathed slowly lest he cough up the hairball the attendant was worried about. *Just breathe, Ember.* "I will be fine. It's overwhelming."

"Well, let's start small. What's something you really want to know about?"

"Um, Dragon physiology." Her chuckle reminded him that not everyone was as verbose as he. "It's the study—"

"Of the physical make up and anatomy of Dragons. I know what it is. Of all the information at your disposal, why would you want to read about such a common field of study?"

"We don't have Dragons where I am from. I just discovered that one of my friends is a Dragomyr. And, um, I have questions."

She planted her fists on her hips and shook her head at him. "Ok. Dragon physiology, it is."

———◦○◦———

Crenthys was surprised at how much her people relied on magic. *Another thing I forgot,* she supposed. The portal she and Vodinar stepped through closed behind them. They stood on a wide balcony that circled a massive pit big enough for ten of their apartment buildings to fit in. Curved chimneys ran along the wall every twenty feet or so, belching smoke out of the top of the massive dome covering the cavern.

When they stepped to the rail overlooking the pit below, a wave of warm air washed over them. Crenthys felt a tingle on her scales and a small part of her mind stirred in the distance. This felt familiar. She wasn't sure she had stood in this spot, but this building felt comfortable. Her attention was suddenly drawn to the pit.

A very young Bronze Dragon crept tentatively into the arena, sniffing the floor as it went.

Crenthys's heart leapt. She squeezed the rail to keep herself from leaping down. *Have I lost my senses?* The drop was at least fifty feet. In that moment, she felt she could glide down. "I have to go to him. Take me down."

Vodinar raised an eyebrow at her demand.

"Please," she begged.

"Why?" Vodinar asked. "Why do you want to go to him?"

"Why? He is my brother. Because he needs me. I—" She couldn't think of a good reason that didn't revolve around her desire to see him. "Because I am all he has," she shot hotly.

"No, Brinka. No longer. He has a family now who are able to care for him and teach him the ways of a Dragon. That is not our place. You and I, we serve. We are outside of that circle. And while you and he are both children of Belendurath, he is not your brother."

That stung. "At least let me see him." Crenthys was a few inches shorter than the emissary, but she was built like a Dragomyr—broad with hard muscle. She squared up to the man and looked up into his amber eyes. "He needs me."

"No." Vodinar didn't shrink from Crenthys's hostile posture. "Not yet. We still don't know if you are well enough to dwell among us." When she opened her mouth to protest, Vodinar held up a finger. "Speak with our Oracle. He is a physician and a gifted sorcerer. If he gives me the peace of mind I require, I will speak to the Bronze Council on your behalf. Perhaps, in time, you will be given leave to train with him. It is the best I can offer."

So I am to be tested? Crenthys felt insulted. It had been a decade. Except for the two or three dozen people she had killed, she hadn't been a danger to anyone. She *had* joined Apostate, the largest anti-Dragon group known in Dorwine. *If this is what is required. I will do it for my brother.* She sighed. "Fine. I agree with your terms. And, thank you."

Vodinar smiled. He seemed to realize how hard it had been for her to say those words.

———◦○◦———

Crenthys had never before considered the burden of having friends. When she entered the common room of their house, she heard Tabir and Ember in the dining room. Tabir laughing at something the Malkin was saying. She would have to tell them about today and hear about their day, and try to seem interested. It was a strange realization, and it made her feel a little selfish. She cared for her friends and their interests, as she did for her brother.

"Cren," Ember called, "is that you? Or is someone stealing our laundry again?"

Tabir laughed harder this time.

"It's me." Crenthys followed a wonderful smell to the dining area where a generous meal sat on the table and her friends lounged. She stood in the doorway and appraised her companions. "Everyone survived, I see."

"Survived? Cren, it was amazing. There were so many books, I nearly fainted." Ember's eyes glistened as he smiled broadly.

"Well, it is a library," Tabir offered.

"No, it's... it's an institution. Like a living thing. Oh." Ember sighed, laying his head on the table. "I am exhausted, and I can't wait to go back."

Crenthys strode to the table and pulled a strip of meat from a platter. "Did you learn anything useful?"

Ember sat up and looked around. "Useful? Not really. Usual library things."

As smart as Ember was, he was terrible at lying. She felt a little less guilty about her reluctance to share. "What about you, Tabir? Did you learn anything?"

Tabir pursed his lips thoughtfully. "After most of my people... died, I felt very alone. Today, I discovered that might not be the case. These Golden Elves are strange, but they are my people."

Crenthys nodded, stripping off another piece of the succulent meat. Ember cringed as some juices dripped onto the table.

"What about you? And what about..." Tabir lowered his voice and looked around the room as if he expected to be overheard. "What about the things you are supposed to be learning about?"

Crenthys chewed the tender meat. "Nothing like that, yet. Not really. I tried to get permission to see my brother."

Tabir and Ember looked up at Crenthys.

"They all think I may still go crazy. Vodinar wants me to speak to a memory witch. That's what we call them." Crenthys cocked her head and squinted. "I just remembered that. Huh. Anyway, he wants me to speak to this physician to make sure I am not going to flip out and start attacking people. Then I may get to help train with my brother. He is still so young. And vulnerable. I'm afraid..." she trailed off.

After a few seconds Tabir said, "You are afraid they are going to corrupt him? Turn him into something awful?"

Crenthys nodded. Cursed emotion welled in her chest and she swallowed hard to push it down. "Yeah. Like a Dragon." She turned away before the tears could fill her eyes.

The Dragomyr's friends were silent while she composed herself. Friends are a good thing, she decided. "I don't know how things are going to go. We may not have much time. Tomorrow, I am going to find out what I can about Shimmer's response to Celebris's murder."

"I will see what I can learn about the item Wave used to control you in Usban," Ember said.

"And I will see what gossip my new Elven friends have heard about politics in the Bronze court," Tabir said.

Crenthys nodded. "Good. Let's just hope that Anuka is getting somewhere with his part of the plan."

Chapter 6

Well Laid Plans

Anuka watched Rigby unfurl the giant map of Barith Shir. *He always was better at this stuff than me.* The bard was an excellent planner and executed those plans very well. Anuka was content to let Rigby run the recovery. It was easier to let the crafty human handle those details while occupying himself with bigger thoughts. The big picture was Anuka's specialty.

Kelios and Offund flanked Rigby as he explained the basic layout of the structure. Felin, the Wild Elf Rigby was training, looked over Offund's head.

"If what the Victorin has told us is correct, I suggest a Chimney Man and a Late Rent." Rigby made the comment matter-of-factly but Kelios and Offund looked at Rigby, then questioningly at each other. *So green.*

"Chimney Man," Rigby said. "You know. Scary guy that climbs down your chimney, creeps into your room at night covered in soot, and steals your stuff while you are asleep."

"What's a chimney?" Kelios asked.

Anuka dropped his face into his palm.

"Chimney Man is a local story. Something parents tell their kids to make them behave," Rigby said patiently.

Yeah, he's better at that than I am, too. I would have slapped him.

"So we will crawl down the shaft here," Offund squeaked, pointing at a spot on the map. When Rigby nodded, he continued, "then we will locate and steal Bog's treasure back?"

"Yes," Rigby said.

Offund stroked his beard. "Pretty simple. What is 'Late Rent'"?

"Somebody is late with their rent, POW!" Anuka backhanded his other hand to demonstrate. "You sock em' right in the mouth."

"Who are we socking?" Felin asked.

"Dark Elf lady. Probably some kind of magic user." Anuka said.

Rigby nodded. "Kelios, that will be you. Anuka says you carry quite a punch."

Kelios nodded slowly and scratched his gills. "Yes. I have... means."

The Triton's gonna need to get in some water soon, Anuka thought. It was one of the limitations of the aquatic race. He could breathe air just fine, but his skin dried out quickly if he didn't keep wet.

Wait until Rigby sees him turn into a bear and eat that Dark Elf lady! Anuka chuckled to himself. Kelios was a druid, whatever that was. Anuka was about to explain what the Triton could do but thought it would be funnier if Rigby saw it for himself. Kelios had also turned into a dolphin a few times but hadn't eaten anyone then. That was kind of disappointing to the little pirate. He shuddered at the thought of Kelios unleashing the bear on the poor, hapless elf lady.

"How's the Dark Elf get up and down the shaft?" Felin asked.

Anuka gave the wood elf a withering look, as if he had just said something stupid. It was actually a good question, but he didn't want Felin to know that.

"Well," Rigby said as he stood and stretched his back from side to side like old people do, "that's a brilliant question. Lebarin says it's a lift of some sort. Probably powered by DragonsBlood."

Not likely, Anuka thought.

"DragonsBlood?" Kelios asked. "Where would she get that?"

"As far as we know, she can't. Lebarin thinks she is stuck down there because she can't get any. I assume the priest who built it had a decent supply of DB smears." Rigby shrugged. "My guess is that she has used all of them. That's good news for us."

"Why don't we take some with us and use it to escape?" Offund suggested.

Rigby pursed his lips and looked at Offund.

Oops, I smell a problem. Anuka was torn. He wanted the mission to go well and for them to all escape alive, rich, and famous. But he desperately wanted the Dragons to lose.

"Lebarin refused to give us any. He says it's a waste to use it just to keep us from having to climb out of the dungeon. Honestly, I agree. The value of DragonsBlood is astronomical since you guys destroyed Usban."

"Hey," Anuka retorted, pointing a clawed finger at Rigby, "that isn't fair. I did most of the destroying myself. Kelios wasn't even there!"

Rigby rubbed his face with his hands. "The point is, we are going to have to make our escape the old-fashioned way."

The group was silent for a few minutes before Kelios asked, "what, precisely, are we stealing?"

"We aren't stealing anything—technically—it's a rescue mission." Rigby said.

"Can we call it stealing? I'm training these knuckleheads, and I want them in the right frame of mind." Anuka said.

Rigby sighed. "We are stealing a knee-high box about the size of a man's torso."

Anuka snickered at the joke the others seemed to miss.

"What's in it?" Kelios asked.

It was the right and wrong question—they shouldn't care what was in it. This was where Anuka and Rigby diverged most in their criminal ethics. The goblin would steal a boat out from under a grandma crossing the river if they paid him enough. Rigby would want to know the grandma's name and what she did to deserve to be robbed. Granted, the bard's standards were pretty low, but having standards made him less effective, Anuka believed. Besides, his companions wouldn't figure it out in a million years.

"We don't know," Rigby finally answered, "and we aren't meant to know. Now, there is a lot of speculation—"

"Dragon Egg," Anuka provided.

"Yes. The most obvious answer is that it's one of Bog's eggs."

"I thought Bog was a male Dragon. How does that work?" Kelios asked innocently. Even Offund rolled his eyes at that question.

"Dragon reproduction is a topic for another day. We have to discern the truth from the rumors. Which is?" Rigby gestured for Kelios to answer his cryptic question.

Don't fail me now, Fish Man! Anuka thought.

After a pensive moment, Kelios said, "it is not a Dragon Egg."

"Why?" Rigby asked.

"Too obvious."

"BOOM!" Anuka yelled, smacking his fist into his palm. "Taught him everything he knows." Anuka gave Kelios an encouraging swat on the rump that made the Triton jump in surprise.

Rigby smiled at the exchange. "Right—so it's not an egg—too obvious. What is it?"

The question hung in the air for a minute before the bard answered himself, "We don't know. Since we don't know, we don't care. I assume it will be heavy. Anuka says that shouldn't be a problem for you, either."

Kelios shifted uncomfortably from foot to foot. He looked at Rigby. "It should not be."

Rigby nodded.

"Excuse me," Offund said. "We know why Kelios is here. And you are the crew leader. Anuka is the comedy, but..."

"Hey!" Anuka protested.

Offund ignored him. "Why am I here?"

Rigby looked at Anuka expectantly.

"Well, bubby. On a job like this, there might be trouble. The sort that requires balls of fire to rain from the sky." The goblin wiggled his fingers to show fire falling from the sky.

Offund stiffened and looked sharply at Anuka.

"Relax, Rigby is good people. We can trust him." Anuka winked at the Hob.

"No offense, but you work for Dragons. You have for your whole life." Offund flexed his gnarly little hands at his sides.

"We all have. Well, those of us who grew up on Dorwine. You learn one of two things growing up here: to love the Dragons, or to hate the Dragons." Rigby counted the points off on two fingers.

That's right, Anuka thought as his rage smoldered inside him. "And you can roll over for your whole life. Or you can bide your time. And then smash 'em!"

Offund caught Anuka's eye. The Hob gave him a single, poignant nod.

Anuka gave the Hob a questioning look, then he remembered the signal. *Well, this part is gonna stink. Nothing for it, I guess. It's time to get this show on the road. I just hope Rigby don't make me hurt him.*

"How is Rosanalli these days?" Anuka asked mischievously after they resumed planning.

"Who?" Kelios asked.

"Rosanalli. Tell Kelios about her, Rigby."

"She's my sister," Rigby replied through clenched teeth. It looked like the bard's left hand was twitching.

"Anuka, you know his sister?" Kelios asked.

"He knew her, once." Rigby's hands had balled into fists at his sides and his face was flush with color.

"Once? I knew her like five or six times!" Anuka protested, grinning broadly. *That should do it.* The goblin knew he had hit his mark when Rigby launched himself in Anuka's direction.

—◦—

Kelios stood, stunned, as Rigby hurled toward his goblin friend. Anuka dove between the bard's legs and came up in a roll. Quicker than Kelios would have thought possible, the human stopped and hurled a plate at the goblin. Anuka ducked the plate and came up glowing. *This isn't good.* The hot-tempered little creature would burn the warehouse down if Kelios didn't do something. The little pirate was volatile, but this was unexpected. Something was off with his little red friend. He had been different since he'd gotten the last letter from his father.

It had seemed pretty straightforward to Kelios: Anuka's father had arranged for his son to get set on the right path. Captain Sandbar's methods were extreme, but had been effective. Kelios had seen Anuka pouring over that letter a hundred times in the past few weeks. What was in that letter that the rest of them had missed? What was causing the goblin such turmoil? Kelios saw Offund placing something in Rigby's secret wall panel, but he hardly had time to discern what it was.

Anuka ducked a punch from Rigby and laid a smoldering hand on the bard's thigh, making him cry out. The goblin scrambled onto the human's back and was working on executing a choke hold on the man. *I must intervene.*

"Anuka, you stop—" Kelios began. Just as the door to the room was blown from its hinges.

A high-pitched whining rang in the Triton's ears. Muffled shouts echoed in the distance, but he couldn't make them out. He strained for air that refused to come in sufficient quantities. He breathed air tainted with the smell of smoke. Something small but heavy lay on his back. "Crenthys..." Kelios croaked. She and Ember broke through the door with the Malkin's magic. *We have to escape.* But that wasn't right. They had escaped Wave's dungeon and Crenthys was gone.

Kelios wiped his stinging eyes with the back of his hand and tried to rise. Someone shoved him back to the hard wooden floor.

"Stay down!" an angry voice yelled.

The fog in Kelios's mind cleared, and he remembered where he was. *Anuka!* His friends were in danger. Instinctively he reached inside his mind where the spirit of the bear waited eagerly.

With a growl and violent twist, Kelios leaped up, sending the person holding him down flying backward. A haze of smoke hung in the air and shards of wood littered the room. Irana, the name he had given the bear spirit, rushed to fill him. Pain racked his arms, legs, and chest as muscle and bone stretched and re-knit. Through blood-shot eyes he saw five men dressed in black clothing. One was subduing each of his friends. One lay groaning from Kelios's attack. The remaining man pointed a crossbow at his chest.

"Don't do it, bubby!" Anuka shouted from the floor.

The men had bound the goblin and the one standing over him drew a long-bladed knife from his side.

It was too late, the rational part of Kelios's mind thought. Irana was coming, and she didn't fear the weapons of man. But the invader didn't advance with his knife. He knelt and laid the keen edge of the long blade against Anuka's throat.

Kelios shoved Irana back with his mind. She was so strong and resisted his pleas for her to retreat. But he insisted. He had spent his idle time on board the *Kargarak* exercising his control over the bear spirit. Slowly, reluctantly, the bear retreated. Her sadness was heartbreaking. Oh, how she longed for bloodshed and Kelios was denying her.

The effort of dismissing Irana in the middle of his transformation was exhausting and Kelios sagged to his hands and knees panting. *Surrender and live. We shall fight another day.*

He looked up toward his attacker just in time to see the club descending. Then his world went black.

"Let them go, you Sum Buck!" Anuka growled, slamming his steaming palms onto Lebarin's desk.

The Victorin looked at the goblin's hands and then locked gazes with him. He smirked with amusement.

Anuka huffed and removed his hands from the priest's desk. Exhaling forcefully, the goblin rubbed his face and spun, his back toward Lebarin. "It's me Bog wants. Why are they locked up, and not me?."

The Victorin smiled. "Rest assured that you know little of what Master Caustimis wants, Mister Sandbar."

It clubbed him like a falling coconut. He turned back and fixed Lebarin with a smug look. "It's not what Bog wants. It's what you want. You need me. For what? You want *me* for the impossible job everyone is blathering on about," Anuka said.

One eyebrow climbed the old priest's liver-spotted forehead. "You are perceptive, Mister Sandbar. You seem to be a man of two reputations. I imagine that makes you easy to underestimate."

Lebarin's yellow-tinged eye was begging for Anuka to ram a dagger into it. *No, bubby. We need this gasbag to get out of here alive.* "Well, let's hear what you want from me. Maybe we can work somethin' out."

"It may be nothing. We may discover that you aren't interested, or even capable of providing what I need. If that is the case, then we end our relationship." The Victorin spread his hands before him and shrugged. "Your friends all die. Aridelle stays here with me, and you suffer your destiny at the hands of our God, Lord Caustimis."

Maybe one dagger for each eye would be better... Anuka had seen the crossbow slits in the wall when they escorted him in, but he was pretty sure he could bring a satisfying end to a well-deserving old twist. *I can't die here.* Papa was close, and Anuka was feeling like he might actually get to him. Deep down, the goblin knew where he would find Papa, but he pushed those thoughts aside.

"Fine," Anuka said. "Okay, I get your point. You've got me stretched over a barrel. What do you want?"

With effort, Lebarin pushed back from his desk, rose from this chair, and paced around the room. "Something dear to our Lord has been stolen."

Anuka didn't like that 'our Lord' garbage but said nothing.

"A treasure of immeasurable value has been taken. This treasure was hidden in a fortress near here. A member of my order named Reimor guarded it until his death. When he died, the knowledge of its location nearly passed as well. Only the old priest and our Lord knew where it was hidden. At least we thought that to be the case. We believe we have found the hiding place." The priest slid open a drawer and pulled a thin book from it. He held it up for Anuka to see, but did not hand it to him. "These are Reimor's collected notes. His assistant was a Dark Elf named Visceria. She took control of the fortress when my colleague died. So far, the Dark Elf has rebuffed my attempts to retrieve my Lord's treasure."

Anuka nodded and rubbed his hands slowly together. "So, this Dark Elf lady has Bog's super-secret treasure and won't give it back."

Lebarin did not confirm the goblin's statement.

"And Bog don't know it's no longer his. With the sky full of Silver Dragons, I'm guessing he needs it. Whatever it is. He will be here soon to get it, so you are about to poop your robe full."

"Perceptive, indeed, Mister Sandbar. I am willing to release your friends to you. All of them. Even Aridelle, should you succeed. I will pretend I never saw you and the church will pay you an unimaginable ransom."

"I don't know. I can imagine a considerable amount." Anuka tried another smile, but the old priest returned a sour stare. "Why me? I mean, I'm flattered. Despite rumors that twenty people have taken your little job and failed, why me?"

"Because, Mister Sandbar, you are the best of what is left to me. Besides, if half of the drivel floating about the rumor mill is true, you could do this *simple* job blindfolded."

"It's all true. But even I can't do it alone. I'm going to need my team."

Lebarin smiled. "Nice try, Mister Sandbar. I'm afraid you will need to make other arrangements."

"Other arrangements? What is that supposed to mean?" Anuka flung his hands in the air.

"It means you are going to have to find some other tunnel rats."

"Where am I going to find people with the right... skills?"

Lebarin fidgeted with the corner of the pile of notes he was holding and smiled to himself. "I believe that Mister Rigby has some associates he used frequently. That would be a sensible place for you to look. Mister Sandbar."

Taking the words as a dismissal, Anuka donned his cheap disguise and left Lebarin's office. Now he had to figure out where in Kentari the bard stashed his criminals.

Chapter 7

Ghosts

C renthys sat on her soft, giant bed, thinking. Ember's soft purring echoed throughout the small living space and Tabir tossed and turned as if caught in some frightful dream.

She hadn't slept, and the night was deep. There were too many questions. Her memories were still locked behind a stone wall. Some had climbed over or wriggled through cracks and she had gotten a few peeks, but most of her past was still walled away. The keys were there somewhere. She knew it. If she could access those, everything else would fall into place.

Sleep wasn't coming, and Crenthys needed some fresh air. She crept to the front door, but paused before opening it. A skinny human with a patchy beard leaned against a building across the street. He looked bored. Lookout, she thought. I'm being watched. Anger welled in her chest. There was a back exit in Ember's room.

Stealth had never been her forte, but she stepped slowly around the Malkin's bed. He looked tiny, curled up in the middle of the giant mattress. With one claw, Crenthys creaked open a shutter and looked out. All clear. She slowly rotated the handle on the door and stepped quietly into the night.

For an hour Crenthys walked around the city. She sorted through the thoughts in her head, trying to make sense of them. Her brother was a big concern. What was in store for him? Would he turn out to be a tyrant like the other Dragons she had known? She feared that was a likely outcome.

What about my memories? Crenthys hadn't said as much to her friends, but the ruby Wave had used to control her had changed everything. Since that attack, tiny pieces of her past had floated down like ashes. Her first memory had been of crawling through rubble out the side of a mountain. A mountain that had just exploded. Remembering anything afterwards had been a struggle. Everything prior to that moment was blank. She felt like she stood near a dam in a shallow river, her previous life beating against the other side. She had felt violated, too. Totally vulnerable. Wave could have killed her with a thought. Had he not been insane, he likely would have.

Crenthys had never been like other Dragomyr. Each was created by a Dragon, for a Dragon. To serve that Dragon until death. If that Dragon died, the Dragomyr followed soon after. They either grew sick and died, or went insane and were destroyed. Only one exception: her. Thought it was widely known that Dragomyr were incapable of such, she began to experience human emotions. Most notably, love. She had developed a crush on her Apostate mentor, Morglun. When he spurned her affections, Crenthys fled. Shortly after that she met Kelios. Why he should plague her thoughts, she did not know. He had attributed his affection for her to the emotional surge he had taken when he shape-shifted into a feral bear. She had agreed with him, but they both knew that wasn't true. Why he was attracted to her was a greater mystery than why she was attracted to him. Kelios was a noble man. He was courageous, selfless, and compassionate. He even—

Crenthys realized she was no longer walking. She stood outside a barricaded compound in horrid disrepair. She could hear her blood thumping through her veins. Before Crenthys could stop herself, she scurried over the wooden barrier and jogged up a cobbled walkway with tufts of grass poking up sporadically. Two more steps brought her to a magnificent door tall enough for a Dragomyr and equally as wide. The handle resisted but opened with a little effort.

Crenthys stepped into a foyer with dirty marble floors. Twigs, leaves, and other debris had been shoved to the corners. Just ahead was a massive pair of mirrored spiral staircases leading up to a balcony. Sconces throughout the room held thick, hearty candles. They were all lit.

What is this place? Crenthys thought. She stepped past the staircases, under the balcony, and into a giant room. It was in various stages of cleanliness. The floor held a layer of grime, but the staircase banisters were polished. Flower pots held the faintest traces of dead plants, but the mirrors on the walls gleamed brightly in the candlelight.

The scurrying of footsteps brought her out of her reverie and she prepared to defend herself. A disheveled old human man shuffled out from a doorway beneath the stairs. He had long wisps of thin, white hair. His suit was like a man-servant's uniform but was worn thin and wildly out of style. The old man stopped thirty feet from Crenthys and put his hands on his hips with a huff.

"Mistress Brinka? It is very inappropriate for you to be here!" the old human said with a stomp of his tattered boot.

"Any why is that?" Crenthys asked.

"Because you are dead!"

The words struck her, but not as fiercely as the voice of the speaker. "Odwin?" Instead of answering, the old man strode toward her and slowly inspected her from head to toe.

Odwin had been their chief servant. While Crenthys saw shades of the man in the creature before her, she couldn't believe this was him. He had tried to shelter her after Belendurath died.

"Odwin, where are your children? And the other servants?"

The old man took on a distant look, and he winced. "My... my children?" Odwin seemed to return to himself. He wiped his hands on his ragged vest, pressing down pocket flaps that were determined to protrude in a rumpled fashion. "Yes. Well. Saralyn and Dalmere have moved up, as they say. Yes. They serve Lord Dovondes in some capacity, as I understand it. Yes. I haven't seen them in quite some time." Odwin slid his hands into his vest pockets and retrieved something from the left one. Crenthys couldn't see it but he rubbed the object nervously.

Crenthys's heart ached for the man. Apart from his stained and torn clothes, Odwin seemed to be waging a losing battle against the wisps of hairs splaying wildly atop his balding pate. And he looked tired. Worn down like the soles of his boots. Heavy bags drooped below filmy, gray eyes that darted about maniacally at times.

The old manservant bowed suddenly and rose with effort, pain twisting his face. "Forgive me Lady Belendurath. I wasn't aware of your coming. Will you require a meal or perhaps some entertainment?"

The old man's words socked Crenthys like a punch in the gut, stealing the wind from her lungs. *What did he call me?* "Odwin. It's me Cre-Brinka."

"As you say, mistress. I've had difficulty keeping things straight lately."

"Odwin, look at me." Crenthys said, stepping forward to grab the man by the shoulders. She grabbed with more force than she intended and alarm crossed the old human's face. "Look at me. I'm Brinka. You called me Lady-." Crenthys stopped, realizing she couldn't say the name. "You mistook me for the Lady Dragon."

Odwin looked Crenthys over with wide-eyes. "Pardon, Lady. Meaning no offense, of course. I don't make assumptions concerning Dragons, Lady. I will address you as Mistress Brinka this evening, if you prefer. Will... will you require a bed in the manor house, then?"

He is mad! Crenthys thought. *Truly mad.* She needed to get away from this place. As the Dragomyr glanced around, the lengthening shadows seemed to ensnare her. Parts of the foyer were spotless, while others were coated in dust and cobwebs. Many pairs of human-sized boots, shriveled from disuse and covered in dust, were lined perfectly by the outer door. Every third wall hook was broken or missing, but every intact hook had a moth-eaten coat hanging from it.

"Master Odwin, I have to go." Crenthys said, releasing the man and turning to leave.

"Go? Mistress, you only just returned home. Where are you going?" The old man's voice seemed pained by her departure.

"I have to return to Slephinax Manor. They are expecting me." Crenthys felt dread rising up, and she quickened her pace to the doorway.

"Slephinax Manor?" Odwin said, "My Lady is very brave to be the guest of the Dragon that killed her."

Crenthys laid on a curved metal table covered with a thickly stuffed leather cushion. There was a groove near the bottom to cradle her tail. She chuckled. It was an odd thing to find amusing, but being a Dragomyr, she had spent a lot time figuring out what to do with that appendage. None of the places she had lived over the past decade made such accommodations. It had been easier to assume a form without a tail.

Along the walls were trays of tools and vials discreetly covered with cloths. Tomes of various sizes, some ancient, filled bookshelves lining the walls. The spaces not covered by shelves were paneled in warm colored woods, including the floors. Apart from a pair of plush arm couches, a tall armchair, and a crackling fire, the room was bare. A soft, floral scent hung in the air. Crenthys saw an aromatic log in the fire. The lengths the physician had gone to make her more comfortable were making her uncomfortable.

The door opened silently and a tall, smartly dressed dark-skinned human with gray hair smiled as he stepped confidently into the room. He continued to smile as he surveyed Crenthys. He wore tan colored trousers and a darker brown shirt, with a thick silk jacket of an even darker brown.

Does he always smile like that? She wanted to ask, but instead said, "Are you the Oracle?"

His smile became a barked laugh, as he sat in the chair next to Crenthys. "Do you know what that term means?"

"Yes." She hadn't intended to sound defensive, but it came out that way. "It means someone who can see the future."

"Correct. I am called the Oracle as a joke. I cannot foretell. I'm not sure anyone can any longer. No, I look backwards: I help people delve into their minds and find things they have lost."

"Are there many people like me? Who have forgotten things?" She dreaded the answer.

"Yes, for many reasons. Some have been injured. Others may have painful events in their pasts that prevent them from accessing those memories." Still the Oracle smiled.

"Which am I?"

"That is what we are here to find out."

"Are you a Dragon?" The question sounded stupid as soon as she asked it.

The Oracle's smile grew warmer. Less clinical. "I am. An ancient Bronze Dragon who no longer enjoys the burden of ruling. You may call me Ivrus."

"I have one more question," she blurted. Crenthys hadn't planned on asking, but was emboldened by Ivrus's honesty. "Would you call me Crenthys? Everyone here insists on calling me Brinka, but that name is painful to me."

"Of course, Crenthys. Now, I would like you to relax." Ivrus stood and walked to the head of the table.

He is a Dragon. Why take this human form? Perhaps it makes it easier to do whatever he is going to do. She wondered if it was too late to call this madness off. Perhaps her mind was protecting her from things that could harm her.

"You are supposed to be relaxing, Crenthys." His chiding was mild but firm.

"I apologize. I... This is difficult."

"I understand. Let me explain how this will work. I will step into your mind with you. Together, we will journey back as far as you can remember. Then I will examine the thing blocking your mind and determine how best to remove it. It will not hurt. Some things you hear and see may not make sense to you. That is normal and we can discuss those things afterward. If I discover something too harmful, we will end the session. Okay?"

Crenthys nodded and tried to relax. She closed her eyes and took slow, deep breaths. A crack like a whip sounded and her eyes popped open. The sun was bright and birds were chirping all around. She was standing in waist high flowers. Crimson flowers. Hummingbirds flitted nearby. "The grove," she breathed. Crenthys's voice sounded odd, as if she was speaking underwater.

"You know this place?" Came another warbling voice. It almost sounded familiar.

"Kelios?" she asked, spinning around. Instead, she saw Ivrus standing nearby. He was dressed as he had been.

"Yes. I know this place. I dream of it often." Crenthys touched a flower and gasped. It was real!

"I see. And Kelios is...?"

"A friend," she supplied quickly.

Ivrus nodded. "We should get started. Take my hand."

She didn't really want to leave this place. It was more real to her than she could remember. But there was work to be done, so she stepped to Ivrus and took his hand. The grove vanished.

Crenthys was lying on her back, staring at a starry night sky. She hurt. Every joint ached, and she had a cut on her face. She tried to sit up, but struggled to rise. A hand appeared, and she took it. Ivrus pulled her onto shaky feet. Every inch of Crenthys was covered in dust and dirt. Her eyes stung, and she wiped them with a dirty hand. She wore a dark yellow uniform and had a curved-bladed sword strapped to her side.

"It's ok," Ivrus encouraged her. "This is a memory. It happened in the past. You are going to be ok."

Of course. I am remembering. This is the last thing I can remember.
She nodded. "Ok."

"Perhaps you should sit." He helped her sit on a flat rock.

They were on the side of a mountain. Crenthys could remember the climb down and the hike back to Clover Crisp. It had taken days. Her hands trembled as she remembered.

"I am going to go inside and see what I can find," Ivrus said.

"You can't," she cried, grabbing him by the arm. "It's dangerous. There is something awful in there. I..." She couldn't think what would be so terrible.

"It's ok, Crenthys. This is a memory. We are perfectly safe. I will be right back." Ivrus squeezed her shoulder and smiled. Then he jogged up the hill toward the hole she had crawled out of.

Crenthys didn't want to watch him. Instead, her thoughts turned toward the future. What would she do once she found out what was inside that mountain? She hadn't really thought about the potential consequences for her brother, or even her friends. What if what she learned here changed everything? The reality of her situation began to sink in and she felt vulnerable. If Ivrus had moved so easily into her mind, what kept another Dragon from doing the same? What would happen if they discovered what had occurred in Usban Port? Or if they saw the things she had done in Apostate's name? What if they saw Kelios and how she felt for the Triton? She didn't understand those things, but they were inside her head.

Distant vibrating sounds drew Crenthys out of her reverie and she sprang to her feet. A building pulse filled the valley and the mountain trembled beneath her feet. A gigantic dome formed on the other side of the mountain. It was so vast that it covered the entire distance between her and Clover Crisp, even engulfing the distant mountain behind Wrythmar.

Ivrus came staggering from the hole in the mountain where Crenthys had escaped. His eyes were wide and wild. The old Dragon staggered forward as the ground shook beneath his feet.

Crenthys caught him as he wobbled forward. He clasped her forearms in a tight grip and stared at her with a crazed expression on his face.

"You should not have come back. Should have stayed away. You should have stayed far away." Ivrus sounded desperate, and his face contorted with fury.

Crenthys tried to step away, but Ivrus held her fast.

"You should have stayed away," he screamed.

Finally, Crenthys tore free of his grip and fell backward. She landed with a start, her eyes popping open to reveal Ivrus's office.

Crenthys flung her legs over the side of the table. Her head swam. Any thoughts of leaping to her feet were dispelled by a wave of nausea.

The door clicked open softly and Vodinar stepped inside.

"Vodinar, what happened? Where is Ivrus?"

The male Dragomyr rushed to her side. "All is well, Brinka. Everything is fine. You should lie down."

"Where is Ivrus? Why are you here?" Her tone was demanding, and Crenthys hoped the volume masked her fear.

"The Oracle is in his study. I am here to collect his report. Remember?"

That seemed a poor choice of words to Crenthys. But she recalled their conversation. "What did he see? Vodinar, he was terrified at the end. He kept saying that I should not have come back. What is going on?"

"Brinka, er Crenthys, it is common to experience oddities in these situations. The Oracle told me as much. I suggest you return to your apartments and get some rest. When you are more relaxed, you can return and he will fill you in on the details."

Maybe he is right. I'm exhausted. Crenthys took the hand Vodinar offered and followed him down the long hallway toward the building's exit. Just before stepping into the sun, Crenthys heard a low chanting from behind a closed door. "You should not have come back... you should not have come back..."

Tabir didn't think he would have much trouble getting information from Payris. The slender elf seemed to love the sound of his own voice.

"Tell me of your homeland, of your people," Payris said excitedly.

They had toured the Golden Embassy and now walked among the beautiful gardens behind the compound. Tabir knew this question would come. That hadn't assuaged his dread of the conversation. "My people lived in a land called Descoran, in a grand city called Eldinel. Descoran is a spur on the grand continent, Hekorin."

Payris stopped and put his hand on Tabir's forearm. "I know nothing of these names. Could they have different names in the Dragon tongue?"

"Perhaps, though I don't think the Dragons of Dorwine pay those lands any heed. It is far from here. Above the line, as you say," Tabir said.

"Above the line." Payris nodded. "Please, continue your tale."

They resumed walking, and Tabir cleared his throat. "Descoran was created when, in anger, the creator god, Rathune, flung the great mountain Scoranthus to what was believed to be the edge of the world. The people of the land fled from Rathune's burning anger as he passed judgment on his fallen avatars and their disciples, committing them to the core of Acos for a thousand years. Some of those who fled passed over the mountains in the southwestern corner of Hekorin. Many of them died and the way of return was shut behind them. Those who survived lived in the mountains for generations until the dust of Scoranthus settled. Slowly they moved south. The dwarves stayed in their keeps in the mountains, humans lived at the foothills, and the elves ventured far south, where they planted the forests. Over time, relations between the peoples grew strained and wars erupted. Making war is all mankind knows. Eventually, my people prevailed—they made slaves of the humans and murdered the dwarves nearly to extinction. My people were villainous tyrants, and I didn't know it. I ran away, found a passage through the impassable mountains, and here I am. With a few stops along the way."

Payris nodded as if he was connecting dots together. "How did you come to Dorwine?"

"I met a friend who has good relations with the metallic Dragons of this land." Tabir hoped the ambassador didn't press too much on that subject.

"Coltimar?"

Tabir nodded.

"Fascinating. You are a fascinating individual. We must have more of these conversations. It has occurred to me that you likely know little of our people here. Our ways. We must remedy that. But first... wine," Payris said, smiling broadly.

Tabir was thinking of ways to politely decline more wine as they entered the compound. They took a different turn than he remembered and soon they were in a long hallway with rooms on each side.

"Where are we?" Tabir asked.

Payris stopped and looked at Tabir. "Oh, yes. These are the private quarters. They aren't part of the usual tour. My apologies. I keep the best wine for myself." He continued on to the end of the hallway and into a giant bedroom. The ambassador moved to a wine rack affixed to the wall. It was filled with bottles.

Tabir stepped in and was about to decline more wine when something caught his eye. Behind a pane of DragonGlass, illuminated with magical light, hung a thin strip of torn parchment two inches wide and a foot and a half long. When Payris stepped up and offered Tabir a glass, he drained the contents in one gulp. His eyes never left the display.

"Interesting, isn't it?" Payris remarked. "It's some sort of ancient writing. It cost a fortune, but I thought it looked classy."

Classy? There were many words Tabir could think of, but classy was not one he would have chosen to describe one of the Slivers of Aracthias.

Chapter 8

The Best of
What's Left

B *e careful, bubby,* Anuka chided himself. He was supposed to be angry, but he didn't want to get carried away and wind up in the cell next to Rigby.

Lebarin wiped the places Anuka's hands had been with a handkerchief. "From what my guards say, you were trying to kill the bard when they arrived."

"I-yeah. It's complicated. We are old friends." That was an oversimplification of his relationship with Rigby, but it was all the Victorin was getting. A few years back, Anuka and the bard pulled off a big job in the capital that had made them legends.

"I have a similar relationship with many of my colleagues." The priest smiled, pleased with himself.

"Yeah, I imagine so," Anuka said under his breath. *It's time to move this along.* "Look, you've heard what Rigby and I can do. I need him. I'm gonna need all of my friends to retrieve your lost treasure. There are things they can do that no one else can."

"Indeed." Lebarin seemed to enjoy making the goblin squirm. "Those things are what prompted His Holiness to issue your arrest warrant, as I understand it."

I hate bullies. Clenching his teeth, Anuka dammed up the tide of vitriol that threatened to come flooding out. Rigby, Offund, and Kelios needed him to keep his head.

"You seem to have some understanding of what I require of you. What have you heard, Mr. Sandbar?"

Anuka frowned and rubbed his eye. "Not much. Just what I've heard on the street and that's pretty thin..."

Lebarin looked impassively at the goblin until he continued. "About fifty years ago, Bog came here and brought his favorite priest some kind of treasure to guard. Everyone thinks it's an egg. So it probably isn't. Instead of keeping it in Kentari, the old priest vanished. Every so often, the priest would show up in Kentari with the treasure. Bog would arrive in Kentari, meet with the priest in secret, disappear for a week, then return. The old priest disappeared again for a few months. Cept' the old priest hasn't been around for a long time—he's probably dead."

"Bog told you where the priest was hiding, told you to go get his treasure, or he would melt your face off. You've been sending idiots after the treasure ever since. The Silver Dragons showed up and bought you a little more time but, despite your calm exterior, you are about to lose your mind. You are desperate enough to put one of Bog's most valuable bard's in jail, imprison his daughter in this church in the swamp, and offer the number one criminal on the whole continent freedom in exchange for this treasure."

This was the part Anuka loved most in life. The old priest seemed to be in the middle of a heart seizure. Lebarin's wrinkled chin sagged and his mouth hung open like a flycatcher. If his eyelids opened any further, the priest's eyes would tumble out of their sockets. The old man panted like an alligator had chased him. Now for the dagger.

"What did I leave out, father?" Anuka made a deep bow in mock obeisance. This was usually when someone punched or kicked him, so he braced for the assault. It never came.

Curious, Anuka raised his head to find the priest taking a long pull from a fluted flask. *I nailed it!*

The hands of the Victorin, the highest-ranking priest of Bog in the region, trembled as he returned the flask to his desk. The old priest took a long, calming breath and turned to face Anuka. The goblin stood and brushed the dust from his knees as the priest glared down at him. "You are resourceful, goblin."

No more Mr. Sandbar? I must have really gotten close.

"Perhaps you are worthy of the better of your two reputations. For your sake, I hope so." The Victorin moved to stand near the little pirate. "I suggest you make haste in assembling your team, Mr. Sandbar."

———⋄———

Anuka paused at the thin wooden tavern door. The room beyond was quiet but not silent. *Amateurs.* He didn't remember ever visiting this tavern. *Maybe it used to be something else,* the goblin thought. It certainly wasn't his first tavern; he knew what to expect.

Closing his eyes, Anuka drew in a quick, deep breath. He fisted his hands at his sides. Then he started to glow.

A crimson radiance emanated from his skin as if a lantern were in his chest instead of muscle, bone, and blood. As he stoked that inner fire, tendrils of smoke wafted lazily from his skin. He used to think about the day his mama drowned whenever he closed his eyes. Now, knowing that she yet lived, he focused on her betrayal. *She didn't die. She left.* His skin tingled, and he felt his pores opening. *Papa left, too. Left me alone.* Another burst of energy surged within and he could smell the wood smoking beneath his feet. He hadn't held this much heat before. Not for something as simple as scaring a few kids. But he was tired. Tired of not being respected. Tired of being ignored. And tired of Dragons telling him what to do. With a roar, he opened his eyes and savagely slammed his tiny boot into the door.

It flew open in one quick, wobbly motion. Through blazing red eyes, Anuka saw the shocked faces of three youths step from their hiding places. The goblin ignored them and strode into the common room, leaving scorched footprints in his wake. A new pair of boots was a small price to pay for the looks on their faces.

One youth, a bald, pear-shaped human, either gained some courage or lost all sense. He stepped into Anuka's path and pointed his long gnarly club at Anuka. He opened his mouth, likely to tell Anuka that he had no business here, that Felin wasn't here, and that he had better leave. Before the human could speak, the little pirate grabbed the business end of the club and ignited it.

The instant his hands touched the club, Anuka released a ball of frustration that manifested in a small conflagration. The weapon-turned-torch blazed with fire and the youth drew it up to inspect it. With a cry, the fat young man tossed the flaming item to the floor and thundered out the front door. Anuka calmly retrieved the club, and grasping the still-burning weapon in both hands, turned to look at the remaining youths. They hustled out the front door after their friend.

Anuka took a couple of deep breaths and stuffed his rage into in the corner of his heart where it lived. It felt good to get mad. Most of the time, he wore a mask for others to see. Keeping his feelings bottled up was getting harder. If he hoped to find Papa, he would have to keep a lid on his rage. For a little while, at least.

The club was really cooking now. Anuka tossed it into the cold fireplace in the corner. A plume of ash puffed from the hearth and floated in lazy motes around the room. Rubbing his hands together, the smoldering goblin said, "I didn't hurt your friends, and I don't plan to hurt you." When no reply came, he said, "I don't blame you for running: that was the smart move."

Another half a minute of silence passed. Anuka let it.

Finally, a voice from the shadows said, "Why did you come?"

Huffing through his nose, the goblin turned to peer into the darkness. *He's pretty good.* "Lebarin took em' all, that Sum Buck. Rigby. Offund. Kelios. He has em'."

"Why you're free?" The voice sounded apprehensive.

Anuka didn't need to see him to imagine the dagger the elf held. "Because that old geezer still wants us to go steal his treasure back."

"Us?"

"Yeah, us. He's kinda holding our people hostage to make us play along." Anuka squinted at the outline of Felin hiding in the darkness. "C'mon out, bubby. I won't hurt you. And it's weird talking to the dark." Anuka climbed up into a chair and propped one elbow on the table in front of him.

Felin slowly stepped from the shadows and tried to be sneaky about putting his dagger away. Warily, he took a seat across from Anuka. "I don't have people."

Anuka snickered. "Sure you do. Rigby told me about some of the jobs you've pulled. How you handle yourself. He's fond of you, kid. You probably remind him of a much younger version of himself. And you follow him like a puppy."

Felin looked at his hands. "He has been kind to me."

"Yeah. He's like that. Look, I didn't see the point of you tagging along on this job from the beginning."

Felin looked up sharply.

"No secret. I'm a world class burglar. You are green as the inside of a snake."

Before Felin could unleash his building indignation, Anuka held up a finger to stop him.

"Rigby thinks you have potential. But now he's stuck. And he needs you more than ever." Anuka let the young elf chew on that for a minute.

"What you're going to do?" Felin asked finally.

"*We* are going to do the job. Lebarin is setting us up to fail, and I'd like to feed him a turd sandwich. I need your help."

The idiom seemed to glide right over Felin's head so Anuka moved on. "Rigby has a handful of criminals in this city that he's worked with before. I need you to help me collect them."

Felin took a moment to mull over Anuka's words. The wild elf was a lot smarter than he seemed. Anuka guessed he had crawled out of the woods recently and was just learning the low Draconic language.

Finally, the Wood Elf nodded. "I like you less than you like me, Anuka Sandbar. But I will do this thing for Rigby. He is a good man."

"Excellent!" Anuka hopped off his chair and clapped loudly. "Let's get to it. Where do we start?"

"Grom."

"Grom? What's a Grom?" Anuka asked.

"Grom is where we start. Have you ever met a giant?"

Chapter 9

Accidentally in Love

Ember had learned so much in the past couple of days it was astounding. He knew enough of Dragons and Dragomyr anatomy he could perform a thorough dissection of one, should the need arise. Yet, he felt guilty. Which was confusing. Of all he had learned, he still had discovered nothing regarding what Anuka had him searching for. There must be another section. High above, on the uppermost floors, were books restricted to all but Dragons and their kin. That must be where his answers hid. He stared up the central staircase for the hundredth time that day. So close, yet just out of reach.

"What's got your fur ruffled?" Yondi asked from her chair at the table behind Ember.

Subconsciously he rubbed the thin hair on his arms until he realized she was using an idiom. "Oh, well... nothing." It wasn't a question, but it came out sounding like one.

Yondi chuckled as she came to stand behind him. Then she touched him. She combed the hair on Ember's head gently with her fingers. "You are a horrible liar."

"Thank you?" He wanted her to stop. She mustn't stop. *Oh dear.*

Then she did stop and drug her chair to his table. Yondi spent the whole day by his side, looking through various books or just watching him. Usually, he couldn't stand for someone to watch him, but he didn't mind Yondi so much. She was strange in a way he couldn't figure out. But the touching...

"What's on your mind? You've been reading the same page for ten minutes."

He looked down at the essay on brain trauma in Dragomyr and realized she was right. "Oh. Well, I am a bit distracted. I am looking for a bit of information that isn't available in these sections."

"Oh? What sort of information?" Yondi asked, leaning forward.

"I really shouldn't say: it's kind of secret." The walls began shrinking in, filling with water. His heart thumped so hard it must be visible outside of his chest.

"Ok. No problem. Why don't you tell me what girls are like where you are from?"

Girls? A mob of angry people had formed a circle and were closing in on him. In the front was his mother brandishing a Thibawhack paddle overhead. "Dragon artifacts!" Ember squealed. He clamped his hands over his mouth as if he might prevent further disaster. His tone was an octave higher than normal and carried considerably more volume than was advisable. Yondi giggled. A metaphorical clunk sounded in Ember's mind. Like the proverbial last tumbler of a lock falling into place. A collage of faces filled his mind's eye. First was his father saying, "women are wise in ways a man can never understand". Then came his brother, "Ember, steer clear of women. They will play you like a double-reed flute and you won't even hear the music. You will just dance along." Finally, Anuka said, "Bubby, a woman is like a honey badger..." The Malkin shook his head violently before the goblin could finish, and dispelled the images from his mind.

He examined Yondi. Ember thought back to their meeting on the steps the first day. Her smile each day, how she made eye contact with him. The way the human flushed earlier today when he made an offhanded comment about her hair. How she had rubbed his hair just now until he nearly purred aloud. He leaped to his feet, knocking his chair over.

She sat up, wide-eyed concern on her face. Yondi stood as well and grabbed his hand. "Ember, what's wrong?"

"I'm not sure, but... but I think you are amorously infatuated with me."

Her cheeks filled with color, and she looked away.

"What's more, I feel a reciprocal response."

Yondi burst out laughing then.

Ember didn't know what to do. He wanted the sink hole beneath the library to swallow him, yet he was afraid they were going to be forcibly removed from the library. So he did the only thing he could think of. In one swift move, he swept Yondi off her feet and carried her from the library. She rested her head on his shoulder and sighed. It sounded a lot like a purr.

Outside, they sat together at the bottom of the library stairs. Yondi was heavier than she looked and Ember couldn't carry her much farther. He refrained from explaining that to her as he had read that women of some species grew angry when questions of weight or age were broached. Yondi was still laughing.

"Ember, you are amazing. Do you know that?"

"I don't know. The tapestry of emotions I am experiencing is pretty broad, and amazement isn't among them."

She laughed again, harder this time.

When she finally gained control, the human girl looked into his eyes and smiled. "Tell me. Are you this straightforward with every girl?"

How do I answer this? Apart from my personal policy of perpetual honesty, which Anuka has already forced me to bend nearly to breaking, I don't want to seem foolish. If I lie, she will know. And I will be a liar. Yes. Honestly, then. "I can't say that I have ever expressed my feelings to another girl. Honestly, I didn't know what I was feeling until just now. I attributed it to indigestion secondary to the introduction of a new diet because it has only been since our arrival here." Yondi laughed again. So did Ember. He didn't laugh often. When he did, he thought it sounded like a cross between a wheeze and a cackling hyena.

When their laughter died down, they looked at one another. Ember said, "I am unsure what we do next. I have read very little about romance and relationships with humans, though I am now well versed in the mating patterns of chromatic Dragons."

Yondi snickered. Then she leaned closer. "Well. The next thing we do is find a way to get you into the restricted book section."

"I thought I would be speaking with Ivrus today." Crenthys tried to keep the irritation from her voice, but was doing a poor job of it. She had slept little the previous night in anticipation of getting some answers. Her encounter with Odwin at her old manor hadn't come up, and she was eager to share that with the old Dragon. She wasn't sure it was a great idea to tell Vodinar about him.

"I understand, but a pressing need of his services has arisen. I volunteered to discuss the matter with you," Vodinar said.

Crenthys stood in the doorway of Vodinar's massive office. It was so clean and ornate she was afraid of tracking something on the carpet if she came in much further. She folded her arms across her chest and clicked her tongue. "Ok, what did he say? Will my memories ever come back? What... what did he see inside the mountain?" Ivrus had seemed deeply upset by what he had seen, and he was clearly avoiding her now.

"He saw the slain body of your master." Vodinar rose from his desk and stepped closer to Crenthys. "She died from the cave-in. It appears she caused the mountain to collapse. A large stalactite impaled her when it did. There was a great release of magic involved. The Oracle couldn't determine whether the collapse was accidental or intentional." Genuine sadness shone on Vodinar's face. "Belendurath was my friend, as I am sure you know."

"How would I?" Crenthys asked, and Vodinar looked at her. This wasn't what she hoped to hear. The story about Ivrus being busy was suspicious.

"Of course. My apologies." Vodinar gave a shallow bow.

"So, is there nothing that can be done about my memories?" Crenthys asked.

"Perhaps the best course is to look to the future and not dwell on what is behind. Especially those things too hurtful to recall."

How could he say that? "My future is tied to the fate of my only remaining blood relative." Crenthys tried to keep the rising anger out of her voice

"Yes—and to that end, I have some news. Lord Dovondes and the Bronze Council will convene in three days. You are officially summoned to attend a hearing where your fate will be decided." Vodinar smiled as if he expected applause.

"That sounds pretty ominous."

"I won't lie to you. There is no precedent for a Dragomyr surviving the death of their master as long as you have. It concerns them. The safety of many people, mortal and DragonKin alike, is at stake."

Crenthys felt anger rising in her. "What will I have to do to prove myself?"

"I can only guess that they will question you about the past decade and try to discern your overall... fitness." He fussed with a tiny string on his crisp yellow tunic. "My Lord and I have spoken at length about your case. So long as you comport yourself properly, I imagine it could go well for you."

"Then what?" She didn't dare spell it out.

"If things go very well, you will be restored to your family name and allowed to join the team tasked with raising your brother." Vodinar seemed pleased with the announcement.

To mortal ears, it likely sounded like a terrible deal, but Crenthys's heart sang. She had friends and owed them her life, and more, but she needed to be in her brother's life as much as he needed her in his. "Ok. I think I can manage that." She was smiling like a little girl, but didn't care.

"Good. Brinka, I feel I must warn you. Dragons have long memories. Some on the Council recall the events of a decade ago and will not be eager to have you restored."

"I understand." And somehow Crenthys did. A tingling in her mind, like a distant alarm, warned her of the folly of running afoul of Dragons.

---‹O›---

"What do you mean you think you are falling in love?" Crenthys asked.

"Well, I have identified the major markers. I haven't finished charting my progress on the timeline I made, but I think I am deep into the infatuation stage of a relationship." Ember explained.

"Ember, you met this girl two days ago," Crenthys said.

"How long had you known Kelios before feelings began to develop for him?"

The question was stated matter-of-factly. It was an honest query. But it struck Crenthys like an oar to the face. *Was that really what was going on? Am I falling in love with Kelios?* Unlike Ember, she had avoided much examination. Tabir didn't seem shocked at Ember's revelation about her feelings toward Kelios. *Did everyone know? Did Kelios?*

"I think this is what Ember means to ask: Is it plausible for feelings to mature so quickly?" Tabir supplied.

He must think I am offended. I'm not offended, just unsettled. "I understand, it's just... you should be cautious, Ember. Very little in the Bronze Court is what it seems to be."

The Malkin cocked his head to the side. "Are you inferring that Yondi Fick is pretending to like me? Why do you believe that coercion would be required to find me attractive? Is it because of my bookish nature? Or my hideous appearance?"

"Ember, I didn't—"

"Because Yondi finds both of those things adorable. She told me as much. Plainly. Perhaps if you were more forthcoming with Kelios—"

"Ember," Tabir said, when Crenthys tensed.

"I believe I will retire early. I have a timeline to finish." Ember picked up his papers, quill, and ink bottle. Then he retreated to his room, smartly drawing the heavy curtain closed behind him.

Crenthys sighed and sat in the chair the Malkin had just vacated.

"I know," Tabir said too softly for Ember to hear, "I am concerned, too."

Crenthys gestured helplessly with her hands. "How was your visit to the Golden embassy?"

Tabir pursed his thin lips and sat silently.

Crenthys had never known the elf to be dishonest, but he seemed to be contemplating doing just that.

"Interesting. Payris is... different than I expected. He drinks a lot of wine, uses a lot of words, but never really says anything. It's strange. When I tried to drift the conversation into Dragons or politics he subtly grew obtuse . . . elusive . . . like trying to catch smoke." He opened his mouth, then closed it again.

"That's frustrating. I'm sure you will get somewhere, eventually." Crenthys tried to keep the disinterest from her voice. The Elves were of little concern to her at the moment. "Did you learn anything else?"

Tabir's smile didn't touch his eyes. "I did. Something incredible, but I don't know how to relate it—how to make it matter to you."

Crenthys folded her arms on the table and gave Tabir a challenging look. "That is an odd thing to say to a friend. Try me."

"Okay. You know what I believe, in whom I believe." It was a statement, but Tabir waited for Crenthys to nod before continuing. "Rathune is returning. Either in judgment, or with peace. Which, I do not know. But we have some clues. There once was a divine creature named Aracthias—I say creature because no one knows what he was—only that he came from Rathune, and did his bidding. Aracthias left behind a decree behind. The decree described Rathune's past judgment on the mortal races, on the land, and on his avatars—Keit and Tor. It also prophesied his return in a thousand years. The decree was later destroyed, ripped to shreds. Its pieces were scattered by the winds. Those pieces—slivers—endured. All of them. When I left my home, I found a brotherhood of priests who were faithful to Rathune and were guardians of these Slivers of Aracthias. Their aim was to assemble them, translate them, and learn how to appease Rathune before his return. Crenthys, Payris has one of these Slivers in his quarters."

The Dragomyr's expression was confused. "Why? Is he one of these priests?"

"No," Tabir said, with a chuckle, then grew serious as he pondered. "No, he couldn't be. He said he appreciated it as a piece of artwork, but I suspect he knows more about it than he is letting on."

"What do you intend to do about it? Contact the other priests?"

Crenthys didn't understand. How could she? Tabir decided not to reveal his plans for the Sliver in Payris's bedroom. "I don't know. It just seemed... odd."

"That does seem odd," Crenthys agreed.

"How did your second meeting with The Oracle go?" Tabir asked, steering the conversation away from things he may be forced to lie about.

"It didn't. I met with Vodinar, instead." Crenthys shrugged at Tabir's questioning glance.

"What did he say?"

"He said that they didn't think I was a danger, and that my memory loss is likely because of physical damage. And can't be reversed." Crenthys kept a neutral expression while she struggled to understand the news.

"Do you believe him? I mean, considering the advice you gave Ember... "

"I will until he gives me a reason not to. What choice do I have?" Crenthys shrugged helplessly.

Tabir only nodded.

"I'm not saying what you said about Ember's friend is true, but I have to wonder; why are we here?" Tabir continued when Crenthys gave him a confused look. "I mean, Ember and I. We are being treated very well. If not for my reservations about trusting our hosts, I would love the consulate. The idea of understanding another group of my people is very attractive. And a massive library for Ember to explore. What could be better? Your people reminded you of the disgrace in which you left this place a decade ago, then they began doling out niceties and privileges. Why go to all that trouble if they think you are potentially insane and dangerous? Why are we all not in a dungeon somewhere?"

Crenthys closed her eyes. Tabir was right. Between worrying over her brother's wellbeing and fretting over Kelios, she had done the very thing she had warned Ember against: trusting Dragons. She nodded and looked at Tabir. "You are right. We must all be cautious. I've been so concerned with my brother and... the others that I have let my guard down."

Tabir laid his delicate hand on her arm. "Your brother will be fine. He has you to care for him." That made Crenthys smile. "And I am sure the *others* are doing fine."

"Thank you," she said.

Tabir nodded and walked toward his room. He stopped in the doorway and looked back. "And Crenthys."

"Yes?"

"Everyone knows about you and Kelios." Tabir drew the curtain closed behind him.

Chapter 10

The B Team

A nuka was miserable as he sloshed along the muddy path toward the river. It had started raining right after he and Felin set out. During the hour they had spent cleaning up Ribgy's hideout, the rain had become a downpour.

Apart from being soaked to the bone, Anuka's head hurt from lack of sleep and his belly was empty. That was a common problem with his small stomach and high rate of activity. To top it all off, now the goblin had to go haggle with a couple of Ferbs to get his Stoneman out of jail. *Perfect.*

At least the Wood Elf was holding his tongue while they walked. Anuka didn't think he could tolerate a stream of mindless blathering from the kid. *Kid? He's probably seventy years old.* Tabir had tried to explain Elves to him, but it made little sense. Apparently, Wood Elves were a different breed entirely. A High Elf would learn a trade and never change throughout his life—he'd do the same thing for hundreds of years. Wood elves got bored and completely changed their entire lives every eight or ten years. That made more sense to the goblin, but he didn't understand how someone three times his age could be so green. *Whatever.*

Now Anuka had to build a crew from the dregs of Kentari, and time was running out. The sea of people grew more dense as they drew closer to the west-end docks. The little pirate reflexively felt for his coin stack. The familiar lump under his tunic was there, but was much smaller than he liked. He should have shaken Lebarin down for some seed money. Coins in Dorwine were small metal pieces with a hole in the center. Some were round. Some were perfectly square or rectangular. They were all made to stack by size and then be threaded onto a leather thong to secure them.

Anuka hated crowds. Being short was a real hassle. And the idea of having people behind him made his palms sweat. Thinking of Felin on his flank made him check his coin stack again. Anuka couldn't see where they were going so he made the Wood Elf take the lead.

One good thing about the rain was it made it easier to hide. A handsome goblin with red skin would stand out in any crowd. So he wore an over-sized jacket that nearly drug the ground and covered his hands with gloves. Rigby had a decent collection of hats at the hideout, and Anuka had found one big enough to obscure his face pretty well.

Up ahead, above the crowd, he saw the sign they were looking for: Half a wagon wheel mounted on a crooked pole. It looked like a sun rising on the horizon. *Stupid Ferb superstition.* This jail was called Sunny Times. Anuka thought it was about the dumbest thing to name... well, anything. Let alone a jail. In Zhazie, the jails were all private businesses. PeaceMen brought the crook to the jailer and announced their crimes. The jailer decided on the punishment. If the wardens did a good job, the person learned their lesson and were considered reformed. The jailers were paid based on the behavior of the criminals they released. Like everything else in Dorwine, Anuka thought the entire system was a joke and totally corrupt.

Apparently, Grom had gotten himself arrested. In Anuka's opinion, it was bad form to work with people who habitually got arrested. He couldn't voice that opinion right now since his friend and their two associates were also in a hole in the ground. The thing that concerned him most was that Grom had gotten arrested because he *wouldn't* fight. If he had busted open a few heads in a bar fight, well, that would be understandable. But to get jailed for refusing to fight? Anuka shook his head.

This jail was run by a couple of Ferbs. Two brothers, Kort and Jens, from the far northwest country of Ferberia had ruled the docks in Kentari for over a year. From what Anuka knew of them, everything they did was strange, but you couldn't argue about their effectiveness. Most contracts—or contractors—made with the church didn't last so long.

The crowd thinned as Anuka and Felin stepped into a series of pole barns and shanties cobbled together along the fairway near the center of the long western dock. Anuka had counted fourteen vessels in port so far; and they stretched on down the wide river bank as far as the eye could see. Kikkabar had been careful not to dock so far upriver. Most of the river here was backwashed from the Dragonblade Sea. The river was wide enough, and deep enough, to make Kentari the perfect port for trade vessels to stop for repairs, news, and supplies. The impressive variety of trade goods from the various mills and warehouses from inland Zhazie kept the port crowded with a mix of foreigners and ruffians. Anuka hoped that made it easier to blend in. He was eager to get indoors.

"Help you sirs?" rasped the voice of a tall, broad fellow. He wore dirty snug-fitting, dark blue pants, and a mustard colored vest over a dingy white shirt with the sleeves rolled up. A worn, squat hat with a flat top and sweat stain around the brim topped his small head. He was a human in his early middle years with an ugly scar on his left jaw. The jagged scar crossed his throat and disappeared into his shirt near his right shoulder.

That explains the rough voice. "Oh hey, fella, me name's Shemin. I'm comin' ta see bout the big fella in yon cage, ya." From his peripheral vision, Anuka saw Felin staring at him but hoped the elf had enough sense to hold his tongue.

The gravel-voiced guard smiled broadly at the goblin showing seven or eight rotten teeth spaced evenly throughout his mouth. "Yo, sir, seems you've a bit o' sense about you, ya. Visited the homeland, have ya?"

"Oh, ya," Anuka lied. He tried not to scream at the site of the man's rotting teeth. *Nothin' worse than letting your teeth go like that.* "Long ago. Say, is one of them fellas Kort or Jens? I've a bit o' business to talk with em."

"Oh, you bet. Wontcha come in outta this rain?" The big man gave another nauseating smile and motioned for the goblin and Wood Elf to step inside.

Felin shot Anuka a questioning glance when they had moved beyond the guard's sight.

"That," Anuka murmured without moving his lips, "is professionalism."

The inside of the shanty was surprisingly well lit. Only one small torch burned, but the cracks in the walls were so big they scarcely diffused the sunlight. Motes of dust filtered lazily through the air. The pungent odor of unwashed bodies in a hot, damp room overpowered the smell of the greasy torch burning. An astonishingly corpulent Ferb sat behind a desk barely as wide as he was. He didn't look up as their grizzled guard escort stopped and folded his hands patiently behind him.

Anuka opened his mouth to speak, but a look from the guard convinced him otherwise. The immensely fat human behind the desk poured over a mess of papers covering his desk. He looked to be reconciling accounts. Sausage-like fingers glided gracefully over the multi-colored beads of a small counting frame. Anuka gasped in astonishment when he realized the wooden calculator was permanently affixed to the Ferb's left arm where his hand should have been.

The man looked up then, dark blue eyes peering from under the brim of a thin visor. Rivers of sweat that had been neatly pooling at the border of the human's bald head and the visor's ring cascaded down onto the papers.

The accountant looked addled, as if coming out of a week long Tent Weed binge. He blinked twice and a broad grin split his face. His front teeth were missing, top and bottom, and the remaining teeth looked to be losing a hard fought battle. "Oh hey," the big man rasped, sending ripples through the impressive collection of fat rolls on his neck.

"Oh hey, boss," the guard growled deferentially, "this'n here is... ". The guard looked helplessly at Anuka.

"Shemin," Anuka provided.

"Shemin, eh? Fine name. Welcome to Sunny Times," the massive accountant said, spraying his papers with spittle as he said 'Sunny'. "What can we do for yous?"

"Well, me 'n me elf friend 'ere was hopin' to free our friend what got himself in a spot of trouble. Name a Grom."

The fat man's smile dropped like loose trousers. "Oh, Grom ya' say?" He gave a sad shake of his head. The movement included his whole upper body and the desk scooted a bit with each wag of his head.

This ain't good, Anuka thought.

"We pride ourselves on rehabilitating our criminals well at Sunny Times." The rotund Ferb looked forlorn.

"Lowest rate of recidivism in Kentari," rasped the gruff guard mournfully.

Anuka was stunned. Not just by the gravel-voiced guard's shocking vocabulary, but by the gloomy mood that had come over the room. It was one of the few times the goblin had ever been at a loss for words. He cleared his throat and said, "Oh, ya. Sure enough he's done bad, but... ".

"Bad?" The fat man said, jerking his head up. The thin desk in front of him scooted forward with the motion, as if it was also outraged. "Grom's a saint of a man. Bless him, but he is."

"Oh," Anuka said dumbly. "Then wha's the problem? Can't just let him go, eh?"

"Look now, them PeaceMen expect our prisoners to leave here better men than when they came in. Improvement is our hallmark."

"Our hallmark," the grizzled guard echoed.

"He got put in here on account of refusing to fight. What can we do with a man set on a life of peace? We cannot improve on them sort of virtues."

"Aye," the guard agreed. "He makes us better men."

"If we just let him go, and he refused ta' fight again, he comes right back here." The fat man's face was beet red. Sweat ran unchecked down his face, leaving clean streaks on his grimy cheeks. Then the accountant ground his remaining teeth together and snarled, "And we don't get paid."

Ah, Anuka thought. Everything comes back to money. The Peace-Men liked to pit the dock workers against one another, especially if they found someone they thought would make a good fighter. Grom had probably refused one of these fights and wound up in jail.

Anuka spread his arms out wide and smiled broadly, "Gentlemen, don't ya fear. Yer lookin' at Grom's physician."

The fat man sat back, confusion twisting his chubby face. "Physician?"

Felin appeared from the shadows to fix Anuka with a curious look.

"Oh ya, friends. He right sick, ya see? I was in the process of trainin' him in the ways of violence 'fore he slipped away into the streets of Kentari for a night of benevolence."

"Right?" asked the guard. "You teach men to be violent? How's that work?"

"Well, secrets of the trade, ya know. But I'm quite good. I once coached a village of squirrels to lead an attack on a bear."

"Ya' don't say?" the fat man asked.

"Oh ya. Let me take my patient back and continue his treatment. Before ya know it, he'll be back in your care. Only next time, he'll have done some real menace." Anuka punched the air to accentuate his point.

The guard and the fat man exchanged looks. The fat man tried to shrug but his shoulders and neck were so buried it was barely evident.

"I reckon then we could rehabilitate him, on account of the violence, eh?" The grizzled guard seemed to warm to the idea.

The fat man nodded. "You really think you can turn him violent?"

Anuka bowed low, "Oh ya, the next time you see him, he'll be a slavering savage. Oh ya."

Once the papers were signed and a small amount of coin changed hands, Anuka and Felin stepped back out into the swampy streets of Kentari with a gigantic Stoneman in tow.

Grom looked like a statue come to life: his skin was gray and stretched tightly over corded muscle. His jaw could be used as a plow.

One of and his hands could easily wrap around Anuka's head. Anuka guessed the half-giant's shadow weighed three stones.

Anuka tried not to stare at the big man as he lumbered along the street behind them. The smattering of workers and other citizens were doing plenty of that. Felin wasn't staring at the giant. He was staring at Anuka.

"What?" Anuka asked.

"What was that?" Felin asked.

Anuka knew what he meant. He was used to people's stunned expressions at his application of social magic in tough situations.

"As I said, young Felin. Professionalism"

———◦———

Crows were a bad omen. Anuka wasn't particularly superstitious, nothing like Rigby, but the ravens all seemed to stare at Grom, Felin, and himself as they trudged along the sodden path. Dead trees were scattered along the road like a wood graveyard. The ravens stared at the troupe from their perches on those terminally-ill branches. *They are just birds,* he chided himself.

Getting the half-giant out of jail had been a simple matter, once Anuka applied sufficient charm—and coin.

The cacophony of croaking, dripping, and chirping that enveloped them grew louder the farther they trudged off the main road. Anuka itched to pull a torch from his pack and light it. He could see plenty well, but having a lit torch provided a bit of comfort. He resisted the urge because he didn't want to show his unease to Rigby's recruits. *Recruits. Ha!* More like projects. The bard was always nursing some greenhorn along. In other circumstances, he would never have dreamed of using such green young criminals on a job this big. In most circumstances, Rigby would be the one worrying about the help.

Grom stomped along behind him, his giant boots making sucking noises with each step. He was big. Maybe the biggest creature Anuka had seen. He was at least as big as Kikkabar and looked very strong. And, supposedly, he hated to fight. Anuka sighed. Grom would have to do. Anuka knew very little of this Westerner or of his people. The few things he had learned about them, however, were enough to make the goblin's eyes pop out. But legends and rumors didn't fill your belly.

Felin was another matter. The Wood Elf was cocky, mouthy, and arrogant. Anuka had told him he was redundant on this job and he had meant it. But there was something about how the elf moved that reminded the little pirate too much of himself. Despite his flaws, he seemed to have a lot going on between his pointy ears. On this job, Felin may end up doing some delicate work he had never done before. His failure could mean death for all of them. *There is so much riding on this job.* Anuka enjoyed laying everything on one bet. For that reason, jail might be the best place for Rigby. The bard was cautious. If he was honest, Anuka missed him. Rigby was a perfect foil to his impetuous nature. Not having someone to keep him grounded was dangerous. It was reckless and a good way to wind up dead. Grom was a smash and grab guy. His job was straightforward.

Suddenly on edge, his feet stopped moving. He held up a hand so Grom wouldn't accidentally step on him. A chill crawled up Anuka's spine.

The others strained to hear what may have alarmed him. Nothing. That was the problem. The forest was now totally silent.

It was like being in an empty warehouse at night. A feeling Anuka knew well. No birds, frogs, or bubbling swamp. Total silence. The narrow path at their feet had nearly disappeared.

"There is something there. A house, or something." Felin said, pointing a slender finger straight ahead.

Anuka trusted the Wood Elf's eyes but couldn't see much besides shapes in the distance. Then he did.

Someone had arrayed a ramshackle collection of blackened wood to form a tiny hut. A dense clump of trees surrounded it like a nest cradles an egg. The trees were black and twisted. Their leafless branches stretched like skeletal arms toward the hidden cabin. A figure stood on the stoop.

The air was as still as death. Yet the stranger's tattered cloak billowed around him like he was in the crow's nest during a gale. The figure held a long staff out to his side and stared at the trio of invaders.

Sum buck. How would Rigby handle this? The bard was good with people. He could talk a Dragon out of his scales. Anuka thought back to previous encounters. He had seen the human negotiate and tried to imagine how to deal with this man. With Offund in the cellar, they would need some magic. And the church had become suddenly stingy with potions and other magical items. So they needed this guy.

Anuka took a breath and fixed his plan in his mind. "Hey!" *Good start*, he thought. "We heard you were a wizard or something. Why don't you come with us to—" A dissonant chorus of caws erupted from the figure. A heartbeat later, a torrent of ravens erupted from where the stranger stood and charged the intruders.

In a flash, the birds swarmed Anuka, knocking his hat from his head and blasting him backwards. The squelching mud held his feet fast, and he careened into the soggy mud. The keening scream of the ravens pierced his mind like a dagger. *Sum Buck!* This was like drowning without water. It suddenly occurred to him that the birds would likely peck his eyes out if he gave them the chance. He reflexively shielded his face with his tiny red arms. Panic gripped him and Anuka nearly cried out. He didn't want the foul birds mistaking his perfect teeth for pearl corn, so he squeezed his mouth shut.

The birds kept swarming and Anuka knew he had to get away. With a flop and a twist, his feet were free of his boots. He sprang into a crouch and looked around. Squinting to peer through the hurricane of black feathers, Grom was where the goblin had last seen him. The giant stood, arms at his sides head tilted back, his eyes closed. He splayed his hands wide open, and Anuka marveled at the barrel-sized mitts and the titanic man. Felin was nowhere to be seen.

I knew that cowardly little slive would run the first chance he got. Anuka couldn't blame him. Part of him knew he was just looking for reasons not to like the Wood Elf. It occurred to him suddenly that the birds weren't attacking him. From what he could tell, Grom wasn't being attacked, either. Anuka planted his bare feet on the sodden ground and tentatively stood. No birds struck him.

The screeches and caws were still sharp in his ears, but some of the panic clawing at him receded. It was still impossible to see more than a few feet in front of him, but he knew where the ravens were coming from. He put his head down and steadily moved in that direction.

Anuka used one arm to shield his face, and just in case his suspicious were wrong, he used his other hand to slide a dagger from his side. He didn't know what he would to do when he got to the figure but negotiating was always easier when he held a dagger in his tiny fist. *Why did Rigby's magic man have to be such a pain?* Offund hadn't been this way. Once they had freed him from imprisonment and certain death, he had joined Anuka and Kelios happily.

He was within thirty feet of the shack before he could see the figure. Ravens still poured from the dark man. *Are they pouring out of his chest?* Anuka had seen some weird stuff, but that made little sense. He didn't want to hurt Rigby's magic user, but this had to stop. A plan had just started forming in his mind when the ravens suddenly stopped.

Sudden silence jarred him. Anuka heard a soft grunt and the dark figure staggered a bit. A second figure appeared behind him. Felin.

The Wood Elf stood behind the cloaked stranger, holding a dagger to his throat.

The stranger dropped his stick and raised his arms. Anuka's tiny bare feet splatted in the mud as he stalked toward him. Felin forced the man to his knees, putting him at eye level with Anuka.

The dark-clad stranger was a scraggly human with greasy black hair and a scruffy beard. His dark brown eyes darted wildly, trying to focus on Anuka as he approached. The man's breath came in ragged gasps. His teeth were yellow and crooked.

Anuka stopped a few feet short of the man and tented his hands on his hips. "Are you Zenzendorf?"

"Xanavor," Felin corrected. The human tried to turn to look at the Wood Elf, but the knife held him in check.

"Xanavor," Anuka said. "Is that you?"

"You've come for me at last," the man croaked. His voice sounded coarse, like he hadn't used it in months. "I knew this day would come."

Anuka scratched his head. *How did he know this was coming?* "Then you should know what we want." He didn't like how unsure his voice sounded.

"You will have to kill me." The man's voice sounded resolute.

Sum Buck. I was worried I wouldn't be able to afford him, but good grief. "Look, man. It don't have to come to that. We need your help, but if you don't want to help, then don't. You'd better believe I'm telling Rigby about this."

"Rigby?" Xanavor asked. "What is this about?"

One time Anuka was lying on his back staring up at a swaying coconut. At one point, the coconut started getting bigger. Part of Anuka's brain told him that the coconut was falling, but it took a bit for the rest of him to catch up. That was how Anuka felt in that moment. "Hold up! We don't work for Bog. We ain't comin' to kill you. We're here to offer you a job."

"A job?"

"Yes, a job. We need you to magic some stuff for us! Rigby sent us."

"Rigby?"

"Ya!" Anuka looked at Felin. "Bubby, let him up."

Felin returned the dagger to his belt, and Xanavor stood.

"Man! This whole approach was stupid. I'm sorry we startled you. Look, we hate Dragons!" Anuka slapped the dark man on his leg.

Xanavor smiled and some of the exuberance drained out of Anuka at the sight of his teeth.

<hr />

"Okay you sorry Sum Bucks, listen up." Anuka paced in front of his three new crew members. Getting Xanavor to come into the city had been difficult. Apparently, the strange man had a mistrust of civilization that was deep-rooted. It took an official declaration from Lebarin stating that he was pardoning Xanavor of all past crimes. It was one of the goblin's best quick forgeries. "Rigby and my boys are stuck in a hole. We gotta do this stupid job for Lebarin, so he will let 'em out. Rigby's daughter, too." He stopped pacing to make sure he had their attention. "The old plan is junk now. We don't have the right personnel. No offense. I'm sure you are excellent criminals. You just don't have the right skills. And I don't trust any of you."

The three exchanged concerned looks before Felin said, "So, what is your new plan?"

Anuka nodded. "I'm workin' on that. It's still coming together."

The door banged open and Anuka almost messed his trousers. A tall human with blonde curly hair and a chin dimple as deep as Anuka's big toe strode into the room.

"No plan? That sounds dangerous," the stranger said in a singsong voice.

"Who in Keit's bushy back hair are you? Grom, rip this Sum Buck's arms off." Anuka knew Grom didn't like violence, but hoped the big man would play along. He didn't.

The stranger dropped a missive on the table and walked up to Anuka. "I," the man began, flinging his hair to one side, "am Fabian. Victorin Lebarin sent me to join you on your quest."

"Fabian? You?" Anuka barked out a laugh that sounded as fake as it felt. "You were a pimply little butt sniffer last time I saw you."

Fabian sneered at Anuka. "Well, some of us grow up."

Oh. Short jokes, eh? "Yeah. You got bigger, but I'm pretty sure you're still sniffing butts. You are the worst bard nobody's ever heard of. Ain't no way. If you're half as stupid as Rigby says, you'll get us all killed."

"Rigby isn't here," Fabian said with a dazzling smile. "The Victorin decreed I join you." The bard pointed to the paper that Xanavor was reading.

"Well, he ain't here either." Anuka put as much defiance in his tone as he could muster, but he knew he was beaten. Having Fabian along would seriously complicate the mission. The older bard had said the young fop was useless. He had forgotten to mention how nice Fabian's teeth were.

"It looks legitimate," Xanavor said.

Anuka snatched the paper from his hand and pretended to read it. Instead, he examined the artistry. If it was fake, it was very good. Sum Buck. *How is this gonna work?* "Ok, fine. Go sit down with the other rejects. We can't do the original plan. Our smash guy don't smash and our wizard don't use magic."

"I am not a wizard. The Mistress of the Harvest has chosen—" Xanavor began.

"Yes, yes. Can you blow up stuff or set things or people on fire with your mind? No. No wizard then." Anuka snatched his hat off and ran a hand over his bald head. With a sigh, he smashed the hat back on his head. "Alright. We do this the old-fashioned way."

"Won't you enlighten us young fellows, please?" Fabian said with a sardonic smile.

Anuka probably wasn't much older than the smug bard. "We make it up as we go along."

"That's it?" Fabian asked, standing.

"Yeah. That's all I got. Your boss has the plan guy in a box."

"That's madness," Xanavor said. "I don't even know what we are doing."

"You aren't the only one," Fabian added.

"We can't just make this up, Anuka. There are moving parts and... complicated things to consider." Felin piled on.

Great. The dimwit posse is ganging up on me. "Look, if you Sum Bucks are scared or want out, hit the door. I can replace you all tomorrow."

Grom stood up from where he sat on the floor beside the table and cracked his head on the low ceiling. "Planning to proceed with no plan is dangerous. Some of us will be killed. You have wasted my time. I am going back to jail." The giant's voice was like thunder over a mountain. The titan ducked his head and lumbered out the door.

Figures—I finally figure out how to get him mad and he quits. "Enjoy your cage, coward! Who ever heard of a thug who won't fight?" Anuka kicked at a piece of the ceiling that lay near him but missed. "Who needs that idiot? Stonemen are three for a copper."

Felin looked at Anuka like he'd eaten the last biscuit. Then the Wood Elf turned and walked out. Xanavor fixed a disappointed look on Anuka but held back whatever he intended to say. He followed Felin out.

"Whelp, we got us a clean slate. You know anybody that'll work on short notice?" Anuka asked Fabian.

"Lebarin will not be pleased." The human tossed his head to one side and stalked out of the room.

"Who cares? When is that old fart ever pleased?"

Frustration stabbed Anuka like a needle in the eye, and he wanted to scream. He balled his fists and gritted his teeth. Growling, he shoved a wooden chair onto its side and raked the remaining items off the table. The memory of the last time he saw Papa came to mind and then slowly faded away.

Chapter 11

Sunny Days

T abir stood in a small study in the Golden consulate. Payris was at court, but Tanila had insisted he stay. She had provided Tabir with a series of genealogy charts that were fascinating. They traced every Golden Elf family for nearly a thousand years. One of the oldest lines belonged to Druindar, the Gold DragonLord. He had taken an Elven bride and even fathered eleven children who had children of their own.

Tabir's legs felt weak. Only then did he realize how long he had been poring over the charts. His intention had been to find someone to ask the questions he had been compiling, but now he was most interested in working out the cramps in his legs. As he limped around the study, stretching his aching leg muscles, Tanila returned carrying a tray of food and drink.

She stopped in the doorway and regarded Tabir curiously.

"I've been sitting longer than I thought, I suppose."

Tanila smiled. "Yes, you have been quite diligent." She moved some of the charts with the corner of the tray as she sat it on the table. "I came twice, but you did not notice."

"Apologies," he said with a small laugh. "This is incredible information. These records are... amazing."

Tanila picked one up and looked at it. "Did you find me on these charts?"

He hadn't even thought to look. That seemed rude to him. Payris was easy to find. He was much older than Tabir would have guessed, nearly four centuries. "I didn't. Actually," he said, limping his way over to pick up another chart. "I had questions about this one." He handed her the paper.

Tanila looked at the paper and smiled. "Why is a Dragon in the Elven lineage?"

"Well, yes."

"Dragons have unbelievable powers. Apart from being immortal, and unfathomably large, they also possess incredible magical power. They wield the power of the elements, they can change the nature of things, and they are incredible illusionists. They are rumored to possess the same creation magic that created our world. Dragons can assume any form they desire. Your friend, Brinka, has similar powers."

Tabir nodded, thinking of the Sea Elf disguise Crenthys had worn.

"Lord Druindar is the most powerful among them," Tanila continued. "So strong is his magic, and his understanding of it, that he doesn't simply resemble an elf. He becomes an elf. So much so that he can father Elven children."

"That is incredible. And a little disturbing," Tabir said.

"No, he is one of us. He loves us as his people. Even more than he loves the Dragons." She spoke confidently.

"Have you heard of the incident in Usban Port?"

Tanila looked at him. "Of course. Everyone has heard of it. That is why you and your friends are here, no?"

"Yes," he said. It wasn't a lie. One reason they were here was to determine what the chromatic Dragons might do in response. "What do you think Lord Druindar intends to do about the situation?" The mess at Usban had been Wave's fault, not his friends. That mad Sea Elf had killed the Silver DragonLord's ambassador, her Dragomyr, and blamed Anuka Sandbar for it. From what they had heard, the Silver Dragons had filled the sky in Zhazie, looking for Caustimis.

"He intends to find the truth, I imagine. That is his way, Tabir. He is fair. Do not be afraid of him."

"What about Lord Dovondes?"

She pursed her lips thoughtfully. "We shall see. Most of the chromatic Dragons, most of the Council of Wyrms, truthfully, follow Lord Druindar's lead. The Dragons will handle the situation."

"It is the mortals who get caught in between I am concerned about."

Tanila looked at Tabir. She seemed about to reply when a call from the doorway interrupted them.

"Apologies, Tabir, my friend. My work kept me over long. Tanila has kept you entertained, I hope." Payris looked tired. He took a long sip from a slender wine glass.

Tabir turned. "Yes, she showed me some of the history of our people."

Payris licked his lips and nodded at Tabir. "Our history, indeed." He took another sip of wine and stood before Tabir. "We are cousins. Of the same blood. Only a bit of geography separates us."

Tabir didn't reply, but he could sense a speech or long tale building.

"As I have already told you, my time here is ending soon. A replacement will be sent and I will return home. Much of the staff will leave tomorrow."

"Yes, you have told me as much."

"Would you consider returning with me? To Theleth."

The unexpected question stunned Tabir. His first thought was that he could not. He had work to do. Rathune's work. But his heart ached to meet more of his people. The sudden demise of so many of his kin, and his role in that demise, had left a gaping hole in his heart. The Golden culture was so different from his own, yet also quite similar. A part of him longed to go back to the days of his youth when he lived in ignorance of his people's ways. Back to the joys he experienced before he knew anything of slavery, demons, and magic. He wanted to live that way again.

"Do not answer now," Payris urged him. "Think on it and we will speak again tomorrow. I must beg off visitation for now. Stay as long as you like, but I must retire. Dealing with Dragons is exhausting."

The self-contained nature of Wrythmar fascinated Ember as he and Yondi walked along the clean cobblestone walkways. Separating the Dragon city from Clover Crisp with portals that used precious DragonsBlood made Ember sad. It was another layer of superiority the Dragons added between themselves and the mortals.

"What are you thinking about?" Yondi asked as they walked.

"Several things, simultaneously. In the front of my mind, I was pondering the social impact of dividing two nearby cities via a wall and guards."

"Oh? Did you reach any conclusions?" Yondi asked. Her voice held a hint of teasing.

Ember didn't mind that. He frequently endured much worse from people he liked far less. "No. I imagine its something my subconscious will chew on for a while. In a few days, I'll pick the question back up and mull it over some more."

Yondi laughed. "You are always thinking."

"Well, sometimes I feel things, but I'll admit to being far less skilled in that arena."

She took his clawed hand carefully in her small human one. "Practice. That's all you need."

Ember smiled. Her hands were rougher than he had imagined they would be, but he didn't mind. *Here we go. Away from the safety and comforts of my mind, and into the barbarous, unknown lands beyond.* "So, you look nice today." She did. Yondi typically wore simple, comfortable outfits. But they suited her.

"Thank you. I made an effort."

How bizarre is my life? Ember thought. It was baffling how he could go from being a side character in a play with important people like DragonKin, princes, and pirates, to starring in his own production. Yondi thought about him before selecting an outfit. Ember couldn't remember the last time someone deferred to his interests.

"So, are you ready to begin your life of crime?" Yondi asked.

"Hmm? Oh, the library. Technically, I am already guilty by association to one of the most notorious crimes on the continent in decades. But yes, I believe I am prepared for our incursion."

"Incursion. That makes it sound so... official," Yondi said.

"Well, you are a duly appointed academic ambassador on a diplomatic assignment. Should we get caught, you can blame me and severely mitigate our punishment." Ember had thought that out. He wouldn't have agreed to allow Yondi to be involved otherwise. This wasn't his first time breaking into forbidden libraries. But the girl didn't need to know that.

The idea of keeping things from the girl he intended to court didn't sit well with him. Even though it was for her own benefit. He thought of what Crenthys had implied and wondered if Yondi was keeping things from him. *Of course she is. It's natural to do so. Certainly nothing as nefarious as Crenthys suggested.* Thinking about the conversation put him in a dour mood.

"What's wrong, Ember?" Yondi asked, concern in her voice.

Ember made an irritated noise. "I was thinking of an argument I had with Crenthys last night."

Yondi frowned. "Is she hard to get along with?"

"She can be," Ember conceded. "Usually not."

"There are so many rumors about her and the... circumstances of her leaving years ago. I was only a little girl."

"The three lowest forms of information are rumor, opinion, and hearsay," Ember recited.

"Oh, really? Is that your opinion?" Yondi asked.

"No, it's empirical."

"Well, do you know what happened? Based solely on reliable information, of course."

Ember pondered as they rounded a corner to avoid walking into the Mallory Gate. "I don't—neither does she."

Yondi looked at him curiously, but didn't press.

In for a drop of DragonsBlood, in for a gallon. He continued. "Cren was accused of all sorts of things. Treachery against the Bronze Crown, murder of other Dragomyr, even killing her master. While she wasn't convicted of any crimes, the Bronze Council concluded she would soon go insane and ordered her destruction. Her words, not mine. I would have said murder."

"Do you think she is insane?" Yondi asked.

"By the largely accepted scientific definition? No. In a looser, more abstract definition of the term? Perhaps. She has done some things that I would argue a sane person would not do. However, some of those have benefited me greatly. Even saved my life. And I have also done things that would fall into this dangerous category. So, no—she isn't insane. No more than I am." Ember smiled.

"What happened in Usban?" She asked in a rush, like she had been building up enough courage to ask.

"Many things. We may have uncovered a massive conspiracy. Very damning for the council of Wyrms. We may have started a war." Said aloud, the list of things he and his companions had done seemed like a fantasy tale.

"Well, then. Umm. So you were part of it? I mean, you know this Sandbar that killed the Silver ambassador?"

"No. I mean, yes." Ember stopped and took Yondi's hands. "Remember what I said about rumors? Anuka didn't kill Celebris. He was framed for that. The Sea Elf who killed him was trying to start a Dragon war. If we aren't careful with the things we repeat, he will succeed. Crenthys hopes to clear up some of those things and—"

Yondi released one hand suddenly and dragged him into a nearby alley.

When they stopped, Ember stood with his back to the street, alarm on his face.

Before Ember could speak, Yondi took his face in her hands and said, "Promise me you'll be careful. You have dangerous friends and I don't want you getting hurt." She wrapped her arms around him and buried her face in his chest.

What brought this on? He gently returned the embrace. "I will be careful. I promise. It's in my nature to do so." Her concern for his well being touched him.

———◆◇◆———

Yondi had seen a large, robed figure pass by the alley twenty feet behind them. Ember was so engrossed in her affections that he didn't notice. She bit her lip and squeezed her eyes tightly shut. Her fearful trembling was genuine as the Malkin returned her embrace.

———◆◇◆———

The knock at the door was thunderous, causing Crenthys to jump. "Sands," she swore as she pulled on a clean shirt and jogged to the door. On the other side stood a tall human with dark brown skin. He had a flat nose and a flat face. The deep set emerald eyes were unmistakable. "Zanderon." Her voice held relief and a little embarrassment. She still expected armed guards to show up to take her away. "Please, come in."

The Dragon, in human form, grunted and stepped over the threshold. He looked around appraisingly. "This place belonged to Slephinax."

"So I have heard."

"He was a good-hearted Dragon. Loyal to our kind." Zanderon continued his perusal of the interior.

Crenthys wondered what the old Dragon would think if he knew what Odwin had said about Slephinax. This wasn't the time for such discussions. "We are alone, if that is what you are wondering."

Zanderon grunted again. "It was. I also like to see how mortals live. The older I get, the more time I spend like this." The Dragon gestured to his human body.

"You train young Dragons," she said. Vodinar had told her as much.

"I do. But I cannot allow you into the Forge where your brother is being trained."

Crenthys released a slow breath. Anger wouldn't help her here. "I don't want you to overstep your authority, I just—"

"I have plenty of authority," he interrupted. "And plenty of good sense. That is why I will not allow you to train with your brother. Not now, at least."

She felt heat on her face and her hands balled into fists. Zanderon wasn't concerned. *Of course not. He is a Dragon.*

"Tell me, Crenthys, why do you wish to train with your brother? Do you have experience training Dragons? From what I have heard, you remember nothing more than a decade hence. Any useful information about rearing Dragons is gone from you. I don't profess to be an expert in how the mind of a mortal works, but I imagine you feel a great deal of fear for the youngling. Perhaps you have a great desire to protect him? Give him the best?"

Crenthys felt like her clothing had been stripped away one piece at a time. Her fists unclenched and she folded her arms over her chest.

"Crenthys." She looked up into the old Dragon's eyes. He continued, "We desire these same things. *I* desire these things. I have centuries of experience. I have been through the process myself. You know the emotions you are experiencing aren't possible for a Dragomyr. Until you have control of those emotions, you will do more harm than good to your brother."

She had nothing useful to say, so she just nodded. The pressure at the back of her eyes made her furious, so she squeezed them shut and forced back the tears. She opened them once the tears were sealed away.

"Your eyes are like hers," Zanderon said. "More so than I remembered."

"I will take your word for it."

Zanderon smiled. "Is that why you asked me here?"

Crenthys hated being rash, but she was getting desperate. *What is there to lose?* "Do you remember a servant of my master called Odwin?"

The old Dragon furrowed his brow. "Odwin was more than a servant. He ran all of Belendurath's affairs. His family kept her mortal homes. He did many jobs you did not have the patience to do. Why do you ask?"

"I saw him. While out for a walk, I found our old compound. He was there."

"I thought he had died or moved into the lower city. He lives in the old manor?"

"Perhaps. He was there a few nights ago. The house looked like he was expecting someone. Zanderon, he is quite mad." She regretted the words, true as they were. He seemed a kind man and was likely a wonderful servant. Odwin didn't deserve derision from her.

"I see. Mad in what way?" Zanderon stood and looked Crenthys in the eye.

Her skin tingled, and she knew he was using magic. *Old wyrm thinks I will lie to him.* "He called me Belendurath. Insisted that I was my master in disguise. He carried on like it was a game I might be playing. When I told him where I was staying, he told me I was brave for sleeping in my killer's house."

Zanderon's silence worried Crenthys more than the anger she had expected. She felt the magic dissipate.

"I should send a group of the guard to find him."

"Don't! Please. He isn't harming anyone." She hadn't meant to sound pathetic, but there it was. "At least let me talk to him."

"Crenthys, you cannot trust his words, or put any hope in them. His mind fractured when Belendurath died, it seems." He put a dark hand on her shoulder. "I know you are eager for answers, but they will not come from Odwin—not suitable answers."

"I don't know where else to go. I spoke to Ivrus, Vodinar's physician."

"The Oracle? What did he tell you?"

"Nothing. I can't even speak to him again. He told Vodinar that I hit my head or something, and that my memories are just lost. Zanderon, how can I just go on and ignore this giant hole in my life?" Crenthys hung her head, anger and shame whirling inside.

After many moments, Zanderon pulled Crenthys into an embrace. "I do not know. But you don't need to sit here alone with your thoughts. If you promise not to interfere, I will take you to see your brother."

Crenthys looked up, hope welling inside. "Yes. Of course."

"From the mezzanine. Watching only."

She nodded and wiped the rogue tear on her cheek.

"I have a feeling I am going to regret this," Zanderon said as he cut open a portal to the Forge.

Chapter 12

Motivations

B eams of sunlight burst through holes in the clouds, occasionally bathing Anuka in glorious light. It was the first time he had walked freely in weeks. He wore no disguise—rather a dapper set of clothing he filched from the warehouse. They were children's clothes, but no matter. He had even slept a bit last night. Despite losing his whole crew the night before, he felt grand.

Gasps escaped the lips of several passersby, and Anuka grinned. Some were astounded at the oddity of a goblin with bright red skin strutting through the Kentari streets. Anuka knew those gasps well. He had heard them all his life. Others were stunned to see a legendary brigand come to life before their eyes. Yet another group of surprised reactions came from those who knew the score. The infamous Brine Slayer was brazenly walking through town. Someone must be told. Those folks made haste to the church or to find a black-robed figure so they could report what they had seen. Regardless of the reason, the gasps were musical to Anuka. They were the forerunner to the next phase of his plan.

He wore a winning smile and took long, confident strides on his march down the major thoroughfare. Anuka knew what was coming, but he plowed ahead. Waving at shop keepers, winking at old maids, and blowing kisses to fair damsels. Still, it was a shock when the black-clad figure burst from an alleyway and tackled him roughly to the ground.

The things I do for my friends.

"Why did you not send a messenger requesting an escort? Do you have any idea how foolish your stroll was to my mission?"

My mission? Anuka thought. *My buddies and I are the ones taking the risk.* "Relax. I didn't see a single Silver Dragon on my way here."

"It is not only the Silvers that need concern you, Mister Sandbar." The spit missile Lebarin launched at Anuka's face was well aimed.

I riled the old priest up pretty good, Anuka thought. "I'm sorry, your holiness. My team left me and I just don't know what to do."

"Do you think this to be a game, Mister Sandbar?" Murder danced in the Victorin's eyes.

Anuka was an expert at making people angry, but he was outdoing himself today.

Lebarin stood suddenly and commanded Anuka, "It seems you need further motivation. Come with me." Then the old priest stalked out of the room toward the pair of double doors at the far end of the hallway. The ones with big chains and padlocks on them.

Anuka smiled.

He followed the Victorin down several flights of stone stairs. The torch the priest carried cast a garish light enveloped in deep shadow. At the bottom of the stairs, they stood on a small landing. Apart from the musty smells he expected in a dungeon, he also smelled salt water.

That made little sense. Even the brackish waters of the river were only a little salty this far from the sea.

"Hold this," Lebarin said, thrusting the torch toward Anuka. From a fold in his voluminous robes the old priest fished out a ring of keys. A tall iron door with shades of rust around the edges loomed ominously. The Victorin slid an ornate key into the slender keyhole and wrenched the lock open.

Anuka resisted the urge to thrust the torch into the back of the old crone. Instead, he squinted in the poor light to get a glimpse of the lock as Lebarin withdrew his key. *Masterwork. Impressive.* The curious goblin couldn't turn off the part of his brain that wondered about the means people used to secure their valuables. Beyond these doors, he knew, were The Victorin's prized possessions. *If you owned a dungeon, why not use it?*

Anuka suddenly realized that the stately priest was waiting for him to open the door. He did so and held it open for the pretentious old man. The Victorin snatched the torch out of his hand as he passed through the doorway. Anuka followed.

The Victorin placed his torch in a wall sconce inside the massive foyer. They wouldn't need it. Along the expansive hallway that stretched before them, Anuka saw torches all along the wall—each made of single slats of solid stone as smooth as creek rock. *Where had they found rocks so large? And how had they moved them here to form walls? Dragon Magic,* Anuka thought bitterly.

The Victorin was patient as the goblin touched the stone wall and marveled at the craftsmanship. Even if it was magically wrought, it was a masterpiece. The floor and ceiling were the same stone for fifty feet beyond the doorway. It was sobering to consider the amount of power that would go into such stonework. The thought of opposing those capable of such things once made a shiver run down his spine. Now he gritted his teeth in grim determination.

"Shall we continue? I haven't all day." Lebarin's patience apparently had its limits.

Excellent. Angry people made stupid mistakes. Anuka gestured for the High Priest to lead the way.

Anuka's boots echoed eerily and splatted in small puddles as they walked along. The scent of salt water grew stronger as they moved along the hallway. "Where did this place come from?" Anuka asked the priest, his voice echoing louder than he intended.

The Victorin flashed a grin over his shoulder but kept walking. At the end of the hallway, the priest produced his keys again and opened a door similar to the first.

Anuka considered lifting those keys and leaving the old man to rot down here. But he doubted he could make it out of here with Rigby and his friends. He feared Lebarin had similar thoughts about leaving him down here. He swallowed hard as the priest unlocked the door.

This time, the door opened, seemingly of its own accord. Beyond the old man stood a tall, well-muscled man in boiled leather armor. When the sentry saw the priest, he fell to his knees and placed his forehead on the floor. Then the guard murmured, *Highest* in Draconic. Anuka pretended not to hear or understand.

"Rise, Josk." Lebarin said. The man complied.

When the guard was standing in the light, Anuka saw patches of blackened skin on the man's face. Dark veins crawled out of the patches like roots questing for water. His eyes were dark and wild. The man looked at Anuka's hand and Anuka realized he had reached for his dagger. He smiled and moved his hand slowly back to his side.

Lebarin walked past the guard into the next hallway. Anuka followed, noting the same dark patches and spidery black veins on the man's exposed arms as he passed.

Sum Buck. Anuka had heard of Dragon fanatics who drank elixirs containing DragonsBlood and Keit knew what else, hoping to change their appearance to look more like their gods. He had also heard of how it altered their behavior, making them aggressive and unpredictable. Papa described seeing horrible things people did in the name of worship during his years working in Dorwine.

Victorin Lebarin made a left turn, and Anuka hustled to follow. In the short hallway they entered an eerie blue light reflected on the floor. The priest entered a small room, and the goblin saw the source of the light.

The wall in front of him was made of the largest piece of glass Anuka had ever seen. It stretched from floor to ceiling and was at least twenty feet wide. On the other side of the impossibly thick glass, water filled the entire space. There was something in the water.

"This is a place I come to think. And to pray in peace." Lebarin folded his hands in mock prayer. A massive fish with a cone-shaped nose appeared and rushed to rub against the glass.

Anuka jumped and swore, causing the Victorin to chuckle to himself.

"What is that?" Anuka gasped. He put his hand to the wall for support and bent down to look at the monster from a different angle, careful not to get too close.

"He is quite magnificent, isn't he? I have two," Lebarin said as he stepped forward to caress the glass lovingly.

Sharks, Anuka thought. *Big uns.* He put his tiny red hand on the glass. *It's warm. What kind of shark lives in warm water?*

"River sharks," Lebarin said as if reading the goblin's mind. "I have raised them since they were small. They have a taste for man-flesh. Apparently, runaways are particularly tasty." The priest moved away from the glass and started up a spiral staircase.

Anuka had a pretty good idea what the Victorin was getting at. Something in the tank's corner caught his eye, and he almost gasped aloud. The little pirate turned away quickly with a cough. "Point taken."

Rigby didn't look bad, all things considered, Anuka thought. Offund and Kelios were different stories. Each was in a separate cell. A wall of cold iron bars between them. Some effort to provide food and water was being made. That was good. The only way into the large room where the three cells were located was across a small retractable bridge. Over a giant glass box with sharks in it. Anuka tried to be angry about the ridiculous measures Lebarin took with his prisoners. Mostly he was jealous he didn't own a couple of sharks.

Offund looked rough. The Hob's face was ashen. His dark eyes appeared glassy through bare slits, and his breathing was slow but steady. He lay on a crude cot that was too big for his tiny frame. He didn't stir at the arrival of guests.

Kelios looked worse. He sat on his cot with his head propped against the corner of his cell. The Triton's green/blue skin had white, dry patches with a pink tint. Kelios could breathe air nearly as well as any human, but his skin required a lot of water to remain healthy. He must have been scratching the dry patches—they looked angry. For the Druid, it would come down to drinking his water to survive or dosing his skin to keep from drying out. Anuka knew Rigby and Offund should gladly share their water with Kelios. He also knew that Kelios would refuse it. *Sum Buck.*

"Okay, you've made your point," the goblin told a self-satisfied Lebarin.

"You are not here, Mister Sandbar, simply for intimidation. I am trying to motivate you. If you fail, your friends will die a terrible death here. But for you and the others, it will be much worse."

Well. This is interesting, Anuka thought.

"You opened a gaping fissure in the stability of Dorwine, beginning the moment your grubby little red toes first touched the sand at Usban. I am to compel you to correct the problem. Restore my treasure and it may be possible to set your mess to right. Fail me..." Lebarin didn't finish his threat.

The goblin nodded somberly. "I understand. Can I tell my friends goodbye?"

After a moment's deliberation, Lebarin nodded his assent.

Anuka stepped to the bars of Rigby's cage and spoke tenderly. "Hey, bubby. Hang in there, okay? I'm going to go get this whatzit and bring it back. We can go fishing then. Maybe catch our own sharks. Then, with your permission, I'd like to look up Rosanalli and try to make things right."

The bard appeared to be moved by the goblin's words and reached his hand through the bars to place it on Anuka's. They exchanged a smile, and Anuka moved to Kelios's cage.

"Hey Fishman. You hang in there. You can bear this. I will come back for you. I need you to take care of Offund. You know he's just little and basically useless. When we get outta here, I'm gonna make Kikkabar build you one of these glass cages on his boat."

Kelios nodded one time.

Anuka slipped his hand in his pocket to stow the paper Rigby had slipped him. As Anuka turned to go, he glimpsed Offund in his cage. The little Hob almost cracked a grin and just about ruined the whole thing.

———•◦•———

The door to the tavern was still crooked on its hinges. Anuka noted the scuff marks left by his tiny boot on his first visit. Anuka sighed heavily. He could pick a double pawl chest lock with a stiff horse hair. No problem. He could peel coins from a coin stack without the owner noticing. *Why is eating a little crow so hard?*

A faint red glow blossomed on his exposed skin, just as it had on his last visit here. Anuka took a deep breath and exhaled his frustration and fear. *Now or never, bubby.* Foregoing his usual flourish, Anuka slowly pushed the door open and stepped inside.

Xanavor saw him first. The shadowy human sat on the hearth swaddled in his tattered cloak, warming himself by a modest fire. The flame at his back cast an eerie glow about the human. His dark eyes were like a raven's. They quested over Anuka standing in the doorway.

The half-giant sat against the wall opposite Xanavor, the pair of them flanking Anuka. Grom's back was against the wall with his tree-trunk sized legs tented in front of him, massive arms resting on his knees. The gray skin of his face was like a clay mask of disappointment. The giant's visage sent a shot of regret through Anuka. *Seas take Kelios and Crenthys.* They had given Anuka something to care about. It had nearly ruined him. This line of work wasn't for the sentimental.

Felin looked like an alligator with a belly full of kittens. "What do you want, goblin? Did you come back to burn the place down?"

What's this punk think? That I can't carve him up? It's not like the giant is going to save him. No. I'm not here for my pride. I'm here for Rigby and for Kelios and Offund. "No, I'm here to—" *Sum Buck. This is hard.* "I'm here to apologize."

Grom sprang up like a river trout and jabbed a sausage-sized finger at Anuka. "Why should we care what you say? You are no leader to us. Rigby would never say the things you say. Do the things you do."

Good grief. Even the pacifist is joining in. "Yeah, well, I ain't Rigby. But he needs us. He's in a bad way."

"Because of you," Felin barked, standing. "He was retiring."

"No, bubby. I pushed him into this job, that's true. But he's been in a bad way since he found out about that girl." Anuka let his words sink in. When they didn't break the silence, he continued. "I know Rigby. Have for a long time. If I hadn't come along, he would have made a play to get his daughter out of Lebarin's hands. Did he recruit any of you for that?"

The three crew members exchanged looks but said nothing.

"I didn't think so. He wouldn't want to put you in danger. At least not the kind of heat he would call down if he tried to get his daughter back. Most likely, he would have tried something and gotten killed. Now, he may have a shot."

Felin huffed. "How? What are you gonna do about this problem? Are you going down the big tube to steal the Victorin's treasure?"

"No," Anuka said with a smile. "We are."

"You are crazy, goblin," Grom said.

"That's debatable." Anuka prepared to lay out his illustrious pedigree as a legendary pirate and thief, but Xanavor suddenly joined the conversation.

"She speaks." The shadowy human didn't turn from the fire as he spoke. "She speaks and I obey. I will accompany you into the tomb of the dead that live." Without another word, he stood, grabbed his staff, and moved out the front door.

Anuka cocked his head to one side. "And you said I was crazy."

"If the man of ravens goes, then I will go." Offering no further explanation, Grom walked out to join Xanavor.

Felin's look of flabbergasted incredulity was worth any indignity.

"Did... did you pay them?" the Wood Elf asked.

"Not yet. Come on, bubby. We'll all get paid." Anuka extended a hand toward the wood elf.

Felin stepped closer and took the goblin's tiny red hand. "Don't get us killed."

"No problem!" Anuka beamed. "Besides, with what I learned from Lebarin's compound tonight, this should be a cinch."

Felin didn't look convinced. They stepped out to join the others.

"One spot of bad news. The butt sniffer is still coming." Anuka nodded as the crew members groaned. "Oh, and Felin, we need to go see a buddy of yours on our way back. A jeweler."

Chapter 13

The Need to Know

"I may have made some headway today," Ember said cheerfully after gliding through the front door.

"For our cause or in your relationship?" Tabir asked.

"Both. Yondi is both a wonderful person, and an ally of our plans."

"Ember, I—" Crenthys began.

The Malkin interrupted her with a raised hand. "Say no more. Another argument doesn't further our plans. And no, I haven't shared those plans with Yondi. She just fancies giving me aid when I ask for it."

Ember could feel the tension between the Dragomyr and himself, but decided ignoring the rift was preferable to making it worse. "We are going to make our incursion into the restricted area after dark this evening, when most of the staff have gone for the day."

"How are you going to get in? And what are you looking for, exactly?" Crenthys's tone was skeptical.

That's right. She still thinks she is the only one with an important job to do. "There is a great deal about inter-Dragon politics to be learned there, I believe. And, about Dragon and Dragomyr memory related problems."

"Ember, Ivrus is the city's best physician and memory expert." Crenthys was trying to avoid being condescending and failing spectacularly.

"If there was such a thing as absolute experts, we wouldn't need libraries, would we?" The Malkin tried not to sound sardonic and failed with equal fanfare. "No memory is flawless. Even a Dragon's. Besides, learning about Dragon memory can't hurt." It wasn't entirely true. Curiosity had ended the lives of many of Ember's kind.

Crenthys appeared to be pondering the statement.

"You didn't say how you intended to get into the restricted section," Tabir noted.

"I didn't, did I?" Ember smiled.

Crenthys and Tabir exchanged a look.

Crenthys turned to Tabir. "Well, did you discover anything useful?"

"No one wants to talk much about Dragons. Although you are a keen topic of conversation."

"Me?" Crenthys asked.

"Yes. They ask me all manner of questions about you." Tabir sipped the strange juice that was provided with the evening meal. "Are you really mad? Why have you come back? Did you kill Celebris? On and on. The rumors about Usban are wild here."

"I've noticed," she said. "Hopefully, I can put a stop to most of those in a couple of days."

Ember saw the concern in Crenthys's eyes and he ached for her. Even though he was still justly angry with her, he didn't want to see her suffer. Much.

"Can we join you for your trial?" Tabir asked.

Crenthys shook her head. "No. DragonKin only."

"Have you no one to stand with you?" Tabir said, concern in his voice.

"Vodinar is as much my advocate as I could hope for."

"Perhaps I could take the guise of a DragonKin and sneak in..." Ember was dying to learn transmutation magic.

"Thank you, but no. We've no one to teach you the spell. And where would you get DragonsBlood?"

Both fair questions. The Malkin's lip poked out of its own volition.

"Besides, I may ask Zanderon to stand with me."

"Do you think he will?" Tabir asked, hopefully.

"I don't know. I'm still not sure where his loyalty falls in all of this. Honestly, I'm not sure whose side I am on sometimes."

The High Elf nodded. Ember thought he understood what she meant. Things had gotten very confusing during their days in Wrythmar.

"In other news, Payris wants to adopt me," Tabir said.

"What?" the Malkin asked.

Crenthys sputtered, nearly spraying the other two with juice.

"He is returning to his home. He has asked me to join him."

"What did you say?" the Dragomyr asked.

Tabir shrugged. "Well, I didn't want to anger him. We still need information. I told him I would think about it."

Crenthys shook her head. "This is taking too long. We need to be ready to run if things go poorly at my trial."

"Will that be an option?" the Elf asked.

Ember knew what Tabir was thinking, and didn't like it. If the Dragons decided Crenthys was a threat, they all would be executed. Quickly.

"Let us hope so."

Ember grabbed a hunk of bread and a healthy strip of meat from the dinner tray. "Well, I am off."

"You're really going back to the library?" the Dragomyr asked.

"Of course. As you said, getting the information we need is taking too long. I'm going to hasten things along."

"Ember," Tabir said. "Be safe."

"Don't worry. I still have four or five lives to spare."

———◦———

Crenthys moved through the misty streets of Wrythmar, but she didn't feel like her legs were moving. Nor did she remember leaving her bed. *Is this a dream?* Suddenly, she stood before an ornately carved door in a rounded doorway. It opened, and she went inside. She closed the door behind her and turned only to find herself lying on her side on a long stone table. A female Golden Elf of surpassing beauty stood looking down at Crenthys.

"Why have you come?" the young girl asked in a dreamy, wistful voice.

"I need to know," Crenthys said, though she didn't open her mouth.

The elf placed a hand on Crenthys's head, and the room melted away. Her ears were cupped with a chorus of unfamiliar noises. Echoes of running water... moans of the dying... and the stench of death mingled with the clean scent of freshly spent magic.

The enormous cavern was strewn with corpses. Two dozen Dragomyr bodies lie crumpled in every corner of the massive cave. Crenthy's feet sloshed in a river of blood as she lumbered around the room. To her right, she saw the unnatural orange glow of magical fire illuminating a dugout in the wall as big as her apartments. Something there called to her heart, but a sound near her feet drew her attention. A Bronze Dragomyr clutched her leg.

"Failed..." the voice croaked painfully. Two bubbles of blood formed on its neck as it spoke.

Tears spilled from her eyes and dripped onto her fallen kin. The Dragomyr's eyes slowly opened and were filled with tears as well. They were fierce and the same color purple as a bellflower. Like her own.

This Dragomyr was familiar to her—but she couldn't pierce the fog of her memory to understand how. Her companion breathed her last and slumped to the floor. She willed her tears to stop and stepped over the body toward the fire.

Crenthys had no fear of fire, magical or otherwise, but the nearer she drew to the smaller cavern, the more fear gripped her. The flames were high, and the heat warped the air, making it impossible to see inside the cave.

Power coursed through her veins. Apart from the distant report of injuries Crenthys had sustained, somehow, she felt strong. She steeled her will as the wall of flame drew nearer. The unknown thing beyond the flame gave her pause, and she stopped a few feet away. A lance of terror shot through her. She had to know what was beyond the flame. With long, deliberate strides, she stepped into the flame.

She opened her eyes, but the flame was gone. The Elven girl stared at her. "What was beyond the flame?" Crenthys asked.

The girl drew her lips into a disappointed line and bowed her head. "I could take you no further. I was prevented."

Disappointment washed over Crenthys. It was muted, like pain from a scar. "I must know."

The girl placed a hand on the Dragomyr's side and whispered something softly. After a moment, she opened her eyes and said, "Your body is strong. There are children in your future."

A dream. She was still dreaming. She was Dragomyr. No children would come from her body. It was not possible. A part of her wished it was so. Crenthys chuckled.

"I am sorry. This must end--the cost is too great." The young elven woman's voice held a trace of apology.

Crenthys started to protest, but the lithe Elven girl snapped the insides of her wrists together, then flung her hands out wide. The vision disappeared in a flash.

Crenthys had assumed the dream would end and she would find herself in her bed. Instead, she was in Ivrus's examination room. Her head swam as she sat upright. Lingering dread from her vision of the cavern clawed at her mind. Profound loss over the phantoms in her mind made her very sad.

What am I? she wondered. My memory fails me. My master is dead. My own people hate me. *I am like a kite with a broken string, carried along by the wind until I get caught in a tree or strike a stone.* Crenthys had prayed--yes prayed--for peace upon returning to her home. Peace was farther away now than ever. The people surrounding her, her own people, looked at her with sideways glances, despite their overtures to make her feel welcome. *They know enough of me to hate me,* she thought bitterly.

Crenthys's mind drifted to Kelios, as it often did when she was alone in her thoughts. Why does he plague my mind? Do I not have enough to fret over? While the Triton defied understanding, her own feelings for him were an even greater mystery. It wasn't puzzling why someone would be attracted to Kelios. He was handsome, in his way, and was an honorable man. He was kind, and loyal. The question was not why she had feelings for the Triton. No. The question was how was she able to feel affection for anyone?

A Dragomyr, Crenthys was created by a Dragon solely to love and serve that Dragon, none other. Belendurath infused all of her loyalty and devotion into her creation. If a Dragon died, their Dragomyr died. Except she hadn't.

She had been over this a thousand times in the decade since her master's death. Why did these thoughts plague her dreams as well? She had always come to no conclusion about what may be wrong with her. She had survived her master's death, yet something in her mind made mistrusting her own kind easy. And she had felt emotions that no Dragomyr had the capacity for. *Have I forgotten how to be what I am?*

Ember had suggested her master's death had been so long ago that she was healing, and that her natural physiology was allowing her mind to heal and develop emotions. The Malkin still couldn't explain why Crenthys had survived the death of Belendurath. Or why she felt the loss so keenly. The cat-man was wise, but he didn't know everything. She only hoped his time in Dovondes's library would yield some answers. She wiped her eyes. When she looked up, she stood outside the door of Ivrus's office. This time, instead of chants of "you should not have come back," she heard a frantic scratching sound. With a push, the door opened easily.

Ivrus was at his desk swimming in an ocean of papers. Crenthys stood ankle deep in charcoal sketches. Each one was the same. She bent and picked up one of the papers. Ivrus stopped sketching and turned to regard her. His face looked angry. He clutched a sliver of charcoal in one soot-covered hand. "Why did you come back?"

Crenthys felt guilty at his accusing words. Before she could answer, a movement on the paper in her hands drew her eye toward it.

When she looked down at the sketch, the eye glared up at her. Then it blinked.

She flung the paper away and turned toward the door. Before she could dash away, something impossibly strong grabbed her ankles, and she fell slowly to the ground. She landed with a painful crash.

"Crenthys," Tabir cried from the doorway. He stood in his bedclothes, looking terrified. "Are you alright?"

She sat in her bed, panting. Her hands trembled as they clutched the sheets.

What was *that?* Her mind raced to separate reality from her dream. "Just a bad dream," she said between huffing breaths. "A very bad dream. I am fine." Even as she said the words, she knew it was a lie. Whether dream or vision, what she had seen tonight unsettled her. She was far from fine.

Chapter 14

An Outing

As strange as it was, Kelios felt proud to have picked the small lock on his cell door. He had learned a new skill. That was commendable. He was also fast on the path to becoming a criminal. That was less so.

"Anuka teach you that?" Rigby asked once the Triton was out of his cage.

Kelios nodded. "Would you like me to open your cell as well?" The sharks splashed violently in their tanks nearby.

The bard shook his head. "Nah. I'm not going anywhere. Besides, one empty cell will be hard enough to explain." Rigby looked at the tanks as though he expected the sharks to climb out of the water and flop into his cell.

The Triton smiled. "Offund?"

The Hob slid from his bunk and closed his eyes in concentration. Soon, a ripple of light in Kelios's cell morphed into a near perfect illusion of the Triton lying in his bed.

"Seas..." Rigby said breathlessly.

"It is a simple spell, but maintaining it requires a great deal of concentration. It will be physically taxing for him. If they bring us food, I intend to share mine with Offund," Kelios said. "You may need to do the same." He added looking at Rigby questioningly.

"I have no problem with that. He needs to keep his strength up." Rigby stared at the Triton. "So, what will you do?"

Kelios smiled again. Rigby seemed to be a kind soul. Anuka should be grateful for his friends. The Triton lifted his hand toward the water and closed his eyes. The savagery of the shark wasn't surprising to Kelios as he touched one of the beast's minds. He was surprised to find that the violent attitude wasn't natural. Something was agitating them. The caregivers were feeding them things they didn't want, like meat from land creatures. Man-flesh wasn't their favorite. They preferred the mud bellied fish of the freshwater. Some details got lost in translation, but Lebarin was also putting something in the water to upset them.

Kelios introduced himself to both of them and calmed their minds. The splashing stopped. Soon, the sharks slipped into a peaceful trance.

"Oh," Rigby said from behind him. "That was... impressive." The bard fidgeted with the hem of his shirt and then said, "I don't suppose you are going to tell me what Anuka is really up to, are you?"

Kelios chewed his lip. He didn't like keeping things from an ally, but the goblin had been very clear. "No. I cannot. I am sorry."

The bard threw his hands in the air and leaned back against the bars of his cage.

With a sigh, the Triton took two steps, then dropped into the tank with the sleeping sharks.

Kelios climbed out of the tank after soaking a short time. He looked across the narrow space where the now retracted bridge had been and whispered to himself. "Please, Anuka. Do hurry."

Moving along the hallway beyond the shark tank, Kelios paused to listen at the next doorway. Lebarin was confident in his prison and, so far, had only sent one guard to check on them periodically. If he held to his pattern, he wouldn't be back for at least an hour.

Kelios wasn't sure where he was supposed to go. The goblin was certain he would find what they were looking for. Lebarin's people had blindfolded them before bringing them down. Kelios had made a point of listening as carefully as he could. Irana made him a keen listener. If his ears served him well, this floor held a lot more than a handful of cells and a couple of sharks.

He hoped he and his two companions were the only guests down here and that Lebarin didn't bother with much of a guard presence. Personnel was bound to be at a premium with the skies full of Silver Dragons. There was no way they could escape their cells, right? Kelios grinned.

Still, it was a risk. While Bog really wanted Anuka, if they caught him outside of his cell, they would kill him. Despite his apparent value to the DragonLord, Rigby would likely be killed as well. *No matter*, he thought. *I'm not getting caught.* He sounded confident, but he felt a twinge of fear.

Kelios walked toward the end of the hallway. The smooth, white stone walls made the Triton feel like he was in a long box. He didn't like that feeling. Especially when he thought about how much dirt and rock were likely above him.

The hallway turned ninety degrees to his right and continued on to the limits of his vision. *Anuka's keen eyes would be handy right now.* Unless he was mistaken, there were stairs at the end of that hallway. He didn't want to go up.

Sweat beaded on the smooth iron door to his left. They had painted pitch or tar on its surface. Despite the coating, Kelios saw rust around the door handle and every nail head. He shook his head. How this whole place hadn't rusted apart was beyond him.

The door had the same lock as his cell door. *That's fortunate.* The goblin had only shown him a few locks.

He listened at the door before slipping his little metal tool into the lock. It unlocked with a smooth clank. The caretakers had oiled this lock recently.

He dragged the door open, lifting the handle to discourage the door from squeaking. It didn't. The hinges had been oiled, too.

This must be a door Lebarin used often. The priest wouldn't suffer a noisy hinge on a door he frequented. Kelios peeked inside once the door was open enough. All clear.

He stepped through quietly and pushed the door closed behind him, then made his way down the hallway. Evenly spaced doors ran along the left side. Five rooms in total. The hall had one door at the end.

Wonderful, Kelios thought with a sigh.

Rigby assumed everything had gone well with Kelios's mission. The Triton returned in one piece with no sign of Lebarin's guards on his tail. Offund faded to sleep moments after his friend's return.

He watched the tiny Hob snoring contentedly. The poor man had only slept in bursts during the past couple of days. Beyond Offund, Kelios was watching the small man just as he was. The Triton felt Rigby's stare and looked up. He smiled.

"He has great courage," the Druid rumbled in his deep, melodic voice.

Rigby nodded his agreement. The bard didn't know how Anuka had come by such companions, but he was glad for it. He thought of the rumors about his little red friend's exploits in Usban. "Where is your female companion?"

Kelios's eyes went wide; "Crenthys," he whispered. "Yes. She—Crenthys isn't with us. Two other companions of ours went west with her to deal with... family matters. They're on an important mission." Kelios looked away and seemed to slide into deep thoughts.

Rigby recognized the Triton's tone. The tender way Kelios said Crenthys's name, and sadness coupled with a longing that coated his words. Interesting.

"She must be a remarkable woman." Kelios looked up at the bard's words. "From the rumors I have heard."

"She is that," the Triton said with a smile.

It was not clear what race Crenthys was. Some reports said she was a beautiful mixed-blood Sea Elf. Other reports said that she was a DragonSpawn. The answer to question itched at Rigby, but he didn't press. "The world has a shortage of those. Remarkable women."

"Yes," Kelios replied solemnly.

Chapter 15

Answers

It had taken Crenthys nearly an hour to lose the human following her. Now, as she crawled over rubble and through a hole in the stone fence around Belendurath's manor, she was wishing she had waited until dark. Stealth was not one of her strongest skills and every neighboring compound likely saw her skulking about. She stayed low anyway as she scurried up to the back of the manor.

The back door was locked. *Perfect. Just great.* Crenthys looked around for something to use to open the door. The only thing at hand was a bone white stone pot with the corpse of a long dead plant in the center. On a lark, she buried two fingers into the soil and pulled out a key. It was thrilling to think that her subconscious memory had done that. Maybe her memories weren't lost, just disconnected.

Crenthys wiped the key clean. With some effort, the lock finally turned. She replaced the key and shouldered the door open. Piles of leaves, dirt, and other rubbish made it difficult to open. She stepped inside. A large marble wash basin sat just inside the room. It was bone dry. There were hooks for hats and a shallow wooden box along the wall for shoes. Everything was caked with a layer of grime and blanketed with cobwebs.

The floor had been swept, but poorly so. It looked like the front of the house had been broomed to the back of the house. The short hallway ahead was dark, but dust motes floated in a shaft of light from a room on the left. *The Kitchen*, she thought, but didn't know why she thought that. Crenthys adjusted the bag slung over her shoulder and moved toward the light.

A low murmuring echoed as soon as Crenthys stepped into the hallway. Sniffling and the occasional sob punctuated the soft speech. Odwin stood at a broad countertop rifling through an enormous pile of refuse he had dumped there. "Odwin."

The old man startled and jerked his head around, fixing a bleary-eyed look of surprise on Crenthys. "Oh, mistress. I am so sorry." He flung his hands over the pile of trash and little flecks of something landed on the heap. Odwin wiped his eyes with the back of his dirty shirtsleeve. "Apologies, my lady. We don't have any proper food in the house. I thought you might come, and I was trying to make the best of what I found." He muffled another sob into his arm.

This is what he eats. Crenthys looked at the frail old man and only now seemed to notice how gaunt he looked. That didn't seem right to her. Then she looked at the rubbish pile. It looked like leavings from cast off food. An array of eclectic unfinished meals. *This is what he eats.* A lump formed in her throat. Crenthys stepped toward the old man and he looked up.

"Odwin, you can't eat this. Come." She took him by the arm and guided him toward a nearby table. "I brought food for you. Proper food. Sit down and I'll get you something good to eat."

The old man turned and looked at her. "Mistress," he whispered, aghast, "I am the servant. I should be serving you."

"The best leaders are marked as the best servants," She said without thinking. No doubt, she had picked it up somewhere in her travels. From Morglun, perhaps.

The old servant's eyes welled with tears, and he smiled. "My lady."

It occurred to Crenthys that Belendurath may have said that phrase. How frustrating that memories came unbidden, but could not be forced out of their hiding place in her mind. "Yes, now sit down."

Odwin eased into a creaky chair and wiped a thin layer of dust from the table with the sleeve of his shirt. "You always were so good to us—so kind. We were so heartbroken when you left."

Crenthys didn't know what Odwin meant. Did he still think she was Belendurath, and she *left* when she died? Or did he know she was Brinka, and regretted her hurried flight from the city a decade ago? She sighed. It was likely that the old servant didn't know what he meant any more than she did. She pulled out the jars of food she had saved from the breakfast Ember hadn't eaten, as well as some staple items from the apartment. "Odwin, do you know who I am?"

The old human pondered for a moment. "Why yes, you are the lady Dragon, Belendurath, of course."

She shook her head and knelt down, taking him by the hands. "No, Odwin. I am Brinka. Do you remember Brinka?"

"Remember? Of course. I—" He seemed to falter, and then he grew sad. When he looked at Crenthys's face, there was an unimaginable weight of grief on it. "Mistress Brinka."

She smiled warmly and squeezed his hands gently.

His lip quivered as he spoke. "I went to the mountain. I took a cart from the lower city and I went... I went to find you."

"What did you find on the mountain?" Crenthys hated to press him. His heart was breaking all over again.

"I found your bones..." The old man cradled his face in his hands and began to weep.

Crenthys didn't want to be cruel, but she had to know the depths of his madness. She gently pulled his hands from his face. "What do you mean, my bones?"

Odwin sniffed loudly, coughed, and wiped his nose with his sleeve like a small child might do. "Inside the mountain, I found the bones of Mistress Brinka. I found them and I brought them home. When I returned to Clover Crisp, I put the bones in a big wooden box and covered it with flowers. Big red ones. I slipped them into the upper city through the Friel gate under the guise of funeral decorations. I guess they were."

Brinka's bones? He must be mistaken. "Odwin, what did you do with my, with the bones you found?"

"Why, I buried them properly under the Haylock tree where Mistress Brinka would sit and read. It was only fitting."

It was so strange a tale. She didn't believe him, couldn't believe him. Yet she stood and moved toward the window. A giant Haylock tree loomed over a back corner of the property. A rectangular patch of delicate red flowers covered a large area of ground at the foot of the tree. Crenthys felt her hands tremble as she stared at the flowers. Red: just like the ones in the grove she dreamed of.

———•◦•———

Ember smiled when he found the window still ajar. He had laid a small stick in the sill the previous evening. Someone had pushed the window together, but hadn't noticed that it didn't close fully. It popped open easily, and he stepped from the thin ledge onto the window frame and then into the first floor of the library. Then he turned, took Yondi's hand, and helped her inside.

She wouldn't make a bad burglar, he thought, but it would take some training. Ember felt proud of the mental notes he had taken watching Anuka skulking about with locks and his general roguish behavior.

The room was dark, though not totally. Without exception, fire was prohibited inside the library. A series of magically imbued stones filled basins that had been hoisted into the air. Polished metal plates were mounted on the ceiling to reflect the light that illuminated the room. At night, some of the stones were removed. Otherwise, the library would glow like a torch in the night and prove quite distracting.

Ember could see well in the dark, and led Yondi on a path to the stairs that were well lit and free of obstruction. They got to the rail, and he glanced around. His heart pounded in his chest and he combed his fur down anxiously. They could be caught, and despite his bravado yesterday, could get in serious trouble. Angry Dragons were never a good thing. *No guards. Good.*

When he was sure there was no one about, he crouched down and crept up the first flight of stairs. He paused at the top and turned to Yondi. "Don't be scared," he whispered. He wasn't sure why, but maybe his second thoughts were gnawing at him.

She smiled and nodded, so he continued.

Ember's logical mind told him that there was no need to post guards in a library at night. There were likely a dozen Dragons in the upper city and twice as many Dragomyr. This was as safe a place as could be found. He also realized that parts of the library were restricted. If someone wanted to access those parts, night time would be the best time to do it. Which is why they were here. But the keepers of these mysterious treasures would also understand this and take the appropriate measures. That circle of thinking was without end. They crept on.

They passed through the second and third floors without incident, though Ember could have sworn he had heard something several times. They didn't see any evidence of guards, so he tallied the sounds to his imagination.

He took extra care as they slowly ascended the stairs to the fourth floor. They ducked even lower and moved more slowly. Gathering his courage, Ember peered over the rail when they reached the top of the stairs. He didn't see any movement.

Yondi was smiling when they reached the door to the restricted floor. Ember was glad she was enjoying herself. His heart thudded, and he was sweating. Wiping his hands on his pants, Ember pulled his little tools out of his cloth bag and examined them. They seemed pretty poor compared to the ones Anuka had used. He peered into the lock from the side as he had seen done, and made some guesses about how this lock worked. One pick seemed a little too stiff, another a bit too soft, but both found purchase on the parts inside with a little effort. After a couple minutes of sweating, pulling the picks out to look in the hole again, and putting the picks back in, Ember's hands began to cramp. Yondi was squatting down next to him, watching his progress, or lack thereof. He couldn't decide if she looked curious, impatient, or both. The human girl looked like she wanted to grab the little pieces of metal out of his hands and open the lock herself. *That would not do.*

With renewed determination, Ember worked the picks around until they gained traction and made a sharp twist. To his surprise, the lock clicked, and the door creaked open. He couldn't stop the giant smile that split his lips.

Yondi released the breath she had been holding.

Ember paused, debating between wanting to allow the young lady the privilege of entering first, as was human culture, or sprinting from bookshelf to bookshelf. He settled on entering first to protect Yondi from the dangers within—another human cultural ideal.

The smell was intoxicating. Old books and secrets. Dried ink and scholarly sweat. The faintest trace of magic lingered in the background. Ember trembled with excitement.

Yondi squirmed past him and whispered, "Wow... Where will you begin?"

He had been asking himself that question for two days. "I have some ideas."

———— ◦ ————

Three hours later, Ember sat holding his throbbing head in his hands. He simply couldn't absorb information fast enough. Yondi was busy duplicating some pages that he would have to interpret later. He felt like a new Malkin. In a week of nights like these, he would barely cover a small percentage of the knowledge in this room.

The shelves of this room were lined with political treatises, written by Dragons for Dragons. There were tomes on magical theory, runes and scripts, and histories beyond belief. He had absorbed more Dragon lore in a few hours than in a previous year's worth of study. His subconscious mind was putting together pieces of the mystery he was here to solve. He would have to examine them later. *When will I sleep?* This was ever the plight of the researcher.

He was shaken back to consciousness a second later by a frantic Yondi. "Ember, someone is here."

That brought him fully awake. With horror, he realized he had left a small puddle of drool on the Chronicles of Ancient Mortal Warfare.

He had no time to mourn. *Where was the someone?* Ember couldn't see anyone, but was aware of a light moving around the room. The doors in the back of the library must lead to sleeping quarters. He felt stupid for not realizing that before. The door downstairs was too far away. They would need to hide somewhere.

Yondi scaled the ancient bookshelves so nimbly Ember wondered if she had feline ancestry. He followed close behind, careful not to make any sound or to scratch the beautiful shelves with his claws. Her instincts were good. The guard might not look up.

Yondi didn't stop when she reached the top of the bookshelf. She smoothly slipped onto a nearby darkened chandelier.

Ember wasn't sure he could follow Yondi. They were very high up. He tried not to look down, but it was unavoidable. With a deep breath, he grabbed the heavy chain securing the light fixture to the ceiling and stepped onto it. The girl guided him to a place where he could sit next to her. He closed his eyes as the chandelier swayed back and forth. It came to rest a few moments later and Ember opened his eyes to see Yondi grinning at him.

The young robed librarian paced below them, his emerald green stone held aloft to light his path. One of the sharp edges of the heavy metal chandelier dug painfully into Ember's rump. Ember bit his lip and tracked the young man as he moved among the bookshelves. It occurred to him then how close he and Yondi were to one another.

She sat next to him with her feet on the bottom of the light fixture, holding a support chain in each hand. Her face was only inches from his. She looked lovely in the pale green light. Even if they escaped tonight, she would likely never forgive him.

Her eyes searched his face. The door clicked shut below them and they each looked around for the young man. He was gone.

Ember bit his lip to keep his celebration quiet. When he turned to Yondi, he could see the elation on her face, as well. Then she stopped and looked into his eyes. He felt the logical part of his brain hang up a signed that read *closed*. His hand brushed Yondi's cheek gently. Then, with no instruction at all, he leaned in and pressed his lips to hers.

The creature currently possessing him must have kissed someone before, because he seemed to know what to do. It was strange . . terrifying . . . amazing.

They parted a moment later and Ember felt his conscious mind reconnect with his body. He felt a moment of panic. Then Yondi smiled.

"That was nice," she said. "But we need to get out of here before he comes back."

In that moment, she could have suggested Ember jump in the ocean and he would have thought it a grand idea.

Most of Tabir's time the past few months had been spent riding boats. The long path out of the city and into the foothills made his legs ache and his lungs burn. He was glad he had accepted the offer of clothes more suited for this journey and felt foolish for denying some new boots. Payris was very generous. Suspiciously so. The elf had even offered to rent a horse for him to ride. He had laughed at the notion. It was a somewhat bitter laugh. His brothers had been accomplished riders. They had used horses to tend and corral the human and half-elf slaves. It had been near the time to begin his own lessons. Except for Rathune's mercy, Tabir would have joined his wicked family.

He had politely declined the offer of a horse and new boots. It was false humility. Pride. His greatest foe. Blisters on his feet would be his reward for being so humble.

When his breath was coming in ragged gasps and his legs could go no more, Tabir stopped, and leaned forward with his hands on his knees. If he sat down, he would not want to get started again. He lifted his head and scanned the climb ahead. There was no trail, but the way was simple enough. If he guessed correctly, the cave where Coltimar camped in was just beyond the next knoll. Tiny wisps of smoke drifted lazily from that direction.

Tabir needed wisdom. He could ask Crenthys but she was so twisted by her past she could offer little help. Ember was smitten, his mind clouded by infatuation. Neither of them could give him what he needed. Plus, Coltimar was several hundred years older than either of them. As fond as he had grown of his new friends, his bond with Coltimar transcended their few scrapes and close calls. His old friend knew secrets Tabir was not ready to share with his new companions. Likewise, he knew dangerous secrets about the big man which would be disastrous to expose.

Deciding Coltimar's camp wasn't getting any closer, Tabir began the last push up the hill.

As Tabir rounded a bend, he saw the mouth of a cave set into the hillside. A low burning cook fire was slowly dying. He trudged the last few steps to examine the camp. There was no sign of his friend. From where he stood, his keen Elven eyes saw to the back of the shallow cave. A healthy pile of fresh bones; two rabbits and three fish, were in a shallow uncovered pit. A large, flat stone that weighed as much as Tabir had been positioned for sitting. Another one, similar to it, sat on the other side of the fire.

"C'mon Colt. Where are you?" Tabir resisted the urge to sit on the stone and milk the fire of the last of its warmth. Instead, he walked to the cave's mouth and peered in. At the rear of the cave a bedroll sat atop a folded blanket. Various tools for cooking were spread out on a leathery cloth. A tent-sized shirt was suspended from a thin clothesline.

"It's not the grandest place I've slept," came a voice behind Tabir.

He jumped and cried out. Coltimar stood smiling smugly just beyond the cave's mouth.

"Not the worst, either," the voice continued.

"Do you have to do that?" Tabir asked sharply. He was an elf, trained in the way of the woods from childhood. Such a gigantic man shouldn't be able to sneak up on him.

"Apologies. I don't mix much with people. I tend to forget how domesticated they are in general. Have you eaten?" The big man held up a stringer, revealing a handful of long, slender fish.

"I have. Didn't you just eat?" Tabir sighed as his friend smiled. Coltimar's appetite was voracious.

"Did you walk all the way here?" Coltimar asked as he looked around for a Dragon or some other conveyance.

"I needed the exercise," Tabir said. When his friend leveled an unconvinced look he continued, "And some advice. Come. I'll help you with your lunch."

To clean the fish, they walked farther from the camp to clean the fish than Tabir's aching feet desired. It wasn't wise to leave animal guts in your camp, he remembered. Coltimar produced a long fillet knife from a sheath on his belt and then another from his boot for Tabir to use.

"What troubles the man of God?" Coltimar asked, sawing the head smoothly from the first fish.

Tabir gave Coltimar a withering glance before cleaning his fish. Not only was his friend's irreverence toward Rathune annoying, it was also baffling. Of all the creatures on Acos, Coltimar's faith in the creator god should be among the strongest. He *knew* Rathune was real, what he had done, and much of what was to come: Colt's own father had stood in the presence of the deity centuries ago. "Your attitude, for one. Though that ranks pretty low among my present worries."

It was an old argument. One where Tabir ended up asking Coltimar why he didn't play a larger role in the resolving one or another of the world's problems. It generally ended with a heated exchange and resulted in the two not speaking for some time. Tabir had neither the time nor the stomach for such arguments right now.

"I found another Sliver." He was aiming to sound nonchalant but ruined that when he smiled at the big man's startled reaction.

"What? Here? Where? Does Dovondes have it?" Coltimar had stepped up and taken The High Elf by the arm.

Despite his friend's feigned disinterest in the business of their god, the Slivers of Aracthias greatly interested him. "Peace, my friend. No. Payris has one in his quarters."

"Payris? The Gold Ambassador?"

"Yes. And before you ask, I don't know why. He has been dismissive about it. Acts like it's just something that caught his eye. I don't even know where he got it." Tabir worked himself free of Coltimar's grip. It was starting to hurt. He put his back to Coltimar, and the silence grew.

"Are you going to redeem it?" the big man asked.

Tabir shuddered when he thought of claiming the relic. *What an interesting turn of phrase. Not inaccurate, I suppose.* It felt more like theft to Tabir. Though the ancient slivers didn't belong to anyone. Or if they did, they belonged in the hands of the few remaining priests of Rathune.

"I am," the priest finally answered.

"What is your plan? What can I do to help?"

That was a good question. If he so desired, Coltimar could go where he wanted, take what he wanted, from whom he wanted. There was little anyone could do to stop him. But the mysterious man chose to live a life of obscurity. Only a handful of creatures in the whole world knew what Coltimar was. Maybe another handful guessed at it. Tabir's friend was committed to a life of solitude, away from the tangle of the world's problems. There was no way Coltimar could aid Tabir that wouldn't jeopardize that. And they both knew it.

"I don't have a plan. Not yet, at least." He looked at his friend and saw regret on his face. "Crenthys is in a difficult state. I believe her past is circling her. We will probably need a quick escape at some point soon. I think that would be a prudent moment for a bit of robbery. Or when Payris returns home—his assignment here ends soon. Either way, I don't want you to get involved." Tabir held up a finger to forestall Coltimar's protest. "Unless I need you." The man's encouragement had been all he needed, after all.

Coltimar didn't like it, but he seemed to accept the answer.

"Do you have a way to return to Wrythmar quickly if needed?" Tabir asked.

"Zanderon left me a means of summoning him, should I need it."

"Like your own pet Dragon," Tabir chided.

They both chuckled.

"Tabir, my friend, if I am honest, I have nearly had my fill of Dragons."

Tabir knew just what his friend meant.

Chapter 16

White Globs of Death

The road out of Kentari turned rough quickly. Anuka supposed that made sense, considering that there was nothing east of the city but trees and swamp. Plenty of that in Kentari already. No one used these roads, and it showed. The paved path faded to a thin trail within a mile. They had left before the sun had risen and would trek all day. Their pace was slow. That suited Anuka just fine. His short legs made it hard to keep up with taller folk. Xanavor obviously walked very little and couldn't manage a brisk pace.

No one talked much. That was also fine with Anuka. If anyone was going to yammer on about nothing, he wanted it to be him. Besides, Felin barely spoke Low Draconic, Grom was too thoughtful for conversation, and Xanavor was just weird. It was Fabian that worried him. They'd been walking for a couple of hours and the bard hadn't said a word. He didn't sing, hum, or whistle. *Odd for a bard*, Anuka thought.

Felin had said it would rain today, but the sky was as clear as could be. Anuka knew it was petulant to revel in the young thief being wrong, but that did little to dampen his satisfaction in the clear, blue skies.

When the silence had finally stretched to his breaking point, Anuka said, "You sorry lot don't have much to say, do you? Let's stop for some vittles. See if that loosens your tongues."

"I could eat," Xanavor said.

"Okay. I brought food." Felin slung the pack from his back and dug for the food inside as they continued walking.

"Oh yes. Dried mushrooms. Can't wait." Anuka doubted his companions caught the sarcasm, but he didn't care. He was used to talking over everyone's head. He scouted around for a place to stop and rest.

Just over a rise, the murky swamp gave way to a small hillock bisected by a pair of thin streams. The streams had large boulders in the middle that would be good to rest on. There was even a clearing with evidence of previous campfires. "This place is perfect." Anuka announced.

The party stopped, and each member surveyed the scene. Fabian looked disinterested.

"Yes. Perhaps too perfect?" Grom said. His voice was like rubbing two flat rocks together.

Too perfect? Sum Bucks are hard to please. Anuka surveyed the area again, looking for different things this time. Then he noticed it. The patches of thistles that had kept them from venturing off the path were absent. Someone had placed nice flat rocks in a circle around the fire pit, which looked like it had never been used. "Sum Buck." *An ambush site.* "How you boys want to handle this?"

"Handle what?" Fabian asked.

Anuka groaned. "Grom, are you sure you don't want to try pulling people's arms off? I bet you'd love it. Kelios does."

The look on his companion's faces, especially the half-giant, was discouraging.

"I am committed to not harming living things." Grom's tone was final.

Fine. The goblin stepped into the clearing and turned a circle as he yelled his challenge. "Alright, you dumb Sum Bucks. Show's over."

"What are you doing?" Felin hissed, reaching for his short bow.

"C'mon before I send my half-giant thrall over to rip your arms off. He drinks the blood of babies, you know."

"I do not!" Grom said with a bellow.

Anuka waved a shushing at him. "My buddy Felin the Heartless killed fifteen people with that bow—before breakfast! It's better to come out before Fabian here has to sing you to death."

Suddenly, one boulder in the stream stood on spindly legs and looked at them. Soon, the others joined in. They looked like swollen torsos stacked on flamingo legs. With the head of a giant frog smashed on top. *Wumpys.* One of the Wumpys stood and hopped forward. Three human strides in one hop. Anuka's hand went to his dagger and he cried out—just to alert his companions. The Frog Man bowed low and tossed a leather pouch at Anuka's feet.

"Now what?" Anuka complained. He stooped down cautiously, keeping an eye on the creature. He snatched the pouch up and backed away a couple of steps. It was a weathered courier bag. Anuka opened the pouch and found a letter inside. The word 'Sandbar' was written on the outside. "Oh, for Keit's sake." He fished the letter out and dropped the bag. He observed Lebarin's seal with a frown. The seal popped open easily. He read aloud, "Mr. Sandbar, the Wumpys are ancient servants of the Black Church. Bumph will be your guide through the forest and will accompany your band to Barith Shir. Signed by Victorin Lebarin."

Anuka wiped his hand down his face and sighed.

"Anuka, what is it?" Felin asked.

"Lebarin just saddled us with *another* useless idiot."

"Hey!" Fabian protested hotly.

The letter had been written in haste. Had anyone but an illiterate Frog Man given Anuka the letter he would have sworn it was forged. "Oh well. The more the merrier."

"Wumpys," Felin said under his breath. "Obviously."

Of all the things the Wood Elf could learn about the intricate Low Dragon tongue, why did he have to learn sarcasm? "Do they speak?" Anuka asked.

Felin shrugged.

I sure wish Fish Man was here. He could probably turn into one of these things. "You boys understand Draconic? Dragon speak. You know, like Bog?"

At the mention of the Black DragonLord's name, the half-dozen Wumpys fell to their faces and croaked loudly. Their chanting was rhythmic. For one with a dynamic imagination like Anuka, it sounded like they were chanting "*Bog*".

"Well," Fabian said. The bard combed his long golden hair with his fingers. "Now what?"

"Bah, they won't be any trouble. I say we go on. We have a long road ahead of us."

"Are you sure you don't want me to rip off their arms and drink their blood?" Grom's face looked the same as usual, but his eyes were laughing.

"Oh, everyone has jokes now. I liked it better when you all were quiet."

———————•◦•———————

The original plan was to make camp just before the spooky forest. The Wumpys escorted them for a couple of hours, but none would enter the forest with them save their leader, Bumph. According to the map, the forest should take about an hour to hike through. They had made good time and still had plenty of daylight left. Anuka encouraged them to press on. "Let's crank it up a notch and put this forest, and our escorts, behind us."

Now, as they stood looking into the blackened tangle of trees, he reconsidered that idea. Long blackened tendrils of leafless branches sagged toward the overgrown path like handless arms clawing for them. It seemed to Anuka that a great fire had devastated the forest long ago, but it refused to die. Thistles and brambles, dark and lifeless, clogged the ground around the spectral trees. They choked the walkway, making it nearly indistinguishable.

"Still want to go in there?" Grom asked.

"What choice do we have?" *Idiot. No one wants to go in there.* "C'mon. Best to get this over with. Somebody fish a torch out. Maybe we can burn our way through."

"I could . . ." Xanavor began. Everyone stopped walking and looked at him. He cleared this throat and began again. "I could send a raven or two to scout ahead."

The goblin shrugged. "Whatever weird thing you can do that will get us to the other side. Go for it, bubby."

The dark-clad human stepped ahead of the group on the thin path and bowed his head. Suddenly, a half-dozen birds flew from him as though he had been hiding them inside his coat. The birds cawed and disappeared into the dark forest.

They had wasted a lot of time deliberating, and the thick black canopy made the path very dark. Bumph trembled as his huge eyes darted along the treetops.

"Fabian, you take the torch. Felin, you go last and watch our backs. Xanavor, you stay with Grom—you've got all our medicine." Anuka snatched the torch from the bard's hands and effortlessly lit it with the power of his Djinn heritage.

"Why do I go first?" Fabian protested.

"Because you can't see without the torch and you aren't being useful in any other way." The goblin shooed Fabian along the path. "Now get—we're losing daylight."

Fabian snatched the torch from Anuka and picked his way along the narrow path.

Anuka grinned widely at the bard's back. He enjoyed keeping Fabian agitated. The Victorin doubtless sent the young bard to wreck the group. That was certain. Lebarin had probably told him to wait until they found the box and then try to kill them in some awful way. Or maybe Fabian was there to keep them from forming any devious plots. He sure didn't offer any useful skills to the party. It didn't matter. The Victorin and his cronies were at least four steps behind Anuka. *Being the smartest person in the room is a horrible burden*, he thought.

They had scarcely walked a quarter of an hour before they stopped. Anuka fell back with Felin, since Xanavor was as blind in the dark as the rest of the human race. He couldn't see past 'Mount Grom' but heard what sounded like Fabian throwing a fit.

"Seas, but these cursed things won't burn."

"Stop it before you set the forest on fire around us," the greasy mage declared.

It had to be bad for the implacable man to scold Fabian so. Anuka forced his way between Grom's trunk-sized legs. Xanavor had a hand extended to the bard who held the torch aloft out of the greasy human's reach. He was trying to avoid touching the dirty man whilst keeping him at bay.

"What are you two festering boils doing?"

The men looked at Anuka with chastened expressions.

Xanavor turned to Anuka and said, "This idiot is trying to burn down the forest around us."

"I am trying to clear our path. It's bad enough that I must lead, but I refuse to continue clawing through these nasty webs!" Fabian looked like he was about to give birth. Tears welled in his eyes and his shaking hands made the fading torch dance strangely.

Anuka looked up at Grom to get an idea about what was going on, but the words wouldn't pass his throat. Lines of sticky webbing crisscrossed the half-giant's face. His chest, too. Anuka turned back to the arguing humans. Fabian looked like he was trying to fling the world's stickiest booger off his index finger. A pair of crows pecked at the webbing on Xanavor's tattered cloak.

Webs meant only one thing: spiders. Anuka felt the tickle of dozens of spindly legs picking their way up his legs, back, and arms. He shuddered and slapped his shirt sleeves and trousers. A scream burst from him like a banshee's keening. Before he knew what he was doing, he blasted past Fabian and Xanavor, running for his life.

Anuka felt like a gazelle fleeing from a thousand tiny, venom-filled lions. His ears buzzed with the imagined sounds of chitinous legs clacking together as his eight-legged pursuers prepared to feast on his blood.

The forest was as dark as the inside of a whale. Anuka glowed like a crimson torch. He realized he might burst into flames if he didn't get control of his fear quickly. He also realized the webs blocking the path incinerated when they touched his skin. The smoldering goblin squeezed his lips together to avoid getting webbing in his mouth or worse; swallowing a spider. The thought made his stomach lurch. Anuka fiercely missed Slobbers right now. She wasn't afraid of anything. One summer, his pet honey badger had saved him from being attacked by fist-sized spiders when he had fallen into their web by mistake. As the translucent wretches scurried after him, Slobbers had interceded. Anuka remembered the milky-bodied beasts climbing all over her, biting savagely. She paid them no heed. Rather, she methodically ate the little Sum Bucks one by one. A few of the spiders had managed to bite through her tough, honey badger hide and inject their venom. Slobbers had staggered around a bit after eating the last one and had slept most of the afternoon. Then she got up as savage as always. The goblin's heart ached for her. Missing Slobbers made him miss Papa. They were likely together and in a far better place than Anuka right now.

On he ran as fast as his legs would carry him. His lungs burned and his feet were cut and bruised. He suddenly realized that his boots had burned away. Along with his shirt, pants, and hat. *Sum Buck*. He had liked that hat.

Anuka had no idea where he was. The path had forked a dozen times, and he had tried to alternate taking the left and right paths. But when the next split came, he couldn't remember which way he had gone last time. *Right*, he thought, angling that way. At the last second, he remembered he had gone right last time and dodged left just a second too late.

Anuka's naked toe caught the edge of a gnarly root and he careened to the forest floor. His fall blasted the last vestiges of air from his lungs, and he rolled to his back, gasping. He tried to get up, but his body wouldn't respond. He conjured mental pictures of buckets of spiders skittering along the path toward him, but his body lay stubbornly inert. *Fine. We die here, then.*

Anuka's vision swam. At the far edge of his sight were unidentifiable white globs in the distance. He coughed, spluttered, and sucked greedily for air. That made him cough more. As air returned to him it brought with it sensation. The muscles of his legs burned and pulsed as his blood carried air to them. It felt like every twig and pebble in the forest clung to his naked, sweaty back.

Anuka closed his eyes and drew a long breath. When he opened them, he saw the white blobs again. They weren't familiar. He had no idea what they were.

An eternity passed as he lay on the ground pondering the shapes. They stood out in the blackened forest like stars in the night sky. They swayed lazily, and Anuka felt their soothing allure. He was on the verge of solving the mystery of the strange shapes when he heard a rhythmic thumping in the distance. It was like the beat of a drum or the fall of an axe. The sound grew louder.

"Hrrrrr," a bellowing voice called. "High hag inn."

A gigantic gray head eclipsed the white shapes. The mouth worked, and noise thundered out, but the words were beyond Anuka's comprehension. *This was Death. She had come for him, at last.*

The need to confess his sins before he expired overwhelmed him. "I drank First Mate Zeelun's wine. Then I put it back... after I was done with it."

The figure kept speaking, but the words were rubbish. The goblin's confession wasn't accepted. "Fine. I didn't really bed Rigby's sister. We just told him I did to make him mad."

The gray head was growing angry. It lifted Anuka from the ground and shook him.

Seas! "Ok, I'm sorry, I'm sorry. I'm a Filgenium. Ember told me. Please don't tell Papa. I'm so ashamed..." Death raked his ears briskly and the world came alive around him as dust and debris tumbled free.

"Is he dead?"

"Why is his skin so hot?"

"Why is he naked?"

Then he remembered. "Sum Buck! Let go of me."

Grom dropped him to the dirt and Anuka sat up. His four crew members knelt in the dirt around him, staring in shock.

"What is wrong with you, goblin?" Xanavor asked.

The mage sounded more angry than concerned. "Loads of stuff, bubby. Let me up."

Everyone stood and gave him some space. Fabian held Anuka's pack and a fistful of charred clothing. He sighed, took his pack from the bard, then looked inside for his other hat.

"Keit and Tor," Xanavor swore.

Anuka looked up to see what the issue was. Everyone stared at the white globs. *Oh yeah.*

It was now apparent that the white globs were bodies hanging from the trees, encased in webbing from head to toe. The urge to flee welled up in him again, but he didn't have the energy for it.

The cocoons hung about ten feet off the ground. Felin and Grom cut them down and laid them reverently in a row on the ground.

"Hey," Anuka said as the pair cut down the fourth and final body. "I appreciate what you are doing, but it would be grand if we didn't end up like them."

They ignored him.

Xanavor knelt beside the first cocoon and sawed the webbing away with a thin knife.

"Weeping death..." Fabian cried.

"Do you know him?" Felin asked.

The bard nodded.

The Wood Elf knelt before the corpse. He closed his eyes and drew two fingers along his own outstretched arm. Then he kissed his fingers and held them above the dead man's face.

Whatever Felin was doing, it didn't work. The guy still looked dead to Anuka.

"Roblando. He was a bard from Finrinkle." Fat tears welled in Fabian's eyes as he knelt by his comrade.

Keit and Tor, but that Sum Buck cries a lot.

They cut the webbing from the other bodies. The bard said they were part of Roblando's crew. There was no time to bury the bodies, so they laid them out respectfully, off the path. Fabian sang a sad song. It was a nice service. Anuka snuck a nice dagger from Roblando's side.

"Despite running like an idiot for ten minutes, we aren't far off course." Felin glared at Anuka.

"You're welcome," Anuka said.

"It's Bumph you should thank. He followed your trail like an expert ranger. I say we get out of these woods and head for the river. We aren't far from the fortress once we get clear of the trees."

Although it wasn't his idea, he went along and they hurried themselves down the narrow path once more.

In their haste, they didn't hear the grinding of chitinous appendages as rows of bulbous eyes watched from the trees.

Chapter 17

Puzzle of Bones

C andle light flickered through the shutters of the front window when Ember glided home. The hour was very late. Dawn was but a few hours hence—no one should be awake. He had left the back door in his bedroom unlocked and had planned to enter that way. But he had started thinking about danger and kisses and forgot all about that plan.

He could see shadows beyond the shutters. The front door was locked, so he gave a weak knock. A few moments later, the door opened a bit to Tabir gaping at him.

"Ember," Tabir breathed, relief in his voice. He stepped aside and opened the door more fully.

Ember entered warily. Crenthys sat on the floor with her back to the wall, mud-caked arms resting on her tented knees. *Goodness.* She had mud everywhere. Then Ember noticed a tattered brown blanket covering something. Crenthys looked up as Ember entered. "What is this? Crenthys, are you well?"

Crenthys didn't answer. She leaned forward and unwrapped the blanket. Inside were the skeletal remains of a large human. No, a Dragomyr.

"Forsaken gods... who was that?" Ember's mind raced. *Had Crenthys killed someone? No, there would be blood. Where did this come from? Why does Crenthys have these bones?* Ember realized his questions wouldn't get answered if they remained in his head. "Crenthys, why is there a Dragomyr skeleton in our sitting room?"

Crenthys folded the cloth back over the bones. "I don't know who it is. Odwin says it's me."

Odwin had been the source of a great deal of unrest of late. "How did he have this?"

With a sigh, Crenthys stood and brushed off the front of her soiled tunic. "He claims he retrieved the corpse of Brinka after Belendurath was slain. He brought it back and buried it at our manor house."

"Do you think he was delusional then, or did your master's death trigger it?" Tabir asked, as he fetched a broom from the kitchen.

"Hard to say." Crenthys went to the basin and began washing the worst of the dirt from her hands and arms.

"You said there were many slain Dragomyr in the cavern when you escaped, right?" A dark feeling began to build in Ember's stomach.

"That's what I see in the fragments of memory that have returned. I suspect this is one of those corpses." She dried her hands on a towel.

"Did Vodinar ever tell you what Ivrus saw when he went into your memories?" Ember was acutely aware of how suspicious his questions sounded, but he couldn't keep them in.

"No. Ember, what is it?" Crenthys's tone was firm and fearful, she was wringing the towel.

"I'm not sure," Ember lied.

"Ember." Crenthys's tone was more forceful.

Why does my curiosity carry me away? "I am just trying to put some pieces together is all." *I have to stall. Change the subject. Flee!* "I found some things in the restricted section of the library."

Crenthys tossed the towel to the floor and took a step toward Ember. "What did you learn?"

Ember swallowed hard. *Well, a great deal about locks and kissing. No, that won't do.* "There is a written history of the death of Belendurath." Crenthys didn't seize his shirt and shake him, so Ember continued. "Their internal account differs from the official report. The official account says that there was an accident during an exploratory journey killing Belendurath and several Dragomyr. The city mourned. But the internal account is less narrative, and more informational. It . . . it paints a different picture."

"Ember, different how?" Crenthys's face looked less angry, but just as rigid.

"Well, the investigations centered on the idea of some sort of treachery from Belendurath." Crenthys screwed up her face at the remark, but Ember pressed on. "These reports weren't specific, but seemed to suggest that Lady Belendurath was not in possession of her wits. The incident was ruled as accidental self death while attempting to destroy her own hatchery."

"Hatchery?" Crenthys took Ember by the arms. "Where? Where did she die?"

"Pelint Peak." Ember's heart was racing as he watched the fire go out of his friend. Crenthys released him and let her arms fall limply to her sides. He continued, "It has another name, as well."

"Scornrock," Crenthys said weakly.

Oh. It seems pieces are falling into place for Cren as well. "Yes. Scornrock. Is that the place Tamris sent Wave's thugs to find an egg?"

Crenthys nodded.

Tamris was an old friend of Crenthys's and leader of the Apostate chapter in Usban. Apostate was a group of anti-Dragon antagonists. Wave's thugs had stolen a Dragon egg from Scornrock, allowed it to hatch, and leeched the baby's blood for months. That baby Dragon was Crenthys's brother and the main source of illegal DragonsBlood in Usban.

"Do you know if Dovondes is your brother's father?" It was simply the next logical question. But based on the outraged look consuming Crenthys's face, perhaps he should have considered the question first.

"Why would you ask something like that?" Crenthys barked, a rough edge to her voice.

"Oh. Perhaps I failed to mention that Belendurath and Dovondes were lovers." *That was an awful omission. truly.*

"Lovers? How do you know this?"

"It was common knowledge, though following your creator's demise, it was rarely mentioned in publication." Upon immediate reflection, it seemed a crude way to divulge familial information to his friend.

With a growl, Crenthys scooped the bundle of bones and fled into the night.

Tabir tried to stop her, but it was a useless gesture. The scornful look the High Elf gave Ember filled him with regret.

"I could have handled that better, I suppose," Ember said.

Tabir sighed and went to his room.

The long day of planning, along with the late night of skulking and climbing, had left Ember exhausted. Still, he knew he could only afford a couple of hours of sleep. He needed to find Odwin.

━━━●○●━━━

Crenthys was exhausted in every way. She had taken the bones back to the manor, and returned to their residence just after dawn. Breakfast came while she was washing. Along with food, the servant had brought a long, simple yellow robe for Crenthys to wear to her hearing.

Ember and Tabir ate in companionable silence while Crenthys held the robe in her hands. She knew what it meant: this was the robe of a servant. *We are all servants of someone; I suppose.* For the past ten years, Crenthys had chosen her masters—more or less. As she searched her heart, she couldn't decide how she felt about being a servant of the Bronze Court again. She scarcely remembered her previous service, but was beginning to wonder if one master differed from another. Dovondes governed a peaceful continent where his servants seemed content. But there were dark tides roiling beneath the water. She sighed as she slid her arm into the robe.

As she stood before the polished metal mirror, she couldn't decide if the robe made her look like an honored guest or a prisoner. Her guts churned. Today was so pivotal and the results were beyond her control. She had skipped at least one meal yesterday and now her stomach was launching a rebellion. A knock came at her door. Tabir was on the other side.

"Your escort is here. Do you need a bite to eat? It might calm you a bit."

Crenthys smiled as the elf pretended not to notice her outfit—it must look ridiculous. "Yes. Thank you."

Tabir returned to the dining area, and Crenthys took one last look in the mirror. Thoughts of Kelios began to creep up, but she crushed them. *I will need all of my wits today. No time for confusing thoughts on confusing topics.*

Vodinar had arrived to collect her today. Vodinar and two guards. She didn't know what to make of that. "One moment, please," Crenthys said.

The lanky Dragomyr's tiny smile was his only acknowledgment.

Crenthys pulled a generous fistful of neatly sliced roasted beef from the tray on the table and quickly devoured it. Her stomach wouldn't thank her for eating in such haste, but she needed the nourishment. Meat was all she wanted lately. When she was disguised as the beautiful Sea Elf, she had taken to vegetables and fruits. Now she couldn't stomach the thought of them.

She wiped her mouth gracelessly and tossed the cloth on the table.

"Can we come with you? As far as they allow?" Ember asked.

Crenthys was surprised at the Malkin's question. She assumed he was still angry with her, so it was touching. "Well?" she asked Vodinar. "Can they join us as far as the palace portal?"

"I suppose so," Vodinar replied, a trace of controlled annoyance in his voice. He likely was concerned about the delay additional people would cause.

"Yes, and thank you. But we must leave immediately."

Tabir stowed a bunch of grapes in his tattered robe pocket and finished his wooden cupful of water. Ember fussed over clearing the table of crumbs and mess.

Soon, the six of them moved along the gleaming city streets in the bright morning sun. The sky was clear and blue—as it generally was. They were on the cusp of the rainy season, but Crenthys hadn't seen a cloud since they arrived. She wished things were as sunny in her mind but her dread grew the closer they drew to the palace portal. Vodinar seemed uneasy at her side. He kept glancing at her friends, and she got the impression that he was ready for them to be gone. Ember and Tabir walked along in silence. It was nice. She was afraid they would try to shower her with encouragement or reassurance. Both were good things, but she wasn't in the mood for platitudes. None of them knew what to expect from this hearing.

The party rounded a corner and stopped before a large, ornate building. Patterns of gilded, inlaid bronze traced the exterior. The deep stairs had been carved from marble and etched with the crests of the great Dragon houses. Far behind the building was Aradian, the mountain where Dovondes built his castle and the seat of the Bronze government. It was unbelievably vast and Crenthys had to remind herself that it was built for Dragons.

"This is where we part," Vodinar announced.

Crenthys turned to her friends as if to say goodbye. The tension of unspoken words hung in the air.

Ember hugged her suddenly. He pulled back to arm's length and craned his neck to meet her eyes. "Be truthful and be brave. Oh, and be yourself." He smiled mischievously and said, "But not too much."

Tabir stepped up and took her massive hand in his slender one. "Go with the grace of Rathune. We will be here when you return."

"Thank you," she said, not daring to say more. The last thing she wanted was to get all weepy in front of Vodinar and his guards.

Her friends walked back the way they had come and Crenthys turned toward the portal house. *Whatever fate awaits me, I cannot avoid. If I am to meet my doom today, I will do so on my terms. It's time I get some answers.*

Chapter 18

A Raven is Never Lost

"Sum Buck," Anuka whispered. He hoped that the crushing defeat he felt in his tiny heart wasn't apparent on his face. Based on how Felin and the boys were staring at him, it likely was. The scene before them made no sense. Instead of a ruined fort, a massive construction project topped the distant hill. There were dozens of Vith. The lithe frog-like creatures resembled humans much more than Wumpys did. At least fifty Kobolds scurried about, carrying lumber or pushing wheeled carts full of large stones. "What did... why don't... where are...?"

"It seems the Vith have enslaved some Kobolds to rebuild the fortress," Grom rumbled as he took his turn with the looking glass.

"You don't say," Anuka said. "Thank you for the update, Grom."

The giant handed the scope to Fabian and said to Anuka, "Rare is the moment you aren't speaking. I took the opportunity to exploit my good fortunes."

"I liked you better as the big, dumb Stoneman. This peaceful poet bit is getting annoying."

"I live to serve," Grom said with a smile. Well, his lips moved anyway. Calling it a smile was a stretch.

Fabian's curse was less elegant and delivered with very little panache, but he made his point. "What are we going to do about them? We can't go down the chute with a bunch of Vith and Kobolds around."

"Yes, thank you Fabian. You're about as helpful as Grom. I don't know what we're going to do. Bumph, you got any bright ideas?"

Only then did the Wumpy join the conversation. He seemed just as content picking through the weeds for grasshoppers as he did hunting for lost treasure. He made one of his long croaking sounds.

"Surrender?" Felin said with a chuckle, "No, Bumph. We must retrieve that box."

"How is it you can understand that guy?" Anuka jabbed a thumb at the Wumpy.

"He speaks to me. In my mind." Felin said with a genuine smile.

"Of course he does. Kindred spirits, you two." Anuka snatched his hat off and rubbed his bald head. He stopped when he realized he was rubbing his head again, but continued when he decided it helped him think.

"The chute can't be the only way down. Wasn't there an old mine entrance on the map?" Xanavor asked as he fumbled in his pack for the map.

"Old mine entra... don't you mean dungeon of death?" Anuka snatched the scope from Fabian. "Bubby, did you not see the little notes about the mine? Did you not see the words 'pit traps' and 'acid pools?'"

"We can't go in there. We have to go back." Fabian was shaking his head slowly and taking small steps backwards into the dark woods.

"We *are* in a pickle if I'm agreeing with Fabian," Anuka said.

"Going back is not an option," rumbled Grom's voice with finality. Everyone looked at him.

When he noticed their attention, he looked at each of them, his face like granite. "We have made a vow. Our honor demands we complete our task."

"See," Anuka began, "The thing about honor is; you can't eat it, you can't spend it, and you can't love on it. It's useless. Especially if you get killed defending it."

"What of your friends, Anuka?" Felin looked at Anuka pitifully.

Sum Buck. Anuka sighed, hung his head, and rested his hands on his hips. *This is too important. Kelios, Offund, and Rigby are counting on me. So is Papa.* "Yeah. Okay. Fine. Felin, go do some scouting. Find us a way in there. Grom, you and Xylitol find us some grub. Fabian, rosin up your bow and warm up your voice box. I'm guessing we're gonna need it."

———◦———

"This isn't even close to the stupidest thing I've done," Anuka said out of the side of his mouth as the five of them crawled through the sand. "One time, I lit a fart on Magistrate Clurpal's funeral pyre for five coppers."

Grom chortled from the back of the pack. He breathed in a mouthful of sand and his chuckle turned into a coughing fit.

"Grom, be quiet," Felin hissed. The dark-skinned elf peered toward the parapet where two sentries stood pointing in their direction. The second one drew his javelin and looked their way. "Run," the elf yelled as he rose and sprinted toward the mouth of the cave at the base of the old fort.

"Perfect," Anuka complained as he sprang and pumped his little legs furiously. Three heartbeats later, Grom blew past him, taking long, ground-eating strides. A javelin sailed over Anuka's head and buried into the sand behind him with a hiss. He spared an upward glance. The first Vith was deftly picking his way down the side of the castle wall. *He's angling for a better throw,* Anuka thought. *Get moving, Sandbar.* Darting to the left, then back to the right again, Anuka tried to make a difficult target. It was times like these that he missed his old pet honey badger, Slobbers. She would have run up the wall and chewed the faces off of those two guards by now.

As Anuka caught up to Xanavor, a javelin sailed in a perfect arc toward him. At the last moment, a raven caught the missile in its chest and fell dead to the sand. Xanavor was panting like a dog in a box full of cats—but he chugged on.

Grom stood in the cave's doorway. Massive beams supported the opening on the top and sides. Carved into squares from incredibly large trees, the supports had withered with age. The half-giant was yelling something Anuka couldn't make out. Not until the giant grabbed the top support and pulled downward with a grunt.

"Grom, you crazy Sum Buck," Anuka cackled. He darted between Grom's legs and stopped to check on his companions. Only Xanavor remained outside the cave. The mage labored on as another javelin zoomed past his head and a raven deflected it. Three strides from the entrance the human stumbled.

Anuka bit down hard on a bubbling guffaw as Xanavor's head collided with the ground in a spray of sand. The human's feet flew up like a scorpion's tail as he skidded to a halt. The mage's hairy legs flopped over his head and Anuka almost lost his composure. Just then, a slender Vith jumped down right beside the human. The creature turned to look into the cave and Fabian screamed.

Wumpys were so ugly they were cute. They looked like big frogs with skinny legs. Adorable. The Vith, however, were a terrifying sight.

First off, his one looked too much like a person. It had long, slender arms and legs, and it moved with a cat's grace. With a slender head and thin, lipless frown Anuka thought it was a devil. It wore a long jump-suit with a hood. Recessed, fathomless black eyes peered from under the hood. In one quick motion, it slid a slender sword from its side and stalked toward Grom.

The half-giant had switched from pulling the beam down to holding it up and was helpless. He focused all of his strength on holding the square beam over the cave's entrance. Grom grunted for help, but Anuka was well ahead of him.

Anuka's newly pilfered dagger sank into the right thigh of the Vith. A second later, Felin's dagger thudded into its chest. Then Felin barrelled his shoulder into the Vith, knocking it clear of the cave entrance. Anuka and the Wood Elf dashed forward and helped Xanavor to his feet. The human was heavier than he looked.

They got the Raven Mage inside the cave and lowered him to the floor near the wall. Felin grabbed his short bow and darted back outside. He returned after a moment. "The other one's gone. Grom," the Wood Elf said with a nod.

With a yell, the half-giant stepped back and ripped the beam free of the support structure just as Felin scurried inside. A cloud of dust enveloped the group, and a cacophony of cascading rocks sealed the cave's entrance. Then the room was dark and silent—save for someone coughing.

Anuka expected total darkness. It surprised him to see an orange glow beyond the fading dust cloud. When the air had cleared, a pair of stunned, dust-covered Kobolds stared at the group. The one holding the torch continued to stare, slack jawed. The second Kobold turned and fled, doubtless in search of help.

———————◦◦———————

"Hello tiny Kobold. I, too, am a creature of an inferior race," Anuka said, smiling broadly.

"Anuka," Xanavor said harshly, "What are you doing?"

The goblin clenched his teeth and replied, "I'm making friends." Anuka gave the Kobold a little bow. "We are here on a mission for the great DragonLord Caustimis."

At the mention of Bog's true name, the Kobold dropped the torch and fell on his belly.

"See? Results." Clearing this throat, Anuka said, "Okay, time to get up and go tell your friends that we are on your side. And that they need to help us." When the Kobold didn't move, Anuka grabbed it under the arms and heaved it to its feet. "There ya' go. Bog don't like layabouts. Run along now."

The Kobold looked at Anuka and his crew. Then it scooped up its torch and ran down a dark corridor.

"See? Easy." Anuka rubbed his hands on his shirt to remove any lingering Kobold ick. He stopped at his vest pocket. Panic hit him. *The Ruby! It's gone*! Anuka released his breath when he remembered the Ruby was safe in his cabin on the ship. But knowing that did little to quell his need of it. The absence of it niggled him like a persistent itch that he couldn't scratch. His attachment to that gem was unnerving. *Focus, bubby*. His crew was looking at him curiously. "Well, let's get moving. If I remember right, there should be a way we can sneak up to the castle from the mine."

"Why do we want to go to the castle? I thought we needed to go down." Xanavor wrapped his filthy robe more tightly around him. Patches of dust marred the dark robe.

"Remember the big shaft we were planning to climb down? If we can come up inside the castle when it's dark, maybe we can slip down the shaft and get what we came for. I, for one, have no desire to go through some mad priest's carnival house." Anuka spat, trying to rid his mouth of the wad of dirt he had breathed in when Grom brought the door down.

"The Vith know we are here. They will be on alert." Grom offered.

"Well, any of you boys have a better plan?" Anuka tossed up his hands in surrender. "I didn't think so. The door is to the north." He turned left and stared into the dark hallway.

"Anuka," Xanavor said. "North is that way." The human gestured to the path on the right.

"Really?" Anuka asked suspiciously. "How do you know which way is north?"

"A raven knows. A raven is never lost."

Anuka thought about the words. That made no sense. "Whatever." The goblin moved in the direction Xanavor indicated.

No one noticed that their Wumpy guide hadn't made it into the mine.

Chapter 19

Trials

L ike so many experiences these past few days, the Grand Chamber of the Bronze Court was new to Crenthys—yet eerily familiar. The ceiling was at least a hundred feet high and terminated in a massive dome of colored glass mosaic. Large half-moon pillars carved in relief from the wall ran from floor to ceiling. Each one was covered in various carvings of glyphs or phrases from the High Draconic tongue.

In the center of the room stood a long marble table with half a dozen Borchwood chairs, each gilded in various precious metals. Three on each long side and a great seat with a rounded back at the end. A huge sun with an etched Dragon superimposed over it decorated the great seat—Dovondes's chair. It was the only unoccupied chair.

Crenthys felt her gut clench as the six Dragons, in human form, watched Vodinar lead her in. He brought her to stand in the middle of an inlaid ring of bronze on the floor. She took a deep breath and met the gazes of each Dragon. From left to right, she recognized Zothit, who ruled Prenya on the country's eastern border with Zhazie. He eyed her with open contempt.

Next to him sat a tiny, dark-skinned human woman of middle years. A red and green ribbon precariously restrained her pitch-black curly hair. This was Vah-mene, sovereign of Fiang on the far western border of the Bronze controlled country of Dirzal. She smiled pleasantly but gave Crenthys an uneasy feeling. Somehow her smile seemed more threatening than Zothit's contempt.

To Vah-mene's left sat Zamyr, a Dragon in a thin human form who looked to be little more than a boy. His patchy beard grew mainly in the shadow of his long, pointy chin. He was an administrator who managed economic and agrarian aspects of the country. His expression was rigid, but his dark amber eyes moved like a hummingbird, sampling everything in the room.

Next was Grenaset. She appeared as a wiry woman with a warrior's build. Her black hair was cropped almost to her scalp and crystal blue eyes brooded at Crenthys. Grenaset's dark brown skin was etched with faded scars. She ruled from the Pelint Plains south to Peleta, where her sister Neersin ruled.

Neersin looked the opposite of her sister. Her dark skin was smooth. Long luxurious waves of curly hair hung around her shoulders and trailed down her back. Her eyes were the same crystal blue, but projected a vigor and joy Grenaset's did not. Neersin's manner was easy and comfortable.

In the last seat was Mondeseth. He looked like a man well past his prime. His white hair was short, like Grenaset, and he wore a mottled gray and black goatee that hung down his chest. His face was unreadable, but he had a reputation for opposing Dovondes, mostly out of spite. Mondeseth once sat in the chair reserved for the DragonLord.

Vodinar had supplied the names, but the impressions were her own. Of late, Crenthys found her randomly returning memory more a blessing than a curse. This was one of those times.

Dovondes entered the room from the back, leaving a cadre of officials on the other side of the door. The members of the Bronze

Council stood and Vodinar and Crenthys knelt as he took his seat and nodded to the other Dragons. They took their seats. "Apologies. The wheels of bureaucracy turn slowly."

Crenthys could feel his eyes upon her, and she thought she heard him sigh. "Rise."

Vodinar and Crenthys stood and raised their heads. Vodinar stepped to the table and declared, "His Majesty, Dovondes, the Bronze DragonLord and Sovereign of Dirzal, I present upon your request, Brinka of Belendurath."

Crenthys thought she noticed a twitch in the DragonLord's eye at the mention of the name. But it may have been imagined. Her heart thumped in her chest. Every instinct told her to flee, but thoughts of her brother's uncertain future strengthened her resolve.

With a nod from Dovondes, Vodinar knelt, produced a slender rod, and tapped it to the floor. Blue energy winked from the spot he tapped and flowed into the circle on the floor where Crenthys stood.

She gasped her surprise and looked at Vodinar.

"Verity Rod," Vodinar said as he stood. "You can render no falsehood while it is active."

That snake, she thought. He hadn't told her about that part. Crenthys's mind raced as she thought of all the things she did not want to be truthful about.

"State your name," Dovondes said in his rich baritone voice.

"Crenthys Larin'hul," she said. The Dragons exchanged a glance and she realized he meant her other name. "Apologies, Brinka of Belendurath." A few of the Council murmured amongst themselves. She had given two names and hadn't died. Was the ring just for show? Crenthys didn't want to test that theory. Something in her mind told her lying would bring unpleasant consequences.

"Why have you returned here?" Dovondes asked. He watched her face closely.

She prayed her fear didn't show on her face. "I found, and have returned, the last survivor of Lady Belendurath. My friends and I wanted to bring him home."

"Home? Hmm." Dovondes looked down at his hands.

Zamyr cleared his throat and flattened the collar of his silk shirt. "Brinka, tell us what you remember about the incident involving the death of Belendurath, Slephinax, and six Dragomyr."

Slephinax had died there? And had she heard correctly? Six Dragomyr? Crenthys looked up at the seven pairs of eyes boring into her. While there were dozens of Bronze Dragons throughout the country, the most powerful were sitting at this table. And the most likely to have created Dragomyr. The weight of the situation settled on her shoulders in that moment. Some, if not all, of these Dragons had likely lost their Dragomyr when her master died. Some may have lost more than one. She shuddered.

"Brinka?" Zamyr repeated. "You are under the influence of the Verity Rod."

The reminder was unnecessary. Crenthys could feel the magical power flowing through the circle at her feet. She didn't intend to lie. "The first thing I remember is sitting on a rock, covered in dust. A Dragomyr guard was there and asked me what happened. He quickly figured out that I couldn't remember anything. He told me who I was and where I needed to go. I ran all the way back to Wrythmar where my mistress's servant cared for me."

"Why didn't you come forward?" Zothit asked.

"I was frightened. And I couldn't remember anything. And the pain..."

"How did you survive, Brinka of Belendurath? Eight others died that day, yet you live." Neersin wore a dour expression.

"I don't know. I can't remember anything before the cave." Crenthys swallowed her frustration before it could build any further.

"Why do you yet live? Why did you not perish with your master—as is custom?" Zothit growled.

They are pushing me. I can't react. I must stay calm. "I don't know why I didn't die when I lost my master. Many times I wished I had. But I didn't."

"Where have you been for a decade?" Asked Zamyr.

Crenthys watched Dovondes. He hadn't participated in the conversation and appeared to be biding his time. She wondered if he knew about Morglun and Apostate. *Of course he does.* "I made some friends. They cared for me and didn't judge me."

"Were these friends criminals?" Zothit asked.

"Yes. Among other things. But they never tried to kill me, so we got along quite well. I did what I had to do to survive."

"So why come back now?" Dovondes asked. The others at the table looked at the DragonLord.

"Because I rescued my brother and felt it was my duty to bring him home." Crenthys took some satisfaction in the discomfort on the Dragon's faces.

"Were you in Usban?" Zamyr asked. "Did you see the red goblin kill the Silver Ambassador?"

"Zamyr," Dovondes barked, "that is beyond the scope of this inquiry. Those issues will be addressed another time."

That was a surprise. Crenthys was expecting to be questioned about that. Vodinar seemed puzzled as well.

"Brinka," Dovondes began, "are you a threat to our citizens, or our way of life? Do you feel any desire for retribution or retaliation?"

"No," she said, and held her breath. She didn't die. The Verity Rod didn't buzz and the blue magic on the floor didn't even pulse. Crenthys didn't want to hurt anyone. Not really. But she was afraid for her brother and she still saw the Bronze Court as her enemy.

As she considered the half-dozen immortal Dragons in front of her, she realized she wasn't the same scared Dragomyr who fled the city a decade ago. She had experienced much of the world. Fought many battles and faced death. Death at the hands of a Dragon Council did not differ from the hands of a crazed Sea Elf. She didn't want to die. In fact, Crenthys had more to live for now than she had the last time she had been here.

"I don't desire anything but peace with my people, and to help raise my brother. He is my only remaining family."

Neersin held up her hand and a clear, soundproof barrier was erected between her and the Dragons. They chatted animatedly amongst themselves for several minutes. The discussion grew intense and Zothit stood abruptly, opened a portal, and stepped into it.

Great. More enemies. Crenthys assumed that some of Zothit's Dragomyr must have been among those slain in the mountain a decade ago. Nothing she did would win him to her side.

Finally, the discussion ended and the barrier was removed.

"Brinka of Belendurath," Dovondes began, it is the decision of this body that you will be renewed to House Belendurath and be given privileges to assist in the rearing of the Bronze youngling in accordance with the will of his trainers."

Crenthys gasped in relief. It was more than she could have dreamed possible.

"Vodinar, you are responsible for preparing the ceremony. This meeting is adjourned."

One at a time the Dragons made portals and left or walked to their chambers within the palace. Crenthys stood rooted to the spot. Of every outcome she had imagined, this was the least likely.

"Brinka, we should go." Vodinar had released the power of the Verity Rod and was beckoning her to follow him.

She wrapped him in a fierce embrace and cried, "Thank you, Vodinar."

The lanky Dragomyr didn't return the hug but patted her head awkwardly. "Come now, we should be going."

He sounded... guilty, but Crenthys didn't care. Today was a good day. A day for celebration. So excited was she that she completely forgot to ask Vodinar what might cause the Verity Rod to fail.

———⊙———

Ember was so flummoxed by their first real argument he forgot which stage of their relationship it was supposed to come in. It was too early for a fight, as far as his chart was concerned.

"We were nearly caught," Yondi hissed. "Now you want to go back?" She glanced around the quiet park outside the library. A few people milled around, but no one looked in their direction.

"Of course I want to go back," Ember replied. His voice was perfectly calm, and just above a whisper. "I have much yet to learn."

"I don't want to get caught." She still kept her voice low.

"You are right. You shouldn't come." Ember immediately understood the error of his words, but wasn't sure what to do about the aftermath.

Yondi's mouth fell open, then a thunderstorm passed over her face and her upper lip curled. "If I hadn't been there, you would have gotten caught for sure." She sneered with a jab to his chest. Her pointer finger was surprisingly strong.

Ember recoiled as much from her words as from the jab. "I only meant that it is unnecessary for both of us to risk getting caught. If I am discovered, I can plead ignorance and talk my way past any real trouble."

"And what of me? I am supposed to be your minder. If you are caught in a restricted area, who do you think will get the blame for the ignorant Malkin wandering around the library's restricted book section?"

He hadn't thought of that. Exhaustion weighed his bones. Things were much simpler when he only had himself to worry about. "I see." Understanding a problem and knowing the solution were two different parts of the equation. "I still need to get in there."

"Why? What is so important that you would risk both of our hides? And *don't* say curiosity."

Some of her hair had fallen down over one eye—it was adorable. He wanted to brush it back but assumed the storm was still raging inside her and he had no desire to be struck by emotional lightning. When he realized she was waiting for an answer, he cleared his throat and rubbed his palms on his trousers. *What can I say? I can't betray my friends. But Yondi is my friend. Maybe more than a friend.* Perhaps he could trust her a bit—see how that goes.

"My friend Crenthys isn't well." *Nice beginning*, he congratulated himself. She didn't seem impressed. "She's a Dragomyr." *Right. She knows this.* "Anyway, her master was killed and she lost her memory. Crenthys did. Not her master. She was dead. Then Cren was chased from the city, where she spent a decade befriending some shady characters and making a series of poor life choices. Then her friend

Anuka rescued me. We killed a Sea Wyrm and fled. I came here with Crenthys."

Yondi's lips wore a crooked grimace and one eyebrow was raised. Ember searched his memory to discern what that expression meant on the woman you are courting, but came up empty. "We don't know what caused her memory issues, but I suspect it was magic. I'm scouring these books, trying to find some answers."

She was looking at him curiously. "Can you use magic?"

Umm. Where did that come from? "You know only Dragons can use magic," he said with a very fake sounding forced chuckle.

"And humans who have an affinity. Do some Malkin have affinity for magic?"

"Let's go see if we can find a book about latent magical abilities in the Tier Three racks. I think I saw one in the restricted section." That was the lamest attempt at a subliminal message Ember had ever heard. Why did she turn his brain into useless mush?

Instead of storming off or attacking Ember, Yondi sighed. Then she stood, brushed the grass from her pants, and offered to help Ember up. "Fine. But we are breaking in my way this time."

That hadn't gone nearly as poorly as he had feared. Next, he needed to figure out how to explain his need to break into the top level.

Chapter 20

A Use for Bards

Anuka stared up at Felin's dangling feet as the nimble elf scaled the back of the staircase. The elf was thirty feet off of the ground and continued to work his way to the top, about another ten feet. *I could climb that. It's just easier to let the gangling Wood Elf get some practice.*

It was ominous to find traps this early in the dungeon, but they had. Did the Vith trap the stairs? Who were they trying to keep out? The questions were a waste of time, but he couldn't put them aside. Felin had elected to scale the outside of the staircase in lieu of disarming potential traps on the stairs.

Craning their necks, Anuka, Fabian, Grom, and Xanavor watched Felin deftly swing his legs up to gain the side of the platform at the top of the stairs. The Wood Elf paused for a moment to catch his breath. Then, he inspected the door. After an interminable amount of prodding and examining, the Wild Elf gingerly tested the "L" shaped door handle.

Felin peered over the side at them, folded his hands in front of him like he was praying, and then pulled them apart like opening a book.

"It's open," Anuka clarified in case one of his companions was being obtuse at the moment. He nodded to the elf and gave an enthusiastic thumbs up.

Felin fully turned the handle on the door. A muted crack split the air and a film of dust curled lazily from the wall the staircase was affixed to. The three companions on the ground startled in unison. A pale-faced Felin stepped quickly over the rail on the top of the platform and began to scale down the way he had gone up.

With a groan and another crack—this one sharp like a dry twig breaking—the entire structure separated from the wall. It listed violently to one side until the five-story platform smashed into the opposite wall.

All thoughts of stealth evaporated and Anuka cried out, "Felin!"

The elf had managed to hang on to the structure and avoided getting squashed between the stairs and the wall. When the staircase rebounded from the wall, however, Felin slammed hard into the opposite wall.

How the elf hung on, Anuka couldn't guess. Felin dangled by one arm from the back of one stair. He was nearly thirty feet off the ground. The main support beam nearest to them groaned.

"Felin, move!" Anuka called up to the Wood Elf. Then he turned to the Raven mage. "Can you do anything?"

"Like what? I can't fly." Xanavor held his hands up helplessly.

Anuka growled and turned to watch the elf's painstakingly slow progress down.

Fabian was quietly strumming a tune while he watched from the hallway.

Anuka turned to rebuke him, but decided the music was nice. The calming effect of it was almost magical.

Grom stepped to the bulging beam with determination: planted his feet, sniffed, and placed his massive hands on the support beams. With a soft groan, the half-giant leaned into the beam, pushing against the bulge. The beam stopped creaking, but the top of the staircase swayed slowly.

Felin gasped as he moved down each step. His arms shook from exhaustion.

Another crack ripped through the structure, and Grom's groaning morphed into a gasp. The huge man's arms shook and his corded muscles drew so tight he looked like a statue carved of granite. Felin continued his descent.

There was nothing Anuka could do but cover their exit and avoid being in the way of Grom's—and hopefully Felin's—hasty exit. Xanavor had already moved out to the hallway, but he frequently peered into the room to monitor Felin's progress.

Sweat ran in rivulets down Grom's bald head, back, and shoulders. His groaning reached a crescendo as he bellowed a fearsome roar. The beam suddenly snapped inward with a shower of splintered wood. Grom pitched toward the structure as it suddenly shifted directions.

Anuka darted back into the room and grabbed Grom by his belt, heaving the big man away from the falling stairs. At that moment, the top third of the staircase tumbled, dropping Felin the remaining fifteen feet toward the stone floor.

Anuka watched helplessly as he and Grom rolled backward together through the doorway. Xanavor brusquely jostled them as he stepped through the doorway into the room.

Before Anuka had time to wonder what Xanavor was doing, the Raven mage flung open his filthy black robe and yelled an unintelligible phrase.

The goblin hit the ground hard and Grom crashed atop him an instant later. Pain surged through Anuka's back and chest as Grom sandwiched him against the stone floor.

His eyes flung open wide as Grom rolled off of him and he saw a torrent of black birds pouring from Xanavor's robe. The birds collected under Felin's wildly flailing body, cushioning his descent to the ground.

The crash of the staircase was horrendous. Metal squeals of bending brackets and crisp wooden cracks blended into an ear-splitting symphony of dissonance. A cloud of dust poured out of the room, followed by the cry of a hundred crows.

Anuka coughed and felt Grom dragging him free of the doorway. Xanavor struggled to pull something free of the pile of wood and stone that had been the staircase. Grom stepped to assist him and soon returned, carrying Felin from the debris.

The Wood Elf's lips peeled back in a rictus of pain. Anuka pushed himself up as the half-giant laid the elf gently on the ground nearby. A foot-long splinter of wood pierced the elf's thigh.

"Sum Buck," Anuka gasped. Blood oozed from the wound to the frantic rhythm of the elf's heart. Could I cauterize that? Anuka wondered. That seemed like a great way to kill the Wood Elf, so Anuka abandoned the idea. Instead, he went to Xanavor's pack and rooted around inside.

The dark-haired human said, "Anuka, what are you doing?"

The goblin answered by producing a tiny metal flask.

"Xanavor, I don't reckon you are secretly a DragonPriest, are you?" Anuka surveyed Felin.

"No."

Anuka shrugged. It was worth a shot. The young bard looked like he might puke. "Fabian, go watch for company."

Fabian didn't move. Instead, he watched Anuka and the others tend to Felin.

"How does that work?" Grom asked as he knelt down beside Felin.

"Um, no clue." Anuka inspected the vial, but found no instructions. He hated dipping into their emergency pack so early in their adventure, but it couldn't be helped. "I'm guessin' one of you is going to have to pull the stick out."

"He could bleed to death quickly. Especially if it hit one of the major arteries." Xanavor didn't shy away from the injury and seemed no stranger to blood.

"I can do this. Have the cloth ready, Xanavor." Grom placed a huge hand on Felin's cheek. The elf grabbed Grom's wrist for support. Then Grom grabbed the shard of wood as Anuka might pick up a toothpick.

"Wait," Fabian protested. "Give me the vial and get out of the way."

"Hey! I'm the bossy one here." Anuka said, holding the flask at arm's length.

"Fabian, what do you know about this?" Xanavor asked. He seemed on the verge of lashing out.

Anuka hoped he would. It would likely be hilarious.

"Are *you* secretly a DragonPriest?" Anuka asked Fabian, who continued to reach for the vial.

"No, but I have experience with alchemy. From... from when I was young."

Anuka knew what the bard meant. Bog sent all children born in the country of Zhazie to the capital city for indoctrination. It was a rough time. Many kids didn't survive. Once they finished their training, those who survived were assigned jobs and places to live by the church. Fabian probably worked for an alchemist in the church. That's likely how he became a bard. Anuka shuddered at the thought of what that life must have been like.

Fabian took the vial from Anuka and then knelt down by Felin's head. The elf reached for the vial.

"Not just yet. Let Grom get that thing out of there."

Fabian unstoppered the tiny flask. Anuka wrinkled his nose . "They use DragonsBlood to make that crap. To me, that's just nasty, but whatever."

"Anuka!" Xanavor barked.

"Oh, right. Sorry." Anuka got behind Felin and helped him sit up. The giant hooked an arm behind the elf for additional support.

Without warning, Grom yanked the shard from the wound. A spray of bright blood spewed from the wound and Felin screamed. Fabian held the vial to Felin's lips. Felin downed the contents and made a face like he was about to retch. Fabian clamped a hand over the Wood Elf's mouth. After a moments struggle, Felin relaxed and the bard removed his hand. The elf gasped and sagged against Grom.

"I'll be the son of a ten-point buck. Look at that!" Anuka pointed to Felin's wound. Blood stopped squirting from the thumb-sized hole in the elf's leg. Instead, it bubbled like a gassy swamp. Little tendrils of smoke wafted from the wound. Anuka wondered if anyone else saw the smoke.

Felin released a sigh of intense pleasure. Then he licked his lips, closed his eyes, and purred like a kitten.

It embarrassed Anuka a little. *Kinda hope I'm the next one hurt*, Anuka thought. Felin had the right idea. A break would do them all some good.

Fabian stoppered the bottle and felt Felin's cheeks. "This would be a good time for us to rest."

That sounded great to Anuka. Until a man-shaped creature with a face like a dog stepped into the mouth of the corridor.

Anuka had probably contracted three blood infections just from looking at the creature's dirty sword.

He had seen a Cat Man, a Fish Man, a Bull Man and a Frog Man. *Why can't there be a Dog Man, as well?* Anuka thought. *Toad stool! We lost Frog Man, Burpie, or whatever his name was.* Oh well, now they had another ugly Sum Buck to deal with. Whatever it was, it *was* ugly. If Anuka had a dog that ugly, he would draw eyes on it's butt and teach it to walk backwards. A foot-long rope of drool hung from the creature's snarling snout. Tufts of mangy hair sprouted from the creases in its boiled leather armor like grass sprouting between paving stones. He thought the thing was wearing pants, but he didn't linger long enough to be sure. And it wore boots. Man sized boots.

Anuka's head was already full of things he could never unsee. The hideous monstrosity loomed large as it surveyed them with its crazy, all-black eyes. Grom stood then and stared at the Dog Man. Some of the snarl leaked out of the slavering beast and it took a step back.

"That's right, dog breath," Anuka yelled, his courage renewed. "Go on and crawl back into your hole. Go lick yourself or chase your tail. Whatever it is you do. Before I send Grom down there to—"

"Anuka!" Xanavor and Fabian yelled.

Okay, fine. He gets the point. The beast backed into the shadows, leaving two Kobolds in his wake. Anuka hadn't seen those before now. They quickly followed the beast into the darkness.

Grom looked down at Anuka. "You must stop threatening people. Especially threatening that I am going to harm them. I will not. You know of my vow."

"Ok, fine." Anuka figured vows were worth less than a good belch when life or death was on the line. *We'll see how strongly you hold to that when the chips are on the table.* "So, what was that thing?"

"No idea," Fabian said. The bard rubbed his sweaty hands on his pants.

It was times like this when Anuka missed Ember—just a little. Stupid Malkin knew all kinds of dumb things no one else cared about. He would know what Dog Man was.

"We need to get out of here," Xanavor said, standing. "Help me." The human began pulling on Felin's arm and saying the elf's name. Soon, Grom hefted Felin up and the groggy Wood Elf stood on wobbly legs.

Fabian went to assist the unsteady elf since Grom was too tall to serve as a crutch.

Anuka didn't like revising his opinion of people, but found himself doing so more frequently of late. Fabian was still Lebarin's man and would kill them all given the chance. The goblin was sure of that. They would still have to watch him closely, but for now, Anuka was glad he was being useful. You could learn a lot about a person from their reactions when the blades were drawn, and the arrows were flying. He was suddenly aware that everyone was staring at him.

Oh, yeah. They're all blind. Anuka picked his way down the dank corridor. His new boots made a gritty sound as he shuffled along the floor. He hated breaking in new boots, but it was what he deserved for burning up his old ones like an idiot. If he didn't get control of his Djinn powers, he was going to hurt someone.

Anuka's eyes were keen, made to see in the dark. Still, he couldn't see far and expected the Dog Man to jump out and slash him with that rusty sword. Distant mumbles echoed off the walls. Grom had spooked that creature, but it would be back with its buddies.

He didn't know which way he was leading his crew, but he had no intentions of asking Xanavor. *I'll figure it out.* He didn't.

Just as Anuka was about to agree with Fabian that they were going in circles, they came to a massive opening. Grom didn't even have to duck here. Twenty feet ahead was a giant, tarnished bronze door set in an iron frame. The door was rounded on the top and covered in weird patterns that were difficult to make out under the layer of green patina. A beautifully crafted lock built into the door was set just above a curved, ornate handle.

Someone was saying his name, but he ignored it. He was short enough that the thin keyhole was at eye level. *A warded lock! Sum Buck.* Anuka didn't touch the lock, or the door, because he wasn't stupid. But he squinted into the keyhole. *Frog farts.* He would need the torch to see this baby. *Will my lock picks even work on this puppy?* He would have to get creative. Maybe the elf knows something about these locks. *Nah. Forget him.*

"Goblin!" came an urgent cry from Fabian.

I've had about enough of these new birds interrupting my work, Anuka thought. He queued up a barrage of disparaging remarks to hurl at his crew like a quiver of flaming arrows. Those died in his throat when he saw the Dog Man and his five big brothers menacing his companions.

———◆———

Oh, Anuka thought. The biggest Dog Man was missing an eye and held a giant club with bent, rusty nails sticking out of it. His ears were pinned to his head. He barked and showered the ground in front of him with spittle.

Over his shoulder stood a black-furred creature with a white ring around one eye. The way it stood in relation to the big dog, Anuka imagined she must be his mate. She seemed to be the most level-headed of the bunch: drool dripped evenly from each side of her snout.

Using either body language or some kind of dog telepathy, the leader communicated to the others that it was time to attack. All of them tensed as one and took a step forward. So did Fabian.

The bard grabbed his lute from his back and slipped something from his pocket that looked like a bar of soap. He began rubbing the soap on the strings of his lute. Anuka wanted to yell out a warning to the foolish human, but he also wanted to see what would happen.

The dogs started yelping and barking at Fabian. The bard jumped in surprise, but kept soaping up his lute. Then he slid the soap into his pocket and began to play.

A bouquet of clear, rich notes burst from the lute as Fabian's fingers danced like faeries along the strings. After the second measure of the complicated musical exhibition, the bard added his boisterous tenor voice to the carnival of notes.

Fabian the Bard, handsome as can be,
He played his lute, as sweet as fruit,
All throughout Zhazie

The mass of mangy mutt men stopped barking and stared at Fabian.

Dragons paid him coin to sing for their feasts,
For the people poor, and nobles dour,
And their perverted priests.

Soon, a glossy look came to their eyes and their jaws fell open. In unison, they swayed slowly from side to side. Behind the Dog Men were a dozen Kobolds. They also rocked to the rhythm of the music.

Sum Buck. Anuka didn't wait to see what happened next. He turned back to the door and peered at the lock. Xanavor had raised the torch to provide illumination for Fabian's show and that gave Anuka just enough light to see inside the lock. *Wonderful*, he thought.

The lock had tiny obstructions inside to prevent anything besides the key from reaching the tumblers. This was a good one. Anuka growled and banged the palm of his hand on his forehead a few times. That didn't open the lock, but he did feel better. He didn't have a key for this, and his tools would be of little use. A lock like this required special tools. Sometimes, you had to bend your tools to fit the lock. That took a lot of trial and error—time they didn't have. He also noted a failsafe: a tiny reservoir just above the lock on really expensive doors. You could put DragonsBlood in that slot and open the door if you lost your key. But that wouldn't do him any good. Anuka only had one smear of DragonsBlood stashed, and they would need that for their escape. There had to be another solution. His foot tapped to the music as he thought. That's weird. Anuka wasn't tapping his foot. It was doing it all by itself. *Sum Buck*.

He looked at Fabian and nearly laughed out loud. The Dog Men, Kobolds, and his crew members alike were bobbing their heads in time to the song. Big, nasty puppy tongues lolled out of the Dog Men's mouths as they gyrated.

Fabian the comely, greatest at his craft.
With hands so quick, and a tongue so slick,
The other bards seem daft.

He's using magic music on these idiots. Anuka noticed that his own head was bobbing now. *The soap.*

Anuka darted forward and slipped the bar from Fabian's pocket. The bard turned to protest, and the goblin yelled, "Just borrowing it, bubby. Keep playin'!"

It wasn't soap. It was resin. Resin infused with DragonsBlood. Bards in Bog's kingdom were used to placate the teeming masses of workers so they would keep working. Despite their exhaustion, sickness, or understanding of how unfair their lives were. It was one little secret Rigby had tried to keep to himself.

Anuka rubbed the resin frantically on the beveled pattern on the door above the lock. Tiny shavings of the waxy substance sloughed off in thin ribbons. The goblin coaxed those into the hole above the lock until it was nearly full. Then he waited.

Things behind him started going poorly. When Anuka swiped the resin, Fabian faltered in his song and had struggled to recover. The bard was making it up on the spot and seemed to be running short on things to sing about.

"C'mon, baby. C'mon." Anuka stuffed a few more resin slivers into the hole, but nothing happened. A snarl and a bark sounded behind him. *We're outta time.*

Anuka drew in a big breath and held it. He put his thumb on the door near the failsafe hole. Pressure ballooned in his mind. Smoke rose from his skin as he felt heat building inside him. A second later, the resin melted like wax over flame, leaving a dark red liquid behind. A flash of bright blue light danced along the patterns on the door like lightning in a jar. Anuka stepped back and watched a branch of the light go down and around the surface of the door in a circuitous path to connect to another line of light at the top. The lock clicked, and the door fell open. *Sum Buck. That was Bog's blood.*

Anuka yanked the door open. A blast of cold air smelling of fetid swamp and dead cats struck him. He nearly gagged. The music had stopped. Anuka looked back to see the Dog Men fleeing. They yelped and ran into the darkness, heedless of the Kobolds they smashed in their haste.

Chapter 21

Be Our Guest

"Odwin, why do you call her Belendurath?" The old house was filthy and Ember was careful not to touch anything. Odwin's random attempts at cleaning up hadn't helped much.

The old man set his cup on the table and rubbed his scraggly beard. "Why do you call her Crenthys?"

"Because that is who she is. She introduced herself to us as such." Ember mentally darted ahead in the conversation to try to figure out where Odwin was going with his questions. He seemed pretty lucid so far.

"Who is Brinka, then?" Odwin asked.

"Brinka is another name Crenthys once had. Well," Ember began, pondering, "I suppose Crenthys is Brinka, when she is in the guise of a half Sea Elf girl."

"So, Crenthys is just a name Brinka uses when in disguise?" Odwin asked.

The way the man asked the question gave Ember pause. It suggested that he was missing an obvious connection. Ember hated that. It was too close to intellectual condescension. That was something Ember abhorred. Then understanding dawned.

For whatever reason, be it grief, madness, or both, Odwin believed Crenthys was an assumed identity—Belendurath in disguise.

Ember put down his cup of goat's milk, leaned back, and folded his arms across his chest. *If Crenthys really is a Dragon polymorphed into a Dragomyr, why can't she remember anything? What magic is powerful enough to erase a Dragon's memories?* The answer seemed simple; another Dragon's. *Why would a Dragon with enough power to erase Belendurath's memories not simply kill her? Why polymorph her, erase her memories, then set her free?* There were too many unanswered questions for that theory to be plausible.

Ember closed his eyes and pictured a slate board in his mind. *Who would be powerful enough to erase the memory of a Dragon of Belendurath's power? It happened here, so I have to assume it was a Bronze Dragon.* He scribbled on the slate board in his mind.

> 1. *Zanderon - No mention of him in political writings. Motive: Unknown. First Bronze to come to Cren's defense. Why do so if guilty? Shame?*
>
> 2. *Ivrus - Very capable with memory magic. Motive: None apparent. Is avoiding Crenthys after entering her memories. He likely saw something disturbing.*
>
> 3. *Dovondes - Former lover, father of her egg. Motive: Jealousy?*

It wasn't much, but it was a start. He opened his eyes to find Odwin considering him curiously. "Okay. I see your logic. Can I speak candidly with you?"

Odwin smoothed down his beard and straightened his ratty shirt. "Please do."

"You disappeared from the city and haven't been seen for a decade. You return when Crenthys does. When she finds you, you say some

outlandish, upsetting things to her, and she concludes you are mad."
Ember saw pain in the man's eyes.

Odwin nodded and said, "Perhaps I am given to bouts of madness.
Mistress Belendurath was killed in the mountain, and I buried Mistress Brinka here. I admit that when I heard of my master's return,
my tenuous grip on reality frayed a bit. I was overjoyed and terrified.
Terrified for *her*, you see. The situation that brought her so much
trouble hasn't abated. In fact, the injustices she stood against are now
celebrated among the Dragons."

"Odwin, I don't know what you are talking about. I read some
things about treason. Is that what you are referring to?"

"Treason," Odwin said the word like it tasted bad in his mouth. "Is
it treason to stand in the gap between victim and oppressor?"

"I know it is foolish to expect any ruler to be completely altruistic,
but it seems that the Bronze Court cares well for its mortal subjects."
Ember mused.

Odwin waved a hand in irritation. "Not the mortals. If you knew
what the Dragons did to one another... " Odwin shook his head slowly.

"Enlighten me. Perhaps my friend and I can—"

"No." The old man shook his head vehemently. "It was something
I saw that lead my master to her ruin. I will not make that mistake
again."

"I thought you believed that Belendurath yet lives." Ember couldn't
help pushing back. He wanted to see the extent of the old man's
madness.

"Ruined and dead aren't the same thing. I can't keep you from
digging into the past. But if you continue to push, you and your
friends will all be destroyed. This goes well beyond illegal Dragons-
Blood on the streets of Usban Port. It goes beyond Caustimis, beyond
Dovondes."

Ember's mind raced ahead. *What could be bigger than a pair of DragonLords?* The need to solve impossible problems chewed at his insides. "Where can I find answers?"

Odwin huffed and rubbed his face with his hands. "Not in the library. Not unless you can get access to the top floor."

Ember couldn't stop his eyebrow from raising at the comment. "Please, Odwin. You know my friends and I came here for this information, even if we didn't know it. The more you tell us, the safer we will be."

"I see the yearning on your face, and I am sorry. I shouldn't have mentioned any of this. Must be the madness."

The old man's regret seemed sincere, but it was tempered regret. Like he desperately wanted someone to get justice for his master, but didn't want anyone getting hurt in the process. Ember made a decision. Perhaps Odwin would soften over time, but if he stayed here his time would be short. If what he believes is actually true, he is in great danger. "Collect your things and come with me."

"Come with you? Where? This is my home."

"No, Odwin. This is a ruined mansion. You aren't safe here any longer. Come."

"Where are you taking me?" Odwin stood slowly, but hadn't moved his feet.

"My brother always complained that I brought home strays. You are coming to live with me."

Crenthys felt better than she had in weeks. Knowing her brother would be safe—and she could train with him—was beyond anything she had expected. She felt like she might float home. Her long legs devoured the path from the portal to the small house where she hoped to find her friends. This news was too good. She was bursting to tell someone. *How will I tell Kelios?* Maybe she would write a letter and try to send it somehow.

Crenthys paused at the doorstep of their small home. A familiar male voice was in the midst of an animated tale. She nearly knocked the front door from it's hinges as she shouldered into the small house. There sat Odwin in her chair. His hands were raised and his mouth hung open, as if he was in the middle of a word. Ember and Tabir stared at her with stunned looks.

What was this? How had Odwin gotten here? "Odwin..."

"Good evening, Mistress Bele—er—Brinka. Welcome home." Odwin smiled and put his hands on his legs.

Ember stood and took a step toward Crenthys. He rubbed his hands nervously on his pants. "Good evening. Um. We have a guest."

"I see that we have a guest, Ember. How did he get here?" There was more anger in her voice than she intended, but she felt like her privacy had been invaded. The elation from her good news had deflated, and she was embarrassed she was suddenly angry. That made her more angry.

"It's a long story. Come and sit. I'll try to explain."

She didn't want to sit. She wanted to rage. But that would accomplish nothing. Perhaps there was a good explanation. If Ember was doing the talking, it would certainly be a long one.

———◆———

Tabir had taken Odwin into the next room for some tea. Crenthys sat quietly, trying to digest the Malkin's words. Ember thought he was helping—he always thought he was helping. Crenthys stuffed down her frustration and breathed. This intrusion stung, she just wasn't sure why it bothered her so much. She resolved to be civil.

"So you wanted to see if Odwin was crazy, or if I was the crazy one?" *So much for peaceful resolutions.*

Ember raised his hands defensively, "Crenthys, no. I just..." He sighed, dropped his hands, and hung his head. "I've read a lot about the human mind. Borthis has an entire volume on the subject. He was a dwarf who studied humans in different habitats. It's a fascinating approach to studying behavior that scholars still... use today. Right. Sorry." Ember combed down the fur on his arms and cleared his throat. "I am sorry if I violated your trust. I thought I might fill in some of the gaps Ivrus left and, well, Odwin was in pretty pitiful shape. I had to beg, but he agreed to come here. If you are amenable. Oh, and I saw someone skulking around the old mansion."

Skulking? "Wait, what? Who did you see?" Crenthys asked.

"Um. I don't know. I've just had a feeling someone has been following me for a couple of days."

"Did you get a good look at them? Is it one of Vodinar's goons watching the place?" *Why would someone skulk around the old mansion? They had to have been looking for me.*

"No, and no. In that order. Though I suppose the order doesn't matter." Ember drew his lips into a thin line.

"Okay. Well, good work. Odwin may be crazy, but he is family—in a way. I don't want anything to happen to him." That was as close to an apology as Crenthys could stomach.

Tabir and Odwin entered the room, small cups of steaming tea in hand.

Tabir knelt down close to Crenthys while Odwin sat by Ember and resumed his story. The Gold elf looked up at Odwin and then whispered to her, "It is good that Ember brought him here, but I don't think he should stay."

Crenthys had expected to hear that. She looked at her friend. "Why?"

"Because if someone followed Ember, they were likely looking for you. Those watching the house now know about Odwin. If they already knew about him, they might try to use him against you. Either way, he isn't safe."

That made sense. Crenthys nodded and asked, "What can we do? I don't dare bring Vodinar into this."

Tabir seemed to be mulling something over. "I could take him to Payris."

Crenthys fought back her initial reaction. "Do you trust him?"

Tabir grimaced. "With some things. I think we can trust him with this."

Crenthys considered their options. None seemed very promising. "No. He needs to stay here with us."

Tabir thought for a moment, nodded slowly, and then stood. "I have an errand in the morning, but I can be back at midday to be with him." The slender elf finished his tea.

Crenthys looked at her Elven friend and smiled. "Thank you."

Tabir returned the smile. "Speaking of errands, it's nearly tomorrow. We should all try to get some sleep. Odwin, follow me. You can sleep in my bed. I'm more accustomed to sleeping on the floor, anyway."

The old man frowned and looked at the others. "But we haven't heard about how the trial went."

"Oh, Crenthys, I'm so sorry. In all the excitement, I forgot to ask. How did things go with the Bronze Council?" Tabir stood in the kitchen looking exhausted.

They all were tired, but the joy she felt earlier came back in a rush and Crenthys couldn't keep the grin off her face.

Chapter 22

Madness, Sheer Madness

O nce Anuka and his crew were beyond the tarnished door, it clicked shut behind them.

"Well," Anuka said. "That was easy."

"Why did they run?" Xanavor asked.

The answer was both obvious and unsettling to Anuka.

"Whatever is in here is worse," Felin said flatly.

The elf gets it, Anuka thought.

"Worse? Worse, how?" Fabian asked. "And what is that awful smell?

Anuka could think of about fifteen dozen things worse than a pack of men with dog heads, but naming them wouldn't assuage Fabian's fear—nor his own. That smell made the goblin's stomach clench and he could taste bile in the back of his throat. Something on this side of that door was long dead.

He looked around as Fabian fumbled with a torch. This area differed vastly from the rough hewn caverns they had just left. No Kobold with a pickax had formed the smooth-edged stone of the walls, ceiling, and floor. In fact, these walls reminded Anuka of Lebarin's dungeon. A thick layer of grime coated every surface, and large, dark stains blotted the floor at random intervals. There was no light until Fabian's torch came to life, nearly blinding Anuka.

Anuka cursed. He missed Kelios and Offund. While they were pretty new to the ways of a hardened criminal, at least they were useful. Of course, if Kelios were here, he would stare wistfully into the dark, pining after Crenthys. He shook his head. Kelios was so worried about whether their parts matched up that he had let her fly off without him. They should have just had a go of it and see what happened. That's how Anuka lived life. No time for anything else.

His tiny heart ached at the hypocrisy of his words. What he wouldn't give to have just a few minutes with Papa. He realized he had ignored the advice he had given Kelios about Crenthys. Some lessons you learned the hard way. He sniffed.

"Anuka," Xanavor called, "you comin'?"

Anuka nodded and padded after the group as they plodded along the long hallway.

———◦———

"Well," Anuka announced through the rag covering his face, "I think we found what stinks."

This room was only one of a half dozen they had found in the latest hallway they discovered. It had been ravaged. A long iron table in the middle of the room was askew. It was stained and rusted. Shards of dark brown glass covered the table and floor. Gashes and dark stains marred the wall in various places. An eerie green luminescence emanated from a clear glass bowl mounted on one long wall. Anuka strained to hear the sounds he expected beyond the door at the opposite end of the room. Those sounds never came.

Felin silently slid to the goblin's side and motioned inside the room, then pointed at himself. With a nod from Anuka, the Wild Elf crept slowly into the room. With the side of his soft leather boot, Felin brushed clean a spot for each footfall.

Seas, he's quiet. The stress of trudging through total darkness for so long—coupled with the possibilities of some wild beast around every corner—was wearing on them all. Fabian's eyes were wide, and he fumbled for the wall with one hand. If they went much farther, their supply of torches would become an issue. They still had more than half of the rugged light sources left, but would need to save some for their return. When Anuka suggested letting himself and Felin guide them through the darkness to save torches, Xanavor and the bard had emphatically said no.

Anuka turned back to see a panting Xanavor waving away Grom's attempts to help him. The Raven mage's head bobbed in rhythm as he gasped greedily for air. The human was in poor shape and the air supply seemed to diminish the deeper underground they went. *Xanavor is pretty tough*, Anuka thought. Most men would have buckled under the horrors they had seen tonight. Xanavor soldiered on. The strange human's magic was taking a toll on him, Anuka guessed.

Grom stood, closed his eyes, and began taking calming breaths. The skin on the half-giant's face was only visible in streaks where sweat had washed away the dirt and grime covering him.

Anuka didn't know what to make of the Stoneman. He was useless in a fight, but seemed willing to help wherever else he could. Grom was the first half-giant he'd seen, but Anuka was starting to understand what type of person he once had been. He was committed to a course of action that—no matter how foolhardy—he was determined to see through. The big man's reasons for non-violence were pretty flimsy by Anuka's reckoning. But the goblin had heard worse excuses for cowardice. One thing was sure, the half-giant was lying to himself. A fire raged inside the massive Stoneman, to be certain. But it wasn't the red flame of simple rage. Rather, a pure, white-hot blaze of destruction. Grom's hard exterior was akin the walls of a forge containing the refining inferno inside. Avoiding violence would not keep Grom from becoming like his brothers. His choices alone would do that. Like so many lessons in life, Grom would have to learn that on his own. Anuka stepped into the room with the elf.

Felin picked his way carefully through the chaos of the room. The elf picked up a nasty-looking hammer from a small table and examined it. *Elf don't want to get dirty. Ha!* It looked like a surgery room in a big city. Only this room was likely for doing more harm than good. Nothing they had seen down here was in need of medical help. Not until Anuka and his gang arrived.

Anuka was about to admonish the elf for messing around when a keening wail from behind nearly caused his bladder to evacuate. Poking his head out the door, the goblin saw Grom staggering backwards as Fabian and Xanavor tried to squeeze past the half-giant on either side. The bard was screaming like a five-year-old girl. Grom turned a little to one side and Fabian squirted between the half-giant and the wall like a calf being born. He hit the ground in a gritty skid, popped up immediately, and nearly flattened Anuka as he plowed into the room where Felin was.

What in Bog's outhouse was wrong with him? Anuka gaped after the bard as he raced past a stunned Felin and began working the handle of the room's other exit. Then Xanavor batted Anuka aside in pursuit of Fabian.

Anuka staggered back into the hallway to see Grom shielding his eyes from Fabian's discarded torch, trying to peer down the hallway. Around the half-giant's massive frame was a pair of vague shapes slinking their direction. With the torch between him and the pair of stalkers, Anuka could see little else.

"Who is it, bubby? I can't see nothin'." Anuka moved and stood beside Grom. A scraping sound, like dragging a rake across stone, echoed down the hallway beyond the figures. There was something else there.

"Anuka," Grom rumbled with an edge of panic in his voice. "Run."

Sum Buck. One thing you learn as a little man is to always run from the thing that scares the guy bigger than you.

Anuka barreled into Felin, who stood in the doorway with a confused look on his face. They managed to keep their feet, and Anuka grabbed a fistful of the elf's tunic and yelled, "Run—well, limp—for your life!"

Fabian and Xanavor were pawing at the door and yanking the handle in turn.

"Why is it locked?" Fabian yowled desperately.

"Move it numb skull!" Anuka barked, pushing the human aside. The door had a flat lock of excellent craftsmanship. It was likely warded from picking as the copper door had been.

"That looks complicated," Felin said. The elf smiled sheepishly as he realized his remarks were not helpful.

Behind them, Grom crammed his massive frame into the room and dragged the metal door closed with a hideous groan. The door didn't fully close. The half-giant pressed his back against the door, holding it fast.

The room grew very still and everyone stared at Grom's panting, panicked face. Then he groaned and pushed against the door with renewed effort. A gap about an inch wide opened in the door and was immediately closed by another grunt of effort. Grom growled and strained to hold the door in place. Anuka and the crew just stared, mouths agape. Then the half-giant's feet slid forward a few inches on the glass covered stone floor.

Anuka didn't need the pleading look on Grom's face to get back to work. He stood just to the side of the lock on the door, eyes closed, muttering to himself.

"Anuka," Fabian cried urgently.

"Shut up!" Anuka barked, holding his hands up to silence the bard. Seconds that seemed like eons passed, as Grom fought to keep the door shut. Though virtually blind, Xanavor had gone to lend his meager strength to the gigantic man.

Anuka's eyes popped open and a huge grin split his face. He slapped his hands together excitedly, then bent down. The goblin flung a thin, filthy rug to the side and retrieved a slender key.

"Lazy Sum Bucks," the goblin beamed.

"Anuka," Xanavor bellowed, cutting short the goblin's celebration.

Jamming the key into the lock, praying to a deity he invented on the spot that there were no traps, he twisted the lock. The door clicked open.

Anuka had made do with short legs all his life. He endured the jibes about his stature. There weren't a lot of things he couldn't do, if he set his mind to it. Being short also held a lot of advantages. None of those involved running.

Once through the door, Fabian morphed into an unparalleled athlete. The bard had snatched the green, glowing rock out of the lamp in the smelly room and used it to light his way. The radiance of it vanished every time he disappeared around a corner. Anuka was so far behind the pack he scarcely glimpsed the bard. Only Grom loped along behind him. The half-giant could have passed him in one stride. *He is staying back to protect me*, the goblin thought. It was a touching gesture he hoped he'd live to appreciate.

Anuka wanted to ask Grom what he was running from but was too busy hustling after the others. He thought back to a time when, as a child he joined a gaggle of goblin children fleeing from a giant dog. He tripped over a cart, landed in a campfire, and the dog got him. It turned out to be a furry little puppy who wanted to lick a goblin child to death. Anuka had seen Fabian's face and doubted there were puppies chasing them. Hideous shrieks and the ring of steel scraping stone hounded them as they ran. Anuka tried to look back once and nearly stumbled. Grom would likely squash him to death if he went down. The other crew members were too far ahead to see now.

"We must go faster," Grom rumbled, scooping Anuka up with a massive hand.

He felt them speed up immediately. It was a good thing, too. Their pursuers were gaining on them. Being carried was embarrassing, but effective.

Over Grom's shoulder, Anuka finally got a look at what they were running from: Dark Elves. With jet black hair, sickly white skin, and pointed ears, there was little else they could be. But something was wrong with them. One of their pursuers swiped the blade of his sword against the wall, creating a shower of sparks. Their gait was weird and graceless, and they lumbered along swiftly—heedless of the noise they made. Disturbing, animal-like groans and grunts indicated their frustration at the chase, but they didn't pant, sweat, or yell. Anuka was pretty sure they weren't even breathing.

He was jostled to Grom's side as the half-giant slammed into the wall before violently changing direction. The Dark Elves ran awkwardly, yet swiftly, careening off the walls at each turn.

A faint green glow ahead signaled they had caught up with their companions. The trio stood panting. Xanavor doubled over, and retched. They were in a moderate-sized room with another metal door. Grom stopped in the room's mouth, set Anuka down, and turned back to the hallway.

The Dark Elves—there were three—stopped chasing them thirty feet away and stalked slowly toward them. It was as if they knew this was the end of the line. The elf in front swung his sword in an arc in front of him, spraying a line of sparks as it raked against the stone floor.

Felin tossed the door mat aside and frantically searched the floor for a key. Fabian held his green light-stone aloft to aid the elf. No key this time.

When the three sword-wielding Dark Elves drew near enough for Fabian's light to fall on them, Anuka gasped.

Their faces looked like skulls wearing Dark Elf masks. Their skin was misaligned and stretched overly tight. There were gashes and scrapes everywhere the skin was visible outside their dark leather armor. The wounds bore no blood. Their eyes bulged and their lips were pulled into a permanent snarl of pain. Each of them carried different combinations of bladed weapons: long swords; short swords; hunting knives; or daggers. One even carried a rusted rapier and narrow-bladed dirk. They held the weapons awkwardly, griping them as a child might, but the lead elf swung his blade in deadly arcs, scoring the floor between the two groups.

"Give me some weapons," Grom grumbled softly.

So stunned was Anuka by the half-giant's words that he stared up at the mountainous man.

Grom looked down at Anuka and repeated, "give me some weapons. And get that door open."

The sadness on the half-giant's ugly face broke Anuka's heart. This was it: Grom would break his vow. He backed away to join the others and to help the giant break his promise. Selfishly, Anuka prayed the giant was better at using weapons than he was at keeping his word.

———— ◦○◦ ————

Grom looked about as ridiculous as someone could look, Anuka mused. In one hand, he held Felin's shortsword. It looked like a dagger in the half-giant's over-large hands. In the other hand he held the hammer Felin had filched from the stinky room they had fled. It looked like Grom was about to ring a tiny bell and then carve some lamb with his dinner knife.

In contrast, the three Dark Elves stood six feet apart in an arc in front of Grom. They held their once-beautiful weapons easily at their sides. None of them moved. No eyelids blinked. No chests rose and fell—like dead beings. Whatever grace they had in mortal life was gone. Replaced by unnatural strength that scarcely remembered the skill once trained in their limbs. They stared at the half-giant with no hint of emotion in their dead eyes.

Then, as one, they advanced on Grom. The big man took a quick stride to his left and met a shortsword thrust with a swipe of his own, knocking it wide. The Dark Elf's other hand brought an over-hand stab at Grom's chest. He had moved quick enough to get inside the swordsman's attack and caught the elf's forearm with the back of his hand.

Grom growled as the middle elf opened a minor cut on his side with a slashing long sword. The half-giant yanked the elf he was fighting by his forearm, hurling him at the middle attacker. The two collided.

Spinning to his left, Grom hurled the hammer with a grunt toward the third swordsman, who advanced on his flank. The head of the hammer buried into the creature's eye knocking it to the ground.

"Whoa," cried, Xanavor, Felin, and Anuka. Fabian gaped in horror.

The first two attackers disentangled as Grom scooped up the third elf's rapier from where it had fallen. His giant fingers wouldn't fit inside the guard, so he wrapped his digits around the hilt, guard and all.

The two Dark Elves stepped forward and raised their weapons. A twang sounded, and an arrow blossomed from the attacker on Grom's right. The Dark Elf stopped to look at Felin, who was fitting another arrow to his shortbow. Instead of crying out, or falling back, the swordsman just stared at Felin. Then it turned to flank Grom.

The half-giant blocked the shortsword with his dagger and again opened a gash on the attackers wrist. The weapon tumbled free of the elf's hand, but no blood gushed from the wound.

Movement to Anuka's right caught his attention. The Dark Elf with a hammer buried in its face stood and strode toward Grom.

"Lookout bubby!" Anuka cried. He whipped his dagger from his belt, sprinted forward and buried it to the hilt in Hammer Face's back.

Without looking back, the Dark Elf savagely kicked backwards—sending Anuka sprawling.

Xanavor screamed and a black mass of twittering birds engulfed Hammer Face. The Dark Elf swiped at the birds with his remaining weapon, but they drove him back, taking savage bites out of the creature's skin.

Fabian was strumming away on his lute. It seemed like a stupid thing to do in the middle of a battle, but Anuka felt his spirits lift and some of the fog of fear cleared from his mind. *The door.* Scrambling to his feet, Anuka dashed over to the door and looked at the lock. Fabian had dropped his green rock in favor of his instrument, so Anuka snatched it up. The handle was on the inside of the door and the lock was like the others. The good news was that Anuka had found the key. The bad news was that someone had broken it off inside the lock.

Anuka darted over to inspect the door pins. They were well concealed with little iron tabs. No pounding them out. He swore and pounded on the door.

Xanavor was still harassing the one Dark Elf with his birds, though they seemed to diminish by the second. Hammer Face looked like a day old deer carcass. The ravens had plucked away hunks of flesh and sinew.

Felin was firing arrows at the two swordsmen Grom faced, but his quiver was running low. Though it sported two arrows from the back of its neck, the Dark Elf with the long sword hardly seemed to notice.

"Fine," Anuka said. "You Sum Bucks stay back. It's about to get hot in here." Resolutely, Anuka stripped out of his clothes and tossed them to the side. Then he placed his hat on the pile and stood naked in front of the door. He filled his lungs through his nose and closed his eyes. Anuka had once heated a blade so hot it burned the man wielding it. He could ignite wood without touching it. This would require a lot more heat.

Anuka had spent the past couple of years trying to put his past behind him, but it dogged his path relentlessly. Now, he reached back to the memories he kept stuffed deep inside for just such an occasion.

A gaggle of children—goblins and humans alike—surrounded him, cursing and jeering him while another child pounded him into the dirt. There were dozens of those memories. Only the faces of the children changed.

Next, he looked up at the laughing faces of his father's crewmen as Anuka fought for his life. His head bobbed in and out of the water, gasping for air and swallowing sea water. Their mocking faces were the last thing he saw as he went under.

Finally, he saw his mother sinking below the waters of the sea. When he witnessed that as a boy, he believed she had drowned. Having seen her a few weeks back, she confessed that she only pretended to drown. She had just gone home to her real family. His mother had important work to do that didn't involve him.

When Anuka flung open his eyes, the entire world was red. He faintly heard his name being screamed, but the voices were in a tunnel far away. Before him, the simple metal door cowered in fear of him. The enraged goblin brought flaming red hands up to inspect them. Then he jabbed his index finger into the lock. The metal squealed and resisted the heat for a moment. Gouts of smoke piped from the lock before the metal around it began to melt. With his tiny claws, he pulled the lock free from the door as metal groaned in protest.

Then he grabbed the iron sheath around the bottom hinge of the door and pulled the metal away like picking a stink bug from a curtain. The door lurched when the pin came free.

He couldn't reach the top pin. Savagely, he kicked the bottom of the door. It squealed as the remaining hinge twisted free. The door opened and flopped crookedly in its frame. A strong draft whistled around the gaps between door and frame.

"Am I so useless, now, Mama? Do you see my power?" His voice sounded strange in his ears. Distorted. Hoarse. "When I get what I came for, we will see who is weak." He stomped at the crooked door again with all of his strength—it broke loose.

When the weakened hinge gave way, a gale of wind sucked the door into the abyss on the other side. Anuka cursed as the wind began pulling him toward the frame. His anger and bravado were swept away along with the door and replaced by a sudden terror. Anuka cursed as the wind began pulling him toward the frame.

Anuka groped the door frame and grasped it with one clawed hand. His body was parallel with the ground and his feet flopped in the wind. When he tried to look up to yell for help, his grip slipped.

As Anuka blew free, he saw Fabian and Felin tumble out the doorway after him. He looked down to see a gaping abyss. *Finally*, he thought. *The fool's errand has ended. I can rest.* Images of smashing against sharpened rocks seemed a comfort to him. Something smacked his face a split second after seeing a thin rope appear in front of him. He was moving so fast, and his skin was still hot enough that he passed through the knot of ropes. Then he struck a second net. This one didn't snap, but stretched for a moment before recoiling. Then he stopped.

Why are there nets here? Sum Buck! I was ready to die. When Anuka tried to sit up, he found his hands held fast. So was the rest of him. He lay there panting and watching his friends as they landed on the net above him. The one he had ripped through. Even Grom, the size of a mountain, was stopped by the net.

Uncontrollable laughter racked him. He sounded mad, he knew. But he didn't care.

This was all so absurd. He decided to just lay there a bit and relax. Deep breath in, deep breath out. It was working. He started to relax. Then he saw the giant spider.

Chapter 23

Some Homework

K elios had seen some horrible things in his life, many in the past weeks, but nothing like this. Every part of his rational mind begged for him to step back into the hallway and close the inch-thick iron door behind him. But he had come too far for that.

Despite the horrid smell, morbid curiosity got the better of him and drew him into this last room. The other three rooms looked exactly like this one—only they were spotless. A long metal table stood bolted to the floor in the middle of each rectangular room. An enviable collection of knives was strewn haphazardly across a small cart nearby. Miniaturized saws and wicked hooks decorated the tables like knickknacks. Large curved sewing needles threaded with coarse, dark string were stuck to a fist-sized cloth ball. Silver basins of water, one clean, another containing murky dark liquid, rested on a corner of the wooden cart. The similarities between the four rooms ended there.

Someone had recently used this fourth room for something horrifying. It was the creature on the table that drew Kelios deeper into the room. Shaped like a person, though a small one, with a stained white cloth draped over it, the body lay unmoving. He stepped nearer and noticed one foot was not covered—fur covered the dangling limb.

He swallowed hard as he approached, and his heart sank. The foot was human-shaped but had a thick, dark padding on the sole, like a cat's. Malkin. *Ember?* Despite his rising instinct to run from the room, he pressed on—he had to know.

With a trembling hand, he grabbed hold of the corner of the sheet near the head of the table. Dark red stained the sheet where he imagined the creature's face should be. Gathering his nerve, he whipped the cover back to reveal a Cat Man with rust-colored fur and white on its hands and belly. Not Ember. In a rush, he exhaled the breath he had been holding.

Kelios knew it couldn't have been Ember, but he had seen too many inexplicable things to rule out any possibility. He looked up at the poor creature and took in its condition. The cuts on its face and chest had been sewn together like a sock doll. Some cuts appeared to have been opened and restitched many times. This poor Malkin must have suffered unbelievably. Kelios noticed its claws were dull, likely from digging into the table, which bore multiple rows of scratch marks. He could have counted all of its ribs even through the blood-matted fur. *They had starved this creature.*

Kelios carefully studied the pitiful creature. He wanted to remember this Malkin. If Lebarin had done his, he wanted to make sure the priest paid for it. *At least the Cat Man rests peacefully now*, Kelios thought. Then its eyes popped open.

With a gasp the Malkin coughed violently. Kelios swore and scrambled back, crashing into the wall. It took a powerful force of will to prevent Irana from bursting forth to protect him. When the coughing subsided, the Cat Man's head lolled to the side, and it looked at Kelios with glassy eyes.

"Kill me..." the Malkin croaked.

Kelios froze as if the White DragonLord Sevaltry had blasted him with her icy breathweapon. He tried to scream, swear, or run, but could do nothing but stare at the pleading creature before him. His hand reflexively went to his side, but it took a moment for him to remember that he had no weapon. The array of bloody knives was a mere step away. It seemed wrong somehow to stab the Malkin with an instrument of his torture. Could he even do it? Kelios abhorred the use of any metal weapon. Perhaps he could make an exception—for mercy's sake.

Kelios would certainly want such mercy for himself if their positions were reversed. With no other option, he stepped up and slid a short-handled knife with a long, curved blade off of the table. The Malkin coughed again and spasmed painfully. *I'm no killer*, Kelios thought. He had killed before to save his own life. Irana's paws had been soaked with blood.

The creature's eyes dimmed slowly. Kelios had seen men die. He let the knife fall to the floor with a clang. Without thinking, he stepped up to the table and stroked the creature's fur near its ear. He wanted to say something but couldn't think of anything fitting.

The Malkin strained to form a last word, but it died on his lips as the light in his eyes winked out. Kelios drew the lids of the Cat Man's eyes closed.

Kelios backed out into the hallway and closed the door. One room left. Unless Anuka was mistaken, the fifth room contained what he had come for.

The lock was brilliant, but Anuka had taught Kelios well. His long, slender fingers and natural patient demeanor made him well suited as a lock picker. Once he had opened the lock, he mustered his courage, pushed open the door, and stepped inside.

A thin wisp of smoke passed over his head and trailed out the open door. A rich, woodsy smell hung in the air. It was intense and laced with perfumed resin. The rancid scent of death waited at the edge of the incense. The room was dark save for an eerie orange glow emanating from beneath an overturned jar on a desk toward the back of the room. He was thankful that Tritons could see fairly well in low light.

Kelios picked his way to the desk and lifted the jar. Brilliant light flooded the room, causing him to recoil at its intrusion. A small stone with some sort of enchantment was the source of the light. Kelios raked it off the desk and into the jar before replacing it on the desk. *That's better.*

With the room properly illuminated, rows of thick wooden book-shelves appeared. Tomes of every size, shape, and color filled those shelves—making the room seem smaller. Some books had tattered leather bindings, while others were clad in brittle wood. Kelios could read a little Draconic, but the writing on most of these books was in a language or script he couldn't understand.

He closed his eyes again and framed his quarry in his mind. He focused on the glyphs Anuka had drawn him. The symbols coalesced and fixed firmly in his mind's eye. Popping his eyes open, he snatched the glowing jar from the desk. Moving with purpose, he began me-thodically scanning the rows of books lining each wall.

Stretching to see the books on top and squatting to see the ones on the bottom, he had almost searched the entire library before a thick, black-spined book gave him pause. The cover was leather but not thick like cowhide. It was thin and slick like a frog's hide. The golden etched symbol at the bottom of the spine was faded.

Kelios's hand paused just short of grabbing the book. The warning he had gotten about the book being dangerous flashed in his mind. With a resigned sigh, he snatched the book off the shelf.

It was cold. *Why is it cold?* He suddenly wanted to fling it into the fireplace, but this room didn't have one. No, he needed to know what it said.

Glancing around the room, Kelios decided that raking the desk clear was a bad idea. So he knelt down on the floor and opened the book near the middle. He tried to, at least. The book didn't want to come open. The cover opened a bit and then snapped shut. It was like prying open a giant clam.

Kelios braced himself to double his effort when he heard a noise in the hallway. He had not bothered to re-lock the door to the room with the Malkin when he fled from there. Straining, he heard someone swearing and then the door across the hallway banged open. He listened as the person moved into the room. Then he scooped up the book, scurried to the door, and yanked it open just a crack. The guard was moving slowly into the room with the dead Malkin—this was his chance to escape.

Moving as silently as death, Kelios slipped into the hallway and pulled the door shut behind him. He wouldn't be able to lock this one, either. But there was nothing for it.

He watched the guard carefully until the stocky human focused on the Malkin. Then Kelios bolted.

Still moving quietly, he zipped down the hallways as fast as he dared. The door at the end of the hallway was mercifully ajar. He cruised through and raced back to his cell with abandon, trusting that there would be only one guard.

Offund sat up when Kelios came bounding across the shark tank bridge.

"Here," Kelios said as he jammed the thick book he had stolen through the iron bars and into Offund's hands.

"What es this?" Offund asked. The Hob's fatigue and stress amplified his odd accent.

Kelios opened his cell, relocked it with his picks, and sat down on his cot to catch his breath. Then he looked over at the bewildered little man and said, "Some homework.".

Chapter 24

A Long Way To Fall

The branches stabbing Ember's back were bad enough. The combination of fear of falling fifteen feet, coupled with his growing embarrassment, had him truly flustered. He bucked and wiggled to get out of the mostly ruined shrub and flopped to the ground. Yondi glared at him with her arms folded and one hip cocked out. The looks of apology and compassion he had expected looked an awful lot like anger instead.

Ember had assumed when Yondi had yelled, 'Halt! By order of the Bronze Protectorate' she had been trying to make a joke. Now he wasn't so sure.

"Ouch," he managed as he stood, brushed the dirt from his hands, and picked sprigs of bush from his fur. "I am certain pretending to be a part of the Bronze Royal Guard is frowned upon in Wrythmar."

"How about sneaking into a highly restricted section of a Dragon library?" She said with a glower.

"Yondi, keep your voice down." Ember patted the air in front of him though he doubted she would listen.

"Why, Ember?"

"Because you will attract attention."

She put her hands on her hips, tilted her head, and glared at him.

"Oh. Why did I go in the tower? Look, Yondi, I told you that I am helping a friend. The things I need are on that floor. Those things and so much more." Ember's voice had faded to a blissful land of possibilities. Her silence told him he had gotten off track.

"Don't worry. I know how to get in and out safely now." Ember's words sounded hollow as he said them.

"Safely? You just fell off the wall." She gesticulated with a hand.

"You yelled scary things at me." Why was she mad? He was the one who fell off the wall.

"What if I **had** been the Protectorate? What would you have done then?"

"I would have talked my way out of trouble. I am convincing when I need to be." Ember smiled proudly.

"Really? Because I'm not convinced that you aren't being reckless and stupid," Yondi said.

Ember's lip twitched. Then he felt his brow furrow. "I'm sorry. Did you just say I am stupid?" He held his tone as flat as possible, but felt his hackles rising.

"Yes. Right now, you are being selfish and acting stupidly." Her words were firm, but her tone had lost some of it's previous bravado.

Ember took two slow breaths. "I am a lot of things. I can be selfish. A coward. I prattle on about things that only interest me. Sometimes I am insensitive and, if I am honest, I have a very hard time understanding what others are feeling. But I am not stupid."

Saying that felt good. He had worked up some momentum and wanted to continue. Why not? "In fact, some have said I am quite brilliant. If I do something that seems risky, chances are good that I'm doing it for someone else. Like using pure DragonsBlood for magic to save my friends. Or manipulating the weather, knowing that it would stretch my body to its limits. Or breaking into a restricted library to try to help a friend who has lost her memory. I think that makes me a pretty loyal friend."

Yondi said nothing, but Ember thought he saw her resolve slipping. He had never won an argument using anything but logic. It felt good, but wrong at the same time. Had he injured Yondi with his words? He didn't want that. But hadn't she just tried to injure him with words?

This argument suddenly seemed petty to Ember. He had to get in that library, but she was worried about him. Surely, they could find a compromise. He opened his mouth to suggest as much, but she beat him to it.

"It's good that you are so loyal to your friends, but what about me? What about what I want?"

Where did that come from? His stunned mind was slow in working out a good way to ask that question when she vomited another abrasive stream.

"Let me put it this way. If you care anything for me, you will keep your furry backside out of the top floor. Is that clear? Or do I need to speak slower and use smaller words?" She hit him hard with her shoulder as she brushed past him.

Ember stood, mouth agape, trying to make sense of what had just happened. They were months away from making ultimatums in their relationship. Maybe his calculations were off. *Did she just break up with me?* He analyzed the available data: yelling and storming off in anger, it assaulted his mind with unfavorable scenarios, and his heart felt like it was in his boots. "Oh dear," he said. "I've been dumped."

Yondi had been speed walking for ten minutes before she realized the rundown old house was just ahead. Anger and fear swirled through her head in violent patterns. Her heart felt like it might burst. "Ahhh!" she growled. Like a stupid little girl. *Focus, Yondi. You have work to do.* She wiped the tears from the corners of her eyes and marched on.

Once inside the old house Yondi had been living in the last few days, she cleared a spot at the table and sat down. The house seemed empty. She blew out a lungful of the emotions clogging her mind and wiped a nearly dried tear from her eye. Once Yondi's heart had slowed, she pulled a tiny smear of DragonsBlood from her pocket and laid it on the table. She then stripped off her blouse and looked over the marks on her ribs and chest. When she found the right one, she pressed the smear to it, and began chanting. After the spell was underway, she slipped a metal claw on her finger and drew a rectangle in the air in front of her.

Bright blue energy filled the rectangle. It rippled like a vertical ocean between Yondi's hands. After a moment, a distorted figure appeared within the frame and a voice warbled out. "I pray you have good news for me, Yondi. My patience is wearing thin."

Crenthys didn't know what to expect when she had come here, but it was not to find Zanderon taking a late night swim in human form.

Now she felt like the one who was intruding. Open pools like this were available throughout Wrythmar.

"You are distraught," He said as he dried himself with a towel.

Like most DragonKin, Zanderon had little regard for modesty. Crenthys took his nudity in stride, but wondered what Kelios might think of the situation. They had seen one another naked in the belly of the Brinery weeks ago. How would he feel about this?

"And distracted." The Dragon said as he pulled on a pair of loose trousers.

"Sorry. Things are getting complicated and I am not sure who I can trust." It sounded like a very human problem.

Zanderon nodded his understanding. "Who are you?" he asked.

The question stunned Crenthys. Her mouth fell open, but no words came out.

"I am not asking who others expect you to be, or who you think you should be. Who are you?"

"That's just it. I can't remember. That's the entire problem." She felt her chin quiver and tears of frustration welled in her eyes.

"So remembering who you were would fix everything?"

She paused for a moment, sensing the trap. "No. But if I knew who I was, I could finally make some decision about who I am to be."

"You believe that? Sincerely?"

"Yes," she breathed.

Zanderon sat in quiet thought for several moments. Then he stood from the edge they sat on with an air of determination. "Come, Brinka. There is a place I must show you." Zanderon leaped from the ledge and his human form was immediately transformed into a massive adult Bronze Dragon. He craned his long neck to look down at Crenthys who now stood.

"Do you want me to...?" She pointed at his back. It seemed more of an indignity for the great Dragon to bear a rider now than it had just a few days ago. Perhaps coming to know the old Bronze had bolstered her respect for him.

"Can you fly?" Zanderon asked impatiently. He knew she couldn't. When she didn't reply, he moved closer to her. "Well, then come. And do hurry. This is important."

Crenthys hustled to the Dragon's side and began climbing. She wasn't worried about hurting him, even with her sharp claws. Scaling his flank seemed wrong—somehow inappropriate. She pushed the thought away and worked her way to sitting, rather uncomfortably, on his bony spine. "Where are we going?"

"A place you need to see." Zanderon burst into flight.

Crenthys cried out and grabbed furiously at one of the bony protrusions on his back. *Old wyrm*, she grumbled to herself. Being cryptic and contrary was bad enough. He didn't have to try and throw her off.

Crenthys ducked behind his massive head to avoid the cool, night air. Tears stung her eyes but she stubbornly held them open. Their trip to Clover Crisp had been marked with concern for her brother. As they flew east, she felt a sense of freedom from those worries and she wanted to enjoy this flight. The landscape below was breathtaking as it unfolded.

Small farmhouses and tiny settlements dotted the countryside. Hillsides covered with dozing sheep or grazing cattle passed below them as they surged onward. They rounded a jutting rock cliff that formed a wide half circle, and her head started to spin. She clung to the bony protrusion to gain her balance.

Although her mind knew what was coming, her heart nearly burst as they spiraled downward toward a stream. Zanderon landed carefully and Crenthys slid hastily from his back. Into a meadow of knee high red flowers. Just like in her dreams. "This place is real?"

Zanderon shifted to his human form. The Bronze Dragon was silent for several moments. "This was your favorite place."

"It still is. A place I visit often in my dreams." Crenthys found it difficult to breathe.

"No, Bel, not your dreams." Zanderon's voice was soft and somber.

A wave of dizziness hit Crenthys again, and she staggered. "What did you call me?"

"What I have called you for centuries. Belendurath was—"

"A mouthful..." She couldn't connect what her ears were hearing with what her mind was thinking. Was Zanderon crazy like Odwin? Or were they all trying to make her feel like she was the mad one? "Zander... what is happening? Why do you think I am Belendurath?" Her voice sounded pitiful.

"I was not sure until tonight. Not totally certain until this moment. I was convinced that someone changed you and erased your memories. You had enemies. Many enemies. I don't understand why they left you alive. I was among the first to arrive at Scornrock. The carnage was incredible. I found your body, in human form, crushed and covered with a dozen slashes. There was no sign of Brinka. Dovondes was beside himself with grief. He forced investigators to search the cavern for her body. When you showed up in the city..."

That made no sense. "Zander, why did they try to kill me when I returned after Scornrock? And why didn't they find the egg when they searched the cavern?"

The old Bronze grew pensive. "I do not know. There were men, Dragomyr, even some Dragons in that cavern for weeks. Even after you fled. Then one day, they stopped and Dovondes put his grief behind him. The destruction was too extensive for their search to continue."

The answer struck Crenthys like an arrow. "They weren't searching for Brinka. They were looking for something else. Whatever it was is the key to everything." She turned sharply to the Bronze. "Zander, help me. I need you to look into my mind."

Zanderon shook his head, "Bel, no. I have no skill in that sort of magic. Ivrus—"

"Ivrus lied to me. And now Vodinar won't let me speak with him. Zanderon, please. I know you think I am Belendurath, but I don't believe that. And I won't until I can break this memory block. I know it is dangerous, but you have to try. You are the only one I can trust."

Zanderon rubbed his short gray hair and groaned with irritation. The old Dragon stared at her for long time. Finally, his resolve broke. "Fine. Sit."

Crenthys hadn't expected him to agree. She paused for a moment, feeling suddenly unsure.

"Now. Before I lose my nerve." The old Bronze put a dark hand on her forehead as she sat among the billowing red flowers.

This is the perfect place to do this. If this kills me, I'll die in my favorite place. Her hands trembled, and she squeezed them together to still them. Zanderon's touch was warm on her head. Suddenly, it turned as cold as ice. She gasped as the moonlit night and swaying red flowers vanished.

Chapter 25

People Change

Lifting his eyelids was like raising a portcullis. Anuka tried to move, but it felt like someone had buried him in mud. His arms and legs were very heavy and he couldn't feel his fingers and toes. He lolled his head to one side and felt his stomach lurch in rebellion. It was the worst hangover he could remember—and that was saying something.

"So you yet live." rumbled a basso voice that thundered in Anuka's pounding head.

"Ouch," The goblin complained at the sound. Anuka licked his lips and croaked, "Grom? That you?"

"Once. Perhaps."

"Once. Wha—." *Oh, great.* "Grom, wha's wrong with you?" Anuka's words were slurred, and he was starting to get agitated. Nothing cured a hangover like working up a good mad.

"It's fitting that they put us in these cages. This is the best place for a couple of savage beasts," Grom said.

The half-giant sounded so melancholy it worried Anuka. With a herculean effort, he willed his leaden arm to cover his stinging eyes with his numb fingers. Visions of a giant spider shooting something at them was the last thing he remembered. "Poison. We were poisoned. How are you okay, Grom?"

The half-giant chuckled mirthlessly. "I have the blood of a giant. And the heart of one, too, I suppose. No poison keeps me down for long."

"Like Slobbers," Anuka mumbled, thinking of his pet honey badger. He let his arm drop and his hand smacked the floor in a way he knew would hurt later. He forced his eyes open again and squinted against the painful assault of a torch in a wall sconce. His vision cleared, and the room came into focus. He was in a prison cell with bars made of thick iron cords that resembled spiderwebs. Fifteen feet away, Grom sat in a similar cell with his knees tented and his arms folded in front of him. The half-giant's head was bowed.

As life slowly crept back into his limbs, Anuka looked around his cell. He jerked despite his lethargy. Two human-like skeletons were piled on top of a Minothos skeleton in the corner. It looked like his captors had shoved them haphazardly to the side to make a spot for the latest occupant. That sent a shiver down his spine. He was awake now. And still naked, he noticed bemusedly.

Anuka doubted the spider put them in these cells, so perhaps there was someone he could reason with nearby. "Grom, where are we?"

The half-giant didn't raise his head to speak. "We're in jail. I think the white-skinned elves brought us down here."

The Dark Elves lived? Oh, fish guts. The Sorceress. There may be a way to talk our way out of this one yet. "Where is everyone else?"

"I don't know. You are the first one awake that I am aware of."

"Hmm... okay, Can you get us out of here?" Anuka whispered in a low voice. Grom did not reply. "Psst. Hey. Big guy. Headbutt your cell door open or bend the bars or something."

"I have no desire to escape." Grom's tone was flat and sullen.

"Oh, okay. That's fine. What about the rest of us?" Anuka didn't mask his building frustration.

"Do not pretend that you care what happens to us, goblin." The shout was like an avalanche. "We came here for **you**. For some treasure. We have failed." Grom's voice was marked with agitation.

A sharp metal clang rang out. The Dark Elf stepped from an adjacent room and slapped his long sword against the bars. His face and neck were perforated with numerous puncture wounds. Felin's arrows had only made him uglier. The one with the short sword walked in behind the other, one arm hanging limply at his side. Hammer Face was nowhere to be seen.

A female Dark Elf strode imperiously behind the two Dark Elf guards. Her steps were as graceful as a cat's and her vulpine expression radiated feigned disinterest—the Sorceress had come. And she was filthy.

Flecks of red dotted her faded purple robes, her face, and her neck. Anuka hoped it was paint. Porcelain white skin peeked from under brown smudges on her cheeks. It looked like she regularly wiped her hands on her sleeves. A wild shock of stringy, unwashed black hair was haphazardly bound in a loose bun on her head. Her obsidian finger nails were chipped.

Except for her unkempt appearance, she reminded Anuka of Jhaldus, the Dark Elf slaver who had kidnapped Crenthys back in Usban. *Where had that Sum Buck gotten to?* No matter. There were larger matters at hand. Anger rose in him as he spied Fabian impishly walking at the woman's side.

"Turd muncher," Anuka growled under his breath.

The party stopped short of their cell doors and the two sword wielding Dark Elves turned their backs to the walls of the hallway.

Fabian stepped forward. He made a little cough into his hand and said, "I present Mistress Visceria, former Archsorceress of the Vel'Jin Mining Conglomerate." The bard stepped back and bowed his head.

Coward won't even look at me. Might be partly because of his nakedness, he supposed, but he also read the guilt on Fabian's face. "Fabian," Anuks said, drawing the bard's eyes to meet his own. "When I kill you, I'm going to remove your eyes with a fork and carry them in my belt pouch so I can play dice with em'."

Visceria gasped. Then a wide smile split her face. "You zaid he was crafty, but did no' mention zo charming." The Dark Elf put her hands to her checks and bent down to look Anuka in the eye.

Anuka gave the woman a lopsided frown and crossed his arms over his chest.

"I am zo glad you are here. You have come at ze perfec' time as well."

Anuka's face shifted from displeasure to confused interest. *What is this trollop going on about?* "Is she crazy?" the goblin asked Fabian.

The Dark Elf licked her lips and clapped excitedly. "Had you come a week before, I would have put you to... other uzez. Zince you come now, an bring me zuch a prize, I am glad."

"Glad huh?. Are you glad enough to let us out of here?"

Visceria chuckled. "For certain. Fabian zez you are in zearch of the box that my late mentor lef' behind. You may have this box as well." She stood and stepped smoothly to Grom's cell. The half-giant didn't move. He just stared at her.

"That sounds great!" Anuka said. "Go ahead and open these cages and we'll be on our way."

"No' yet. Iz safer for you to remain there until I have finish' my work."

"Aww, C'mon. We won't lay a finger on you or your dead bodyguards."

She spun and cackled at Anuka. "I know dis. You mus' remain inside for *your* protection."

Our protection? Don't this moo know that I'm a hardened killer? What is she talking about 'finish my work'? "Fabian, can you translate this for me?"

The bard looked at his Mistress questioningly. She nodded, and he cleared his throat. "Mistress Visceria has labored here for many years on a special task. Tonight, she will complete her work and cross the barrier between life and death." Fabian looked at the crazy Dark Elf who fanned a hand encouragingly. "She will bring forth the spirit of a mighty warrior, long dead, into a worthy vessel."

Anuka looked between Fabian and Visceria. "I know less now than before you started talking."

The Dark Elf woman rushed forward and jabbed a bony index finger in Anuka's face. The jagged nail stopped an inch from his nose. "You blind fool!" she screamed. A wild look danced in her eyes as she stood back and fanned her arms dramatically. "I am zending my magic into the core of the world to free a captive soul. An' bring it back to our world."

"Are you insane?" Xanavor's voice echoed distantly.

"Oh, good. He's alive," Anuka said.

"You can't touch that power. You'll kill us all," the Raven Mage screamed. Then he launched into an expletive-laced tirade that would have cleared the deck of the Sea Pocket.

"Dang, bubby," Anuka remarked under his breath.

The wild Dark Elf woman ignored the raving human. "I have you to thank for bringing me ze necessary vessel. Dis magic requires a living male who has never known a woman."

Oh crap, Anuka thought as he pondered who he had doomed. *Surely Felin had... he was a hundred years old. Or could be it Grom?*

He was so virtuous, not wanting to be like his brothers. Carousing and philandering were likely not things he aspired to. No, wait. Xanavor. Poor guy. All smelly and weird. Holed up in the woods all his life. Pity welled up in Anuka for the human.

Visceria frowned and nodded over her shoulder. The dead guards stepped forward and grabbed Fabian and dragged him down the hallway. The bard tried to resist, but their grip was too strong. He began yelling for help.

Anuka stared, slack-jawed. "You? No way. All that talk of conquest and how your silky voice drew wenches like flies to honey." He chuckled his disbelief. Anuka shook his head and said to Visceria, "You think you know a guy."

She smiled like a drunken cat eying a mouse in a jar. "Again, I am grateful. Please ignore ze screaming." She turned and glided down the hallway after the pleading bard.

Anuka thought about what she had said and shuddered to think of what Fabian's fate was to be.

———◆———

Anuka revised his thoughts on the bard. Maybe he hadn't turned them in. He was likely the victim here. *Well, that stinks.* Even though Fabian was an annoying boot licker, he didn't deserve to have the soul of some long-dead warrior jammed into his body. I mean, that guy had his chance at life. *Poor Fabian.*

Anuka looked across to Grom, who was back to brooding. *Great. Now he feels sorry for himself **and** thinks we are all going to die. He might be right.*

"You are upset, Grom. I get it. You don't want to become a tool for killing, like your brothers. And now you feel like you've started down a dark path. Why? Because you lost your mind and ripped apart a couple of monsters?"

"You know nothing!" Grom's roar made Anuka's ears ring from three strides away. In an instant, the half-giant was on his feet, glaring at Anuka through his bars. "You don't know what I feel. What I have lost. What the things I have done will cost me." The last phrase came out as a helpless plea.

Anuka understood what Grom was feeling. He knew the balm the half-giant needed. "You are pathetic." Anuka let the phrase waft over to Grom's cell. The half-giant recoiled as though he'd been struck. "You look so big and strong. And it doesn't bother you to intimidate people with your silent glares. When the truth is; you're a coward. The first time you have to get a little blood on your hands to save someone you bellyache like a child."

The shock wore off and Grom gripped the bars of his cell so hard they groaned. He opened his mouth, but Anuka cut him off.

"Being big doesn't make you tough. Took me a while to figure that one out. And being nice and smiling at people doesn't make you good. It don't matter what blood you've got, either. It all spills the same. Don't let your fear of ending up like your brothers be your excuse. When the chips are down, you do what you have to do. Period. And if your blood is on fire and you feel like snapping some necks, good. We're going to need some of that if we're going to survive this. But would you please, for the love of Keit's furry naval, stop whining so we can get out of this?"

It was like the sun had set on Grom's face. The flickering torch light from the hallway danced on the half-giant's face giving contrast to the deep shadows on his darkened expression.

Anuka felt small under the weight of that glare. The sound of the big man's teeth grinding was like two millstones rolling together. He had seen murder in a man's eyes before, and he felt a pang of guilt. Grom had changed. The brooding philosopher was gone; a barbarian stood in his place. A line had been crossed when the giant man had decided to fight. There was no going back.

"We will finish this discussion, goblin." Grom's voice was coarse and rumbled like distant thunder.

Anuka simply nodded.

Grom stepped back and brutally slammed his booted foot on the door of his cell near the hinges. The hinge pins squealed as they twisted, then snapped in two. With a loud crash, the door bounced onto the stone floor between their cells. Ducking, Grom stepped out of his cell and stared down at Anuka.

The goblin suddenly felt very naked. Then he realized he actually was naked. Anuka swallowed to keep the quaver out of his voice. "Good work, bubby. Let's let the others loose before someone comes to see about the noise."

Grom grabbed Anuka's door on either side of the food slot, where the metalwork was strongest. With a grunt, he shoved the door, and dust flitted down from the ceiling. He grunted again and yanked the door free of its hinges. Without a word, the half-giant stalked down the hall toward Xanavor's cell.

Sum Buck. Kikkabar was a literal animal and yet was not nearly as strong as Grom.

Felin had given Anuka the lock picks hidden in the sole of his boot. Junky old rust-caked things that a professional wouldn't be caught dead with, but they did the job.

"Anuka," Xanavor said, as he knelt in front of him, and took Anuka's shoulders in his hands. "We must stop her. She will destroy the world."

The human's eyes were wide and his hands trembled on Anuka's arms. His bottom lip quivered as he stared futilely at Anuka.

"Bubby," Anuka said, removing Xanavor's hands and taking a step backwards. "First, don't touch me. I'm naked. It's weird. Second, don't touch me when I have clothes on. Third, what are you talking about?"

Xanavor sighed, raked his hands through his greasy hair, and mumbled to himself. When he looked at Anuka again, the mage had achieved some control. "My Queen, the Raven Lady, the Mistress of Keys, she... she is a guardian. A prisoner for her sins, yet entrusted to guard the doorway between mankind and the lesser gods. Keit. Tor. Their avatars."

"This is the person you worship?" Xanavor nodded at Anuka's question. "Who gives you your power?" Another nod. "And she guards a prison for... gods?"

Xanavor was shaking his head. "No. Well, yes. The prison is for these lesser gods, but not to keep them from escaping, rather to keep us mortals from getting to them before the time is complete."

Anuka looked at Felin and Grom, who only shrugged.

"Look. You don't have to believe me in anything but this: if the Dark Elf lady can touch the realm of the dead, and bring their kind here, we are all doomed. These are creatures who destroyed armies and razed cities a millennium ago. They were judged for their crimes and hidden away, so their knowledge could no longer empower men to destroy one another. One day, in the fullness of time, the door will be opened and these lesser gods will judge man. On that day, we will fall on our swords and curse the day of our birth. But this is not that day. It is too soon."

Anuka thought about it for a moment. *Xanavor is nuttier than squirrel poop. That's certain, now. But some of what he says makes sense. In the same way the stuff Ember says makes sense.* "How do you know this ain't the day?"

"Because," Xanavor said confidently. "The Raven Lady has not told me so. She has promised to spare her faithful on that day. She would have told me."

"Okay. I think stopping the Dark Elf is a good idea. She's crazier that you, Xanavor. Now we just have to find her."

The familiar screech of long sword on stone told Anuka their search wouldn't take long.

———◦———

Dang it. I can't bemoan the bad guys for having good timing. "Okay, we give up."

Xanavor looked incredulously at Anuka. Grom looked relieved. Felin was—he was gone. *Sum Buck. I can't say I blame him.* "Yup. We surrender. Take us to see the insane pale-skinned lady." Anuka put his hands in the air to make sure his intentions were clear. In case dead people didn't understand low Draconic.

The sword-toting corpse pointed his long sword down the hallway behind them. Anuka took his cue and marched along in compliance, his hands held above his head. He guessed this hallway connected to the other up ahead. *The hallways probably make a big rectangle.* On their left were additional cells. None looked to have been used recently.

Most of the doors on their right were closed. The door to the last room was ajar and Anuka glimpsed Hammer Face's corpse spread out on a metal table like the ones they had seen earlier. He shuddered.

Felin was nowhere to be seen.

The hallway turned left at the end and they came to a "T" intersection shortly. As Anuka had guessed, the hallway continued back toward their cells. They likely would go right. The underlying stench of rotting flesh like back in the lab, was very strong here. When one of the dead Dark Elves gestured for Anuka to turn right, he did. Within moments, they entered into a giant atrium with a high stone ceiling. Fabian was bound to a stone pillar in the center of the room. Two more Dark Elves with gray skin stepped forward to block their entry.

"Iz good. Come, come." Visceria continued pacing around Fabian. She waved them into the room without looking at them. The guards moved aside so Anuka and his crew could enter.

Stone stairs circled most of the room, sloping down to form seats. It was like a cemetery collapsed to form an underground theater. Bits of rock and dirt covered the seats, and nearly every row sported the corpse of some creature. Support pillars were located strategically throughout the auditorium. Three other top-level entrances, like the one they had come through, were evenly spaced throughout the room. They made Anuka wonder just how large this facility was. A putrescent odor was thick despite the size of the room. The ceiling above was domed and made of dark green glass, or perhaps some highly polished stone.

Anuka walked down the stairs toward the center of the room. The steps were steep and uncomfortable for his tiny legs, but he didn't really want to use the stairs as a crutch and risk putting his hand on some dead guy's face. Ordinarily, Anuka had a strong stomach, but the funk in this place could gag a maggot.

Great, this is the part where the Débutante of Destruction makes a big speech about her plans and then we attack.

"Grom," Felin's voice called from behind a column. The Wood Elf made a tossing motion and suddenly a gigantic, two-headed axe sailed straight at the half-giant.

In one smooth motion, Grom grabbed the weapon by the handle, spun it once into an overhand arc, and split the Dark Elf to his right like a rotten log. Instead of blood, dark brown ichor, thick as molasses, splattered from the ruined corpse.

Finally! Skipping the monologue is much better. Anuka glanced around.

The Dark Elf standing near him reached for his weapon and stepped toward Grom. Anuka was quicker. The goblin grabbed the Dark Elf's rapier in a reverse grip and snapped it free from its hanger. The dead elf stopped when his hand groped for empty air. When it looked at Anuka, he jammed the tip hard into its eye socket. The sharp point erupted from the back of the thing's skull and it slumped to the stone floor. *Well. That was easy.*

Another of the dead Dark Elves stalked toward Grom, and Anuka hesitated. *He can handle himself.* Instead, with giant leaps he charged down the stairs, taking two at a time. With a quick glance around at the chaos, Anuka found Visceria. Her gore-splattered face was twisted with rage.

She grabbed a long metal handle on the column holding Fabian and yanked it downward. The brass canister her minions had put in place earlier jolted. A piercing squeal barked from the metal container as it started to quaver.

Anuka charged ahead, not eager to see what she was up to. "Dad always said 'you can't call yourself a brawler until you've been beat up by a woman.'"

Visceria noticed him then and slipped a foot-long translucent shard from her belt. It looked like a dagger made of ice.

Three more strides.

The Dark Elf jabbed the dagger into the metal lid of the canister and darted to the other side of the pillar.

Oh no you don't. When Anuka got to the second step from the bottom, he leaped at the woman just as the world upended.

As Anuka became airborne, a brilliant blue light flashed and a crack like thunder reverberated from the column. A gust of wind sufficient to capsize a war ship blasted Anuka backward and he tumbled onto the stairs.

Pain shot through the red-skinned goblin in shocking waves. It radiated from his back and hip. An otherworldly whistle blared in his ears, and he rolled from his back to protect his ears with his hands. It didn't help. He could only hear the ringing in his ears. He forced his eyes open and saw the room's other occupants to be in much the same shape as he. Even Grom had been hurled to his knees beside his two prone attackers. Felin was leaning on a nearby pillar and yelling something Anuka couldn't hear. The goblin shook his head and banged his ear with a fist. That helped a little. Now the Wood Elf was pointing down the stairs.

Anuka looked down at the column where Fabian was tied. The bard sagged limply against his restraints. A trail of blood trickled from one ear. Meanwhile, the Matron of Mayhem was unsteadily cloying her way to her feet.

Anuka tried to stand but his legs failed. *Sum Buck.* He ground his teeth and put a shaky hand on a nearby step. Right on a dead guy's face. He shuddered.

Anuka lurched to his feet and started flinging his hand. Since he was still naked, he had nothing to wipe his hand on. His mouth filled with spit and he felt his jaw muscles clench. He ventured a peek at his hand and saw a small piece of white meat sticking to his palm. With all the power he could summon into his index finger, he flicked the hunk of flesh across the room. He found a clean stone and wiped his hand on it several times. The crimson glow of his skin rose unbidden. Anuka drew his brain-stained hand up and willed his rage into it. His hand burst into flames.

Visceria stood staring at him, her mouth agape. She drew a ward in the air like Anuka had seen Ember and Offund do—then she ran.

Feint echoes of yelling and clanging wriggled their way into his ears. He bolted after the Harlot of Homicide. Praying there wouldn't be any more explosions, he flew down the stairs as fast as he dared.

When he reached the bottom, he heard a pained groaning. He skidded to a halt. *Fabian.* The Butcher of Barith Shir darted into a door just ahead. *I can't let her get away!* He growled as tendrils of steam curled up from his naked body. Anuka knew the right thing to do.

"Alright, bubby. Let's get you out of—ohhh Sum Buck." Anuka stumbled backward and nearly fell on his rump.

Fabian's once handsome face had elongated like some hideous hairless monkey. His skin was red, splotchy, and covered in sores. His black-pupiled eyes were bloodshot and bulging. He opened his mouth to scream and a long, thin tongue rolled out and wagged side to side. Massive horns as black as onyx sprouted from his head. It was like watching Kelios turn into ten horrible animals all at once. Anuka wanted to scream or vomit but couldn't find enough air for either.

Fabian's body writhed and wriggled in agony as the bard gasped for breath. The ropes binding him were digging into his flesh, but Anuka didn't dare cut him free. A roar from Grom alerted Anuka that the function of his ears was returning to normal. The half-giant positioned himself behind a prone dead elf with his massive knees pinning the creature's shoulders to the ground. Grom jammed fingers from each hand inside the thing's mouth and arched his back, pulling at the Dark Elf's jaw with incredible force. With a sickening crack, the half-giant fell back and the elf's head spiraled through the air. Gasping for breath, Grom rolled to his hands and knees, then flung a nearby animal corpse at an advancing dead elf. He bellowed a cackling howl and launched himself at the distracted attacker.

Anuka looked away. *What have I done? He is a monster.* Movement to his right caught his eye, and he saw Xanavor charging him with panic on his face. Instincts sent his hand to retrieve a dagger that wasn't there. The greasy human flung his palms at Anuka and a stream of ravens swarmed him. With little time to react, Anuka covered his vital parts and ducked his head. Not a single crow touched him.

A whoosh and a crack sounded behind him. Anuka spun to see the Succubus of Slaughter frantically unrolling a scroll. With a flick of his wrist, Xanavor sent another bird. It tore through the parchment with a brilliant flash. Through the slivers of ruined scroll, the Dark Elf glared seething hatred at Xanavor.

The Raven Mage stepped in front of Anuka and addressed Visceria. "I will not let you perform this abomination. You have no right to the powers on the other side of the veil. Their time has not yet come."

The Vixen of Violence shook with rage. She fished something from around her neck that hung on a chain. Then she showed Xanavor her middle finger.

On second glance, Anuka realized it wasn't her middle finger, but someone's middle finger. It had been severed and threaded onto a chain. Xanavor looked over his shoulder at a still-writhing Fabian, who had nearly doubled in size. The thin ropes binding him were stretched near to bursting. And he was missing the middle finger on his right hand. *Sum Buck.*

Xanavor and Anuka looked at the Crone of Calamity in time to see her stuff a tiny golden whistle in her mouth. As she frantically blew into it they only heard the sounds of air forced through a metal tube. No keening whistle issued forth.

As a bright green light illuminated her face, the Wench of Woe smiled.

Anuka marveled that her teeth were perfectly clean and straight, yet jet black. Xanavor was yelling his name and grabbing his bare shoulder. Hadn't he warned the mage about doing that? When he turned to confront the man, Anuka saw an enormous creature squeeze out of one of the giant green gems embedded in the wall. When it landed and raised to its full height, Anuka thought his head might explode. Venom dripped from a pair of pincer-like fangs as it stalked toward him. Had Anuka known he was in a world with fifteen foot long spiders, he never would have gotten off Kikkabar's boat.

Chapter 26

Getting Out Alive

E mber's wall climbing skills were improving. Anuka would be proud. He would chide Ember and never let on that he was proud, but he would be. He thought Yondi would have been impressed given her own tendency toward acrobatic feats, but doubted anything he did would impress her now. The ever-present knot in his stomach tightened when he thought of her.

He pushed on the window frame until the clasp on the inside opened. The lock worked like the ones on the fourth floor. Then he pulled the window open and stepped inside the restricted area of the library tower. This window was situated between two rows of ancient wooden bookshelves. The carpeted floor was old and worn. Faint traces of mildew hung in the air of the quiet room. With a sigh, he headed toward the section he needed. This would be his last visit. Time simply didn't permit any further exploration.

This place, like many in Wrythmar, made him think of Yondi. He wondered where that crazy human girl was and if he would ever see her again. Suddenly she was there.

Yondi stood in the center of the open study amongst a gaggle of round tables and haphazardly arrayed chairs. The sight of her warmed and chilled him at the same time. She looked much the same as she had a day ago, but her demeanor had changed. As well as her clothing.

Yondi wore boiled leather armor that covered her from head to toe. Her unruly golden locks were tied into a ponytail with a leather thong. At least two daggers rested in sheaths, one on each hip. Her eyes were different, too. Harder. His remorse at their previous argument and her abrupt departure was gone.

"Good evening, Ember," Yondi said.

Technically, it was morning, but he didn't mention that. "Hello. Nice outfit."

"I warned you not to come back here."

"Yes, well, I was fairly clear about my reasons for doing so." Ember tried not to show too many teeth as he smiled. His mother said that made him look sassy.

"I haven't been honest with you, Ember," she said as she stepped closer.

She didn't sound regretful about her dishonesty. In fact, she sounded pleased. Ember felt betrayed that she might have lied to him. Until he remembered his own secrets. Still, he didn't like the sound of this. He took a step forward, as well. Only he moved to stand behind the massive lectern to his left. "What are you talking about?"

Yondi stopped about three strides from Ember. She swiped a rebellious strand of hair out of her face and looked coolly at him. "I'm not your Dragon appointed tour guide. Never was. In fact, Vodinar and his Dragon masters have no clue I am here."

Ember made a face like he'd found a scale in his fish soup. "What are you talking about? You were waiting for me on my first day in the city."

"Aye. I was. My plan was to act like a lost little girl in need of help. As it turns out, I just let your assumptions run wild. Yours was a much better story. More believable."

That isn't how it went. Ember was trying to get angry, but the emotion slipped away. Instead, he felt like he was standing outside of himself, watching his meeting with Yondi in slow motion. He had a sinking feeling in his gut that he was about to do something stupid. *Sand and seas...* She had never said she was his escort, just agreed with him when *he* said she was. He replayed the scene in his mind. When they got to the front check-in, the librarian eyed Yondi suspiciously. Not him. They expected him to come, but not to bring a guest. *Sum Buck.*

"Why?" Ember's heart pounded as he played through their scenes together. Were he a man of faith, he would have been praying not to see the thing he feared most. If she had been pretending to care for him... *No*, he told himself. *Anything but that.*

"Because of your brother," Yondi said flatly. "Aegis."

Ember's guts turned to water and his tail fell limply to the floor. *Aegis? DragonsBreath. No!* He gripped the podium fiercely to keep from succumbing to the dizziness racking his mind. A million nightmares danced through his head like torch wielding marauders in a city made of straw. His legs could barely hold his weight and his grip on the lectern tightened. "Wha— how... how do you know that name?"

Yondi didn't bask in sadistic glee at Ember's meltdown. If anything, she looked fearful in a way Ember understood. It was the way his brother made everyone feel.

"He sent me here, Ember. Sent me for you." Her voice was strained, but did not falter.

"How did he know I would be here?" There was no logical way for him to know that.

"He's been tracking you for a long time."

That much was true. Ember had spent half a decade on the lam.

"Once he discovered what happened in Usban and made sense of the rumors, he knew there were only a few places you could go. He sent us to those places. I was sent here." Yondi seemed sad.

His head throbbed, and his blood pumped violently in his ears. He loosened his grip a little to test his legs and looked down at the slender drawer where quills and inks were kept. Looking back to Yondi, he crept his hand down and slid the drawer gently open. "Us?" Ember asked.

"The other girls, his other girls." She swallowed hard, but held her face a placid mask. "He calls us his Sanguine Dolls."

"So you are what? An assassin?" It seemed a surreal question and one he wasn't sure he wanted her to answer.

"Something like that." Again, she wore an inscrutable barrier over her thoughts and feelings.

Keit and Tor. Aegis had always been a bit of a megalomaniac. "I'm sorry." He offered a weak smile. "I know what he is like."

Yondi swallowed again and fiddled with a bracer that didn't need adjusting. "Well, you should save your pity for yourself. It's you he wants. And I don't aim to fail him."

Oh, right. He had nearly forgotten that part. With as much stealth as he could muster, he slid his hand from the drawer and pressed his thumb to his bottom rib and his pinky near his navel. "I'm sorry, Yondi."

She made a confused face. "You already said that. And I told you to kee—"

Ember interrupted her with a flick of his free hand. With a grotesque slurping sound, a glob of off-white goo splatted Yondi in the face. On impact, the ball unfolded like a fishing net to wrap her head and torso in a thick web. Then Ember hissed an incantation, ripped his finger painfully from his side, and dove out the window he had come in.

A smoking square of paper drifted down in his wake. The center of the paper was burned out where the smear of DragonsBlood had been.

———————◆———————

Her vision was blurry with tears. Acrid smoke and the coppery smell of blood filled the air. She could not move. A dozen corpses lay scattered around an enormous cavern. No, *the* enormous cavern. From her visions. This was Scornrock.

She glared down from a high place where a bedraggled Dragomyr stood holding a gem that glowed red in his fist. The terror gripping her was familiar. So was the gem.

It was like the one Wave had used to control her in Usban. The thoughts of her present self were mingling with this memory. Wave said he found his gem in the ocean. This gem looked bigger, but she couldn't be sure. The Dragomyr below started speaking, and she came back to the memory.

"I'm sorry, Belendurath. I'm so sorry. You know I have no choice. If the others discover what we have been doing, what we must do, thousands will die. I hope you understand that."

He's going to kill me and my baby. With all her strength she strained against the magic that bound her. Centuries of mastering her power and immeasurable strength in an immortal body were useless. Like a fly trying to move a mountain. Terror and grief crushed her heart. Never had she felt so helpless.

A mix of pity and blind rage filled her when she looked at the Dragomyr holding the gem. *Poor Vodinar. He should not be here.*

The over-tall Dragomyr sobbed bitterly. The oppressive heat of the cavern dried his tears as they tumbled down his leathery cheek. A change came over him then. Drawing in a deep breath, he wiped his eyes. Resolve filled him and he shook his head. "No one else will die for this." Vodinar made a fist with his empty hand.

Crenthys felt the power of the ruby compelling her mind. Instead of being held in place, her hands began to move of their own accord and an incantation escaped her mouth. While being held fast was horrifying, being forced to use her magic against her will was an even greater violation.

Soon the ground grew closer as she shrank in size and settled on two legs.

Vodinar drug the corpse of a Bronze Dragomyr across the stone and dropped it at her feet. *Brinka!* She had felt the loss the instant her sweet girl had fallen, but hadn't had a moment to mourn her. Then she found herself casting again.

The corpse of her Dragomyr child shifted to resemble a stately human woman with braids of ink-black hair, smooth dark skin, and brilliant purple eyes. *What is he doing? Why doesn't he kill me?* She saw it in his eyes, then. Vodinar had been sent to kill one of his oldest friends, but he hadn't the heart. *He is trying to save me.* She wanted to scream at him, to provoke him to end her life. There was no life for her now. After discovering what her lover was doing to other Dragons, at the behest of the Council of Wyrms even, she could never be left alive. The knowledge would destroy her.

Her feet started moving toward the exit. Vodinar walked backwards in front of her, brandishing that cursed gem. They stepped into a long tunnel that would lead them out of her beloved hatchery.

The Dragomyr stared at her piteously. "Forgive me, my old friend." He worked a bit of magic and she felt the ground tremble.

No!, her mind screamed. *My baby! Vodinar, please.* But he could not hear her thoughts.

He turned back to her with a mirthless smile. "One last spell, old friend."

Her hands raised and worked in intricate patterns. Motes of blue light danced around in the air. She felt the cool touch of the spells as the little bits of light settled on her face.

The ground was shaking. She opened her eyes and saw a tall Dragomyr throw something into a dark cave. A gust of air sprayed her with dust and rocks and she shielded her face with her arms. The shaking grew violent, and she instinctively ran toward the dim light at the end of the tunnel.

She staggered out into the light, coughing violently. There was a flat spot near the cave's mouth where she sat trembling, trying to remember who and where she was.

A deafening explosion erupted behind her and she turned to see a massive, translucent dome blink into existence. She struggled to get to her feet when a voice startled her.

"Lady Brinka," the voice called again.

"Pardon me? What did you call me?" She asked the human guard who appeared beside her.

"You are Brinka of House Belendurath. You've been in an accident and your master has been killed. Are you alright?"

Accident? Master? The thoughts jumbled in her mind as she tried to make sense of them. So distracted was she that she didn't notice that the human wore the same clothes as the man she had seen throw something into the cave.

Crenthys gasped, fell to her hands and knees among the red flowers, and retched violently. Her throat burned and her eyes stung. Her heart raced. Zanderon was at her side then. "Come on Bel, breathe."

She tried to speak, but her breath came in rapid bursts. Her arms trembled. Zanderon held her tightly, supporting most of her weight. After a couple of minutes, she calmed enough to gasp, "I remember. I remember." And she did. She remembered enough. *I am a Dragon. The Lady Belendurath. I was imprisoned in the body of my slain Dragomyr, Brinka, to hide a terrible secret. And I am going to burn the mountain down around those who did it.*

Chapter 27

What Secrets Cost

All Anuka could do was watch his friends engage the arachnid. His feet were rooted firmly to the ground. He didn't even have the wits to make up names for the Dark Elf woman. Felin launched an arrow at the beast, but it careened harmlessly off its carapace. Grom screamed and charged with reckless abandon, his newfound axe held overhead. *I can't help them.*

When he realized he would be useless against a creature he was too terrified to look at, he turned his attentions to a fight he could manage. Xanavor and Visceria were hurling magic at one another, taking turns ducking behind a column for cover. Anuka looked down at the rapier in his hand. It was a bit rusty and bigger than he preferred, but it would serve.

Xanavor clamored behind a pillar on the stairs just as a glowing green arrow landed where he had been standing. It exploded on impact, sending globs of acid splattering about with smoky hisses. That was close. But now Anuka had a bead on the Dark Elf lady.

He skulked to the side of the pillar she was hiding behind, not knowing which side she would eventually emerge from. If the satchel stuffed with scrolls indicated how many spells she could cast, they were in a fix.

Fabian continued to wail, making it hard to listen for the pale-skinned witch.

Suddenly, a pair of blue spectral creatures that moved like dogs but looked like lizards scurried up the stairs toward Xanavor's position. Anuka wanted to cry out a warning but didn't dare. At the last moment, a flurry of swooping crows assailed the dog-lizards and ripped them to shreds. Xanavor didn't even look at the fracas. Instead, he fired a column of ravens at Visceria.

Clever. Anuka knew she would be watching the progress of her spell and would be distracted. *This is my chance.*

Anuka slid around the pillar and saw the witch's exposed back. She was stabbing the air, fighting off the ravens with the crystal shard she held. Anuka didn't hesitate. He leaped forward and stabbed the woman in her kidney with all his strength. The rapier bent nearly in two.

Leaping back in surprise, Anuka realized three things at once. First, his stab hadn't even broken her skin. Second, the crows weren't attacking Visceria. They were after her scrolls. And third, she knew he was there.

With a flourish, the witch dispatched the last raven and turned to glare at Anuka. A wide, black-toothed smile split her thin lips and she whipped her hand diagonally through the air in front of her. A thin beaded bracelet glowed on her wrist. Then a ball of red fire the size of Anuka's head flung from her hands to strike him in the chest.

He fell back with an agonizing wail. The rapier fell with a clatter and Anuka slapped at the fire on his face and torso. Wildly, he rolled around on the floor, screaming.

Visceria looked on with sadistic satisfaction. Until Anuka started laughing.

It was too much for Anuka to take. He couldn't keep up the charade any longer. He stood up, dusted himself off, and picked up his rapier. Then he raised one eyebrow and fixed a sardonic glare on Visceria. "Are you stupid? Fire? Seriously? Look at me, woman! I am forty pounds of buck naked, flame retardant fury."

Visceria's confidence broke, and she glanced around warily, suddenly afraid her spells might be failing her. She also seemed to recall the Raven Mage at her back. She was on the verge of running when a roar pierced the air.

Grom sounded like an earthquake when he cut loose. Anuka's best friend could turn into a twelve foot bear. He had once looked an adult Sea Wyrm in the eye. None of those roars compared to this. Anuka thought the world had farted. The ground shook, his ears rang again, and the floor jumped up and slapped him in the face.

From where he lay, Anuka saw a pair of hooves the size of water barrel lids stomping the stone floor. Fabian was gone. He had been replaced by claw, tusk, and corded muscle.

The grotesque creature pawed at the ground, snorted at the air, then... it spoke.

"For ages have I waited. Pressed against the invisible barrier between our worlds, for centuries have I languished. At long last, I am come."

Each step the creature took was like a tree falling. All was silent as the room's newest occupant considered the corpse of the giant spider where it lay twitching. Anuka realized the creature had spoken without moving its hideous mouth. And he heard the words in his native tongue.

"Welcome," Visceria beamed, proffering the talisman at her throat. "It is I that have summoned you, great king. And I who binds you."

The creature looked curiously at her, cocking his monkey head to one side. With a sudden clap of his huge hands, a shock wave exploded throughout the room. It was little more than a gust of air to Anuka, as he worked his way to his feet. The effects on Visceria were much different.

The scrolls in her bag turned to ash and scattered into the air. Little red beads shattered on the floor as her fire bracelet fell apart. Visceria gasped at the rapidly withering finger on her chain.

Uh oh, Anuka thought. The beast smiled as the Dark Elf began to tremble. A squelch from across the room drew everyone's attention to the spider. Grom's fist punctured the beast's side and the half-giant clawed his way out of the dead spider's belly. He stood, sticky green goo dripping to the floor. The barbarian was oblivious to the proclamation of godhood the creature formerly known as Fabian had just made. Grom exchanged appraisals with the creature. Then he covered his nostril with a massive thumb, blew a glob of goo onto the stone, and searched the floor in front of him until he found his axe. Then he charged.

———◦———

From the corner of his eye, Anuka noticed Visceria dashing for the nearby doorway. He wanted to go after her, especially with her scrolls all burned up, but it was hard to tear his eyes away from the sheer savagery of Grom. How could someone so averse to violence be so good at it? The half-giant feigned an overhand chop at the creature, and ducked under a vicious claw swipe. He tucked into a roll as the creature's attack whizzed past and sliced the beast's side with his axe as he rolled away. It wasn't a deep cut, but he drew blood. A moment later, Felin began firing arrows from behind a column. Xanavor was distracting the monster with bursts of ravens.

"Anuka," Xanavor cried. "Don't let her escape."

Right. If he was honest, Anuka wanted no more of the Fabian monster than he did of the spider. He gave one last glance to the battle, then darted after the Dark Elf woman.

This was the moment Xanavor had waited his whole life for. But he wasn't ready. Seeing the demon shrug off Grom's attacks and casually kick the half-giant aside confirmed that.

You are ready, my faithful child.

The voice was sweet in his mind, and it warmed him.

"Thank you," he murmured aloud. He felt embarrassed for saying it. Embarrassed for existing, really. The Queen of Keys had come to him unbidden, when he was nothing. A young boy who lived in a beer barrel, philandering, and working as little as possible. She took a wasted life and gave it purpose. Put his feet on a straight path. He had no idea why.

The demon grabbed Grom by one ankle and flung the half-giant into the stairs. Xanavor sent his ravens to catch the fighter and set him gently on his feet. The demon turned his attention to Xanavor.

Run, child.

He was already hustling behind a nearby pillar. Thankfully, Felin put another arrow in the creature's back, distracting it long enough for Grom to reenter the fray.

Xanavor felt weak. Not because he didn't have Grom's strength or Felin's skill with weapons, but because he was filled with doubt.

Hold fast. Just a little while longer. Your faith will soon be made reality.

The Raven Mage's heart swelled, and he stepped from cover to fight on. The demon grabbed Grom again and tossed him into a wall with a thud. Then the abomination looked at the Wood Elf as Felin fit his last arrow into his bow with trembling hands. The only sounds he could hear were his own exhausted gasps for air. An arrow thunked into the demon's head, slowing the screech of razor-tipped claws scraping on the stone. The demon recovered and continued to move toward the Wood Elf.

———◦○◦———

Moving as swiftly as he dared, Anuka padded on bare feet around a corner. Visceria knelt on the floor and was rifling through Xanavor's bag. *That hag!* She was looking for something. All of their stuff had been dumped in a pile in a dirty little room filled with refuse.

How do I do this? If that Fabian monster removed her magic, I should be able to make holes in her. If not, this will be a quick fight. He blew out the breath he'd been holding and stalked toward the Dark Elf. Anuka winced with each step. *Why do I always forget to go pee before a battle?* Too late, now. When he got within ten feet of her, she cried out, "Yes," and stood quickly.

In an instant, she had turned and was staring at Anuka. "You," she growled.

"Look, lady. I have a sword and a lot of training. You have a smear of stolen DragonsBlood and a metal stick of some kind..."

"Dis? Oh, doan worry about dis."

Suddenly, he was worried about the stick. More so when she pointed it at him and shot a blue bolt of energy at him. Pain like Anuka had only imagined shot through him from head to toe. It was like every muscle in his body was suddenly drawn tight. Then he simply fell over. The pain stopped, save for the knot he knew would soon form on the back of his head. All he could do was pant while his muscles tried to figure out what had just happened.

The Dark Elf cursed him in elvish as she walked past. Anuka didn't understand, but had been cursed enough times to recognize the sentiment.

He wasn't dead. Slowly, his muscles responded to his commands again. That was good. He had to follow her. She couldn't get away. With great effort, he rolled onto his belly and stood slowly. There didn't appear to be any permanent damage. As he started after the Dark Elf, he was thankful for something else; he no longer had to pee.

———◦———

Xanavor shook his head in disbelief. The creature had stretched Fabian's body to ridiculous proportions. The demon stood a head taller than Grom and was as wide as he was tall. Pimply skin was stretched tightly over corded muscle. Blood-red eyes sat deep in black sockets in the thing's misshapen face. A long string of black saliva dribbled from one corner of its mouth and hit the floor with a sizzle.

The arrows Felin had planted in the demon's chest and legs reversed out of their holes to the floor. The wounds began closing rapidly.

To his credit, Felin stood defiantly with his meager dagger in hand.

The creature looked at the elf the way a cook examines a side of beef in a butcher's shop. Clawed hands bigger than Felin's clanked like stones as they flexed into fists at his sides.

Once it decided which fillet it preferred, the demon took a step toward Felin. Then it arched its back and screamed.

A blinding arc of lightning struck the demon, pouring a stream of power into its back. Visceria held the other end. Like the wail of a thousand dying kittens, the massive demon bellowed in agony and spun wildly around. Felin was nearly skewered by the barbs on the demon's tail as it flailed wildly about.

The witch continued to pour lightning into the demon until it fell to its knees. Acrid smoke rolled off of it.

Visceria tossed a metal rod to the floor with a clank. One end glowed an angry red. Then she walked past the gasping demon to the stone pillar. She held something in her hand that Xanavor could not see. With an incantation, she placed it on the pillar. Streams of blue light danced along the column, illuminating invisible runes. Then a wide doorway appeared in the column, revealing a hollow tunnel illuminated with a pale blue light. It thrummed with energy and a gale force torrent of air flowed down the tube.

Xanavor's insides screamed.

Go, my son. Now is the moment. Be brave!

He summoned all of his strength and sprinted for Visceria. She was so focused on Anuka, who had suddenly staggered into the room, that she didn't see him come for her. So intent was Xanavor on stopping her he didn't see the demon rise.

⚬

She ain't gettin' away. No way. Anuka felt sluggish. His legs were like apple jelly as he staggered toward her. Out of the corner of his eye, Xanavor charged the Dark Elf. Anuka had her eye, so he winked at her curious expression. A second before Xanavor tackled the witch, the monster sprang up and backhanded the human into the opening in the pillar. With a fading cry he was gone.

"No! You Sum Buck." Anuka's fists balled up, and he exploded into flame from head to toe. Then he charged the Fabian monster.

The creature snatched the Dark Elf witch by her waist and hefted her to his eye level. "So... you would ascend from the maggots and rule me? A thousand years heretofore I slaughtered your kind by the hundreds. I returned your champions to the mud whence they came. And sullied uncounted maidens as my spoil. Why, pale elf, should I spare your pitiful life?"

Tears streaked her face as Visceria fought in vain against the creature's hold. The Dark Elf, resigned to her fate, stopped struggling and lifted her chin to stare at the monster's hideous face. She would die with dignity. The creature chuckled.

The decision to break the witch's neck showed on the demon's face. As he reached to twist her head, he jerked suddenly, sucked in a quick breath, and dropped the Dark Elf.

Grom landed a running punch to the thing's midsection, dropping it like a sack of potatoes.

The beast roared as it climbed to its feet and flexed its claws. It took a step toward Grom with murder burning in its pitiless eyes. Then Anuka showed up.

"Sully this, you murderous nether boil!" Anuka grabbed the beast's leg with both hands and poured all of his rage into his hands. Fire poured from Anuka and the monster roared. He avoided a savage kick, but had to release the beast when it flopped to one side.

The creature rolled to his hands and knees and stood slowly on shaky legs. When it looked up, the innermost part of his hideous face receded. For a brief moment, Fabian's face pushed to the surface like a dolphin cresting the water. Fabian gritted his teeth and met Anuka's stunned gaze. "Kill... me..." The bard repeated the haunting plea once more before his face was pulled back inside the monster's head.

Anuka observed the burns he had left on the creature's leg. *So fire does hurt it. But how to kill it?* Grom was bent over, resting his hands on his knees. Then he started waving his arms over his head and yelling nonsense.

The hulking beast regarded him with curiosity. Then moved aggressively toward the half-giant.

Anuka saw Visceria scoop up the crystal dagger she had dropped and stalk behind the creature. She raised the weapon to strike the distracted monster. In the blink of an eye, it batted the weapon across the room and picked the woman up by her neck. A swift back kick knocked Grom hard to the floor.

"I will suck the marrow from your bones and fashion for myself a crown from your ribs."

No matter how much she struggled and fought, he held her fast. Her face began to turn purple, and he walked casually to the mouth of the tube and looked down. "A trap for me, perhaps?"

Visceria couldn't have responded to the rhetorical question. She hadn't taken a breath for many moments. Anuka was trying to make his way to the crystal dagger, but he didn't know what he would do with it when he got it. Grom was trying to stand, but kept falling over. Felin crept up and aided the half-giant.

The monster relaxed its grip on Visceria, and she sucked in a gasp of air. "I supposed it was you who brought me to bear." He examined her like a man might scrutinize fruit from a street vendor. "Perhaps you can learn a modicum of obedience."

The Dark Elf was nodding and pleading with the creature.

"No. You die." The beast grinned and tossed Visceria into the tunnel.

Her screams disappeared quickly, as Xanavor's had.

"Who is next?" The monster looked at each of the companions. "You, man with the blood of Septarim?" He pointed a long, ebony claw at Grom. "Or the feral elf, perhaps. I think I would enjoy the brief screams of the Filgenium."

Anuka froze with his hand inches from the crystal dagger. A look of incredulity screwed up his face, and he glared at the monster. Anuka stood, arms akimbo, shaking his head. "Is every Sum Buck I meet gonna know what sort of creature I am?"

The beast raised the lump over his eye where an eyebrow should be. "Yes. You shall serve." The look of surprise on Anuka's face was genuine, but the monster didn't look over his shoulder. Apparently, he hadn't survived for nearly a millennium to be fooled by half-wit mortal tricks. So he didn't see Xanavor rise from the pit on a cloud of ravens until the bloodied human had wrapped his arms around the beast's legs.

The Raven Mage screamed and hugged the monster's knees with all his strength.

Anuka moved without thinking. He dove for the crystal dagger and rolled to his feet. Using the momentum of his roll, he hurled the dagger at the beast. The translucent weapon impaled the creature in the chest, and it howled with fury.

Grom ran at the beast, then leaped, feet first, to send it toppling backwards.

Xanavor clawed for purchase on the stone floor before his fingers found a tenuous grasp. He locked eyes with Anuka, knowing his fate. "Prepare them, Anuka. Prepare the people. The day is coming." The current of the portal gripped man and beast and pulled them into the chasm. With a flicker, the blue light inside the column winked out.

⸺◦⸺

Everyone stared at the dark hole in the column. Xanavor and Fabian were gone.

"Where.. where did they go?" Felin asked. His expression showed hurt and a little embarrassment that his voice had cracked.

"It was some kind of portal, bubby. Magic and whatnot." It was all Anuka could manage. He feared to say much more or his voice might falter.

"Why?" The voice belonged to Grom but was almost unrecognizable. Absent were the traces of compassion and contented curiosity that usually accompanied his low-pitched words. The question sounded less like a peal of thunder and more like a rough whetstone dragging on a dull blade. The half-giant looked at Anuka and took a step in his direction. "Why are we even here?" he bellowed.

Anuka was glad for his recently evacuated bladder as the gore covered mountain loomed over him. *This is it, old boy. Are your secrets worth dying for?* He swallowed hard and considered. His fear had always been that, were he truthful, no one would follow him. The reasons he did what he did, why they all did what they did, were beyond insanity. He felt ashamed that he had given Ember a mission and made him swear not to tell Crenthys. Her own part in Anuka's plan was utterly ridiculous. They all walked on a razor's edge; Ember,

Crenthys, Kelios, Offund, and himself. Even Tabir had some crazy plan to resurrect a dead god or some such foolishness. This was just the next step on the tightrope. Either these men would sign on with his impossible plan, or Grom would toss him into the abyss.

Squaring his shoulders and straightening his back, Anuka looked up into Grom's eyes. "We are going to kill Bog."

Anuka had seen Grom mule-kicked by a creature that crawled from Tor's literal abyss. He hadn't looked as stunned as he did in that moment.

Felin snickered. Then chuckled. Then he guffawed in an uproarious bubbling way that was kind of funny to hear.

Anuka chuckled as well. It was pretty ridiculous to hear it said aloud.

Grom looked between them. "This is no time for your jokes, goblin."

Anuka held up a forestalling hand. "I know. I am serious. This is the first time I've said it out loud. I—give me a moment." Anuka composed himself as best he could. He bent at the waist and blew out long breaths.

Felin was still laughing, though Grom's sobriety was helping to reign in his humor.

"I came to Kentari to kill the Black DragonLord, Caustimis."

"Impossible," Grom grumbled.

"No. Not impossible." Anuka grabbed the half-giant's wrist as the man turned to walk away. "Listen to me, Grom. It isn't impossible. Things haven't always been the way they are. Dragons and men once co-existed. People, humans mostly, started giving the Dragons' power over their lives. A couple hundred years passed, and now they are gods. Why? Because we made them gods."

"This is nonsense. You cannot fight a Dragon," Grom protested, snatching his hand free of Anuka's grasp.

"We can! There are weapons that were forged for doing just that. For fighting the Dragons."

"And you have such weapons?" Felin asked, finally recovered.

This was where Anuka had to tread carefully. He wanted to trust his companions, but had never been good at trusting anyone. "Yes. Some. We came down here for more."

"Lebarin's treasure? Why would he send us after something we could use to kill Bog?" Felin asked.

"He didn't—look, there's a lot to it. Lebarin did send us after something that could kill Bog, but it isn't here."

"What?" Grom's tone and volume sucked the steam out of the room.

Anuka took a cleansing breath. This would be a poor time to lose his temper. "Lebarin has what he sent us after. It's hidden in the church, and I know where."

"Then why did he send us down here to look for it?" Felin asked.

"So it would look like he was trying to retrieve it."

"That makes no sense," Grom bellowed.

"Unless he wanted to use it himself and blame us." Anuka fanned his hands out as if he had just explained everything. The other men didn't immediately object to his reasoning. Before they could, he continued. "Lebarin is furious with Bog for promoting someone ahead of him for some stupid office in the church. So much so that he is conspiring with another Dragon to unseat Bog. Permanently."

"How do you know all of this?" Felin asked skeptically.

"Rigby."

"What?" Grom and Felin asked simultaneously.

"Rigby is a bard. He trades information. I spoke with him about two weeks ago via a magic portal. Don't ask, I will explain that part later. See, I have some other friends who see the gears turning in Dorwine in a way most folks don't. One is a DragonKin and the other some kind of librarian. Anyway, that doesn't matter. When I spoke with Rigby, he told me about everything going on around here. The Silver Dragons, Lebarin's crazy job. Rigby had already turned the old fart down because he pieced together what's going on. Being a smart bard, Rigby wanted no part of an insurrection. He especially didn't want to be the fall guy. I took what Rigby told me, and we made a plan to sail for Kentari."

"Why did you lie to us?" Grom asked. He furrowed his brow into a line so hard you could cut steel on it.

"Well. If I came and said, 'Hey, I need to go steal a magic treasure from a Necromancer so I can kill Bog', what would you have said? Instead, we said 'Let's go smash some things and get super rich". That still holds. I have no need of treasure. Whatever spoils we find are yours."

"What if I am smart, like Rigby, and I want no part of an insurrection?" Felin asked.

Grom nodded his approval of the question.

"Well, that's what you each have to decide. Remember, after Rigby thought it through, he came over to the insurrectionist camp."

"Why is Rigby in Lebarin's jail, and you are here? I thought the plan was for Rigby to lead us." Felin crossed his arms. He looked smug, like he had finally stumped Anuka.

"It was always fifty fifty as to which one of us would get pinched. Lebarin is a bit unstable right now. The plan would have worked either way."

Felin and Grom exchanged looks.

"What does it matter? We are stuck down here."

"Well, Felin, that's not entirely the case." Anuka walked over to the part of the column Visceria had put the smear of DragonsBlood on. "If my feline friend is correct, and he usually is, then I know how this works." He looked back at them with a solemn expression and sighed.

"I didn't intend for anyone to die down here. Especially not Xanavor. He was...strange, but he had a good heart. Even Fabian was starting to grow on me. I don't want to kill Bog for selfish reasons. I don't want treasure or fame. The people of this land have suffered under these Dragons for far too long. They are tyrants. Bog the worst of them. It has to end. The witch piled all our stuff up in a room over there. I intend to get poor Fabian's DragonsBlood resin bar and bust out of here. Then I intend to finish what we started. I haven't been straight with you, but, starting now, I will be."

"So we get to know *all* of your plan?" Felin asked.

Anuka grinned. "Know it? You Sum Bucks will be part of it!"

Chapter 28

Justice Be Done

Zanderon stared solemnly at Crenthys. "Do you realize that helping you will probably result in my demise?"

She knew. It was surprising to realize how easily she had gone from risking her own life to risking the lives of others. That was a sobering thought. Not only Zanderon but also Ember and Tabir were in grave danger. Even if they didn't take the path she was on, they all were in peril. Nothing could change that. They had been in unspeakable danger before they arrived at Clover Crisp. Only they hadn't known. If Dovondes continued using the ruby to control other Dragons, none of them would ever be free.

"Do any of us have a choice?" She asked.

Zanderon's expression was grim. "Only one. Choosing the path that leads to death after centuries of life is difficult. I doubt many beyond myself, and you, would take such a path."

"My friends will. They already have."

Zanderon nodded once and began moving his hands in a circle between them. Glowing motes splinted from the sphere of orange light he drew in the air. He finished with a flourish. A flap folded down like a cloth, creating a large hole in a field of red flowers.

"I will be swift," Crenthys said, stepping forward.

"No." Zanderon put a hand on her chest to stop her. "You are teeming with emotion and your thoughts are scattered. Besides, I know where I am going."

She wanted to stomp her foot and rage in protest, but he was right. Her mind burned with the influx of new information, and her anger was close at hand. *He is right.* She gave a curt nod and folded her arms over her chest.

Crenthys felt the absence of her friend and then saw the portal seal behind him with a faint pop.

Fatigue and the eerie quiet of deep night made her edgy. She had napped fitfully for a few hours the day before, but had eaten little. Her eyes burned from tears and sleepless nights. There was no sleep to be had tonight and her confirmation into the Bronze community was just a few hours away. Fire burned in her belly at the thought of rejoining Dovondes and his cronies. The memories of their deeds were strong, and so was her anger. Rage from her former life was layered on top of her fresh understanding of the sins of the Dragons.

The Dragons had become weary of their rule and grown corrupt. The days of long hours in debate over care for the mortal creatures had been replaced by bickering over territory and squabbling for material trappings. Some of the older Dragons were obsessed with accumulating artifacts from bygone eras. Younger Dragons weren't interested in anything, seemingly. They lived to fill their bellies and put the wind in their snouts.

"What a mess. How did we let things get so bad?" Her skin tingled at the rapid changes in her thoughts. Two hours ago, she was weeping over lost memories. Now she had memories dating back centuries, but her perspectives on the lives of those around her had shifted. Even she, who thought herself so noble among the corrupt Dragons, was only looking to her own cares.

She thought of her brother and jolted as if stunned. *He isn't my brother... he is my son.* He hadn't hatched before she was forced to leave Wrythmar. Dragon eggs won't hatch without constant heat. But he had. And he was her son. Her thoughts went to Kelios, and she nearly laughed aloud. If their relationship was complicated before, what would it be now? "Yes, Kelios. I am a centuries-old Bronze Dragon. Oh, and I have a son." The thought was too ridiculous to entertain. *My boy will need a name.* The baby hadn't been given a name. It was strong Dragon custom not to name a whelp until they were mature enough to understand their name. Many Dragons named themselves. *I can't go on calling him 'baby'.* The idea of calling him son seemed too strange for her to verbalize.

Behind her came a faint tearing sound. Zanderon stepped through another portal, a lanky Bronze Dragomyr bound and slung over his shoulders.

The burden of the Dragomyr was obviously a lot for the old Bronze to bear, but Crenthys took the prisoner's face in her clawed hand and glared at him. "There will be much to answer for this night, Vodinar."

———◆———

The world raced up to meet Ember as he plummeted. The magic seemed to take an eternity to coalesce around his outstretched arms. He wanted to curl into a protective ball, though his logical brain ardently protested. It occurred to him belatedly that he shouldn't scream as he descended. Too late.

A powerful force slammed into Ember, like a giant net, and his plunge to death became a glide. His vertical momentum became horizontal acceleration, and he soared above the city. He had used this spell before and knew how to control his flight, but he had never used it to flee from... what was Yondi?

Pain stabbed his ribs as if a spear had pierced him through the chest. *She works for* him? It was the most disgusting, surreal thought he could imagine. Ember's brother was a monster. Aegis had tormented him from the moment of his birth. Ember was always too weak physically and too soft emotionally. His older brother made it his job to correct those flaws. Endless torment and merciless chiding were Ember's only companions growing up. It had perplexed him why Aegis was so enraged when Ember finally left. That rage had chased Ember across the world. Now Aegis had found a new torment for him; Yondi.

His stomach clenched and roiled, threatening to empty its contents. Ember imagined what it would be like to vomit while flying and forced this stomach to calm. He busied himself with trying to figure out where he was. In his haste, he had angled himself in the wrong direction and had to circle back. The magic engulfing him created a translucent shape, like a magnificent bird. Tiny specs of glowing red sparks filled the shape and, no doubt, made him stand out in the night sky.

I have to get to the ground. He found the correct street, dispelled the magic and landed on all fours, close to where they were staying. Ember scanned the street for signs he had been spotted, but all was clear. His legs wobbled as he slowly stood. *Malkin were not meant to fly.*

With the fear of imminent death waning, his thoughts went to Yondi. This time, he couldn't stop his rebellious stomach from emptying itself on the cobblestones. *How could you be so blind?*

Yondi had been right. He was stupid. Tears stung his eyes as he hacked, wheezed, and spit the awful taste from his mouth.

He didn't want to get up and go face his friends, but he knew he must.

The last few steps to the house were the hardest. Lights filled a couple of windows, and his feeling of dread grew worse. His friends were awake and there would be no avoiding telling them about her. He couldn't even think her name.

It would be better to go in, lay it all out, and deal with it. He didn't know what she was capable of, and his friends needed to be aware of her purpose for being in the city. His stomach cramped again as he thought of explaining about his brother.

He opened the door and stepped inside to a frightful sight. The Dragomyr Vodinar was bound to a chair in the middle of the room, sobbing. Crenthys paced the room angrily. Everyone looked up at him with alarm as he entered. An older human with dark skin and gray hair stood over Vodinar. *Zanderon, likely,* Ember thought numbly. "What is this?"

Tabir appeared from Ember's peripheral and pulled him farther into the room, closing the door behind him. Still, no one spoke. They all stared at him. Even Vodinar raised his head to stare at him through bleary eyes.

"Umm, a lot has happened tonight, Ember," Tabir said.

No kidding. Ember looked to Crenthys, who seemed suddenly very shy.

"Ember. I... My memory has returned." The words gushed from Crenthys like a cork flying from a bottle.

"Cren, that's wonderful. That's—"

Crenthys held up a hand, stopping Ember. "I am Belendurath."

The room grew as silent as a tomb. *I thought my problems were big.* Ember was often right when he made conjectures, but this one had seemed pretty far-fetched. His mind raced to connect the dots he had already discovered. All he could do in response was nod.

"I told you as much," came the voice of Odwin from the sitting room.

Crenthys breathed out a nervous chuckle. "I should have listened to you both. Even now, it's hard to believe."

Ember nodded, "I understand. There is much to discuss then, but my first question is; Why is the Dragomyr administrator of the city tied to a chair in our kitchen?"

The anger Ember had seen before returned to Crenthys's face and her hands trembled at her side. She worked her mouth like she wanted to speak, but the words wouldn't come.

"There is a conspiracy. Among the Dragons." Ember figured now was as good a time as any to lay out the theory he had been building.

"Yes. Ember, how—?" Crenthys began.

"I haven't only been playing kissy face at the library the past few days. The higher you ascend in that tower, the better information you find." Ember swallowed and pushed away fresh thoughts of Yondi. "DragonLord Dovondes, and likely the full Council of Wyrms, are controlling other Dragons, compelling them to do their bidding."

The shock on Crenthys's face disappeared, and her eyes narrowed. She leaned closer to Ember. Her hands flexed at her sides.

The problem with spilling the beans was that Ember never knew quite how many beans to spill. "This is my theory, at least. A lot of what I have read points to this possibility, though I can't sort out why."

Crenthys didn't really relax. Rather, she turned her ire toward Vodinar. "Our guest was just explaining this."

Tabir gave Ember a concerned look.

———————◦———————

The fire burned low as Coltimar paced. He should stoke it, he knew, for he was getting hungry again. He was always hungry. The darkness was full, the air around him teeming with the sounds of the wild. Crickets chirped, frogs croaked, and coyotes howled in the distance. Beneath all of that, a steady mountain wind whistled as it snaked up the pass. The wind was cool, but the chill didn't touch him.

He poked the fire with a booted toe until a tiny blue flame came to life. An uneasy feeling settled into his bones. He felt exposed. Not just because he was camped in the open where a million stars winked down on him. Because of people. He had lived most of his life in solitude. All of that time had been peaceful. It was times like these, when he'd been dragged into the world's problems, that trouble found him.

Coltimar loved Tabir. They were as near to being brothers as two men of different blood could be. Both were children of Rathune. Tabir was glad of that fact, Coltimar was not so much. Each of them was born with long lives to span the centuries. Tabir despised that gift while Coltimar did not. Usually. They both had been raised by hard, principled men who, though misguided, wanted the best for them.

No, Coltimar didn't mind leaving his home for some adventure with his friend. But things in Dorwine were getting out of hand. He would need to be cautious. If he stirred up too much mortal trouble, especially among the self-proclaimed Dragon deities of Dorwine, his father would not be pleased.

Kingdoms fell, and the world was sundered before his father's wrath. Soon Coltimar's father would force him into hiding for a few decades, or until Tabir called on him again and he was able to escape his exile. That was the cost of being a loyal friend.

A foul odor on the wind ended his distraction, and he grimaced at the pungent scent. Had some creature died that he hadn't yet discovered on his walks? *No.* Coltimar realized he wasn't breathing the scent into his lungs, it was perceived by his spirit.

He growled and plunged his hand into the fire for a fistful of burning coals. Agents of the dark usually despised fire. His other hand ached for a sword or axe, but he had set that path aside centuries ago. He put his back to the fire and scanned the ridge. The light of the fire had spoiled his vision and he could see very little in the piercing darkness.

The spiritual funk hit him again, and he spun around in time to catch a flying stone the size of a barrel right in the chest. The ground disappeared from under his feet and he soared into the air. With the speed of a racing horse he collided with a stone wall near the cave entrance. Light exploded in his vision and he fell face-first to the ground.

Instinct told him to get up, and he obeyed. His ears were ringing, and he tasted blood. Rhythmic thunder rolled toward him and his blurry vision cleared enough to see what was charging him. "Golem," he growled.

The rock creature was half again as tall as Coltimar and heading straight for him. He bent his knees to spring to the side but was squashed between Golem and the wall before he could escape. It blasted the breath from his chest and he felt his bones protest. He slid to the ground again, landing in a heap. Before he could move to stand, the creature picked him up with one massive, stoney hand. It hefted him off the ground by his neck. It looked like a rock tower children would build. Each joint and limb was made from a smooth boulder. It's face was smooth with no eyes or mouth. This creature needed neither.

Coltimar slammed his fist on the arm holding him aloft to no avail. DragonsBlood, this thing was strong. His nerves were on fire, reporting injuries to his brain. He hadn't hurt like this in ages. Coltimar raised his legs and stomped on the thing's face, trying to fling himself free. The Golem pinned him to the wall and raised a giant fist, ready to pulverize Coltimar.

"Enough," came a command in an outlawed tongue that took Coltimar a moment to place. Elvish. It was unlawful to speak any tongue but Draconic in Dorwine. The voice was warbled and reverberated weirdly, but the creature obeyed it. Small mercies.

The creature relaxed its grip a tiny bit and Coltimar greedily sucked in air. Ten strides away stood a small, shapely female in dark clothing. Her eyes glowed a phosphorescent green beneath her cowl. It hurt to swallow, but Coltimar licked his lips and croaked hoarsely to the figure, "are all elves possessed by demons in this age?"

The figure moved toward him, sliding her hood back. "Not all, godling. Your friend carries a different sort of host."

He had been scouring his mind for enemies among the elves he knew, but stopped at the allusion to Tabir. *What was this?* It wasn't uncommon for him to be recognized by a denizen of the spirit world and be mistaken for one of the demon hunters his people often became. *But who knows about Tabir?*

When she was just a few strides away, Coltimar noted her features and the tone of her skin. A Gold Elf.

"Have you come to kill me?" If he could get her to talk, he could likely figure out who she was.

"That would be pointless. I've come to detain you." With a motion of her hand, the golem wrapped Coltimar in a bear hug and sat down on the stone, holding him like a child.

The grip was like iron. *Detain me?* Coltimar thought of Payris and how the ambassador had insisted Tabir come with him to Theleth. "I don't understand."

"You don't need to understand," the elf said as she pulled her cloak tight around her shoulders and walked into the darkness.

Struggling against a Rock golem was pointless. The elf had sealed off the magic in the construct. Coltimar closed his eyes and drew in a deep breath. He began exploring ways he might escape but images of Tabir being dragged away kept invading the peace of mind he sought.

———◦O◦———

With a sharp poke from Crenthys, Vodinar gasped and looked up. He looked from face to face, trying to retain as much dignity as he could muster. "I am an instrument of my master. None of you can understand that. *None* of you," he added before Crenthys could protest. "The Dragons create us and use us like a farmer uses a plow. We are implements. Nothing more." His stare lingered on Crenthys for a few moments to accentuate his point. "I have been compelled by the Bronze DragonLord to use an ancient artifact to compel certain young Dragons to fulfill their duties. They are like children, unwilling to do their part."

"What duties?" Tabir asked, looking at the two Dragons in the room.

Zanderon and Crenthys exchanged a look. With a hesitant look on her face, Crenthys regarded her friends. "When Dragons speak of their sacrifice on behalf of mortals, we aren't speaking in metaphor. Each of us is required to take a sojourn and make a blood offering at a secret altar."

"Bel..." Vodinar rebuked.

"No, Vodinar. This is the secret they slew Brinka for. That I was supposed to die for." Now it was her turn to offer a silencing stare.

"Who is this sacrifice made to? And what is its purpose?" Tabir asked.

"Some details are not my secrets to reveal. Suffice to say that my disdain for Rathune isn't rooted in unbelief. Rather in a different perspective of your god than you have. As to the purpose." She looked at Zanderon for support.

"The sacrifice does many things. It provides stability to certain magic that would otherwise run wild throughout Dorwine," Zanderon added.

"And relegates the use of magic to Dragons alone." Ember said in a cool tone Crenthys didn't miss.

"The magic in Dorwine is not like magic in other realms. It is wild, requiring the strongest of wills to wield it." Even as she spoke the words, she understood how arrogant they sounded. But it was the truth. Crenthys had been indifferent to—even grateful for—the magic Ember could wield. Now, it made Belendurath feel uneasy. It was strange to have your mind suddenly changed about everything. Reconciling those two people would take time.

"What is the Nexus?" Ember asked.

The question was startling. Like a flash of lightning. "I... Ember, how do you know that word?"

"I translated it from a High Draconic word. In Low Draconic, it means a series of things that are connected at one point. The term was repeated frequently in discussion of this mysterious duty."

He doesn't trust me. The idea was hurtful, considering what they had been through together. Hurtful, but understandable. *He knows I am of two minds concerning his secrets.* The fount of collected facts he enjoyed sharing freely would likely run dry. Unless she could make him trust her. *Is trusting me a good idea? I am a Dragon. I have responsibilities that transcend my temporal relationships.*

Crenthys sighed. "In this context, the Nexus is a point of connection for seven different worlds: ours and six others similar to ours. Another function of our sacrifice is to prevent the barrier at Nexus from wearing thin. If that happens, creatures could pass from those other worlds into ours."

"The Similseptus..." Ember breathed the phrase with holy reverence, as if the word was smoke and would vanish if spoken too loudly.

Crenthys hadn't heard the term, but guessed at its meeting. "Ember, we can discuss this more later. Right now, we have a series of gigantic problems to deal with."

"What are those?" Tabir asked, rubbing his arms nervously.

"Soon, Vodinar's absence will be noticed. They will look here eventually. Second, I am going before Dovondes and his council tomorrow to be made a part of the family once more. Vodinar, does he know who I really am?"

"He does."

"Does he suspect I know who I am?"

"No. He doesn't"

"He will use the ruby to control you," Ember said in his matter of fact way. He was usually right. Not surprised that he was right, only that he said it out loud.

"Yes. And I suspect a Dragon cannot wield the ruby, is that so?" When Vodinar nodded Crenthys continued. "Third, we have to rescue my son." Saying it out loud was odd. Everyone looked at her as the realization dawned on them. "Finally, we must escape."

"Why don't you revert to your Dragon form or use your magic to create a portal?" Tabir asked, thinking them to be simple solutions.

"Because I cannot. When Vodinar forced me to remove my memories they were locked away securely. I am the only one who can undo it, but without my magic, it's impossible. He created a paradox. I can't transform and I don't have access to my magic. It's as if my body doesn't believe what my mind is telling it." It was embarrassing to admit that she was still so limited.

"Could Master Zanderon make a portal large enough for all of us?" Tabir asked.

"No," said Ember. "He could make the portal, but only to somewhere he has been. We need to find our friends in Zhazie. I doubt he has been there."

"The Malkin is correct," Zanderon said.

"And we have another problem," Ember said with a resigned huff. "Yondi is an assassin sent by my maniacal brother to bring me home."

"What?" Crenthys and Tabir blurted.

"I know. I would prefer not to discuss it beyond what is necessary. In the short, my brother rules my people, or nearly does. He was upset that I left my responsibilities behind and he has been hunting me for years. I know little more than that."

Poor Ember. Crenthys felt bad for her attitude about his ill-advised relationship. A part of her knew the human girl was trouble, but this was no time to gloat. Instead, Crenthys put a hand on his shoulder. "I'm sorry, Ember."

Ember smiled in response. Pain was evident in the Malkin's drawn brow and made his eyes glisten with tears.

"We can talk about it later, if you like," Crenthys said as sympathetically as she knew how. Tabir put an arm around their friend. "Right now, we have to figure out how to get out of here alive."

———◁◉▷———

Odwin walked quietly beside Tabir, a contented smile on his face. Tabir hadn't wanted to bring the human along, but had decided leaving him in the house with Vodinar was too dangerous. Tabir dreaded making this trip, but he felt he should bid Payris goodbye. The Elven ambassador had been kind to him.

No one was around when they arrived at the embassy. It felt lonely.

"What is the proper decorum for entering an Elven domicile?" Odwin asked.

Good question. Tabir knew his culture, and had come to learn much of the Golden Elves over the past few days. "I suppose we go in." The door wasn't locked, so Tabir opened it and stepped inside. He wasn't sure if letting an unknown human enter before him was wise.

The front room was empty. Tabir didn't know whether he should call out or hope someone would pass by. *Was there anyone left to pass by?* Many of the Elves had likely returned home and part of Tabir worried he had missed telling Payris goodbye.

"You brought a friend," a female voice said.

Tabir jumped in surprise. "Tanila," he gasped. "I didn't see you there."

She bowed from the doorway to his left where she had appeared. "Apologies, Master Tabir."

He placed a hand on his chest and returned the bow. "I'm sorry I came unannounced. I wanted to speak with Payris before he left."

Tanila drew her lips into a line. "So you will not join us, then?"

It pained Tabir to let them down. "No. I'm afraid I cannot." An awkward silence stretched on for many moments before Tabir asked, "Is Payris here?"

"I will fetch him. May I find your guest a comfortable place to wait?"

Tabir looked at Odwin who just shrugged. "That would be wonderful. Thank you, Tanila."

Tanila lead Odwin deeper into the building and Tabir took a chair. He blew out a long breath. *What will I say?* Tabir knew the truth was always best. He thought about the disappointment Tanila showed when he told her he wouldn't follow them to the Golden Lands. *Would Payris do the same? Would he be angry? Does it matter?* Tabir knew it did not. He was on a mission from Rathune and couldn't let personal entanglements get in the way of that. No matter how painful.

His mind drifted to the Sliver he knew Payris had. Tabir had thought a lot about how to get the item safely away from Payris. He would have to steal it. It was a shameful thought, but he had no other choice. There was little chance he could talk his new friend out of the item.

A strange scent made the hairs on his arms stand on end. He tried to stand but a hand clamped over his mouth and nose. Tabir fell back into his chair with a muffled cry. He clawed at the hand with his fingers but found nothing. An unseen force was suffocating him. Panic gripped him and he thrashed wildly about. *That scent.* He remembered that metallic smell from decades past. His uncle Folred was an evil sorcerer. When he put those memories together with his current predicament his panic doubled.

Tanila stepped in front of him. "Peace, Tabir. Elves are resistant to sleep magic, and I am afraid I wouldn't be able to subdue you without harming you."

Her words made no sense. His eyes bulged and his muffled plea went unheeded. Blackness came into the corners of his vision and he slid to the floor. His lungs burned for air but his limbs were too weak to resist. Payris peered down at him as everything went black.

"State your name," Vodinar said.

This is it. "I am Belendurath, the Bronze Lady." Gasps erupted from the Bronze Council. *So some didn't know.* She clamped her jaw tight to hide her trembling. Her eyes burned, so she blinked languidly.

"Vodinar?" Dovondes asked.

"She is being truthful, my Lord," the tall Dragomyr replied.

"So you have discovered the truth, at last. That makes things easier." Dovondes rubbed his chin in irritation. "Bel, my love. I believe I have solved the riddle of your escape. It is irony that your clever plan to escape me drew you inexorably home. You knew you had nowhere to run. You destroyed the chamber inside the mountain to destroy evidence of your betrayal. Then you hid, and cleverly so. You assumed the form of your slain Dragomyr, Brinka and changed her appearance to match your human form. Afterward, you fled through a tunnel, collapsed the mountain so we would assume you were dead. Your memory loss seemed authentic. I assume that your last act as a Dragon was to destroy your memory. Is that so?" Dovondes changed his vocal inflection, so the question sounded like a command.

"Yes," Crenthys said, smiling.

Vodinar exhaled.

Dovondes nodded, stroking his beard. "I don't understand what brought you here. And why have some of your memories returned?"

Crenthys tensed, but kept her cool exterior. She paused long enough to draw the DragonLord's attention. Then she said, "A Sea Elf called Wave produced a ruby artifact like this one." She gestured to the Ruby Vodinar held aloft. "He controlled me with it."

"A Sea Elf?" Dovondes bellowed. His astonishment was echoed throughout the chamber. "Where is this Wave now? And how did he come upon a Blood Bane ruby?"

"Gone. He cut a portal and vanished before my companions could apprehend him. We never learned where he got the relic."

"He must be found. That ruby must be recovered."

"Yes, my Lord," Crenthys said.

"Continue." Dovondes began pacing around the room.

"Some time later, I had a sense that the ruby should not have worked on me as it did. That it was meant for a True Dragon. My curiosity brought me here for answers."

Chatter around the table grew as Dovondes pondered her words.

"Am I to return to your side? To raise our son?" Crenthys asked, voice thick with emotion.

The DragonLord stood and nodded as he continued to pace. "According to our physician, your memory cannot be significantly altered by magic again. The modifications simply would not hold. I cannot risk you rebelling a second time. The work we do here, that our people are commissioned to do by the god who made us all, is too important. My desire is for you to be by my side, as it once was. For you to live. But it cannot be so."

Crenthys felt her knees weaken at the proclamation.

"Vodinar, my old friend. I am sorry to ask you to do this." Dovondes hung his head. "Crush her heart."

"My Lord, may I know why you control so many young Dragons with the Blood Bane ruby? Is it not a curse upon our people?" Crenthys asked. It was like swallowing a bee. She regretted opening her mouth and now waited for the sting.

Dovondes looked at Vodinar and shrugged.

"Apologies, my Lord. I let my grip slacken." Vodinar bowed his head toward the DragonLord.

"It is surprising that you don't remember the thing that turned you into a traitor. Very well. Despite your treachery, you have returned our son to me. I will indulge a question. You will die knowing that you fought against me wrongly."

Vodinar slipped his hand into his pocket and looked at Crenthys. She gave the slightest shake of her head and he withdrew his hand.

"The god the mortals once called Rathune brought our kind into this world. When he departed, he tasked our ancestors with the burden of fueling the Separation between our world and six other worlds. The Separation is an altar where a blood sacrifice, the Blood of Dragons, must be brought at appointed times. This sacrifice is paid by the magic in our blood. If the sacrifice isn't paid, the Separation weakens. If it weakens, our world will be flooded with unimaginable horrors from other worlds.

"Throughout the generations, the resolve of the Dragons to keep this vow has wavered. Many believe this to be a myth and that our precious blood is wasted. And Dragons would rather peddle their blood as currency and surround themselves with wealth. Our need for participants to offer their blood for our sacrifice has become so dire that the Council of Wyrms has tasked me with... encouraging reluctant young Dragons to do their part. The Blood Bane ruby, or Crimson Sovereign, is an ancient relic forged by powerful sorcerers who warred against the Dragons. We lost most of the rubies in time. The Council holds three, including the one my servant uses now. It is unpleasant work that must be done. For the sake of our kin and mortal kind."

Crenthys's mind ran in circles around the information. On one pragmatic hand, the fate of the world hung in the balance. On the morally astute side of the argument, compelling someone to do something by force was wrong. She thought of Kelios then. For him, the answer would be simple; find another way. The room had grown quiet. "I see."

All eyes were upon her, so the nod she gave Vodinar was barely perceptible.

The tall Dragomyr slipped his free hand into his pocket. He made a show of switching the ruby gem from one hand to the next. "Master, am I to continue?"

Dovondes squeezed his eyes tightly shut and breathed, "Yes."

Vodinar held the gem high and whispered, "Remember."

A dam shattered in Crenthys as a torrent of memories flooded her mind. She heard herself screaming as centuries of recollections overwhelmed her. This wasn't merely recollections of old relations and events, but of power and knowledge. Crenthys grabbed her head in her hands as if to hold it together. White noise cupped her ears, and she staggered. On the fringes of her mind, she processed other voices, but they couldn't compete with the tsunami in her head.

Someone was shaking her. Slowly her mind began to settle into a calm pool of clarity. Dovondes gripped her shoulders in his iron grasp.

"What went wrong? Why isn't she dead?" The DragonLord screamed at Vodinar, who recoiled in terror.

"Love," she said. Her voice and tone drew Dovondes's attention and his rage turned to confusion. With a wave of her hand, her Dragomyr form melted away and her beautiful human form stood in its place.

Dovondes gasped, along with several council members.

She stepped close to him and placed a hand on his chest. "Dovondes. Twice you have tried to kill me. I'm beginning to think you don't want me around." Crenthys pulled her hand from the DragonLord's chest and made a quick fist. Thick bars of iron encased his human form from ankle to neck.

The Council members sprang to their feet, but froze when she pointed a dark, slender hand in their direction.

"Do you think I would let you poison our son with your lies?" She stepped up and put her face inches from his. "You can tell yourselves what you want, but we aren't gods. We don't get to force the world to bow to our will." She wanted to rake his throat out, but that wouldn't solve anything. With a wave of her hand, Vodinar melted into Ember. He squealed in shock. She continued, "I am going. And my son is coming with me."

Dovondes gave a roar, and the iron restraints tore apart with a terrible screech. Pieces flew around the room with a chorus of clanging and scraping. In a flash, he had Crenthys by the neck and lifted her off the floor.

"I *am* a god! The lives of these frail simpering mortals are in the palm of my hand. For centuries, I have spilled my blood to protect these people. It is time for others to stand in the gap and make that sacrifice, even if I must melt their minds to force them to do so. I won't fail to kill you a third time, my lover. Your blood will be the next sacrifice made."

Crenthys felt her limbs weaken from lack of air. She pounded at his hands, but his grip was unbreakable. She had no weapon and couldn't concentrate on bringing her magic to bear. Kicking her legs only exhausted her further. Darkness crept into the edges of her vision.

"Master!" cried a voice behind her in Ember's voice.

Dovondes raised his head to look over her shoulder. The Ruby Ember held aloft bewitched him in an instant. His face went slack

"Flee," cried the voice in a high-pitched squeal.

Dovondes dropped Crenthys like a sack of potatoes and ran at full speed for the exit.

Crenthys coughed and gasped for air as Ember pulled with all his strength to get her on her feet.

"Come on Crenthys, it's time to go." Ember was looking at the line of angry and confused Dragons moving from behind the table toward them.

Crenthys drew in a deep breath, coughed, and then stood. She thrust both hands into the air and pulled down sharply, like ripping curtains from a window. Tons of ice fell from the sky on top of the Dragons. Even as the ice was piling up, she turned to Ember and said, "Get on."

The Malkin stared at her. "On what?"

With a roar, Crenthys burst into a mass of glistening bronze scales. Her heart sang the way it did in her dreams as she circled her grove. Only this was a thousand times better. She felt Ember scurrying up her side and nudged him into place with an elbow. "Hold on as tight as you can." He nodded.

She saw the Bronze Council breaking free of their icy prison. With a flick of her tail, she swatted Zothit across the great hall. With a great leap, she burst into the air and raced toward the glass ceiling overhead. Just before impact, she covered Ember with a magical shield to protect him from the broken glass she was about to create.

Chapter 29

When the Trap Closes

Anuka lay trembling on the rough wooden floor. He was glad to have clothes on again, and didn't want to puke all over them. It took all of his will power to keep the few strips of dried meat down. Grom wasn't faring any better. The big man was doubled over, a giant hand clamped over his mouth. Felin tried to stand, teetered, and stubbornly corrected himself, using the wall as a brace. He sat down on the smooth onyx chest they recovered from Visceria's lair.

The ride up the shaft had been nothing like Ember had described. The Malkin was likely laughing up a hair ball right now.

Anuka had melted a sizable chunk of Fabian's DragonsBlood resin and smeared it on the appropriate runes. Then they had all been sucked up the tube like a reverse waterfall. Without water.

They had tumbled head over heels before smashing into the top of a building that looked a lot like a huge well. Then two halves of a round, wooden floor came together and dropped them like a bad habit.

Anuka tried to spare some concern for the dozens of armed Vith likely outside the thick wooden door, but was still quite concerned over keeping his last meal down.

"Is everybody ok?" Anuka croaked.

Grom retched violently, and the others had to press against the wall to avoid getting drenched. The half-giant emptied his stomach for several more moments.

Anuka had seen beer casks burst and make less of a mess. The goblin was pretty sure he saw a boat anchor come out of the big man. *We gotta get out of here.* The smell hit him a second later, and he flung open the door. Whatever Vith were waiting to kill him had to smell better than the mess Grom had just made.

The door opened into the vast courtyard of the keep. The once-crumbling battlements were in various stages of being repaired. Broken stone was being replaced, as evidenced by tall wooden scaffolding in various places along the wall. There were no green-skinned assassins ready to skewer him. None living, at least. Broken bodies of the thin frog-like killers littered the courtyard. Piles of bones, like someone had been melted on the spot, dotted the horrific scene.

Felin stepped up beside him and said, "What are you about? Trying to get killed?" Then the elf looked out over Anuka's head at the macabre scene. "Onvara," he breathed.

Elvish, Anuka guessed. The air was thick with a pungent odor, like sulfur from small swamp ponds. "It smells like the world's worst egg fart."

"I may yet," Grom began as he finally rose to his feet, "have one more murder to commit."

"Better hold that thought, bubby." Anuka's voice sounded grim, even to his own ears.

A vile smelling Grom muscled his way past his smaller companions and out into the courtyard.

"Keit and Tor," Grom swore as he surveyed the carnage.

Must be bad. He swore by two fake gods. Anuka scurried to catch up to the big man, who was picking his way around the keep. "Uh, this might not need to be said, but don't step in the wet parts. It's acid."

Grom stopped and looked at him.

The goblin put a finger on his nose. "That awful stank. Acid. I mean, look around. What do you think did this?"

Grom spun in a slow circle.

Felin climbed onto a nearby parapet and looked "Gods..."

"Well, one at least. If my guess is right." Anuka shrugged.

"You don't suggest that this was done by..." Grom seemed hesitant to say the name.

"Bog. Yeah."

Grom and Felin shared a look. "I thought he wasn't stupid enough to show his face with the Silver Dragons in the skies."

"Well, I don't see no Silvers just now. I mean, they can't be everywhere." Anuka squatted to inspect a pair of bodies that had been piled together by a gout of Bog's breath weapon.

Felin hopped down and looked at Anuka, a mask of concern stressing his ageless face. "What does this mean? For us, I mean."

Anuka stood and shuddered as his mind processed the gruesome scene. "Well, it means that Bog is likely out in the open. Which means I still have a shot to finish my mission. And it means it's time for the two of you to cut bait or fish."

"Does it not seem like folly to fight a creature who can do this?" Grom gestured at the surrounding slaughter.

"Grom, how many times in your life have you met someone bigger than you?" Anuka asked. Grom didn't answer. "Everywhere I go there is some Sum Buck tryna' push me around. After a while, no matter how big he is, you have to push back. Felin, what if your village is his next stop? Could happen. I mean, your people don't hold to Bog's laws. You have your own language for cryin' out loud. That's a death sentence. Worst of all, you don't pay any taxes. What's to keep Bog, or any of the two dozen Black Dragons lurking around his country, from takin' five minutes out of their day to turn your people to goo?"

"Enough," Felin barked. "I get your meaning."

"Grom, what about you? Do you have a nine foot mama stashed in a cave back home? Crenthys, my friend, has spent years hiding from them. And she's a DragonKin. There's no hiding. We have to fight. *You* have to fight."

He looked from Grom to Felin and back. "Well? I ain't gonna beg you."

"Yes," Felin said, though somewhat reluctantly. The look Anuka laid on him was accusatory. "Yes. I will go and help you kill a god."

"That's better, bubby. What about you, big guy?"

"You have lied to me, and lead me to become the thing I hate most." Grom took great gulps of air through his nose. "I will do this for Xanavor. He was a worthy companion. I will avenge him."

Anuka clapped loudly, "Alright. We need to hustle back to Kentari. I recommend we make a quick stop at the river. Grom puked all over Lebarin's treasure chest."

———◦———

The warmth of the hearth was almost Anuka's undoing. He hadn't slept in almost two days. The running and fighting, not to mention the scheming, was taking its toll. Grom snored softly in the corner of Lebarin's waiting room. They had awakened Felin's jeweler friend straight away and given the man nearly all of Anuka's remaining coin. Then they had used the rest of Fabian's resin to set their trap. Finally, they had marched into the church, declaring themselves to be conquering heroes and demanding their bounty. That was an hour ago. They had been languishing in the stuffy little room outside Lebarin's office, under the watchful eyes of two guards, ever since.

Rigby is gonna kill me. Anuka didn't know how they were going to rescue the bard's daughter. He hadn't counted on losing Xanavor. That one hurt. The idea that more could still be lost laid a heavy weight on his tiny shoulders. *As long as Grom and Felin stick with me, we should come out ok.*

Lebarin's door clicked open and a wisp of a girl stepped into the room and spoke to the secretary.

"Grom, wake up," Anuka said in a soft bark.

The half-giant's eyes popped open, and he gasped. He mumbled something about drifting off, but Anuka wasn't paying much attention to the big man. The secretary, a much smaller man, was gliding toward them.

"The Victorin will see you now," the thin assistant rasped.

"Grab the box," Anuka said as he hopped off the bench. *It's show time.*

Anuka strutted into the Victorin's office like he had just signed the deed to the place. His lips were pressed in a curved line and he bobbed his big red head to music no one else could hear. The number of people in the room did not surprise him. A half-dozen guards stood at attention around the room. *So few?* Two pretty young acolytes in black robes flanked Lebarin's desk. The old man himself was lazily rifling through papers as he sat in his chair, pretending not to notice Anuka's entrance. Bumph was squatting like a giant frog against the far wall. *Hmm*, Anuka thought. "Bumph!" he said, grinning widely. "You lived."

The Wumpy croaked in reply. That got Lebarin's attention. The old crone looked up from his papers as Anuka came to stand in front of his desk.

The goblin gave a deep bow at the waist. "Your holiness."

"Mr. Sandbar," Lebarin said flatly, standing on feeble legs. "I trust you come with good tidings."

"Yes. And I have good news." He didn't see the Victorin's eye roll as he turned to motion Grom over with the box. "Whoop! Here is your box."

The old priest made a convincing show of excitement as he hustled around his desk to examine the box. They were able to wash most of Grom's puke off of it, but Lebarin still crinkled his nose as he knelt beside the box.

"Jozmyn," Lebarin said without taking his eyes from the box.

One of the young girls produced a key on a thin chain and removed a slender box from the Victorin's desk. She opened the box and pulled a small, waxy piece of paper from it. DB smear.

Here we go, Anuka thought. He rubbed his hands together excitedly.

Lebarin opened the box and stared inside. When he looked up at Anuka, his face was screwed into an angry snarl.

"Where is it?" The Victorin growled, slamming the box shut and grabbing Anuka roughly by the shirt. "What have you done with it?"

"With what? We didn't even know how to open it." Anuka pawed at the old man's hands as the sounds of blades clearing scabbards filled the room.

"Search them."

"Hey, you are wasting your time, man. The box was empty when we got it. That's not our fault."

The search was brief. They didn't have much on them any longer.

"Where did they go when they entered the city?" Lebarin asked, never taking his eyes from Anuka.

"They stopped at a jeweler's shop. And the little one stopped to buy a hat," a guard with a nasal voice said.

"Take them. Find where he hid the treasure. Then burn their ship."

"No," Anuka screamed. Lebarin shoved him to the ground and one guard picked him up roughly.

"Bring the little one. Send the other two to the laboratory." Lebarin moved toward the door leading to the dungeon.

⸻◦⸻

If Offund looked bad, then Kelios was on death's door. The Triton lay against the back wall of his cell staring at Anuka through half-opened slits. His skin was gray, covered in ruptured blisters. It looked like the worst sunburn Anuka had ever seen.

The sharks swam lazily below them as they crossed the small bridge to the area of his friend's cell. Rigby needed a bath and a biscuit, but otherwise seemed ok. He stood and pressed his face to the bars when the procession approached.

"Did you get it? Can we go free?" Rigby asked.

"Your friend, it would seem, isn't much of a friend after all." Lebarin smiled widely. "Mr. Sandbar found the treasure and decided to keep it for himself."

"Don't listen to this old windbag. He's dumber than—" Anuka cut off as a swift kick from a guard knocked the wind out of him. "Ow, bubby. Oh, you almost got my ding ding you Sum Buck..."

"Pick him up." Lebarin stepped closer to the bars and looked at Rigby. "My apologies, Master Rigby, but your friend didn't keep his end of our bargain. Open his cell."

A guard opened the lock on Rigby's cell.

"Lebarin, you have to let Kelios out. He's dying," Rigby pleaded.

The Victorin looked the Triton over and said, "I see. Don't worry. We have other plans for him."

Anuka didn't like how that sounded. He forced himself to his knees, wary of flying feet.

The guard with the key yanked Rigby out of the cell and another ushered Anuka inside.

"I assume you saw the masterful work Mistress Visceria was performing in her laboratory. Well, we are working similar miracles here." Lebarin nodded to the guards. They took Rigby by the arms and began dragging him toward the bridge.

"Regardless of your treachery, goblin, I win. Either you tell me where my treasure is, or I let my alchemists take you to my lab. Before they have finished their work, you will tell all you know. I guarantee that. Telling me now could ensure a painless death for you and your friends."

Lebarin looked at Rigby and sighed. "Except for him. I am afraid we have conducted ample experiments on humans."

Rigby's eyes grew wide as the guards holding him tossed him into the tank, where three hungry river sharks waited.

———◇———

Felin's screams could likely be heard throughout the compound, with the room's door open as it was. The DragonMarked guards slammed the door behind them once the elf was secured to the table. As soon as the door shut he stopped screaming. He raised his head off the cold metal table to make sure they weren't lingering. When he couldn't hear the guards any longer, he dropped his head back down. The cold of the table felt good against his thumb as he pressed the knuckle against the metal surface. Then he began huffing in quick bursts. With a scream laced with fear and dread, this one real, he popped his thumb out of joint.

Waves of electric pain shot up his arm. Sweat instantly covered his body and his breathing was quick and strained. With as much care as he could manage, he slipped his throbbing hand out of the manacle and looked at it. The shape of his hand was grotesque, and it made him nauseous.

Tears streaked his cheek, and he growled again. Then he slammed his palm against the table, putting his thumb joint back in place.

He had done this to himself a half dozen times. It never got easier. He clutched his damaged hand, white-hot with searing pain, to his chest and rested as long as he dared. Thoughts of Rigby in a cage, or worse, spurred him on.

His thumb would be mostly useless for a while, so he raked open the fastener on the other manacle with his fingers. Then he sat up and freed his feet.

The tile of the floor was cool against his feet. The guards had removed his boots to apply the shackles. He preferred going without them. In a few seconds, he found some tools, no doubt intended for some evil purpose, and began to work on the lock.

"Stupid goblin. I can pick a lock, too." He didn't hate Anuka. Not really. But he didn't like the goblin's attitude. He was so arrogant and dismissive. The little guy was a good thief. And an excellent lock pick. Felin had watched him and learned what he needed to know. Soon, the door lock clicked open, and he poked his head into the hallway. All clear.

With his lock picks held tightly to keep them quiet, he silently padded down to the next room. He listened but heard nothing. Just as he moved to the next room, he heard whimpering across the hall. Grom wouldn't be crying. It sounded like a girl in there. The door adjacent to the one he was about to check was open a crack. He peered in.

A young human girl was leaning over the corpse of some hair-covered creature, weeping softly. She wore the soft black robes of an acolyte, the silky hood pulled up. She raised her head from the table and a barely discernible point appeared in the hood. Not a human, then. An elf? His breath caught.

She turned at the sound and gave a startled cry. Felin stepped into the room and pulled the door closed behind him, confident he could pick it open.

The girl's eyes were wide, and she held a shielding hand in front of her. "What do you want?"

"Aridelle?" Felin asked.

Her frightened look melted into one of confusion. She lowered her hand slightly and stood a little straighter.

"I'm sorry. I've come to rescue you."

"Rescue me?"

"I am a friend of your father." Felin let his words sink in. In an instant, a myriad of emotions crossed her face as she processed his words.

"My father?" She said, the words a tangle of anger and confusion.

He suddenly realized that Aridelle could likely use Dragon magic. Why else would she be here, so close to Lebarin and his priests? "Your father. He is here. Looking for you."

Aridelle rolled her hand into a fist. "I don't have a father."

Felin raised his hands defensively. "He didn't know about you, either. Amaria didn't tell him about you. He didn't know you existed until a few weeks ago."

She thought about the words for a moment. "If that's true, why didn't he come and find me?"

Felin dropped his hands and sighed. "Do you think Lebarin would let that happen? Let him offer to take you away from here?" His words seemed to tumble around in her mind. "We know what you are. What you can do."

"Then you know I can never leave. They will never let me."

"We have an arrangement with the old priest."

"If you believe he will keep his word, then you are both fools," she said.

"We don't. But we have another plan. Come with me. Please. We can sort this out later. Right now, my friends are in grave danger." Felin held out a hand to the girl. Tentatively, she stepped forward and took it.

"He is excited to meet you, you know?" Felin gave her hand a squeeze and then turned to work on the lock. A set of keys appeared as he was peering at the lock, preparing to work.

"This will be faster," Aridelle said, choosing the correct key.

———◦———

They found Grom sleeping soundly on one of the metal tables, his legs dangling off one end. The guards had bound him with a chain that Felin doubted would hold the man were he determined to escape.

The giant startled awake and nodded to Aridelle. "Who is she?"

"Ribgy's daughter. Let's get out of here. They need us." Felin worked opened the lock on Grom's chains with another of Aridelle's keys.

"Rigby? The master bard?"

Felin hadn't had time to tell the girl much and now just nodded at her question.

Soon they were padding down the hallway. Aridelle knew the way and led them along the narrow corridors. Soon they came to a giant glass wall filled with water and three river sharks.

It was unlike anything he had ever seen. As Felin neared the tank, the fish startled. Then someone plunged feet-first into the water and thrashed wildly.

"Rigby!" Felin cried.

Chapter 30

Desperations

Tabir calmed his mind amid the throbbing pain in his head. He didn't know how long he had been unconscious, but he had to get free, find Odwin, and escape.

What about the Sliver? It seemed selfish to think about such things with Odwin likely in danger. That thought made him angry. Tanila had attacked him. With magic! A fresh wave of pain in his head reminded him to relax.

Soon his hands were free of the soft rope he was bound with and he searched the room for something useful. This had been the quarters of one of Payris's staff, and was mostly empty. Inside a small crate he found a small figurine made of bent wire. It was a piece of art. *Pity.* Tabir tore it apart and bent two pieces of thick wire until they broke free from the little statue.

Say what you will about Anuka Sandbar. Most of it would be true, but the little red goblin loves teaching his tricks to people. Tabir had stolen before, but hadn't considered himself a proper burglar until now. He dragged the door open and rubbed the raw skin on his wrists.

The halls were dark and quiet. Most of the inhabitants' personal effects were packed into a few small crates. They had lived in this city for fifty years and had but a few scant boxes of personal items. *They are nomads, like me.* Tabir was a minimalist to the extreme. His lifestyle necessitated it. Payris was leaving so much behind. Tabir wondered if he was planning to leave the Sliver behind as well. Doubtful. He kept the artifact in his own bed chambers. Tabir would not count on it in any course.

The scattered rugs were his only reprieve from the cold marble floor on his naked feet. He stalked slowly through the compound, simultaneously looking for a weapon and watching for elves. *They are all gone;* he thought as he stepped into the last room. Payris's room.

The massive bed of intricately carved Borchwood was centered on the far wall. No blankets covered the half-foot thick down mattress. A narrow metal storage case with thin wire shelves was bare. The neatly folded fine silk tunics that had been there just days ago were gone. The night table was clear of keepsakes and the floor had been swept. Only a stack of sturdy crates remained. That, and a thousand year old Sliver of Divinity.

Tabir had seen more of these than perhaps any living person. It still enthralled him. It was but a tiny piece of a giant puzzle that held incredible secrets. Secrets concerning the fate of mankind. And he had been set apart to unravel those mysteries.

His hands ached to touch it. To liberate it. So strong was his desire for the shard, his mouth watered. Soon it would be safe with the few dozen others Tabir had rescued. His thin, pale hands trembled as he reached for the shard.

"Fascinating, isn't it?" Payris asked breathlessly from the doorway.

Tabir jumped in surprise. He looked chagrined as he backed away from the artifact.

"I wouldn't have made you for a thief, cousin."

"Payris, you don't understand." Tabir said, unable to keep a hint of desperation from his voice.

"Oh, I do. It's only fair, I suppose. I lock you in a room, intending to whisk you to a land a thousand miles away. Despite your desires otherwise, you escaped and decided to take something of mine."

"I'm not robbing you." Tabir began. A raised eyebrow from Payris made him pause. "This doesn't belong in someone's bedroom. It's... It's not some decoration." Tabir growled in frustration. "I don't know how to explain it."

Payris shrugged, "It's a Sliver of page four of Aracthias's treatise on mankind. Phrases thirteen, fifteen, and eighteen. Unless I am mistaken."

How? Most of his Order was dead. Payris knew the coding system they used. Part of Tabir wanted to embrace Payris as a brother, another part wanted to attack him.

"No words? I understand completely. Fortunately for you, I have decided not to take you to my homeland. Unfortunately," Payris said as he slid a slender blade from a scabbard with a whisper, "I cannot leave you alive."

"Payris, what are you—" a wild swing of Payris's blade cut Tabir off, and nearly cut him open. He ducked the awkward swipe and stumbled to put some distance between him and the Gold Elf. Oh, how he hated swords. Payris wasn't overly fond of them either, judging by the awkward way he used the slender blade. Tabir thought of the long walking stick he had seen behind a stack of crates in the foyer. No way to get to it.

Payris took the sword in two hands and stepped toward Tabir, a snarl on his face. As the Gold Elf stepped forward, Tabir lunged to his left toward the door. Payris raised his sword for a killing blow, but

Tabir reversed his feint and the unskilled swordsman sliced through wall paneling instead.

Tabir put one of the wrist-thick bed posts between Payris and himself. "How do you know about the Slivers of Arachthias?" He didn't want to hurt Payris, but he had to stay away from that sword.

Payris smiled. "You aren't the only one who survived that mountain, Nal'vir."

Tabir felt the strength drain from his limbs. When he left his childhood home so long ago, he fled through the mountains. There he discovered an ancient dwarven stronghold inhabited by a fanatical brotherhood determined to collect, and destroy, the Slivers of Arachthias. Tabir had joined them hoping to convince them that the Slivers were a map of salvation, not damnation, as they believed. In the end, Tabir had destroyed the magic holding the mountain together, destroying the End of Days Brotherhood. Or so he thought.

"Yes, Brother Skavrag reacted much the same way as you when I described the strange elf who was so taken with my Sliver."

"Skavrag..." Tabir whispered, as if saying the name aloud might summon the old dwarf. Having no love or reverence for Rathune, the Brotherhood did not shy away from using any means necessary to further their plans. Skavrag dabbled in dark magic. Powers that likely drove him mad.

"Yes. He has found favor as an advisor to the most powerful creature in the world and enjoys resources he never could while living in that mountain."

Skavrag advises Druindar. Tabir didn't have time to consider the ramifications of that awful revelation. Payris sprang forward and carved a gash in the thick Borchwood post, missing Tabir's face by two finger widths.

Tabir gasped and fell backwards, tripping over a crate. He scattered the stack of belongings and lay atop the ruined boxes. Something sharp stabbed him painfully in the back, but the gleam of Payris's blade in his face prevented him from moving.

"Good sword," Payris said. He glared down the length of the metal at Tabir.

"You need me. To find the other Slivers."

Payris laughed. "No, cousin. I only need your blood. Brother Skavrag told me how you hid the other Slivers."

A loud crack resounded, and Payris pitched into the wall with a groan. Odwin stood where the Gold Elf had been, holding a long shaft of wood.

Tabir's heart leapt at the sudden appearance of the old man so he rolled off the boxes and gained his feet. His elation turned to panic as the Gold Elf rebounded off the wall with a shove and clumsily stabbed Odwin in the chest.

"Take me by the mansion!" Ember yelled over the sounds of rushing wind and flapping wings.

"Why? Tabir is with the elves."

Bronze Dragons had short, powerful wings compared to other Dragons and could accelerate and turn at incredible speeds. At this rate, Ember would fall off and walk to the mansion.

"I'm not going for Tabir. I have to find Yondi."

"Yondi?" Crenthys asked incredulously as she banked around the library tower. "That treacherous little tramp betrayed you."

"No, Cren. She did what she had to do. I just figured it out. Yondi is a slave. My brother owns her."

Crenthys was silent, but she altered her path from the Golden Embassy back to the north. "Why the mansion?"

"She has been taking care of Odwin since she arrived here. That's who has been cleaning up and the two of them have been living off the scraps she can scavenge." Speaking the truth out loud almost broke him. He felt a great sob building, but he swallowed it. Maybe she didn't love him. Maybe he was just a target. But he couldn't leave without trying to make things right. He loved her. *I do?* The thought made him bark out a teary laugh. *I do. Regardless. I love her.*

Crenthys turned toward the mansion and began to slow.

She knows, he thought. That strange resonance in your being that disrupts logical thought, fills you with distraction, and leads you to places you never wanted to go. *She knows.* Ember smiled as they neared the house and he prepared to once again leap blindly into the path of heartbreak.

⸺◦⸺

The house was quiet. He expected nothing less. The initial betrayal of learning that his beloved was actually a highly skilled assassin was endearing itself to him. As long as her sharpened bone daggers were pointing away from him, he could appreciate her talents. She had been cleaning again, he noticed, as he walked into the atrium. The stairs were freshly swept and the Dragon head bust was centered on its pedestal.

"Yondi. It's me, Ember." The volume of his voice surprised him. It would have been prudent to be circumspect given their circumstance, but he was done being coy. "Come on, Yondi, we need to talk."

He nearly let out a hiss when she materialized behind him. Ember reviewed his assessment of his appreciation of her talents. His heart thudded as she strode intently toward him. Her eyes were red and blotchy. The look on her face could spoil milk. Still, he smiled at her.

She stopped a stride away from him, crossed her arms, and looked him up and down. "Shouldn't you be fleeing the city?"

His eyebrow shot up and betrayed his curiosity.

"I found Vodinar," she continued. He had a lot to say, with the proper incentives. I would have guessed that Crenthys already had what she came for and you would be flying south. Or maybe east."

"Can't go yet," he said. "I forgot something."

"You should go. There is nothing here for you but trouble."

Ember saw her stony mask falter. "I know. But I'm starting to enjoy your kind of trouble." She flinched as he leaned toward her, her hands flew to her daggers, but he ignored that. He put his hand gently on the back of her neck and pulled her to him. He leaned down and kissed her. Everything burned away like dross. Dragons, his cruel, relentless brother, his broken heart, all faded away in the burning bliss of that moment. Her hands moved from her daggers and wrapped him in a trembling embrace. The warmth and energy of her nearness were like a potion filing him with vitality.

He pulled back, stared into her eyes, and saw so much that he had overlooked.

"We can't stay here." Yondi's voice was full of concern.

Ember smiled. "Don't worry about my brother. I can handle Aegis."

"You can't handle a dagger, *gatin*." The words were spoken by a familiar masculine voice in the Malkin tongue and dripped with disdain.

"Aegis," Ember growled, hoping the anger in his voice masked his terror. There was nothing he could do in a fight against his brother.

Ember had never seen anyone stand against Aegis and win. Ember had stopped trying years ago.

Yondi slid a dagger from her belt and pushed Ember behind her protectively.

This is ridiculous. I would never let her defend me. It was an archaic thought that came unbidden, but he stood behind it. He grabbed her hand, intending to swap places with her. She stuffed something into his hand, slid her other dagger free, and stepped into a low crouch. Ember looked down at what she had passed him. A smear of DragonsBlood.

He looked up to see Yondi begin a deadly dance with his brother. She made a quick stab for his eye that he easily parried, then slapped away her second weapon with a snap of the same hand, and rammed the palm of his other hand into her chest. She tumbled backwards with a grunt but landed in a crouch.

What can I do? He cycled through the list of spells he could quickly cast that might be of use. Any spell that was possible to dodge, Aegis would avoid.

Yondi moved toward the deadly Malkin again, more cautious this time. Aegis still hadn't drawn a weapon.

"Have you suddenly mastered those daggers in the months since we last danced this dance?"

The girl executed a complex attack routine, but Aegis stepped outside her jabs and sent her flying past him.

"I thought not." Aegis worked his feet to prevent leaving his back open to his brother. "Perhaps you'd not be so disappointing if you had spent more time training and less time canoodling with my brother."

"Ember run." Yondi cried, "curse you," she yelled as she charged Aegis once again.

Aegis lurched forward and planted a quick kick just below Yondi's sternum. She managed a swipe at Aegis's leg as she tumbled forward, but his high black leather boots prevented the slash from doing much damage.

Aegis felt the cut and pulled back a bloody finger. "You little tramp." Yondi started climbing to her feet but her attacker grabbed her before she could stand. She cried out as Aegis twisted one arm into a tight hold. "Oh yes, Ember. Please do run."

Ember stepped forward, fists clenched. "Let her go. This is between you and me."

"As you say." Aegis drove an elbow into Yondi's contorted arm and it broke with a sickening pop. She screamed in pain as he dropped her to the floor.

Ember sprinted toward the back door.

Aegis laughed as he chased his lanky brother. Ember wasn't very quick or agile. So he used what he had. He pressed the smear of DragonsBlood to a place inside his left arm just as Aegis grabbed him from behind.

The stronger Malkin slammed Ember into the wall near the kitchen and spun him around. Ember's head swam from the motion. Aegis, smiling, pinned him to the wall as Ember panted.

"I should tell you to give up. But after all these years chasing you, I don't want this to end. This is the dance I've dreamed of."

"Dance to this," Ember reached for Aegis. When his hands were an inch from his brother's side a blue light arced from Ember's palms. He grabbed Aegis and screamed in his face. The swordman jerked and was blown backwards with a thunderclap.

Ember slammed against the wall again. Spots of color filled his vision. The stench of scorched hair burned his nose. Aegis lay under the kitchen table twitching. Every hair on his body stood at attention.

Wisps of smoke trailed up in thin tendrils from where Ember's hands had been.

Aegis groaned.

Seas. He isn't dead. Ember glanced around the room frantically for a weapon. He didn't want to kill his brother. He didn't want to kill anyone. But if Ember didn't stop Aegis now, he would never know peace. His tongue darted out to wet his lips and he grabbed the knife from the kitchen table.

Crenthys ducked into the skylight of the Atrius and opened her wings to glide to the floor of the training area. She hadn't entered that way in more than a century. It was difficult to stay focused. The past few hours made her feel like she had three hundred years worth of books stuffed in her head. Everything she touched, every doorway she passed through, reminded her of another time. She pushed the pleasant thoughts away and focused on the task at hand. Her son needed rescuing.

This facility was rarely used, and it almost never held more than one youngling. Still, there were eight massive arched doorways blocked by strong metal doors. The building was designed like a giant wagon wheel. Each of the spokes was a long hallway. Each hallway lead to an open room where the younglings lived, locked away. Crenthys hated the necessity of imprisoning the young Dragons. Until trained, they were far too dangerous to be allowed to run free.

She knew which hallway held her son, and she stepped to the door leading to his room. He sat watching her a couple hundred feet away.

He doesn't have a name yet. I can't call out to him. That thought broke her heart, and she yanked the sturdy lock with a clawed hand.

They didn't have time for her to fool with lock picking or casting a spell. She tore the lock free from the door with an awful metallic scrape. The baby Dragon flinched. "It's ok." She had been practicing what she would say in this moment since she first realized it would happen, but could remember none of that. "I, I am your mother." It sounded insane, even to her ears. The baby didn't respond. He continued to stare at her warily. When she pulled the massive door open with a screech, he disappeared into his room.

He doesn't know me. His own mother and I am a stranger to him. The world seemed unbearably cruel at that moment. She cursed Rathune. If he was the sovereign god he claimed to be, then he was to blame for such injustice. "It's ok, son. I've come to take you away from this place. Do you understand? I'm not going to hurt you."

This wasn't going like she planned. What had she hoped would happen? That he would run out and embrace her? Earning his trust would take time she did not have. An idea struck her.

Fixing an image of her sweet Dragomyr Brinka in her mind, she summoned power from her blood. As quick as falling, her body condensed into the form of her lost DragonKin.

A commotion from above set her in motion. *Dragons.* She sprinted down the hallway and into her son's half-circle shaped room. There he was, crouched in the corner ready to pounce. When he saw her as Crenthys, he relaxed and took a tentative step toward her.

Everything now made sense. Her mad need to protect him. The longings she felt when they were apart. The lances of joy that pierced her heart when next she saw him. This was her son. Even if her mind hadn't known, her heart always had. Crenthys wrapped him in an embrace and wept.

She stayed that way as long as she dared. Growing echoes from the training room forced her into the moment. "My son, we have to go."

He scrutinized her face when she broke their embrace. Intelligence and determination filled his violet eyes. A week free of torture with care and meals had done him some good. But he was still a baby. He may learn to speak in a year. In a decade, he could begin to learn to use magic. How could they hope to escape and outrun the Dragons pursuing them?

She would have to revert to her true form and fight them off, hoping they could escape.

The baby took a step forward suddenly and knelt beside Crenthys, and it shamed her.

Necessity had made a mule of her son. He didn't know that Dragons don't bear riders like a horse or griffin. It was beneath them. Their flight from Zhazie had been desperate, and they had done many things beneath the dignity of a Dragon. Now he expected to bear her. What choice did they have?

The whooshing of Dragon wings beyond the hallway told her they had none. She jumped onto his back and immediately he started running down the hallway.

When they had nearly reached the end of the hallway, the head of Kilkus appeared in front of the gaping metal door. The baby Dragon roared like a lion, causing the Dragomyr to recoil. They exploded out of the hallway into the training room, running full speed. Once they were clear of the door, the youngling leaped into the air and flapped his nubile wings. With a lurch they caught wind and sailed up to the viewing balcony where Crenthys watched him that day with Vodinar. Another flap of his wings and they blasted over the railing toward a pair of wooden doors.

Zothit soared through the roof and swooped down toward them. He roared behind them and Crenthys heard him leap onto the balcony to give chase.

When she looked ahead again, they were a dozen feet from the doors. She gasped, but the youngling didn't slow. He roared again and sailed head first into the doors, splintering them violently.

They burst into bright sunlight and were airborne in two strides.

Crenthys looked back and realized the doors were too small for their pursuers. Her heart swelled with pride at the clever move to escape. With unspeakable joy, she whispered, "My son."

Chapter 31

Gods and Goblins

"Get him outta there, you Sum Buck." Anuka yelled, banging on the bars.

Victorin Lebarin smiled. "It is too late for Master Rigby. We haven't been feeding my babies in preparation for today. Tell me where you have hidden my master's treasure so I may return it and no more of your friends have to die."

"Cut the crap. We all know about Zogros."

Lebarin blanched at the name. "What are you—?"

"Zogros Thoneth. Huge, Black Dragon. Rules the southern provinces of Zhazie. I reckon you two have been in bed for a while. This whole stupid scheme of yours is about stealing a pair of anti-Dragon artifacts and giving them to Zogros so he can unseat Bog. Permanently. 'Cept it was never lost. You've had it all along. You bring us in, accuse us of stealing it, then use it yourself. That way, you get revenge on Bog and hand the DragonLord seat to Zogros. Then you get the seat Bog denied you. Head Jerkface, or whatever."

"Lies..." the old priest breathed. He was backing away from Anuka, as if the goblin could harm him from his cell.

"I am a master storyteller. Yet, even I couldn't have come up with something so crazy."

Lebarin smiled, and confidence returned to his face. "What does it matter? In time, you will all join your friend in my tank. And I will sit at Zogros's right hand in the capital. As you said, I have the item."

Rigby launched from the tank with a gasp and fell on his face in front of the priest. The bard coughed and spluttered, then pushed himself to his knees. With a smile, he held up an odd looking, bronze-colored object in a trembling hand.

Lebarin gasped.

It was a fist-sized bronze eyeball constructed to the greatest of detail. You could see veins in the eye. Thick, scale-covered lids were parted to reveal a violet iris. A tangle of nerves and sinew from the back of the eye held it fast to a smooth rod.

"You don't know what you've done," Lebarin growled. He flashed a look at Anuka and snarled, "You have no idea what that is."

"Vacik's Plunderer? Or The Eye of a Dragon, if you prefer." With a twist of his wrist, the lock on his door screeched opened, and Anuka stepped out of his cell.

"Guards! Kill them all!" Lebarin took a step toward the bridge when an enormous river shark exploded from the tank. In a blur, it bit the old human around the waist and fell back into the water. The old priest barely had time to scream before he hit the water.

Rigby leaped to his feet and raced to the tank in time to see the surface churn with air bubbles. The water turned pink and then red.

The guards on the other side of the bridge froze, their weapons half drawn, not knowing what they should do. Bumph stared impassively.

"No way that just happened," Rigby gasped.

Offund sighed with relief and Rigby and Anuka turned to see the Hob slump to his cot. The emaciated figure of Kelios in his cell winked once and then vanished. Another splash erupted behind them as a river shark crested the water, made a mid-air spin, and transformed to a healthy-looking Kelios. The Triton splashed into the water and then deftly climbed up to stand by Rigby and Anuka.

"That," Anuka began, "is how you make an entrance." He hugged Kelios's leg. It surprised him how much he missed the Fish Man.

"I can't believe it worked..." Rigby said between gulps of air.

"Ha. Never doubt me, bubby. Always a poor bet." Anuka knew they should flee, but the last few months had taught him to enjoy moments like these. They rarely lasted.

The sounds of blades clearing scabbards drew everyone's attention. Lebarin's guards had decided to fight. Four humans, all transitioning slowly to some sort of grotesque Dragon hybrid, held naked steel and began advancing toward the bridge. Then Bumph croaked loudly.

The wumpy arched his back and grunted. A tornado of daggers materialized and began spinning around Bumph at incredible speed. The four guards screamed as the blades ripped them apart. Blood sprayed from open throats and gashed legs. Within seconds, only Bumph remained. He was covered in blood and staring impassively at Anuka and his friends.

"Tor's Abyss, Kiern's pits, and everything else a man can swear on." Anuka shook his head slowly.

"I commend you, Mr. Sandbar, on collecting the items you came in search of." The Wumpy's voice grated like a bow on rough strings, but the diction was perfect. It would have been comical had the implications of the words not been so sobering. "Also, for eliminating a mutual enemy—in an enjoyable way—in the process. Ordinarily, I would congratulate you on successfully evading capture, despite a generous bounty on your head, these weeks past. But, alas, your efforts were antagonistic to my own. Indeed, when the Kargarak docked here those many weeks back, I was compelled to rake the deck with acid and magic. Only the presence of my enemies filling the skies prevented it. You are responsible for those glimmering pests roaming freely over my lands in search of my person; Unless I am mistaken. I rarely am."

"Uhhh..." Anuka said.

"Come now, Mr. Sandbar. Tales of your piercing verbosity have almost reached legendary proportions. Don't disappoint me now." Bumph finished speaking, then wiped away a stream of blood that threatened to trickle into his eye.

Oh Sum Buck. We can't get past him. "What do you want, anyway?" Rigby hid the Plunderer behind his back. "Besides the obvious."

"I want to lie in my true form, covered from tongue to tail in gold coins that I have earned. I want to slowly rake out both of Druindar's emerald eyes in recompense for my own eye. I want to circle the continent of Dorwine and never look upon lands that I do not rule."

"That... sounds like a lot of work. So we'll leave you to it." Anuka pointed to the door behind the Black DragonLord in Wumpy form.

Bog laughed a rough, throaty guffaw through the wumpy's mouth. "Indeed. Your wit is laudable for a mortal creature. I would normally consider exposing and removing a traitor in my church as fair compensation for the minor troubles you have caused me. Unfortunately, your level of understanding of situations beyond you warrants your extermination. Alls the pity. I could benefit from a soldier who is immune to DragonsFire to fight my fire-breathing cousins. But I must take no chances."

Anuka trembled. Rage rose from his gut to warm his face. Here they were again. He and his friends were pinned in a corner by a bigger kid with a bigger stick. "You won't always be the biggest. One day, someone bigger than you will put you in your place."

"Mr. Sandbar, there is no one bigger."

The door behind Bumph flung open and Grom burst into the room, ready to fight. Behind him, Felin stood in the doorway with a young half-elf girl.

Sum Buck. "Grom, he's Bog!" Anuka screamed.

Grom looked at Bumph for just a second, then raised his massive booted foot into the air and blasted Bumph backwards into the shark tank.

Well, we are in it now, Anuka thought as they raced up the smooth stone stairs into Lebarin's office. Felin and the girl led the way with Grom at the rear. The half-giant was ushering Offund tenderly along.

In the Victorin's waiting room, Felin and Aridelle doubled back, issuing panicked cries.

"What the—crazy elf!" Anuka cried. He saw a piece of the air fold over and Bumph stepped out. *I have got to learn how to do that.* "Back. Go back."

Bedlam ensued as Grom's end of the group smashed together with the front end of the group.

"I am a god," Bumph announced with thunderous clarity. Bumph held forth a slender hand, a flash of blinding green light exploded from his fingers in an instant. Everyone went flying.

When Anuka's vision returned, he peered through the crack in the splintered door to see the walls, floor, and ceiling of the room emanating a faint luminescent green glow. Bumph calmly continued his stroll into the waiting room. His long, three-toed feet pattered silently on the cold tiled floor.

"You can't expect to escape. I am an immortal god."

"Immortal doesn't mean unkillable," Anuka coughed through the haze of settling dust.

Bog laughed heartily. "There is the spirit I've heard about. I have lived for six hundred years and my power is in its infancy. You understand this. I sense a modest degree of intellect in you, Sandbar. For a mortal. You have three things that I require." The Dragon disappeared from view, but Anuka heard the crunch of sundered stone under the polymorphed creature's feet as he continued his circuitous path around the room.

"What are we going to do?" Rigby asked in a panicked whisper.

"We are gonna kill this Sum Buck." Anuka ignored the incredulous stares fixed upon him. He needed his new toys. Offund looked like he took last place in a turd dodging contest. "If only we had some DragonsBlood."

Aridelle produced two slender vials from her robe.

Anuka smiled. "Offund. Good news old boy—"

The wall above Anuka's head exploded, sending fist-sized rocks cascading around the small room. Anuka ducked and covered his head with his hands. An instant later, pain erupted in his side as a giant fist hoisted him off the ground. Between the hand crushing him, and the air filled with dust and debris, his breath came in ragged bursts. He faintly heard someone yelling over the ringing in his ears.

"Get off me you Sum Buck!" Anuka yelled.

Rigby groped around, trying to find his legs.

Kelios was at Anuka's side trying to free Anuka by punching one of the phantasmal fingers. The druid's arm below his wrist suddenly turned into a massive fur-covered arm festooned with sharp claws at the tip of a massive paw. Kelios roared bestially and began slashing the hand, raking large sections of blue material off in chucks that turned to a gelatinous goo when they splatted to the floor.

"I smell your fear, Sandbar." Bog said, his voice cold. "You should feel honored. Rarely do I have the occasion to do my own killing."

"I'll give you somethin' to smell you—bah." The force of the hand's grip tightened and Anuka felt like he would be pinched in two.

Rigby wobbled to his feet, supporting himself with one hand on the door. He glanced to Lebarin's office where Aridelle hid. She looked terrified. The bard seemed torn between helping Anuka and saving the girl.

"Rigby, get Offund the DB," Anuka yelled.

Rigby took a tender step toward his friend, trying to decide what to do. The magical hand suddenly dropped Anuka, grabbed Kelios, and smashed him against the opposite wall. Kelios crumpled limply to the floor. The stone on the wall was cracked where he had been smashed into it. Rigby shuffled to the desk where his daughter was. In a flash, the hand grabbed the prone Anuka and yanked him through the hole in the wall, into the adjacent room.

The hand dropped Anuka in a heap in front of the Dragon. With a slight nod of Bog's head, the hand dissipated into smoke. Bog looked down at Anuka as he struggled to rise from the floor.

"You have hurt me, goblin," Bog growled. "No one has done that in a very long time."

"I've seen your ugly mug. Ole Druindar tore your face up pretty good." Anuka panted.

Bog extended a hand toward Anuka, and a torrent of icy wind pinned him to the floor. Steam billowed from the goblin with a hiss and he released a primal wail.

———◦———

Rigby shot a glance at his old friend as Anuka screamed, but kept moving across the room. The bard slid toward the hole in the wall, then stopped next to Offund. When he offered the two vials to the little man the Hob looked at them sorrowfully. With a sigh, he uncorked both and drank the dark liquid down. Offund gagged and fought to swallow the contents. Rigby couldn't imagine what DragonsBlood tasted like.

Rigby looked back through the hole to see Grom stalking like a seven-foot cat toward Bog. With a sudden twist, the warrior's long-handled axe was spinning end over end at the Dragon. Then it wasn't.

A half dozen Black tentacles sprang from the stone floor. One batted the flying axe aside while three others wrapped around Grom like a boa constrictor. The half-giant screamed in rage and another tentacle shrank as slender as a snake. It darted at Grom's face and nearly plunged into his open mouth before the barbarian turned his head to the side.

Anuka shook violently on the floor, like a man having a seizure.

I can't just let Bog kill him. Rigby stepped to the hole in the wall when a small hand grabbed him from behind.

"Father," the soft voice said.

Rigby spun and stared at Aridelle with eyes wide. He worked his jaw but couldn't speak. *She called me Father.*

"See to your friends," she said, compassion in her eyes. She laid a small hand on his cheek and said, "I will help the goblin."

"Aridelle," Rigby whispered, "you can't. Bog will kill you. You have to stay hidden."

"No, Father. We have all hidden for so long. We must fight him." Tears rimmed her eyes, but did not fall. "Even if we die. We must fight. Mother was a fighter. You didn't see that in her. But I did. She just fought the wrong fight."

Rigby knew what she said was true, but couldn't move. He placed his rough hand on top of her smooth one on his cheek.

"Go, Father. They need you." Aridelle pulled her hand away and handed Rigby his lute.

He took it with a sigh. Then he nodded and stepped through the hole.

Papa once told him of a trip to the peak of Mount Borman'gariss to pay homage to Perdition. He talked of snow and wind so cold it cut you in two. "You could spit on the ground and it froze before it ever landed," Papa had said. Like most of Papa's tales, Anuka didn't believe him. It couldn't be that cold anywhere. He was wrong.

The tips of his fingers felt like someone had jammed dull needles under his fingernails. The skin of his legs felt to him what burning must feel like to others. Every nerve ending was raw and sent crippling waves of pain to his mind. Anuka thought his pee was probably frozen inside his bladder.

"Sss... sss... sssummm Bbbbbbuck," he stammered through clenched teeth. With an effort, he forced his eyes open, saw the glow of green light in the room through a milky haze. His ears popped, and he heard the most awful combination of sounds. Men were screaming, rocks were breaking, someone was roaring. He blinked and tried to summon the strength to move. He could not. When he opened his eyes again, a pale, fuzzy creature loomed over him.

"You are going to be ok," the feminine voice said as a gout of flame burned up a handful of crows behind her.

"That's a sssstupid thing to sssay," he said, blinking again until the figure came into focus. *Ah. Rigby's girly.* "We gggonna die, ssssweetie."

"Maybe, but we are alive now."

At least she sounded confident.

"What do you need to be better?"

Another stupid question. She was definitely Rigby's kid. "Cccold. I'm ffffreezing my Ssssprickberries off."

The girl pursed her lips and leaned back calmly as the battle raged around her. Anuka heard the half-giant screaming unintelligible words in a language Anuka didn't know. But he understood swears when he heard them.

The girl closed her eyes and did something strange with her hands. *She's cute*, Anuka thought. *Rigby, you poor schlep, you are toast.*

The girl stood slowly; her face a mask of concentration. Then she held her hands over Anuka and blue flame poured out, engulfing him. *Even Grom won't be able to keep the boys away from her.*

It felt like landing on a foot-thick feather bed. The flames tickled his skin and drove away the agony of Bog's icy spell.

"I'm so sorry!" the girl exclaimed.

Anuka looked up to see her clasp her hands over her mouth, her eyes going wide.

"I've never done that before. Are, are you okay?"

"I'm great, thanks! What—" the girl looked away and seemed to be hiding amusement now instead of shock. She covered her eyes with her hands.

"What is it?" Anuka asked, trying to sit up to inspect the damage. He was naked. Again.

His clothing had burned to ash. *Sum Buck.* He sighed and climbed to his feet in time to see Offund fire a peal of lightning at Bog. "He's got his juice back..." He turned to Aridelle and shouted over the tumult,

"Go help Kelios. The er—Bear Fish Man. Just go help your dad." Once she started moving away, Anuka raced to Offund's side.

The Hob nearly roasted Anuka's face off when the goblin came upon him suddenly. "Whoa! Bubby. It's me."

Offund turned back to the fight. Grom had retrieved his axe and was engaging one of Bog's creations. "I'm busy."

"Yeah, well, I see that. But I got somewhere I need to go just now."

Offund looked at him curiously, then nodded when recognition dawned on him. The Hob murmured some nonsense and whipped a hand through the air. A flap fell away, revealing a wooden room on the other side.

Anuka didn't hesitate. He leaped inside.

———— ◦ ————

Rigby dashed around the room, yelling curses at Bog and encouragement at his companions, all the while strumming a wild tune on his lute. The half-giant was covered in black goo as he stooped to retrieve his giant axe. Offund was distracted by Anuka who was buck naked. With a nod, the goblin suddenly disappeared. The Hob wailed as Bog spit a nasty-looking glob of acid that hissed as it smacked against a magical shield the little man raised just in time. Felin fired an arrow from his short bow that drew Bog's attention away from the Hob, but when the elf reached for another, he found his quiver empty. "Sum Buck. Here we go."

Aridelle was helping Kelios to his feet. The Triton seemed to be weeping and was chanting "Irana" in a desperate voice.

It occurred to Rigby then that he hadn't seen Xanavor. Or Fabian, the bard he could do without. A pang of worry for his friend squeezed his guts.

Worrying for his friend nearly cost Rigby his life. A trio of purple/black daggers soared for his head. He barely avoided being impaled as he ducked behind the remnants of the wall between Lebarin's waiting room and the antechamber where Bog battled his friends. Shards of plaster and stone pelted his face as the magical daggers flew apart.

Rigby wiped his eyes with the back of his hand and searched for his daughter. She was working some magic on Kelios. Magic. *Keit and Tor*. He had guessed as much, but seeing her use magic turned his stomach. She stepped away from Kelios suddenly. The big Triton's face was twisted into a snarl. He sucked in air through his nose in rapid gulps. Then he changed...

Eight chitinous, hairy legs as thick as Rigby's wrist sprouted from Kelios's back. He fell forward with a pained cry and his face peeled away. A pair of multifaceted, bulbous eyes popped forth and a long pair of pincers unfolded from where the Triton's mouth had been. A giant wolf spider, nearly as big as the bear had been earlier, scurried into the fray.

Rigby wanted to crawl out of his skin. A shudder wracked his body, and he thought of his goblin friend and shuddered again. "Anuka would crap his pants full if he saw that."

The bard shook off the horror of the events around him and went back to his playing. Aridelle had produced a half bar of resin from a bag she had found. It looked like the old leather satchel Xanavor carried. The resin, combined with his considerable skill, bolstered his companions as they fought. Keeping to well covered areas, Rigby switched to a Parqir scale. Played at a frenetic pace, the dark, dissonant notes would be exciting for his friends and would instill a sense of foreboding in Bog. If Dragons were susceptible to such things.

Offund was hiding nearby, concentrating fiercely, tapping his foot to Rigby's beat. Then Anuka jumped out of what the bard thought was a painting. The goblin wore the straps of two large satchels across his body and carried a quiver of arrows. He had found a pair of pants and a thin leather vest. Anuka tossed the quiver to Felin as the elf dashed by.

Anuka held up two fingers to Offund and shouted, "Two more." With a wave of the spellcaster's hand, the air warped strangely. Anuka dove into a black hole the Hob cut into the wall.

Two measures later, Anuka jumped out of the blackness and it collapsed behind him. The goblin pulled a dagger from one bag and stuck it in his belt. Trails of steam wafted from his skin as he barked to Offund, "Last one."

The Hob made another portal. This one looked like the courtyard outside the church. Anuka whistled at Aridelle. The girl produced the bronze eyeball from her pouch and tossed it to the goblin. Anuka winked at Rigby and leaped into the hole.

Rigby didn't know what to make of it. He had seen some casters do amazing things in his day but was amazed by the ease with which the Hob handled the magic. His playing nearly faltered when he heard Anuka's tiny voice yelling from beyond the building.

"Caustimis freaking Bog. If you don't come out and face me, you swamp born Sum Buck, then you don't have a single hair on your rump!"

Chapter 32

Here Come the Dragons

E mber couldn't do it. He had used his magic to cause devastation and even death. But this was too personal. To stab a prone man, killing him in cold blood, was more than he could stomach. Besides, this was his brother. Despite his misguided ideology and his cruelty, Aegis was blood.

He dropped the knife with a clang and ran back to Yondi. She tottered while trying to stand and nearly fell over. Ember rushed to her side. "Are you ok?"

She gave him a withering look, and he nodded. "Let's get you up."

With his help, she got to her feet. She winced, cradling her broken arm to her chest. "Did you get him?" she breathed.

"Umm, kind of."

"Ember."

"I know. He is down. For now. We need to get outside. Crenthys should be along soon to get us." Ember steered Yondi toward the door, but she didn't move. He looked at her.

"Us?" she asked.

It was a valid question. She had betrayed him from the very start. Even if he had forgiven her, which he wasn't sure he had, his friends would likely be less inclined to do so. Finally, he nodded. "Yes. Us. I won't leave you here with Aegis."

Her face reflected a gratitude she didn't have time to verbalize. So she smiled through her obvious pain.

Ember checked the hallway for Aegis and saw no sign he had recovered. "Come on," he said, leading her by her good arm out the front door.

They stepped into the sun, and Ember shielded his eyes to scan for a pair of Dragons. He saw one.

Cren's son was winding his way toward them in a sweeping circle. *Perfect timing.* Even after more than a week of flying from Zhazie to Clover Crisp, the bronze youngling was struggling. He likely hadn't gotten to fly much since they arrived in Wrythmar. The trainer had been appalled they let him fly so far.

Ember squeezed Yondi tight as Crenthys and the baby came in for a wobbly landing. They were going too fast and nearly bowled him and Yondi over.

The baby took up much of the street and turned around with difficulty. Crenthys slid from his back and stepped quickly to where Ember and Yondi stood. She fixed the human girl with an icy stare and looked questioningly at Ember.

"She is with me." Ember's tone was firm.

Crenthys simply nodded. "Very well. We can sort that out later." Her tone suggested her expectation for an excellent explanation when they were safely away.

"Um, you are you. I mean, why are you Crenthys? And not..." Ember gestured with his hands that she should be much bigger.

"A massive Bronze Dragon?" Crenthys suggested. She motioned toward the baby. "He doesn't know me like that. This is the only way he would follow me."

Ember nodded. "We need to go."

Something in Ember's tone caused Crenthys to raise an eyebrow. "Trouble?"

Ember nodded. "Cren, you may have to help Yondi. Her arm is broken."

The Dragomyr paused briefly before picking the small girl up and hoisting her carefully onto the young Dragon's back. Crenthys gave a cry and grabbed the back of her leg. A pearl knife handle stuck there.

Ember turned in time to catch a punch to the face that filled his vision with a flash of light and knocked him to the ground. He heard Yondi scream. Crenthys yelled something he couldn't understand. Ember shook his head to clear his vision and saw Crenthys pulling at the knife in her leg, maw clamped tight in pain. Aegis had Yondi by the leg and was dragging her from the young Dragon's back. The baby Dragon spun nervously in a circle.

Ember's arm buckled when he put weight on it and he landed face-first on the cobblestone road. Another cry from Yondi—followed by a roar from the young Dragon—spurred him into action. Aegis had been pounding him his entire life. His brother had taken every opportunity to use him as a training bag whenever his parents weren't looking. Which was often. Ember lurched to his feet and staggered toward his brother.

Aegis saw him out of the corner of his eye. Ember knew what was coming. As soon as the Dragon turned again, Aegis launched a powerful side kick at Ember, but met empty air.

A similar kick had caught Ember many times, and he had decided not to be where it would land. Aegis staggered awkwardly and dragged

Yondi from the Dragon's back. Ember tackled him to the ground. As quick as, well, a cat, Aegis twisted his body and launched an elbow into Ember's face. It was like being struck by a club. Ember's head bounced off the pavement, but he hung on. He tucked his chin so the next blow caught him on top of the head. It still hurt, but it didn't stun him or break his hold.

Ember clawed at his brother's face and clutched at his boiled leather chest piece. Aegis was all business. He slammed his head into Ember's and spun around to pin him to the ground.

"It's good to see some fight out of you. Finally." Aegis held his forearm across Ember's neck, slowly squeezing the breath out of him.

Nearby, Crenthys was getting to her feet. The baby stepped clumsily into her, knocking her back to the pavement.

"I wanted to leave you, you know? I told mother you were worthless, but she begged me to come for you. Now I am wondering what use you will be, really. You've cost me much. Cost the family a great deal. Our family is better off without you."

Ember grunted and shoved at his much stronger brother, dragging in a mouthful of air. He pushed Aegis's arm back slightly. "That's ok *brother*, I have found another family. So it is I who doesn't need you." Ember shifted suddenly, and Aegis's eyes went wide.

With a gasp, Aegis leaped to his feet and clawed at the knife sticking in his back. Ember had stabbed him low, so he couldn't reach the blade. He staggered in a wobbly circle as blood seeped through the creases in his armor.

The baby Dragon spun and, with a loud crack, smashed his tail into Aegis. The Malkin flew ten feet through the air and crashed through the front door. The bronze youngling gave a primal roar and belched forth a twenty-foot gout of bright orange flame.

Ember had rolled onto his stomach and watched the carnage in horrified fascination. Crenthys limped to her son with her hands wide in front of her. She sensed something Ember could not. When the baby Dragon turned to look at the other three, Ember saw savagery and a lust for destruction in his eyes. He wanted to burn the world. Was drawn to the flame like a kitten to milk.

"It's over. It's ok. You can stop now. It's all over." Crenthys continued to reassure her son with soothing words. It wasn't until she touched him that the spell was broken and the terrifying look faded from his face.

Ember got to his feet with some help from Yondi. The look on her face told him he wasn't alone in his concerns about the baby Dragon losing control. He looked at the house as black smoke poured from the front windows. His brother could be there, burning alive. It seemed callous that he didn't care.

"Ember, help me." Crenthys was clutching the dagger in her leg. "Help me get it out."

Ember shuffled to investigate the wound. It was bleeding, and the blade was likely in the bone. "We can't take it out. You will bleed to death. We need to get to Tabir."

Crenthys huffed, but nodded.

"Can he bear us all?" Ember asked.

"For a short way, he can."

"Then let's be about it. If we have bad—" Four Dragons loomed in the distance. They raced toward the pillar of flame and smoke. It was as if they had lit a beacon for them.

"Seas," Crenthys swore as the Dragons drew closer.

Odwin slid from Payris's blade with a groan.

"No," Tabir cried. The ambassador raised his sword to prevent Tabir from going to him.

"Fancy that," Payris said cheerfully. "Father tried to make a swordsman of me. I never took to it." The hand holding the sword trembled, and he was breathing hard. "Swordplay is popular in Theleth, which I never understood. There hasn't been a war since I was a child. We have no armies to speak of. It seemed foolish. Did your father make you learn the sword?"

"Payris, let me go to him."

"And do what? Will Rathune heal him of his wound?" Payris laughed nervously, then continued, "Rathune is dead. Or gone. And if not, he cares no more for them than the grass of the field."

"Payris, please." A pool of blood formed on the ground around Odwin. Tabir stepped toward the old man. Payris whipped his blade to the side and opened a gash on Tabir's forearm.

Tabir gasped, grabbed the wound, and stepped back. The cut burned and a red stain blossomed on his tunic.

Payris dared Tabir to try again with a menacing sneer. "Blood. It's all I need."

The Gold elf was mad. Skavrag had twisted the elf's mind and Tabir knew he would kill them both. He closed his eyes. *Why does it always come to this?* He had promised Rathune decades ago that he would not spill blood. That had proven to be a hard promise to keep of late. Evermore he was forced to use the skills he learned as a child at the hands of murders. Peace, it seemed, was not his lot in life.

"Praying, are we? Please give Rathune my regards when you meet him."

Tabir opened his eyes and met Payris's sneer with an icy stare. He searched the elf's eyes and felt that sneer falter. Payris wasn't a killer.

Or he hadn't been. Stabbing Odwin was a lucky thrust of an unsteady blade. Tabir could spare him. *No*, he realized sadly. Tabir's life was about collecting and understanding the Slivers of Aracthias. Payris had devoted his life to their misuse. He wondered—not for the first time—if his promise of non-violence had been made from his own guilt.

Master Salk had never trained Tabir to use a sword, but had made sure he could defend against one. First, he would need a weapon of his own. He spun to his right, dropped low, and extended his leg. The startled Gold elf was swept off his feet.

Tabir hadn't done that in years and was nearly knocked to the floor beside Payris. Fear drove him and he recovered quickly. He snatched the staff Odwin had used.

Payris scrambled to one knee, his sword arm down. Tabir spun left and brought the end of his staff crashing into the Gold Elf's upraised arm. The bone snapped. Tabir reversed and spun again. Payris's shriek rang out as he pivoted for another strike.

The Gold elf dropped his sword, rolled to his back, and cradled his broken arm. Tabir's next strike whistled through the air before smashing the prone elf's face.

Tabir spun the staff and jabbed the prone elf hard in the throat, crushing his windpipe.

Panting and shaking, Tabir's body buzzed with battle lust. Those old moves had come back to him like a flash of lightning. His elation soon mixed with revulsion as Payris lay writhing on the floor, gasping for air that would never come.

Nausea hit him like a wave from the ocean. Not only had he killed another elf, he had enjoyed it. Reveled in it. How could he ever atone for this? Only seeing Odwin laying not far away kept him from vomiting.

He rushed to the old man's side and rolled his head gently over. His eyes were glossy and distant. Tabir placed a slender hand on the man's chest and began to pray. His people had worshiped devils and wicked spirits, allowing them to dwell alongside their own soul. Tabir sheltered a different kind of spirit. The old priests had called them angels. He reached for the power embodied in the spirit inside him, but nothing came.

In panic, he reached out again, but no surge of healing power came. Rathune had made Tabir a vessel. The first priest in a thousand years. Tabit could use his life force, his spirit, much the same way Dragons used their blood. Only Tabir's spirit did not replenish. The magic would exchange his life to bind the wounds of others. Once he used his spirit to heal a person, his own lifespan was diminished. It could not raise the dead.

Tabir looked at the old man's face. It was peaceful. "Thank you," he breathed. The old man had saved his life. Crenthys would be crushed. Despite her misgivings about the old man, it was clear she held affection for him. Now, with her memories restored, his loss would break her heart.

Footsteps in the hallway drew his attention, so he sprang up, staff in hand. Ember, face bloodied and bruised, stood in the doorway, gaping at the scene. Two bodies, Tabir holding a staff in a threatening position. He looked up with shock on his face.

"Ember, it... Odwin is dead."

"You are needed. Cren is hurt. Yondi, too." Ember looked scared.

Yondi? I am not the only one with much to explain. "Ok, I will come." Ember nodded and jogged back down the hallway.

Tabir looked sorrowfully at Payris and Odwin. *Needless.* Then he walked to the case holding the thin Sliver of Aracthias. It was beautiful.

They all were. He supposed they held a special beauty for him. Gently, he pulled the supple shred of paper from the cabinet and looked at it.

Ember called from down the hall. He was out of time. He took a pair of deep breaths, steeling himself for what must be done. Lifting the Sliver up to eye level, Tabir ate it.

Crenthys gasped as her wound began to knit together. It was agony and ecstasy. Zanderon had arrived shortly after her, and lent her a strong hand to squeeze. There was a sharp bite in her leg bone, then the dull throbbing from the dagger vanished. Tabir was in the throes of his own agony. Sweat beaded on his forehead and his face twisted with concentration. Crenthys didn't know what this cost him. Was it more of a strain to heal an adult Dragon, though she was in her Dragomyr form? She hated to think of the price he was paying.

A series of sharp pinches from deep in the wound told her that Tabir was stitching if from the inside out. And then it stopped.

Crenthys looked to Tabir for an answer, but he seemed just as puzzled that the process had stopped. The entry hole still gaped and a slow trickle of blood oozed out.

"DragonsBreath," she swore, "they're here." Crenthys beckoned for Zanderon to help her up from the floor of the Gold embassy. He obliged.

"How?" Tabir asked, his voice rimmed with panic.

"They have put a shield over us. Presumably over the entire building," Crenthys replied, looking out the hole where the giant skylight had once been. A thin film hung in the air between them and the sky.

"Oh, how does that work?" Ember sounded more fascinated than afraid.

"Ritual magic. They must all be here." Zanderon's tone held an edge of grim finality, as if reading their obituaries.

Tabir looked stricken by the possibility that even his magic could be severed. He seemed so weary.

"This is what the missives claimed you did a decade ago at Scornrock." Ember looked into the distance, the cogs in his mind churning.

"No lone Dragon could do that. Save for Druindar, perhaps," Zanderon said as he tried to peer out a shuttered window.

Crenthys said nothing. This wasn't the time to argue magic theory. She looked at her companions in turn. Tabir. Zanderon. Ember. Yondi. Her son. She would lose little sleep over the death of the treacherous human girl, but the thought of her friends dying on her account was unbearable. Her baby filled most of the large sitting room. He looked around, concern on his innocent features. They had lain the body of Odwin on the luxurious couch in the adjacent room. He looked so peaceful. Memories of decades of friendship with the stubborn old man flooded her. She seized the sorrow she felt and turned it to a divining rod to focus her mind.

"We have to get out of here. Zanderon, see how far back the shield goes. It may not encompass the entire building." The larger Dragon nodded and strode toward the back of the building. "Ember, Yondi, help Tabir find a place to rest. The elf opened his mouth to protest, but she cut him off. "Get what rest you can, my friend. We may have to move swiftly."

"Can you still transform? If we get out, I mean," Ember asked as he and Yondi helped Tabir onto weak legs.

"No. Not while within the circle." Sometimes Crenthys hated how Ember stated the problem so academically.

"So, magic comes from DragonsBlood, but can't function if it isn't connected to... what?"

"Ember," Yondi said curtly, "help me."

The Malkin apologized and returned to settling Tabir.

"Belendurath," boomed a voice from outside. "You are surrounded by Dragons and guards. You are cut off from your power. There is nowhere for you to go."

Crenthys hated when anyone vocalized her problems. Zanderon returned from the back and, with a shake of his head, confirmed her fears. They could not escape.

"Send out my son and you and your friends can go," Dovondes boomed in his distant, powerful voice.

"Our son, you heartless wyrm," Crenthys screamed, startling her companions. Even the baby Dragon whipped his head in alarm. "He is our son. And I know what you wish to do with him."

"We all are servants, Belendurath. We all have a duty. Our son is no different."

Crenthys cried out in frustration. Her son had already had his blood taken by force. That would never happen again.

"He isn't part of the ritual," Ember said, drawing the eyes of everyone. "He is beyond it. Otherwise he couldn't enhance his voice."

"So?" Yondi asked.

"So we only have him to contend with, if you make a run for it," Ember said.

"Malkin, he is a DragonLord. He could destroy us all." Zanderon sounded like he was explaining something simple to a child.

"But would he? If we are near his son, he wouldn't dare attack. It may give us time to get beyond the barrier." Ember held his hands out as if presenting the prefect solution.

"What about the other Dragons? There are five more out there," Yondi said.

"Six," Crenthys supplied. "And no, we will not use my son as a shield." Ember was probably correct, and the plan was a good one, but she wouldn't endanger him unnecessarily.

"Belendurath, if you press me, I will rain fire on this place. Buildings can be rebuilt, but your friends will not fare so well against Dragon fire."

He was right. Crenthys, Zanderon, and her son could endure the fire. Her friends could not. Dovondes would pluck the ruby from the ashes and make a slave of whomever survived the flame. She considered having one of her friends use the ruby against Dovondes and his council, but the thought repulsed her. That ruby was an abomination and she would not use it.

"Surrender our son, Belendurath. And go free."

Crenthys knew the words were lies. No one could ever leave Wrythmar with the secrets of the Council of Wyrms. "I am sorry," she said at last. Looking at her beleaguered friends, she fought to keep her tears in check. "I have brought this on you all."

Ember untangled himself from Yondi and moved to her side. "Cren, we aren't going to let them take your son while we live."

"We can't beat them, Ember."

"Then we fight. All of us. Full assault on Dovondes. If the others break the shield, they will be too weak for several minutes. We will engage Dovondes. You and your son get beyond the shield and vanish. Get him somewhere safe."

"Ember," Crenthys said. She didn't hide how absurd she thought the plan was. "I can't ask you to sacrifice yourselves for my son and I."

Ember took her massive, leathery hand in his slender one. "You don't have to. We are friends."

"So be it," Dovondes boomed from the courtyard. "Their deaths shall be on your head."

Crenthys nodded. "Then grab Tabir and get ready to charge."

Chapter 33

Fighting Fair

B umph stepped out of the building, strode toward Anuka, and stretched into the gigantic form of the Black DragonLord. The sensation to vomit and excrete his pants full warred within him like two pigs in a sack fighting over an ear of corn. The fear he had known as he crawled beneath Ermagash's orc brothel all those years ago seemed a happy memory now. Anuka didn't consider himself brave. He had once run from a chicken. Granted, it had been an ill-tempered rooster with murderous intent, but he had no business standing before one of the most powerful Dragons on the planet.

His friends spilled out of the building and fanned out behind Bog. They gave him strength and reminded him of what he came to do.

"I have answered your call, goblin." Bog stopped thirty feet from the sodden ground Anuka stood on. The Dragon filled the courtyard almost entirely. People were screaming and running away at the sudden appearance of their god. The great Black DragonLord tilted its head to one side and looked at Anuka with his good eye. "I have been trying to decide whether you are brave or foolish."

"Oh yeah? What did you settle on, you big ugly Sum Buck?" Anuka had decided not to chide the Dragon further but had forgotten to tell his mouth.

"I have decided that it doesn't matter." He raised one clawed hand toward Anuka.

"That s'posed to scare me? I'll tell you which I am after I'm done moppin' the cobblestone with your sorry—" the words died in Anuka's throat and, for a brief moment, every muscle drew taught. *A hold spell. He cast a hold spell on me. Idiot.*

Bog grinned as much as his ravaged face would allow. "You see, Mr. Sandbar. It matters little whether you are brave or stupid." The Dragon sucked in a torrent of air. His torso rippled like he had a kicking baby inside. Then he opened his mouth and spewed forth a hissing stream of clear liquid.

Instantly, everything within four strides of where Anuka stood was engulfed in a shower of acid. The grass, the stone, even the building behind him melted like hot wax. But there were no goblin bones among the refuse.

A quick dagger thrust in Bog's belly brought a roar from his dripping maw.

"Who's stupid now?" Anuka called from under the Dragon. He immediately realized it would be him if Bog sat on him.

Bog swiped his tail violently from side to side, but Anuka hid behind one of his giant legs. Grom narrowly avoided being swatted into the swamp on one of the tail's passes. "You Sum Bucks stay back!" Anuka yelled.

The Dragon raised his foot to stomp, but Anuka moved to the other side. He opened a tiny gash in Bog's tail as he dashed by, just to keep the Dragon moving. Anuka sprinted out near Bog's front leg, but the big DragonLord saw him.

A flash blinded Anuka, and something sent him flying. He landed painfully, but quickly rolled to his feet. A giant crater was now in the spot he had just vacated. His friends all stood with their mouths hanging open in shock. *Shock. Oh.* Anuka looked down and saw tiny trails of lightning dancing up and down his body. There was a shard of glass buried in the sand at the bottom of the crater.

Bog looked on with his one eye wide and a mask of consternation on his face.

"Oh, you think a little lightning is gonna hurt me? I'm a Femagilligan!" Anuka tried to keep the bravado in his voice. The leaves of all the nearby trees were burned away, leaving only charred limbs behind. Offund had been too close to the blast. The hair on his head and chin stood straight out. It was kind of comical, so Anuka chuckled nervously.

"My dagger," Bog bellowed.

Anuka, still laughing, held the Biazo blade up for him to see. "Oops." Anuka laughed in earnest.

"That dagger is in my vault," Bog roared.

"*A* dagger is in your vault. You should assume none of your stuff is safe." Anuka sobered up and wiped tears from his eyes.

"No magic can touch you, goblin. But I assume your friends don't have such protection." A wide grin split the onyx Dragon's leathery face. He thrust his hands in the air and the sky cracked open. Chunks of ice the size of Anuka's fists rained from the sky, pounding his friends.

The cries of his companions were drowned out by the thunder of the ice storm. His friends would be pulverized in seconds. Anuka had to stop this. He slipped his shoulder bag off and tossed the Biazo dagger into it. "Okay, you win. Stop!"

Bog let the ice fall for several more agonizing seconds before the last bits fell like stones from the sky. The silence that followed chilled Anuka's blood. To his right, Offund rose from where he had huddled under a magical shield, his hands trembling. The others were either too far away or buried under a mountain of ice.

"Oh, great Caustimis, you have made your point. Take this crap. Just let us go." Anuka gestured to the bag on the ground and put his hands in the air. He was dangerously close to the acid pool that threatened to consume everything it touched.

"Toss me the dagger. Gently." Bog commanded.

Anuka moved to the bag and drew out the sheathed dagger.

"Anuka, no." Offund cried hoarsely.

With an underhand toss, Anuka ignored his friend and sent the dagger sailing harmlessly toward the Dragon.

Bog snatched the weapon out of the air. "There are entirely too many magic users in your group for my liking."

"Offund," Anuka cried. "Light him up."

Bog looked from Anuka to Offund, who shrugged helplessly. "Anuka. He *has* the dagger."

Caustimis clutched the dagger, so tiny in his massive claw, and leaned down to peer at Anuka. His foul breath nearly overpowered Anuka. "Yes, Mr. Sandbar. *I* have the dagger. It would appear that you are, indeed, quite stupid, after all."

A tiny feral roar erupted from Offund, followed by a look of pained surprise on Bog's mangled face. The great Dragon whipped his head around to where the Hob stood pumping bolt after bolt of magical projectiles into the Dragon's flank.

Bog brought the dagger up as a shield, but the bolts kept coming. Each one carved a small gash into the Dragon's hide. Despite the pain and shock, the old wyrm began accumulating magical power in his fist. Then Anuka darted forward.

He snatched up his satchel and slung it over his shoulder as he ran past. Then he fished something out that looked like a mace and smashed it into the Dragon's toe. Power streamed from Bog, through the bronze Eye of a Dragon and into Anuka. It was like being struck by a thousand lightning bolts. His tiny red hand was stuck fast to the artifact, and he ground his perfect teeth together. As the magic continued rushing into him, Anuka felt like he was inflating from the inside. It was like every fart he ever let suddenly returned the way it came. He squeezed his eyes shut lest, he feared, they would fly out. Then it stopped.

The ground flipped up and smacked Anuka in the head with a large piece of pavement. Through bleary eyes, Anuka saw Bog stagger and fall to the side, crushing three buildings.

<hr />

The building-crushing earthquake jarred Rigby awake. Something was pressing up from the ground and he imagined a fissure opening to swallow him. Then he realized he was still on top of Aridelle, protecting her from the falling ice. He rolled painfully onto a sizable chunk of ice and cried out. They had been near the doorway of the church when the storm began. Rigby had immediately covered his daughter with his body and been stuck several times for his effort. Shooting pain lanced up his left leg where a ball of ice had struck his thigh.

"Are you okay?" Aridelle asked, hovering over him.

"I, I think so." He did a quick check of everything. Getting older had trained him to be good at self diagnosis.

"Good. The goblin is yelling for you." She stood and offered him a hand up.

She was small, but pretty strong. Rigby flung water from his hands. All of him was soaking wet from the fast melting ice covering every surface. He quickly scanned the carnage. Grom leaned against a pillar in obvious pain. Large welts were raising on his back that would be purple bruises before the day ended. Blood ran down his face into his eyes. He spit out a stream of pink through swollen lips.

"Father," Aridelle said at his side. "Go. I will tend to him."

Father. It sounded like it was as odd for her to say it as it was for him to hear it. Taking care not to slip on the ice, he limped slowly toward the goblin. He was a frightening sight. Buck naked and covered with dirt and black streaks. He held a hand over the head of the titanic Dragon. Bog did not move.

He passed Offund lying face down on the cobblestones. When Rigby stopped to check on the Hob, Anuka said, "leave him. He's just exhausted." Rigby wasn't sure, but continued on to his old friend.

"Bog is held, but he is still very strong." Anuka fished something out of his pack and handed it to Rigby. A small ruby gem. "I need you to control him for a bit."

Rigby took the gem and looked at it. "How?"

"Put it up to your eye. You'll figure the rest out."

"Anuka, are you sure about this? What's this going to do? To me." It wasn't that Rigby didn't trust the goblin, but... well, he didn't trust the goblin.

"Remember that night we were captured by the half-giant women who wouldn't let us pass through the Serv Ravine without... paying the toll? Well, it's a bit like that. Just try to hang on."

Sand and sea. Why would he bring that night up? Especially in front of my daughter. He looked at the gem in his hand before succumbing to the inevitable. Rigby put the ruby in front of his eye, and the world around him changed.

Everything was red-hued, as he would have expected, but nothing else was the same. He could see *inside* the great Dragon laying before him. Bog wasn't asleep, he was held as Anuka had said. Every muscle in the great creature's body strained uselessly against the magic. He scanned the length of the Dragon and was amazed. Not only could he see everything, he *knew* everything. Which organ did what and how they all worked together. Rigby knew where the acid for his breath weapon came from. He also saw what was missing. The magic.

Blood was still pumped through Bog's body by his massive heart, but it was a lifeless thing. The blood should have shone like diamonds as it moved. *Anuka stole his magic.* **All** *of his magic.*

Indeed, when Rigby looked at Anuka, he saw the sparkly blood surging through his tiny body. It was so bright and dense and glorious.

"Rigby, stop messing around and hold him. I've got work to do."

It was a simple matter. Rigby looked at Bog's mind and found where his will to escape was, and he turned it off. Instantly, the Dragon sagged.

Anuka released his spell—Rigby saw the tendrils of it waft away—and rummaged in his pack again. With a clanging sound, the goblin produced a wicked-looking contraption. A long, sharp metal rod with a hole in the end, connected to a metal box. A fat metal protrusion hung from the end.

Rigby knew what that was. More accurately, Bog knew. So he knew. "That won't work."

Anuka stopped and looked at him like he was the naked one.

"It won't work, Anuka." Rigby repeated. "You have stolen the magic from his blood. His blood is of no use to you now. You need the blood of a DragonLord. You stole that mantle with the Eye of a Dragon."

Rigby wasn't sure how he knew, but he did. Somehow, Bog's thoughts had mingled with his own. In time, Rigby could plumb the depths of the Dragon's mind and know all his secrets.

"Sum Buck..." Anuka breathed as he thought about what Rigby said. "Aaaahhhhh!" the goblin screamed. He tossed the Blood Letter to the cobblestone walkway with a crash of metal. He stalked back and forth in a rage until he spied a broken hoe handle on the ground. Anuka snatched up the shaft of wood and proceeded to savagely attack the prone Dragon. "You rotten, grub eatin', toe lickin', butt sniffin', winged son of a nightcrawler."

Bog didn't register any pain from the attacks. His mind raced with an odd sensation that he hadn't known in centuries: fear. He wasn't afraid that Anuka might break the skin with his stick or his caustic swears, but that the goblin would remember the magic coursing through his veins.

"Anuka, stop it," Rigby chided. It was difficult to hold his concentration and yell at his friend at the same time. He felt like he had a firm grip on a tiger's tail. One slip and he would be a meal.

Anuka stopped and tossed the freshly splintered stick aside. He doubled over, panting and shaking his head.

Offund finally woke up, likely because of Anuka's rant, and waddled over to comfort the goblin.

"Keit and Tor, Offund. The whole plan is shot. How—" Anuka's voice cracked. His pain sang to him, and his hold on the Dragon nearly faltered. "How am I going to find Papa now?" Anuka whispered.

"It's ok, my friend. We should go. Bog isn't the only Dragon we have to worry about." Offund looked up as if mentioning the other Dragons would summon them.

Anuka's head popped up and his eyes went wide. "Rigby, give me that ruby."

Despite the urgency in the goblin's voice, Rigby didn't want to give up his new treasure so soon. Anuka was soon clawing at his face, and Rigby tore the ruby away. As soon as he did, Bog flopped to the side, sprang to his feet and roared. Or he tried to. His bellow was cut off as Anuka quickly put the ruby in place.

"Easy there, you big Sum Buck. Settle down." Anuka slashed a hand through the air and Bog laid down in the rubble of the buildings he had crushed. "It's time you did something useful. I need to find another Dragon."

Chapter 34

Count Your Dragons

D awn had come and still he sat hugged by the immovable construct. The Elf—Tabir had called her Tanila—had taken to her bedroll shortly after returning in the night. She stirred just after sunrise and took some meat from her pack without offering him any. When he asked, she had given him water.

Everything hurt. He had stolen a little sleep in the night, but awoke to terrible neck pain each time he nodded off. The sun climbing into the sky painted a beautiful portrait. He basked in the array of a multitude of colors dancing across the horizon. It was likely the last time he would see it. Dragons were long lived and had long memories. This excursion out of his hermit lifestyle had been like the ones before. Tabir had called, he had answered. Now he would return to his solitude.

Coltimar allowed himself a moment of sorrow for what he would leave behind. Then he turned his attention to the elf. "What is his name?"

She looked up sharply from where she sat, stowing her belongings in her pack. "What? Who are you talking about?"

"Your guest. Do you even know its name?"

"*It* is a she, and her name is of no concern to you." She cinched the bag shut with a fierce yank of the leather thong and gave him a sharp glare.

Coltimar drew in the scents of the mountain. The ash of the cold fire. The morning dew. The scent of a nearby patch of wildflowers. He leaned his head against the stone Golem and closed his eyes. He would miss this place. "It's a courtesy, that is all. I like to offer the name of any demon I vanquish, one final prayer."

The Gold Elf looked at him with a hint of concern on her face. "What are you going on about? Shut up."

Coltimar smiled and seized the Golem's thumb in both hands. Then pulled it off.

Tanila leaped to her feet, eyes wide.

With another yank, more of the Golem's stony hand broke away.

The elf fell into a chant and the creature came alive once more. It clawed at Coltimar's arm with its ruined hand, to no avail.

Coltimar grabbed the broken appendage and bent it down savagely. He tumbled free with a groan. The Golem stood and Coltimar stood to face it. He launched a thundering punch into the construct's chest, cracking the stone.

The Elf snarled behind him.

With another punch, the chest was fully sundered. The Golem swung at Coltimar, but he easily ducked the blow. Then he jammed his fingers into the crack in the Golem's chest. The stone creation jerked as Coltimar pressed deeper into its chest. With a grunt, he split the stone chest, and it fell away. With a squelch, Coltimar pulled a beating heart from the center of the golem.

Tanila stared with wide eyes as Coltimar squashed the heart.

The feelings he had spent so long cultivating in himself shriveled like the dead heart in his hand. His pity and sorrow vanished like dust in the wind. In their place burgeoned purpose. His purpose: righteous vengeance. He was the hammer that pounded flat all that was wicked against the anvil of divinity.

The elf fell on her back before him. The demonic glint in her eyes winked out. All that remained was a pale, thin Elven girl. Coltimar knew the truth of the matter. When a host accepted a demonic spirit, it forever would darken their path. There was but one way to separate the body from the corrupt spirit.

Coltimar knelt down beside the girl. He knew his appearance had changed. Soft, human eyes now glowed with holy fury like blazing white torches. His shadow fell over Tanila and her horror was complete. There was no where for her to go. Her lip trembled as she cried, "What are you?"

"I am the Harbinger. I come to reap the harvest of righteousness. The weeds are bundled and cast into the fire. You have defiled your vessel by inviting a damned soul to dwell within you. The gift of life you were given is now revoked."

Coltimar's fist fell like a smith hammer onto the girl's chest, crushing it as surely as he had the Golem's.

He stood then, gore dripping from his hand, and unfurled a pair of snow-white wings. With a leap, he sprung into the air and took up flight toward Wrythmar.

As soon as her friends charged through the embassy door, Crenthys knew she could not allow them to sacrifice themselves. Not even for her son. They would die or escape together. The baby Dragon climbed through the hole he had made in the ceiling a quarter hour earlier. His claws made great gashes in the ceiling as he charged forward.

Once out of the compound, she saw the other Dragons. All the council was there forming a half circle around the building. Each one held a part of the magical shield in place. Crenthys pondered attacking one of them to weaken the shield but changed her mind when she saw human guards leveling crossbows at her charging friends.

Her son would be of little use against Dovondes but could wreak havoc on those guards. Crenthys cried out before the men could release their volley and they turned their attention to her instead. The sight of a Dragon charging, even a small one, took the fight out of the men and they scattered. She leaped from her son's back and landed hard on the ground. While the baby chased the men away, Crenthys scooped up one of the discarded weapons and leveled it at Dovondes.

The DragonLord, in human form, watched his attackers with amusement. He was preparing a spell to hurl at her friends. Crenthys had lived for centuries and learned to use most weapons. Regrettably, crossbow was not one of them. She yanked the trigger, and the bolt skittered harmlessly in front of the DragonLord. He looked across the courtyard at Crenthys.

It occurred to her he likely didn't know any more about crossbows than she did, so she raised her empty weapon and took aim again. A lance of energy streaked between them in a blur. Even though she expected the attack, she barely dodged to the side. The crossbow fell under her as he dove and she crushed it. No matter. She didn't know how to reload it.

Zanderon burst out of the magical shield and launched a thunderous, magic-enhanced punch to the DragonLord's jaw. The shot cracked like thunder, but did little more than turn Dovondes's head to the side. He quickly countered with a burst of energy to Zanderon's chest that hurled him into the air and onto the roof of the embassy. Tabir didn't hesitate to strike Dovondes in the face with the staff he found in the embassy while Ember hurled menacing spells meant to trip or slow the DragonLord.

Tabir was a credit to warriors. He moved with speed, grace, and purpose. But he was ridiculously over-matched. Dovondes nearly crushed his skull with a barehanded swipe. She had to intervene.

Crenthys took off at a sprint through the magical barrier and exploded into her true form. Dovondes grabbed Tabir's staff and hurled him across the courtyard. He pivoted toward Ember, but a giant clawed hand tossed him into the air before the blow could fall.

She turned and began ripping council members, in their human forms, from the ritual and hurled them in different directions. It wouldn't stop them, but it would buy them time. They would be weak from the ritual for a few minutes at least. Just as she tossed Zothit, with a little more force than required, Dovondes came soaring from the sky. His bronze scales glistened in the morning sunlight as he plummeted.

"Run," she screamed at her friends and soared up to meet him. They clashed fifty feet in the air with a meaty thump, punctuated by the leathery flap of their wings.

Through the air they tumbled. Her magic was strong, but she was not a match for his strength and ferocity. He was older, stronger, and his veins were filled with the blood of a DragonLord. More than just a title, it was a distinction made based on gifts he enjoyed from birth that set him apart from other Dragons. Something about the coronation as DragonLord amplified those gifts even further. On she fought.

Every punch and bite was countered and riposted. In seconds, she bled from a half-dozen wounds. They continued to spin in a circuitous path toward the ground. Crenthys heard her son cry out. Dovondes heard it, as well, and his reaction to it doubled her determination. He would not have her son.

She gathered her power and released her grip on the DragonLord. When they were separated, she sent a powerful blast of magical energy, like a shower of black rods, hurling at him. The force of the magic sped her descent toward the ground. Dovondes brought a wing up protectively and Crenthys saw the majority of her bolts burst onto a magical shield. She landed with an earth rending crash.

The air blasted from her lungs, and her head struck the ground with a thud. Stars burst in her vision and pain from her wounded leg stabbed her sharply. She felt like a turtle stuck on its back as she groped around, trying to rise.

Dovondes filled her vision, hovering just above the ground. Anger burned in his dark eyes. Zanderon rejoined the fight then, finally in his true form. He tangled with Dovondes as Crenthys struggled to gain her feet.

The old trainer was no match for the DragonLord. He tossed Zanderon around much the same as he had Crenthys. She finally got to her feet and steeled herself to help her old friend against her former lover. Then she saw the first Dragon return and her heart sank. The Dragons Crenthys had scattered were returning to the fight.

Yondi was helping Tabir stand on an injured leg, and Ember was scrounging through his pockets. Zanderon crashed to the ground not far away and Dovondes immediately struck him with a bolt of lightning.

The DragonLord landed lightly beside their son. They eyed one another warily. *Be the sky full of Dragons, he will not take my son,* she swore and stalked toward them. A shriek from above drew their attention, and everyone looked up in time to see a winged figure plow into one of the council Dragons. Whatever it was, it hung onto the Dragon's neck and punched it savagely.

The whirling Dragon and its rider fell like a stone. They separated moments before the Dragon crashed into the embassy. The winged figure glided gracefully down.

"Oh, Coltimar," Tabir moaned and hung his head.

Moments later, the winged figure, who closely resembled Coltimar, strode out the front door carrying the sword Payris used to kill Odwin. The blade dripped with blood that hissed when it hit the ground. Like her own blood was doing.

Then she remembered. Coltimar was a godling. The fabled child of a divine being who mated with a mortal. It was rare for those creatures to sire a child. Coltimar's father had thirty. Crenthys hadn't known that Coltimar was one of those children, but Belendurath did.

"Send your council home unless you wish for more blood to be spilled," Coltimar bellowed as he stalked toward Dovondes.

"I rule here, godling. Not you. These are my lands." The DragonLord pushed out his chest and leered at Coltimar.

"Justice recognizes no jurisdiction."

"Do you then presume to judge me? Mortal?" Dovondes growled in Coltimar's face.

"Do you presume to deny the judgment to come, drake?" Coltimar paused long enough for the DragonLord to answer. He did not. "How many years hence until the judge of the world comes? Your people should have the counting. Have you time to atone for your sins before that day?"

Crenthys could only gape at the exchange. *Who speaks to a Dragon, nay a DragonLord, in such a way?* The rest of the Bronze council floated to the ground, filling the streets near Dovondes.

The return of his council brought the steel back into the DragonLord's spine. He pulled himself to his full height and glared down at them all. His cronies sidled in close around him. Five adult Bronze Dragons.

"My father slew your kind by the dozens before the world was sundered," Coltimar said.

"You are not your father. That blade in your hand does not frighten us." Dovondes opened his mouth to continue his bluster, as a large portal sizzled to life behind Coltimar.

What further horrors has Dovondes summoned? All eyes turned to the portal as a tiny red-skinned goblin stepped through and looked around.

After a moment of stunned silence, he said, "Man. Y'all are some dour Sum Bucks."

Anuka beamed like the cat who caught the mouse.

"Anuka," Crenthys barked. "You shouldn't be here."

"Cren? Girl, what happened to you?" *Oh seas. Is she one of them now?*

"Kill them all." Dovondes roared.

"Sum Buck. We'll talk about this later." Anuka stepped up to the cadre of Dragons and thrust a glimmering ruby into the air. "Dance," he commanded.

Dovondes and the rest of his Bronze council stood on their hind legs and began dancing. Each had their own idea of what dancing meant. They spun and gyrated hilariously, shaking the ground as they moved.

"Doh, not you, big guy." With a gesture of his hand, Dovondes returned to his place on the ground. Another Dragon, a badly injured old boy was hobbling around trying to execute some ballroom moves.

"Anuka, he's with us." Ember shouted.

Anuka released the Dragon and turned his attention to the Bronze DragonLord. Just as he opened his pack to retrieve his tool, a powerful arm spun him around.

It was Crenthys, looking like Crenthys again. Anuka didn't miss the storm on her face. With all the eloquence he could muster, he asked, "What?"

"Anuka, you mustn't. That thing is an abomination. I forbid you to use it." Her grip was firm, almost painful, and her look determined.

"Crenthys," he said in a soft voice, "let go of my arm." She did, and she seemed to be deciding whether he compelled her to do so with the ruby or the force of his mighty voice. Either way, she eyed him warily.

"Listen to me, Anuka. That thing is evil. Wave used it on my son, and on me. You have to understand. It takes away their will."

Oh. That. Anuka had forgotten about the ruby. Maybe he was getting too comfortable with it. Then he remembered Crenthys wasn't supposed to know about it. *Oops.* He thought she was talking about the blood letter. *Well, isn't this a pickle?*

"Takes away their will, eh? The Dragons?" Anuka nodded, put a thumb on one nostril, and blew an impressive ball of snot out the other. "I wonder what it would be like to live with someone else controlling your life. Sounds like a bad deal." He snapped his fingers and Dovondes and his council reverted to their human forms. With a beckoning gesture, they scurried over and sat in a circle at Anuka's feet.

Crenthys balled her fists and glared down at him, but his words shut her up.

"The thing about power is, once you get it, you can't live without it." Anuka hooked a thumb toward to the DragonLord. "This Sum Buck had all the power in the world until I showed up—"

"Until we showed up," Offund corrected.

"Until *we* showed up. Thank you. How has he done with that power? Don't you think a little humility might do him some good?"

Crenthys's eyes darted wildly about and she seemed about to burst.

"He's right, Cren," Ember said. "You know what he's done. What all of them have done."

"That doesn't make it right. That makes you a tyrant." Crenthys stared at Anuka.

"A tyrant for a day," Anuka conceded. "Look, I don't know what happened during your homecoming. Obviously, things have changed. My goals have not. Maybe my plans, but not my goals. Your high holy Bronze god Donuthole—"

"Dovondes," said nearly everyone.

"Dovondes, has something I want." He held up a hand when Crenthys opened her mouth. "I need a little of his blood. If you tell me not to kill him, I won't."

Crenthys's mind raced behind her eyes. "You killed Bog."

"Why does everyone assume that? Sheesh. You kill one Dragon and you get labeled. No, I did not kill Bog. I domesticated him. Look, it doesn't matter. I'm here now to get what I need, and then we go. No one else has to die. *That* is what power should be used for. Best solution for everyone, minimal losses."

A loud crack sounded as Anuka's arm was batted into the air. A tall, skinny DragonMan appeared out of nowhere. He was holding a square chunk of wood in his hands and gave Anuka a look of shock.

Pain lanced up Anuka's wrist and he cried out. He grasped his shattered wrist with his other arm and sucked in sharply. Everyone moved at once.

The DragonMan dropped his stick and reached into the air for something. *My ruby.* Crenthys lurched awkwardly toward the gem, as well. The six polymorphed Dragons in front of Anuka jumped to their feet and began reaching for magic. The baby Dragon roared. Anuka staggered as the pain made him swoon.

Oh, Sum Buck. He was no stranger to pain, but that had been a sucker punch. If he didn't do something quickly, those Dragons would rip them all apart. He wasn't able to heal his broken wrist, but he could fix it. The world around him was a garbled mess of chaos. Everyone was yelling and screaming. Anuka pushed the sounds as far away as he could and reached into his wrist with his new DragonLord senses. He could see the break. It looked clean and he fought hard not to vomit. Everything around him moved slowly as he reached with his magic to wrap tiny fingers of his power around the broken bones. Then he snapped them in place.

Anuka awoke with a gasp as the world crashed in on him. He was lying on his back on the stone while battles raged around him. Crenthys and Coltimar were twirling around a trio of Dragons high above him. He squinted against the sun and noted that the fight was going poorly for the home team. Another Dragon, who looked like a bad guy, had Tabir, Ember, and some cute little human girl cornered in the remains of a building. Offund had his hairy little legs wrapped around the tall DragonMan's neck, launching punches with a tiny glowing fist into the things snout. A giant gray wolf straddled Anuka, growling at a pair of dark-skinned human women. *Sands but I hope that is Kelios.*

The pain in his arm came in sharp waves. He found a spell in his now vast repertoire and encased his left arm in a protective sleeve as hard as stone. It was crude, but would work. *I've got to have Ember teach me to use this magic before I kill us all.* With his other hand, he yanked on the tail of the wolf, "let me up, bubby."

Wolf Man looked at Anuka and got clobbered by a phantasmal fist. Kelios yelped and rolled to the side.

The mantle of the Black DragonLord pressed on his mind. He growled and mentally pushed the weight of the DragonLord power back. Anuka understood the basics of elemental magic from his time in Bog's head. He rose to one knee and slapped the palm of his unbroken hand against the ground. Violent blasts of wind slammed the women battling Kelios from each side, crashing their heads together. They stumbled and fell back, but Anuka wasn't watching.

With a flick of his wrist, a gigantic translucent hand fifteen feet wide fell from the sky between Tabir's group and the Dragon stalking them. The hand landed with a spray of broken stone and opened in time to catch the brunt of a fiery blast of the Dragon's breath weapon. The girl screamed, or maybe it was Ember, but the flame didn't touch them. The phantasmal hand was charred black but still standing. One finger lazily raised in a rude gesture toward the Dragon. *Sum Buck.* Anuka hadn't consciously used a spell. He had done that with Bog's innate magic. He shuddered to think about the power a DragonLord with centuries of study would have.

Anuka grabbed the stick that had broken his wrist with a fistful of unseen will and slammed it hard between the legs of the lanky Sum Buck who attacked him. His knees and eyes crossed, he sucked in a breath and staggered forward. Offund seized the moment. He bit the

DragonMan on the hand holding the ruby and wrenched it free. The DragonMan recovered and a wrestling match ensued.

Grom, Felin, and a hobbled human man—likely the injured Dragon—were playing peek-a-boo with the remaining Bronze Dragon while Rigby and Aridelle took shelter nearby.

Sizzling drops of DragonsBlood rained down from the group fighting above them. The big human, Coconut, fought like nothing Anuka had ever seen. His sword dripped with blood and he swiped, kicked, and punched at anything in arms reach. For her part, Crenthys held her own against two Dragons. She seemed to be tiring though and some of the blood raining down was hers.

All of his friends were exhausted. Between giant spiders, undead Dark Elves, and demon possessed bards his crew was on the verge of collapse. No telling what Crenthys and her battered crew had been through. He had to get his hands on that ruby.

The Dragon harassing Tabir's crew was raking at the magical hand with wicked claws. He would soon be through the barrier. Too much was happening for Anuka to be everywhere he needed to be. A cry from behind him spun him around. Grom had a Dragon by the tail as it angled it's long neck to bite him. Felin was out of arrows and the crippled man was... crippled. Anuka launched a rock-hard blast of force into the Dragon's face before it could take Grom's head off.

A wail from the baby Dragon drew Anuka's attention to the skies. Crenthys fell like a stone rolling end over end. Thrusting his hands skyward, Anuka shot the first spell he could think of at his plummeting friend. With a loud crack, feathers exploded in the air and cradled Crenthys's descent to the top of a long, flat-roofed building. The DragonLord descended toward the goblin.

Anuka groaned as the toll of throwing so much magic quickly settled over him like a wet blanket. His head throbbed and his hands shook. He would have to regroup if his friends had any chance at surviving. The two women he had addled earlier had recovered and now marched toward him.

A keen whistle split the air and drew every eye to Ember. The Malkin stood on Tabir's shoulders, supporting himself on the wall of the adjacent building. "Fly to Inri you Sum Bucks!" Ember yelled. And they did.

The women in front of Anuka jumped into the air, transformed into Dragons, and flew North. The same with the ones attacking Grom and Tabir's groups. Even the baby leaped into the sky before Ember called him back. Only Dovondes and the hobbled human remained.

The old DragonLord had ignored Ember and touched down in the ruined courtyard, still eying Anuka. He pointed a clawed hand at Ember and the Malkin froze.

"You will find me harder to subdue than Caustimis. I can smell his magic on you, goblin." Dovondes shifted to his human form. He seemed no less imposing. Anuka could sense the power in him. Truly, much of Bog's power came from his cunning and treachery. If ever Anuka met a god, it was standing before him.

Crenthys groaned and rolled to her side. The baby Dragon clawed his way onto the roof beside her and muzzled into her side.

"There is no victory for you here, goblin. Take what is yours. Leave what is mine. And go. Otherwise, you measure the might of your stolen power and the godling against my own. We shall see how your friends fair in the wake of such a battle."

Anuka wanted to be glib. To yell something absurd in the DragonLord's face like he always did. But he couldn't muster the words. Dovondes was right. Even if he and Coltimar could give the DragonLord a fight, many—if not all—of his friends would die.

The lanky DragonMan flung Offund to the ground with a thud, and limped over to the DragonLord. With some effort, he knelt with his head to the ground and looked up at Dovondes from his knees. "Master."

Dovondes looked at the DragonMan, *his* DragonMan Anuka supposed, "Do you have my ruby, Vodinar?"

"Master," the DragonMan said with a cry that was part sob and part plea. "We can't continue this course. It's madness. *I* cannot continue this course. Please, my Lord."

"Vodinar, you weak fool. Give me my ruby. I command it."

The words hit the DragonMan like a slap. He whimpered and doubled over.

"You are of my blood. I *made* you. Do not force me to unmake you."

"Can't..."

"You will obey!" Dovondes roared.

The tall DragonMan's whole body shook as he planted one hand on the ground and slowly stood. When he was at his full height he looked down at his master through tear-streaked eyes. Then he brought his arm up quickly and brandished a sparkling ruby—larger than Anuka's—before the DragonLord.

"This madness must end, my Lord. If I can't stop it, then I refuse to be a part of it."

The DragonLord in human form went rigid, eyes wide. Then, he moved his hand mechanically to his hip and drew a slender short sword.

Sum Buck, what is this idiot doing? "Kill him. Crush his heart. Something!"

If the DragonMan heard Anuka, he didn't let on. He stuck his chest out proudly as the DragonLord drew back the short sword and rammed it into his chest.

"No!" Crenthys wailed from the rooftop where she watched.

Vodinar gasped and grabbed his master with his free hand. He coughed a spray of blood onto the DragonLord's horrified face. The DragonMan slumped and the hand holding the ruby dropped. The gem bounced off the stone courtyard and careened wildly to the side. Offund pounced on it like a frog on a Dragonfly.

A thunderous crash, followed by an explosion of rock and dust rose from a nearby building as a Dragon corpse fell onto the structure, crushing it. Coltimar, covered from head to toe in DragonsBlood landed softly a few seconds later. The blade of his gore- splattered sword was bent at an angle. He let it clang to the ground.

Instead of turning on the group with rage, the DragonLord sagged to the ground holding Vodinar. He flung his head back and wailed sorrowfully.

Crenthys limped forward with aid from Grom. She knelt by Vodinar and Dovondes and gently stroked the DragonMan's cheek. It was about the saddest thing Anuka had ever witnessed.

"Why, Belendurath?" Dovondes cried with anguished sound and doubled over onto Vodinar's corpse.

"He couldn't live with the things you made him do, Dovondes. The things we all have done. He saw the evil in what the Council is doing even before I did. It's over, now. It has to be over."

Dovondes didn't answer as he held Vodinar, rocked back and forth, and sobbed bitterly.

Crenthys looked up at Anuka. Her own eyes were red and filled with tears.

"If you ever use that on me, or my son, you will have to kill me. Do you understand?" Crenthys's voice sounded on the verge of breaking.

"Yup."

"Do you swear it?"

"I swear on my dead mother. I will never use this ruby on you. And I'll never use it on the baby." *Never again, at least.*

Crenthys nodded once and hung her head.

"I still need some of his blood, Cren."

She didn't look up. Only nodded.

"Okay, Kel, get this bunch of banged up louts to the ship. Offund and I will finish up here." With a lazy flourish, Anuka opened a huge portal in the courtyard.

———◆◇◆———

Crenthys struggled to hold her composure. *Was this Ember's secret? Has he known all this time that Anuka had one of those blasted ruby gems?* She knew it had been Wave's. There was no other explanation. Their relationship had a rocky start aboard the Sea Pocket. Now she felt she could never trust the little goblin again. Her son, her precious baby, nuzzled affectionately with the goblin. She took a step to intervene, but a strong arm stopped her. Her breath caught. *Kelios.*

The Triton helped her stand on her good leg. He wrapped his big arms around her and stared warmly at her.

What can I say to him? How do I tell him I have a son and that I am Belendurath? How do I tell him we can never be together? And that I want to be with him more than anything?

Kelios smiled knowingly and kissed her gently on the forehead and said, "Later".

She closed her eyes as the confluence of her two lives staggered her for the hundredth time that day. Ember and Yondi held hands as they passed through the portal. Crenthys shook her head. She looked at Anuka, who held open a portal five strides wide, one he had created, with barely an effort. Whatever power the goblin had stolen from Bog, it was bad news for the world.

Tabir and Coltimar shared a quiet farewell before the big man flew west. The rest of the group, including many people she did not know, stepped through the portal. She had sent her baby through with Kelios. Only she, Anuka, and Offund remained. It was revolting to watch Anuka use the device Wave had used to drain her son of his blood. She guessed it was the same one. Somehow, the goblin had kept it. Another reason not to trust him.

True to his word, Anuka did not kill Dovondes. Crenthys was surprised to realize she was conflicted about that. Instead, the goblin had commanded him to transform, and then put the DragonLord to sleep. The other Dragons Ember sent North to Inri would return as soon as they entered the neighboring country. She came home hoping to repair bridges she had burned in the past. Instead, the number of people she counted as enemies was growing exponentially. From what she learned during her time in Wrythmar, she didn't care. There was a world of evil that she had been part of for far too long. She was ready to stand on the other side.

"Sum Buck," Anuka said. He and Offund had finished their work and were staring at the sky.

A line of Dragons filled the horizon to the northwest.

"Time to go," Anuka announced.

For once, Crenthys agreed.

<hr />

Kelios found the sway of the *Kargarak* soothing once they reached the open sea. With some instruction from Ember and Offund, Anuka had erected a magical canopy over the ship that hid them from the myriad of Dragons zipping up and down the river leading out of Kentari. Ember had gushed over the display of magical skill the goblin had wielded in making the veil. It made the Triton uneasy.

Anuka sat cross-legged on the bow of the ship, meditating. A look of stern concentration puckered his face. Kelios didn't know if he was in the midst of a spell, or some titanic inner banter. He wasn't sure about much concerning the goblin lately. Anuka's manic drive to find his father had cooled to an icy determination. They were on course to a secret port Anuka knew of, but the goblin hadn't revealed many details.

Once there, they would part ways. Rigby declared that as soon as they made landfall, his adventuring days were over. Zanderon, the Dragon who had aided Crenthys, was determined to seek asylum from the Brass DragonLord until his wounds had healed. Tabir was nearly despondent over the trouble he had caused his friend Coltimar, but was determined to head for Theleth as soon as was feasible. Crenthys was of a mind to join the elf.

Kelios felt a deep, primal tug on his heart to return home. Something told him that the time was drawing nigh to go back to his people and set things right. But that could wait. He had no intention of being separated from Crenthys again. Not for a while, anyway.

Crenthys? She was Belendurath now. Well, she always had been, he supposed. She was concerned how the revelation would change things between them. Initially, the news was shocking. After a week at sea he found the strange situation changed his feelings very little. Whatever the future held, he wanted to share it with her. Now he just had to figure out how to convince her of that.

Crenthys and Anuka had agreed that the rubies should not stay together and each took one. Cren didn't like the idea of having such a vile item any more than she liked Anuka holding one. The goblin's meteoric rise in power was disturbing on many levels.

Kelios sighed as the ship slid through the smooth waters. There were rumors of open fighting between metallic and chromatic Dragons all across Dorwine. Shimmer, the Silver Lady, had placed a bounty on Anuka's head so astronomical Kelios considered turning him in. The backlash from Wrythmar would carry it's own set of troubles. On top of all of that, Ember had grown paranoid that his brother had survived and would crawl out of the ocean and slit his throat in the night.

Had he not smelled the leathery metallic scent of her, the tap of Crenthys's cane would have alerted him of her approach from three strides. She laid the cane against the rail beside him and wrapped her arms around his waist from behind. He touched her smooth dark skin and smiled. She was Belendurath, in human form. The thought that she could become anything she wished was a little disturbing. Maybe she could become a Triton and he could take her home to meet his mother. He chuckled at the notion as she laid her head on his back. He closed his eyes and basked in the embrace as the cool sea water misted over them.

Tomorrow may bring showers of fire falling from the sky, but today was a day of sweet gratitude. Come what may, all was quiet on the deck of the Kargarak. For now.

The End

Epilogue

Anuka's head pounded. He had come below deck for rest, but had found none. Apart from a few fitful hours of exhausted slumber, he hadn't rested since leaving Kentari. The pressure of the Black DragonLord mantle caused an ever-present ache in his mind. Now, the burden of the Bronze DragonLord crushed his mind as well. He was under a constant barrage of suggestions, questions, and demands. The urge to set the ship on fire had nearly overwhelmed him just an hour ago.

It was like having two gigantic dogs. Each hating the other, and each one desiring your full attention. Anuka battled every moment to keep the two incompatible powers in his mind from destroying him. Whenever his mental barriers slipped, one of the mantles of power would creep into his mind, filling him with a grandiose sense of power and purpose.

Anuka gasped and made a pitiful noise of desperation. He was losing his battle against the Dragons in his mind. He finally had all he needed to find Papa, and the power to get to him. And it was destroying him.

Anuka winced in pain at a sudden banging on his door.

"Anuka," came Crenthys's voice beyond the door. "We need to talk."

...you should kill that one before she destroys us... The Black Drag-onLord mantle whispered.

...she must take this mantle. Only she is fit for it... The Bronze mantle countered.

Crenthys beat on the door insistingly and Anuka winced again.

Anuka drew in a breath and exhaled slowly. He licked his lips and clawed free of the two Dragons in his mind. "Okay," he croaked, "hold your tater." Standing on wobbling legs, Anuka walked to the door, reminding himself with each step that he didn't need to kill his friends or set anything on fire.

Aegis hissed as he slid gently from the tall bunk bed in the massive jail cell. The skin on his thigh burned when he moved. The pain was nearly as bad as when the injury happened. His arms, too, were burned. The hair singed away and the skin on his arms was covered with angry blisters. He hadn't seen his reflection yet, but assumed his face was much the same based on the stinging tightness he felt.

Aegis had underestimated his brother and his friends. Yondi had betrayed him. He flexed his hand painfully into a fist. The burning from his skin fueled his anger. A muffled cry outside brought rational thought back to his mind.

He drew a deep breath into his smoke-damaged lungs, and coughed. When his cell door clicked open he mastered himself and wiped spittle from his swollen lips. "You took your time, Dragon Man," he croaked.

"Dragomyr," the basso voice replied.

Aegis nodded to Kilkus. "Then let us be gone, Dragomyr. You have secured a portal for our escape?"

"Of course. I have kept my end of our bargain completely," Kilkus said.

"And I shall keep mine. Come, I must recover and prepare." Aegis limped past the Bronze Dragomyr as swiftly as possible.

"Prepare for what?"

Aegis paused in the hallway, but did not look back. "Vengeance," the Malkin growled.

<<<<>>>>

Also By

Thank you for reading *The Eye of a Dragon*. If you would like to read more of my work, you can get the short story *The Vustaan Incident* detailing the escapades of a young Anuka and his pet honey badger, Slobbers, by going to:

https://authorjackadkins.com/free-short-story/

Be on the lookout for the final book in the first trilogy in *The Dragons of Dorwine* series coming fall 2023.

About Author

Jack Adkins has been spinning tales for over thirty years. He is a seasoned veteran of Dungeons and Dragons, Top Secret, Vampire, MechWarrior, and almost every RPG in between. Jack has finally gotten around to sharing his unique humor and imaginative stories with the world. Before he began writing novels Jack enjoyed building lightsabers with his four boys, moving props and equipment for the marching band, and studying Reformation Era Christian Theology. In his spare time, Jack has built a twenty-five-year IT career.

Made in the USA
Middletown, DE
27 October 2024